I0566198

Seeds of Farsil

The Chronicler's Awakening, Book 3
J M Samland

Copyright © 2022 by J M Samland

All rights reserved.

No portion of this book may be reproduced in any form without written permission from the publisher or author, except as permitted by U.S. copyright law.

Cover art by Jim Williams

www.jimwilliamsartist.com

Interior art and map by Ryan Allen

Instagram @gimble_nackle

Ash,
It wasn't the same writing this without your laying over the keyboard.
We'll never stop missing you.

INTRODUCTION

I started *Realms of Terswood* in earnest as I was prepared to test for my black belt. I published it within a week of me testing for my second degree. I published *Trials of Throk'tar* within a week of testing for my third. I churned out *Necromancer of Urbus* for NaNoWriMo 2021, meaning I wrote the first draft start to finish in the month of November. Now as I close out this tale of Alishia coming into her power, I take a deep, calming breath and examine what I learned.

Trilogy for my first publication: Bad idea.

Time travel for my first publication: Bad idea.

But hey! I learn and improve everyday. I'm only in competition with who I was yesterday, last week, and a year ago.

I had a conversation with Grandmaster Rose (aka who *Realms* was dedicated to) the other day about how hard it is to measure progress. It's difficult to see that you've gone a foot when you're just focusing on moving forward an eighth of an inch at a time. I know my taekwondo skills, after countless hours of training, have improved in the time since drafting *Realms*. My writing has as well.

After four books and 1200+ pages, I'm ready to set aside Alishia and Lone for a while to let them breathe. Yeah, I know, 1200 pages is like what Brandon Sanderson writes on a holiday weekend, but I'm only comparing myself to me.

Each of the hundreds of characters lived in my mind with brilliant lucidity. From the indoctrinated Delphin Carter to the starstruck Dehset Tekin. Morally ambiguous Siraas vass Soss and morally dark-gray Cazlandt. I channeled my own grandmother into Lone's grandnan. Daelin was a combination of many of my father figures.

Being an indie writer is so damn hard. There's a constant mix of imposter syndrome mixed with the depression. It's a mess. Writing happens in all the hours that were once full of anime and video games. Not to say I regret the sacrifices made to flail endlessly at the keyboard. It's been a wild several years and something I hope to continue to do for several more.

I could ramble, but there's a book to get to. This trilogy wasn't my work alone and could not have happened without those that support me. So basically... you. You that are reading this line, thank you. What you hold in your hands is the sum hundreds of hours of my effort. My only hope is that it will give you six to ten hours of enjoyment to you. Just the fact that you're reading these words, when so many skip the "from the author" and prologue means so much. Thank you.

Don't skip this prologue, it's important.

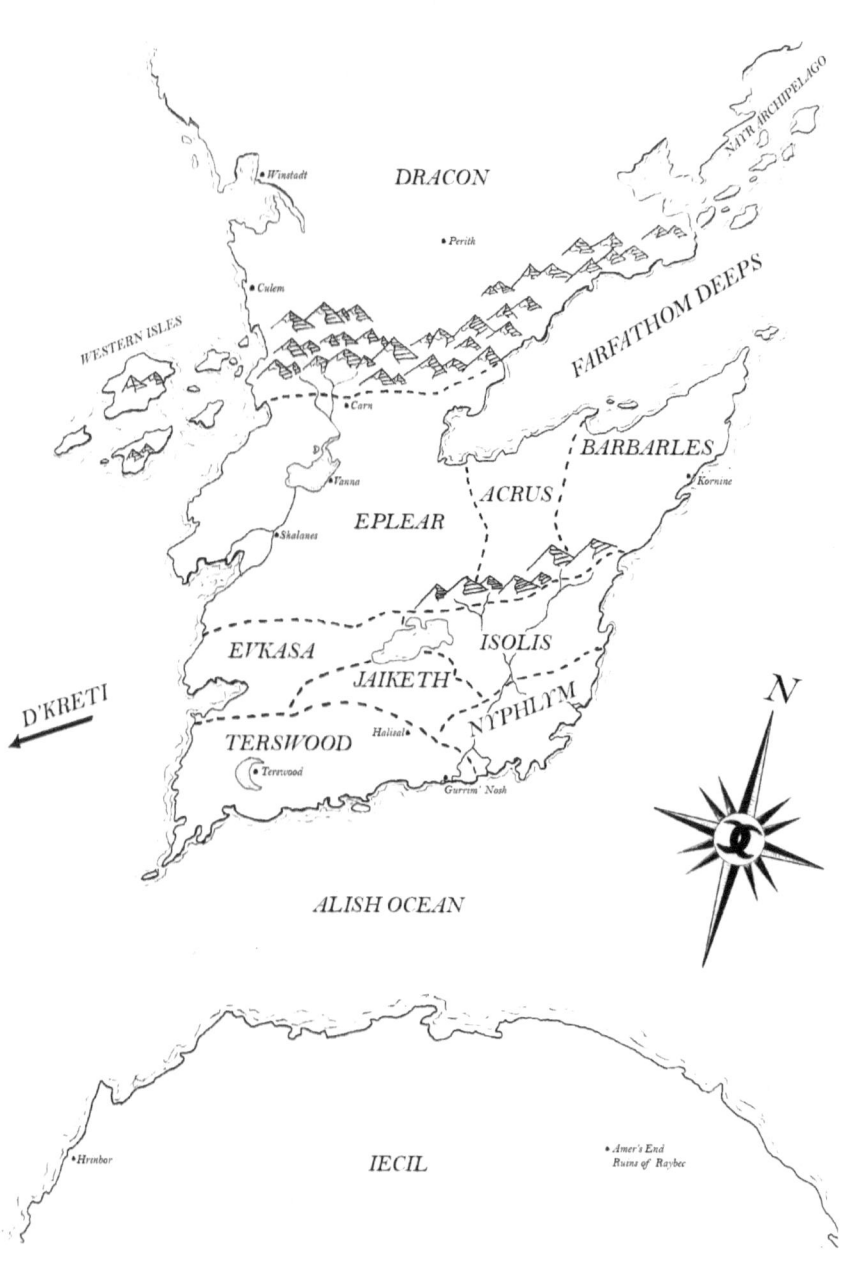

PROLOGUE

1

Seeds are fascinating to study. To think a world tree can come from such a small thing.

B efore the Mists

Endren waved slender fingers over the tome, gracefully turning the page without touching the crisp, weathered parchment. The ancient volume contained stories of the mundane lives of mundane people who were now nothing but dust. This was one of the few items in the archives that Endren had yet to read, and she was a completionist.

The mage stifled a yawn with the back of her hand and looked out the narrow window overlooking the gleaming spires of her city. She ran her hand in the other direction, and the tome gently folded closed. These stories could wait until after a snack.

Endren stepped out onto the spiral stairway attached to the outside of the spire and began the long climb down, over thirty levels. Other than a slight grumble in her stomach, she was in no rush that day. As she rounded the far side of the spire to a view of the city unseen from the reading room's window, she noticed, between the soaring tower and empty market squares, a flash of color far below in front of the Symposium.

They were raising the Protectorate Banner. Endren could see its cobalt and silver snapping in the wind even from her distance. That would mean a guest had arrived from outside of Tidecrest, but there had been no guests since the days of legend, since the days of the book she had just been reading. Endren hurried her pace around the narrow stone steps. Surely if there were a guest of importance, they would ring the Toll, calling all avaryll to the Symposium.

As if they heard her thoughts, a sudden, deep pulse in Endren's chest reverberated through her bones. She pressed against the wall to her left and wished a railing was on the other side. She glanced over that edge and the twenty levels still to descend. Over two hundred feet from the ground, Endren stepped from the stairs and, with only the barest tug from her Shadow Step, stood on the cobblestone square before the Symposium. Other avaryll similarly appeared around her and filed into the vaulted palace of the Protectorate. All coming at the call of the Toll.

Endren ran a hand through her brass hair, smoothing it while adjusting her flowing hakama and the heavy iron bangles around her arms. As she entered the Symposium alongside dozens of her kind, the temperature dropped, and the humidity rose sharply, just as the Protectorate preferred his space. Endren crossed the tiled, marbled floor without looking at the ceiling nearly a hundred feet overhead. Well-tended trees grew in this space, almost reaching the top while moss drooped from their branches to brush the cool floor. She strode through the gathering of avaryll, not pausing to greet or acknowledge them as she passed.

Protectorate Gundil sat on his throne atop a dais at the head of the long chamber. A shaft of light from the tall windows cut through the haze to illuminate his radiant cobalt hair. Two dozen mages flanked him in rows, curving into a semicircle on either side. Endren took her place at the end on the right side.

Two men stood before the Protectorate. One wore a long leather jacket with dark, shoulder-length hair loosely tied back, the other in shining golden plate mail and eyes that twinkled like polished amethyst. Neither appeared to be armed as they calmly waited to be addressed. The one in plate even looked bored by how he tapped at his armor's tasset as if drumming out the rhythm of a melody. Other than their attire and hair, they were nearly identical. Brothers, perhaps even twins. They were not of any race Endren knew of in Poas. They lacked the ears of the avaryll or svarters, were far too tall to be a dirge and too short for a kalvyr, and were obviously not feybeasts or Mraasil. Could they be from another realm? Though the men looked young, something in their eyes hinted at a deceptive age.

Eighth Celestial Mage Wrost, standing at Endren's side, leaned over and hissed in his high, strained voice. "These two were caught strolling through the city."

Endren nodded and said nothing, keeping her gaze locked on the two invaders.

Avaryll continued to file into the Symposium for another five long minutes, filling the space while not gathering too tightly.

Protectorate Gundil looked over his people with a somber eye before focusing on the two standing patiently before him.

"Guests," Gundil's words shook the marble under Endren's feet, vibrating her body as the Toll had. "We have not entertained guests in living memory. I, Protectorate Gundil, Keeper of the Silven Rings of Anshamot, welcome you to Tidecrest. Now, who are you, humans?" He smacked his lips as if tasting something sour.

Humans? Those are a rare sort, Endren thought and craned her neck with renewed interest.

The man in plate armor started to speak, but the other pushed forward. "Thank you for granting my brother and me an audience without advance notice, Protectorate. Our names are unimportant, and we have had many titles in our time. We only come offering a gift."

Gundil sneered. "A gift? The avaryll have no interest in accepting gifts and becoming indebted to others. Much less to a human, to the race that unleashed the Gods of Naught and brought ruin to a thousand realms."

The armored brother smirked and rolled his eyes. "You do not want it? Fine, we keep it and leave."

"Quiet," the other hissed and focused back on Gundil. "We ask for nothing in return but to ask you to care for it. Any realm lacking a living world tree is fated to decay and eventual death. What Ters did four thousand years ago may have saved countless other realms, but Poas is doomed to a slow end."

Gundil leaned forward again. "How does any of that relate to why you are here now?"

The brother in leathers reached into a pouch at his hip and pulled out something in his fist.

"It will take time and effort to nurture, but I offer you the very thing that will save your realm." He opened his fist, revealing a large acorn. Endren squinted and could sense the energy of it as it radiated a cobalt-blue aura, not unlike Gundil's flowing locks.

A hushed mummer filled the chamber as some gasped while others craned their necks to identify what the human offered.

Gundil's eyes widened as he pushed himself from his seat and stumbled down the steps of the dais. "Is this from..." his words were lost in his awe.

"Yes, the only one," the brother said, pressing the acorn into Gundil's eager palms. "The first Seed of Farsil to create the final world tree."

Protectorate Gundil held the acorn close to his nose for a moment before raising it carefully, reverently, over his head. "Poas will be reborn!"

The room roared with cheers. Gundil finally looked back down at humans, more than a head shorter than himself.

"Take it. Care for it. Let it grow," the brother said. "I will be back to check on it."

Gundil nodded. "Of course." His eyes glinted blue with the power he held. "Others must know of this event. What might we call you in the retelling?"

"We have had our share of names and titles," said the one in leathers. "The Forged, the Scions of Flayme, but if you need individual—"

"The Gilded Warrior!" his brother cut in. "Call me the Gilded Warrior."

The other closed his green eyes with a slow breath and continued. "I will visit often to tend to the tree. You can call me the World Tender."

With a stiff bow, the humans turned and strode through the mass of avaryll and out of the Symposium.

2

They referred to it as "The Final Daemon War." Very optimistic.

At the beginning Etharis touched the rough bark of his world tree and felt, with each breath, her roots cut through the rocks and soil below. Around him, the once perfectly flat world of Tempus Fa slowly took shape as mountains pushed into the clear skies and oceans dug deep and wide into the world.

"Archdruid Etharis," said a soft voice behind him. He had not heard his name said out loud in so long that he did not recognize it at first. To hear anything in his realm was a reason to look, as he was the only living creature besides the plants.

A short woman with dark skin and long-tipped ears stood there wearing an elegant blue dress that swept around her ankles and a wide leather bracer around her right forearm. Etharis narrowed his glowing amber eyes, instantly recognizing her despite having no memory of their meeting. "Chronicler," he said and stood, brushing the dirt from his hands. "I thought I might be alone here forevermore."

A warm grin spread across the Chronicler's lips. "You will never be alone, Etharis. Well..." She looked out to the horizon, where the clean air eventually became too thick, fading the world to mist at the edges. "I mean, once the other Mraasil are born and the realms begin to populate."

Etharis felt a pang of sadness mixed with a spark of hope. He had no means of measuring how long he had been alone to wander Tempus Fa, and though he knew nothing but solitude, the concept of others like him gave him a quiet thrill. "When will the other Mraasil be born? Before they left, the Ascended said something about me seeing to them, but they weren't really talking to me." He shrugged.

"That sounds about right for them. They crafted Farsil as the first world tree and laid the ground for the first realm. You were born of it, Etharis. Your journey will be strenuous and lonely as you travel the realms and tend to the trees. Eventually, your siblings will be born to offer companionship, and the mortal races later still. Everyone is, for at least an instant, the youngest living person in all the realms. For now, you are both youngest and eldest, Etharis, and you will always be the eldest."

He followed her silvered gaze across the landscape of his realm with a rush of excitement, wondering how other worlds might look and smell. "I have only vague memories of the Ascended as they left me alone so long ago. Yet I'd no doubt of your identity when I saw you. I think they said you named me. Were you there when I was born?"

The Chronicler nodded and pushed a stray lock of auburn hair around the long tip of her ear. "I named you what I already knew you by, a cyclical name without origin, a mistake of my younger self." Etharis cocked his head, unsure of her meaning, but the Chronicler waved off the topic and continued. "I'm on a journey not unlike what you will take, Etharis. I came to see and speak with you to suggest it may be time for you to get yours underway."

He blinked at her. "To travel the realms and see to the other world trees?"

"My role is to observe and record the history of all realms across all time until the end. Yours is one of guardianship, protection, nurturing."

"It will all end?" Etharis glanced around at the endless plains stretching away to the infinite.

"Mana creates life, and life creates mana, but there is a little lost in the exchange. Eventually, yes, there will not be enough of either to sustain the realms, and they will collapse. That's so far in the future; you've no reason to concern yourself with it now." She smiled and gestured to the massive tree behind Etharis. "The Ascended planted the world trees from the Seeds of Farsil. Not all will produce viable realms, but your role is ensuring as many survive and thrive."

She stepped forward and reached up to place a hand against the archdruid's soft, lavender cheek. "I envy your journey. You will see and experience your share of hardships and horrors across the realms, but there are equal or greater joys. The former makes us appreciate the latter. Keep heart, archdruid."

The Chronicler disappeared in a blink, leaving Etharis alone again, but now with a sparking desire to see what worlds lay beyond his own.

3

Necromancy exists in other realms without the stigma it has in Poas. The people of one realm even use it in their reproduction.

Delphin Carter, Halberdier Second Class, flinched at the sudden pop as another group teleported into the courtyard's center. The marble tiles before the Six Steps leading to the Gilded Basilica were among the holiest grounds in Acrus, in all of Poas, yet the Archetype allowed heathens to use the Ascended's gifts here. They flaunted it.

"Regent King Lone of Dracon has arrived," said one of the five now standing before him, the one wearing plate armor and holding a spear. Despite the imposing gleam of armor, the voice was feminine.

Another woman stood beside her, wearing a drab gray dress with a satchel of books over her shoulder.

Disgusting heretics. Not only do they waste the gift of the Ascended, they bring women to this holy site.

At least the three men were dressed well, but it was well known that the regent king was in an unnatural relationship with the island savage he hired to train his castle guard. Delphin gripped his halberd tighter to keep his hand from shaking. There was nothing to be done for the heat in his helmet and the drip of sweat running down his back.

He curled a lip behind his visor and watched the group meet with Lord Patriarch Shenna Quey. The revered holy man had been reduced to a common escort as he led them across the marble tile and into Suanh's Chapel. Delphin had served for a decade and only once had been invited to enter that shrine of knowledge, where Archetype Dalbinth the Redeemer was said to be today. Delphin was never aware of being so physically close to the Archetype, only a few hundred yards away.

Delphin prided himself on strictly adhering to the old teachings of the Scrolls. Not *old*, the *correct* teachings. That rigidity allowed him to rise to his rank at only twenty-three, a feat rare even among those ten years his senior. Delphin intended to make captain before he reached thirty-four. Then, he could make some real changes in how things were done. Women would remain at home, where they belong. Using the Ascended's gift, so-called "magic," would have the highest possible retribution.

While he fantasized about punishments worse than death, a couple swaggered into the courtyard from the west. They wore light traveling clothes with delicate, yet complex, goggles around their necks. Their dark skin and pale eyes heralded them from Jaiketh. Behind Dracon and Terswood, Jaiketh was easily the most sinful of nations in Poas.

The couple approached a guard standing a few down the line from Delphin.

"Lady and Lord Bismat!" said the woman, and they both bowed deeply.

The guard said nothing as he gestured with his halberd to the entrance of Suanh's Chapel.

"Thanks, pleasant talk," Lord Bismat said with an exaggerated smile, and they both pivoted on the heels of their heavy boots toward the Chapel.

Delphin watched them enter and continued his thoughts. The leaders of both Dracon and Jaiketh allowed women to introduce them. Women led Terswood and Evkasa. Barbarles and Eplear had mages among their retinue in the Chapel at this moment. The nation's leaders in Poas were all infected with sin. Acrus was truly the only pure nation, the only pure people.

"Second class, attend me," ordered Major Bennus, and Delphin's line snapped to follow the Bismats toward the Chapel's entrance.

As Delphin neared those simple double doors, elation and deep reverence swelled within him. He could barely hear someone within speaking in an unnaturally deep voice but could not make out the words. Delphin entered the sanctuary of knowledge to see two tall figures with silver and gold hair in the center, with all the other dignitaries of Poas forming a ring around them.

"Seize them!" Lord Patriarch Shenna Quey commanded, and Delphin swept forward.

His armor suddenly weighed a thousand stone, crushing him to the ground. Around him, his fellow guards and the rulers of Poas fell as well.

"We represent the High Court of Isolis," said the silver-haired woman in that terribly deep voice. "We have watched the actions of your child race and found you wanting, dangerous. As such, the avaryll are retaking our rightful place within this realm to restore order."

A man, resplendent in robes of pristine white, standing tall despite all others in the room being helpless under the magic of these invaders, stepped beside Delphin and looked down at him. "Guards, stand down."

That must be Archetype Dalbinth, Delphin thought, despite the effort it took to breathe. *Of course, he could defeat their feeble magics. I lie here almost close enough to kiss his feet.*

The invader's spell lifted as suddenly as it hit him. Delphin leaped to his feet, halberd ready to slay the pale enemies with their long-tipped ears, but Archetype Dalbinth waved to Major Bennus, and the guards were led back outside the Chapel. As he followed the others, Delphin could do nothing for the weight of impotence slamming against him. Years of training, endless sweat and blood spilled, broken bones and noses, concussions, unyielding faith in the Ascended, and his calling to protect those nearest to them. When he finally stood beside the holiest of men, heretical magic laid him low. He acted instinctually as he snapped back to position beside the others of his rank. Rage heated his armor more than the sun overhead and he held his weapon in a grip that would shatter one of inferior make.

Curiosity was not one of Delphin's flaws, but he felt the temptation of it now. The details of what occurred within Suanh's Chapel would not be told to someone of his rank, and no one in the barracks would dare to speculate and start rumors. Yet he would know what had happened within the Suanh's Chapel. Somehow, he would find out.

A group of clerics stormed from the door of the Chapel, led by one wearing a pristine white hat, stole, and a cloak inlaid with gold—the Archetype. Archetype Dalbinth was walking directly toward Delphin Carter, Halberdier Second Class.

The Archetype passed close enough that Delphin could have reached to kiss his ring.

As he passed, Delphin heard Archetype Dalbinth the Redeemer whisper something, almost as if muttering under his breath.

"Scragging avaryll."

PART ONE

4

I've tried to trace Cazlandt's parentage, without success.

The Tersguard standing before the house marked the approaching regent king, but did not stop him. Lone passed them without a glance and entered the home assigned to the delegation from Terswood. The layout was the same as the house Lone used on his first visit to Acrus two months ago. The foyer held a grand staircase to a second level and a dining room to the right. A packed sitting room was to his left.

"Five weeks," he shouted over the din of conversation. He spotted his father standing tall over the collected svarters and strode to him.

Queen Teiris looked at him from where she stood, speaking with the new svarters prelen. Lone could not recall her name.

"Regent King," Teiris said sharply, and the dozen svarters between them parted as if by the force of her words. "I appreciate the strong bonds between Terswood and Dracon, but this is a private space. Entering without a summons is not appropriate."

"Tell that to your king," Lone muttered under his breath and continued. "The avaryll have given us five weeks to prepare for some mystery event in Isolis. I'm taking my father to Siraas vass Soss for treatment. We need him lucid."

Teiris closed the gap between the two and lowered her voice. "I would have words with you, Regent King. In private." She continued her pace toward the door leading to the gardens at the back of the house.

Lone looked over the gathering of svarters dignitaries and to his father's vacant stare before turning to follow the queen.

The garden at the rear of the two-story house was as well-manicured as any other Lone had seen in Acrus. Topiaries expertly shaped into the forms of animals surrounded a lawn of trimmed grass. He remembered Chief Arborist Gadrial

Drock leading the tour of the gardens south of the Gilded Basilica and wondered how many tenders smelling of sunshine and fertilizer Acrus had in its employ. An oval-shaped fountain featuring a tall, cloaked cleric pouring clear water from a jug stood as the centerpiece. Lone was accustomed to the gardens of Terswood or Eplear and again noted the lack of flowers here.

"Teiris, we don't have time for formalities. We have five weeks to prepare for whatever is to happen in Isolis. My father's mind is mush, and Alishia is still missing after two months."

Teiris crossed to the fountain and placed her palms on the wide ledge. It was a seat for humans but was a comfortable waist level for svarters.

"Can Siraas cure him?" she asked while looking into the pool.

Lone stepped beside the queen and followed her gaze into the bubbling water. "Siraas has studied magic-born illnesses for close to four centuries. It was she who named Red Bloom and a dozen other diseases. She diagnosed the svarters man in Halisal a few months ago."

"I'm still not convinced that was accurate, that a svarters man contracted Red Bloom," Teiris said with a thoughtful hum.

Lone continued. "Even if my father's condition is not caused by his mana cultivation, I have absolute confidence that Siraas will determine the root of it and define a treatment schedule."

Teiris nodded. "I'll take him." She reached to trace a finger along the water's surface.

Lone watched his stepmother in profile for a moment. He did not expect her to fight him on this decision, but he was unprepared for it to be so easy.

"What of Alishia?" He asked. "I need something greater than you saying that Enid says she's safe."

Teiris turned to him, leaning her hip against the fountain's ledge with a deep breath. "I can't keep this a secret," she said, more to herself. "Lone, I have told no one of this. Not your father or my great-aunt Wynlen, but I can't keep it from you. Not any longer."

Lone raised an eyebrow and waved a hand for her to continue.

Teiris opened her mouth with a deep breath and let it out with a sobbing laugh. "It sounds like insanity. I know it's true, yet I'm questioning myself as I'm about to say it."

Lone waved his hand while keeping his expression level. "Say it."

Teiris took another deep breath. "Alishia is a god." She paused, waiting for Lone's reaction, but he gave her none. He knew his sister had power beyond his ken.

"The Ascended," Teiris continued after a moment. "Enid, Elphame, Suanh, all the beings of reverence and worship representing their individual fundamental concepts are not at the pinnacle of our cosmology. There are layers of beings above them. The Sundered, the Primes, the Gods of Naught."

Lone half sat on the fountain's lip to face Teiris. "I can believe that. If the Ascended are so advanced over humans and svarters, any beings with a similar power gap above them would be unknowable to us. What does this have to do with Alishia?"

"I'm getting there. This has been difficult for me." She wrung her hands nervously. "This goes against ten thousand years of doctrine, and I've learned it all in the last few days. It would be easier if I just…" She raised two fingers at Lone's forehead, and he caught her by the wrist.

"Memory magics? No thank you, Teiris. We can stick to words."

She dropped her arm with a huff. "Time is vital, Lone. I could show you in twenty seconds what would take me an hour to describe. We wouldn't want anything lost in translation."

Lone bit his lip and looked down at her hands, now folded in front of her. There were rural areas of Poas where the parents would scare their children to sleep, telling tales of svarters using memory magic to turn their victims into slaves or worse. In reality, there were no known cases of it ever being used for ill deeds. Despite Lone's personal feelings for Teiris, stemming from the loss of his mother at an early age, he knew the queen of the svarters to be well worth every ounce of his trust.

Teiris had a good point about things being lost in translation. Though they both spoke Svarters, Lone knew Teiris simplified the words and dialect for his human ears. Even if Teiris switched to speaking the native human tongue, the spoken word was rife with simple misunderstandings—tone, inflection, body language. Memory magic was just a broad term for a linkage of the minds, converting every thought to a means of natural understanding. He would know things exactly as she did.

"It's perfectly safe," Teiris urged. "You won't walk away thinking you're me. I'm not implanting memories. You won't think my memories were yours or that you were present to see things firsthand. You'll view memories from a third perspective and be aware you're viewing a scene. Like a play. Just without a language barrier."

"It sounds like a reminisphere."

Teiris shrugged. "I don't know what that is, but sure."

"They're orbs containing memories. Jazelyn said they were based on svarters magic. We found one in The Stacks a couple of months ago with some of Cazlandt's memories regarding the Shadow Reaver."

"It's probably the same sort of thing, then. Rather convenient, you just happened upon one about the Shadow Reaver when you did, huh?"

"Very convenient..." He looked down at her hands with a deep breath. "I'm sorry, Teiris, I can't. It's not that I don't trust you, of course. I just can't. I'm the ruler of a nation. I have to set a hard line on some things. Not just for my safety, but for those I serve."

"I get it," Teiris said quickly, drumming her fingers of one hand on the other arm. "I'm the queen of the svarters, the beacon of Enid's light in Poas, etcetera, but there are two things in this world that I love more than any of that, Lone." She held out her hand to count them off with her fingers. "Your sister and your father. You and I have always had a rocky relationship; I know much of the blame is mine. In almost twenty years, the only thing your father and I have fought about was you. I wanted you to live with us in Terswood, but your father wanted to leave the decision to you."

"Really?" His father never strongly insisted that Lone come to live with them, so Lone always assumed Teiris had no input on it. He even assumed she was against the idea.

"Yes, but I recognize now my reasons weren't purely altruistic. I was a twenty-year-old maiden when the high prince archmage widower with a young son came courting me. I knew if you stayed in Dracon, my new husband would spend half his time there with you."

Lone leaned back with arms crossed. "So you wanted me close to keep my father in place."

"Yes. It's terrible, but yes. I'll admit to it. It's no tremendous secret that your father and I started as something close to an arranged marriage. He needed to escape Dracon and the memories there, and Terswood needed to build ties with the human nations. That isn't the case now. Your father, even with all his grunted replies and drinking he thinks is a secret from me, is the love of my life. So Lone, because of him and your sister, you and I are bound tightly. We should work together, completely in the open, with full honesty."

Lone nodded absently. Images from the last twenty years flashed by. Every celebration or trip his father missed, Lone blamed on Teiris, allowing bitterness to fester. Perhaps he could have done more. Perhaps he could have spoken out and asked his father directly to be when and where he wanted. Perhaps Teiris was not the sinister villain he made her to be. It would take time for him to work through it all. "So what of Alishia?"

Teiris sighed and looked down at her hands before folding them in her lap. "I doubt your father told you the full story of our trip to Tempus Fa and Elogah'an." Lone shook his head, and she continued. "Long story short, I got a missive from Enid through the Prophetess Mylaerla. She told me that because of Alishia's mixed blood, she would not be the queen of Terswood, that her destiny lays elsewhere."

"Because she is the Chronicler." Lone had been so focused on his duties in Dracon and worried for his missing sister that he never considered the crisis of leadership in Terswood. Without Alishia, leadership would pass through Teiris's younger brother's future children.

"And what is the Chronicler?" Teiris asked. "After Alishia disappeared, I begged Enid for some spark of hope and received nothing. I begged any of the Ascended, and the response I got was from a being above them, calling herself one of the Sundered. She explained what lies above the Ascended and Alishia's place in the structure of our gods. I believe her fully that Alishia is safe where she is now."

Lone bit his lip, knowing a dozen questions to pick apart and dissect Teiris's story but unsure which to ask first. "I'll trust you, Teiris." He paused to rephrase his statement. "I do trust you. I know there must be so much more to your story, but we both want to get back to dealing with everything else. You can tell me all the details later. I, ah... I also have talked to someone who knows about Alishia."

Lone told Teiris everything about Dalbinth the Redeemer, Archetype of the Holy Seat of Acrus, actually being a kalvyr, a race of dragonmen from the far west shores of D'Kreti. Not only a dragonman but a light shaper, a type of magic user instructed by Aiden, the man playing the part of Dalbinth at the summit and self-proclaimed long-time friend of Alishia. He felt good to confide in someone other than Bard. Between their two tales, they shared more words by the fountain that afternoon than they had combined in twenty years. Lone felt like a crazy person as he heard his words spoken aloud, but Teiris nodded along, doubting nothing.

5

I quietly visited Prince Erusa's tomb once. I don't know what I expected thirty-thousand eggs to look like, but I expected to be impressed, for some reason. I wasn't.

Queen Teiris strode back into the house and directly to Prelen Kaermys. The newly appointed commander of the Tersguard did not wear the heavy plate armor of her predecessor but wore a brooch in the shape of a war hammer pinned to her leather breastplate in his honor.

"Prelen," said Teiris, "please return to Terswood immediately. Gather and mobilize the Tersguard. Prepare them for the march to Isolis."

"Of course, My Queen. What route will we take?"

Teiris considered for a moment. "I won't risk our forces through the fey wilds of Nyphlym. Going through Evkasa requires we cross the Loch, but we have no boats. We don't have the time to negotiate with the Bismats. We sail around the east," she decided. "Captain Hihowl will recall the fleet, and we'll make it to Tidecrest with time to spare."

"Yes, My Queen," Kaermys said with a stiff bow.

"Regent King Lone," Teiris called to her stepson as he was about to exit the room. He turned and crossed to her.

"Queen Teiris?"

"I have a favor to ask of you. Please assist the prelen to Terswood with a teleport."

Lone's lip twitched. "It would be my pleasure."

Kaermys looked at her queen with confusion. "You are remaining here?"

"No, I am taking the king to Barbarles for treatment."

The prelen touched Teiris's forearm. "My Queen, you must allow me to select an escort. The king is not well. He could not protect you, should you need it."

Teiris looked down at Kaermys's hand and up to her dark blue eyes. "We will be quite fine. I appreciate your concern." She looked around at the other dozen svarters in the room before focusing back on the regent king. "I have another favor to ask, Lone. Your father brought us here with a series of teleports. I can't guess how long we'll be gone or how your father will be afterward. Might I impose again upon the northern mages to see my people home?"

Lone took a slow breath. "I'll see it done. Anything else?"

"No, thank you."

Lone stepped beside Kaermys, placed a hand on her shoulder, and they both disappeared with a faint pop.

Teiris turned to her husband. "Daelin, you've been to Siraas vass Soss's tower before, yes?"

Daelin's gaze floated down to meet Teiris's with a smile. "The healer? Yes, dear. I went for Siraas when Lium started getting sick. I told Lilan it was Red Bloom, and there was nothing to be—"

"Take us there." She clasped his right hand in both of hers.

"What? Now?" He bent closer to her and lowered his voice. "I am not feeling my best, Teiris. Perhaps an upset of the humors. I just saw Lone leave. Maybe he could take you when he returns."

"Daelin, it's not I that needs to see a healer."

"I... I think I understand. Though I still think it safer to wait for Lone to return."

"I've imposed upon him enough for the moment. You can do this," she hissed.

The king shrugged and took a deep breath. With a pop and jarring tug, the two stood at the doors of a tall, unevenly built tower. Smoke plumed from chimneys at three levels, and old scaffolding stretched five stories on the east side, either for repairs or enhancements. Teiris could see rusted tools lying on the wooden planks and tall grass. A long-abandoned and barely recognizable vegetable garden was staked out a few yards from the entrance.

The door opened with a loud creak before they could knock, and a wave of fresh-cut herbs and wood smoke buffeted Teiris's senses. A human woman looked them over with a smile. Her wide, white, calf-length dress was trimmed with red, and her silver hair streaked with white. Her age was impossible to tell by her unlined face, but her eyes gave her away, holding deep wells of knowledge.

"Ah, good afternoon, Queen Teiris. I was wondering when the king would come to see me. Please, come in."

"Thank you, Siraas," Teiris said and entered with her husband close behind. Inside, the smell of a dozen potions brewing at once dazzled her senses. Acrid, bitter, sweet, earthy. Vanilla mixed with vinegar, citrus, and ash. She breathed through her mouth, but it barely helped. Tables and chairs were heaped with texts and scraps of equipment. Teiris had met the legendary healer before, and she always seemed to be calm and meticulous. This was not what Teiris expected her home to look like.

Teiris turned to see Siraas already examining Daelin. She looked into his eyes, turned his hands over, and checked his height against her own.

"I'll need to see him in my lab on the sixth floor," Siraas announced while looking into Daelin's mouth. "I assume I have permission to perform all needed tests, including, but not limited to, the extraction of fluids or other samples?"

"Y-yes, whatever you deem necessary," Teiris stammered, trying not to suffocate through the fumes. She pulled at her internal mana to create a thin bubble around herself to filter the worst of the air. She sighed as her lungs relaxed.

Siraas led Daelin to the steps at the far side of the cramped space, and Teiris had a sudden memory of scaling Gurrim'Nosh in Tempus Fa with Daelin, Dryon, and the Mraasil. That seemed like so long ago now.

Siraas had no problem with the steps being at irregular heights, but Teiris and Daelin did, as they tripped frequently. The levels of the tower they passed were also inconsistent. The second floor was barely high enough for the mage to stand upright, while the third and fifth were three times the average height for human architecture.

"I had to ask them to stop," Siraas explained as they passed a window showing the top of the scaffolding outside. "They were making too much noise."

Teiris wondered how many decades ago the builders had been asked to leave. If they were human, were they even still alive?

The stairs continued upward, but the sixth floor was a clean space of white-washed walls and a floor pristine enough to serve dinner upon. Siraas waved Daelin to sit on a long iron table and mixed a thimble full of some draught using ingredients on another table beside it. She poured the contents into a glass vial, covered the opening with her thumb, and shook it vigorously.

"Drink this," she said and handed Daelin the small vial. He downed it without hesitation. Siraas moved to the workbench across from the metal table. Candles of every color and shape sat below a shelf on the wall stocked with clearly labeled jars of reagents, herbs, and stoppered vials. Short metal rods were next to a handful of daggers next to cubes of wood ranging from black to white and every color between. Siraas carefully selected items, arranging them on a silver tray.

Teiris paced the edges of the room, examining a shelf reaching to the ceiling full of creatures and portions of creatures suspended in murky fluid. She could barely guess what most of them were.

"It is a shame about Red Bloom," Siraas said without turning from her array of vials and tools.

"How do you mean?" Teiris asked and gently pushed aside a jar with the right side of something's head to see behind it.

"I studied it for twenty years and was so near to understanding. We had the first case of it jumping to svarters, which was also the first case of recovery, involving a feybeast, no less."

Teiris turned from the jars. "The symptoms were similar but not identical. Your diagnosis cannot be confirmed."

Siraas faced Teiris with a shrug. "The Sisters of the Moons called it Red Bloom before I arrived. That's why I traveled there to see it. But, as was said, Red Bloom is always fatal, yet the svarters subject is alive. Perhaps I was wrong. It matters not. With the affliction in the realm's mana resolved, those with Red Bloom will now die and no one else will contract it. Why continue a study when it will now resolve itself? I studied a disease for twenty years to cure no one. Such a waste." She turned back and picked up her tray of tools and jars.

Teiris stepped closer to Daelin, who was staring drowsily at his hands, seeming to hear nothing around him. "I understand the disappointment, but even if you didn't find a cure, I'm sure you learned much in your study, learned to ease the suffering of hundreds. It's enough to know Red Bloom is gone."

Siraas sat her array of tools on the table beside Daelin and sighed as she ran a finger along the flat of a dagger inlaid with runes. "I almost hope that isn't true. If someone else contracts Red Bloom, my research may continue."

Teiris cringed. "Those aren't the words of a healer."

"I am a researcher. The theory states that Red Bloom was a corruption in the world's ley lines caused by Amer's defeat. Queen Lilan pulled Amer's essence in the attempt to flush it to the Afterlands, but instead, the necromancer took over the risen body of the prince, killed Queen Lilan, and raised her body as an undead puppet."

"You know a lot for someone who hasn't left her tower in years."

"I leave my tower often to care for my garden," Siraas said defensively. "The theory of the disease's origin was my own. I told the late queen about my suspicions of Red Bloom, and she took action. Queen Lilan and I often spoke at great length on many topics." She sounded proud of her relationship with the late archmage queen.

"King Daelin—"

"The king is suffering from a cytotoxic hypersensitivity to ley energy brought on by his recent resumption of mana cultivation," Siraas spoke quickly and flatly as if bored by the diagnosis.

"Could you say that again, but assume I won't know what any of that means?"

Siraas let out an exasperated breath. "He's allergic to mana."

Teiris looked at the tray of tools and vials and back to Siraas. "But you haven't done any tests."

The healer shrugged. "His condition is exceptionally rare but not unheard of. Do you think someone with my experience requires extensive testing?"

Teiris brushed off the statement of overconfidence. "Then do you have a cure?"

"No. The king has not cultivated ley energy in over thirty years, and it's now destroying him from the inside, focusing on his brain. He could reduce the rate of cultivation or stop completely, but this sensitivity to ley energy is, as I said, rare. Archmages don't just stop mana cultivation unless they're very old and want to die. It's the cornerstone of what makes us... us. Daelin was in his late teens when he met a mundane human girl he wanted to marry. He gave up immortal for Lady Aaislin." Siraas waved a hand over her equipment. "I will need to run tests to know if the damage is permanent and to model the best route to full health, but your king is mortal now. He cannot cultivate ley energy, meaning he will die at the age most humans do."

Daelin heaved a deep breath and blinked rapidly as if struggling to pull himself from a nightmare. He looked at Teiris with surprising lucidity and spoke with strained effort. "I cannot stop, Teiris. I can feel it, feel the confusion, and it terrifies me. But without cultivation, I have at most another thirty years. That is not enough time."

Teiris took Daelin's left hand in both of hers. Even Siraas paused adjusting her instruments while the two shared a silent look. Teiris's heart clenched as Daelin's eyes glazed over and drifted to the middle distance.

Teiris looked at the healer. This was a woman with a drive to discover truths but also with a frighteningly cold distance from any compassion. "Tell me more about mana cultivation," Teiris said, releasing her husband's hand and crossing her arms.

Siraas picked up a dagger and ran her thumb down the blade's edge. She smeared blood into the runes carved on the flat side, and they glowed faintly in response. "Do you want me to run these tests or explain to you the basics of what it means to be an archmage?"

"I want you to do both," said Teiris.

"I don't know what busy looks like in Terswood, my queen, but I assure you I don't have time for that."

Teiris pushed down the healer's hand holding the dagger. "I will not sit idly by here without being of some help." She considered the old researcher. Most archmages of Poas focused their skill on a few types of magic. Daelin was an expert in teleportation. Jazelyn could travel the ley lines of the world. Lone was... Teiris was not sure where her stepson's specialty lay. Siraas was famous for projecting herself, creating simulacrum to go into the world while remaining in the weird comfort of her tower in eastern Barbarles. Siraas vass Soss could very well create a copy of herself to tell Teiris everything she knew about mana cultivation and its functions within archmage physiology while still working on Daelin.

"Fine," Siraas sighed. "Meet me one floor up." She turned back to Daelin and raised the glowing dagger.

Teiris grumbled to herself and returned to the stairway.

"Wait," Siraas called after Teiris. "What happened to his left hand?"

"He used it to channel the energy to destroy an inter-realm gateway at the base of a world tree. Then he used mana crystal to teleport, which exploded, embedding crystal into the flesh. Archdruid Etharis repaired the damage a little and svarters healers and his son have attended to him since."

"I see," Siraas nodded, unimpressed by the list of events. "Not what I would have guessed. I'll see if I can do better. Carry on, I'll meet you upstairs."

Teiris rolled her eyes and turned back to the steps. One level higher, and she entered a room filled with slate boards lining the walls and freestanding on wheels for mobility. It reminded her of General Jazelyn's workshop in Castle Dracon. Siraas stepped from behind a board, her fingers and dark smock covered with chalk dust. Though she knew it would happen, meeting a copy of the healer was jarring. Or perhaps this was the real Siraas.

"Queen Teiris, please join me over here," Siraas spoke cheerfully and led Teiris to a board showing a carefully drawn human outline. Thick lines spread down the spine to trace the legs and arms. "Where should I start with a lesson on mana cultivation?"

"At the beginning," said Teiris. "Svarters don't do it, and in the almost twenty years Daelin and I have been together, he's never much talked about it. I don't know why only the smallest handful of humans can cultivate."

"Hmm, not exactly true about svarters. I haven't studied your kind in great detail, but I suspect you naturally cultivate, or at least something akin to it." Siraas waved away the topic and pointed to the diagram on the board. "We can discuss that another time. The defining feature of an archmage over other humans is that archmages can draw ley energy into their bodies through their nervous system. This alters our spell-casting abilities, as we can draw the energy through ourselves first, giving greater control over the result. The ley energy also constantly rebuilds every cell of our bodies, giving us accelerated healing. By doing so, our bodies become dependent upon it. After a few decades or a century, we no longer require food, water, or even sleep. A constant stream of mana is enough for us."

Teiris wrinkled her nose in thought. "Svarters passively absorb mana from our environment. Our capacity limits are determined by our practice and some innate ability. This all happens naturally from pubescence. If an archmage can choose not to cultivate, does that mean it isn't a natural process? That it's a skill that is taught?"

"Cultivation is a learned ability, yes. It would be as natural as breathing in your husband these last decades, but he actively suppressed it. Like holding his breath for thirty years. The first archmage, Cazlandt, King Daelin's grandsire, developed the technique. Do you know about Cazlandt?"

"Yes," Teiris huffed. "I am aware of him."

"Before Cazlandt, archmages were little more than powerful spell casters. They could pull mana to fuel their spells from ley lines rather than requiring mana crystals or the like, but not live indefinitely as we do now."

"What's involved in learning the technique?"

"Oh, it's really very simple." Siraas laughed to herself. "It's no more complex than learning a basic spell, taking an hour at most. Many archmages later laugh that it wasn't conceived of sooner."

"When did Cazlandt come up with it?"

"He was perhaps in his mid-sixties."

"And when was that?"

Siraas's brow furrowed with confusion. "I don't understand the question."

"I mean, when was he in his sixties? He raised Castle Dracon about twelve hundred years ago. How old was he at that point?"

"Oh, of course. No one is sure of that. There is no mention of Cazlandt prior to his gathering of the first archmages."

"And he taught those archmages like Jazelyn and Mage Varon the cultivation technique, who taught it to others. That millennia-old technique is now killing my husband. So then, the obvious question, is it the technique or ley energy itself? Can another method be developed to produce the same results?"

Siraas frowned and shook her head. "No, Queen Teiris. Cazlandt's technique is how mana cultivation works."

"Don't be lazy," Teiris said through her teeth. "There is always more than one route to a solution. The first mages used Ley Slip to teleport, not knowing what it was doing to their bodies. Now, at least the few my husband has allowed to learn the magic use a much less efficient variation of teleport that doesn't destroy themselves in the process. Two types of teleport. Two very different spells with the same results. There *is* another method for mana cultivation, and you *will* find it."

Siraas looked confused and angry before amusement spread across her lips. "Thank you, Queen Teiris. I have been working only within the realm of known theories. I fully understand the biological process of mana cultivation, so why shouldn't I be able to find another means to the result? I'll even name it after myself. How grand would it be for future generations of archmages to learn the 'vass Soss Cultivation Technique'? I'll work on the name."

Teiris looked down at the wide silver band on her left forefinger. She might have asked for Siraas to provide accommodations while she worked, but she felt rushed with the preparations needed for the events in Isolis. Teiris closed her eyes with a deep breath. "Do what you must, but the king must be ready to travel in five weeks."

"To Isolis, yes." Siraas nodded.

"How can you know that? How do you know so much?"

"I watch. Well, not me personally, but another of me."

"Have you been inside Isolis?"

"The protective wards surrounding Isolis are neigh impenetrable."

"That isn't the same as saying 'no.'"

Siraas sighed. "No. I could never create a simulacrum within Isolis, but have one on her way there now, formed from the one that examined the svarters man months ago." Her gaze took on a glassy, distant look. "She's at Tolnach Loch now. The waters are so still, perfectly reflecting the clear skies above." A smile traced across her lips.

"You're in contact with all your simulacra?" Teiris asked, taking a curious step closer.

Siraas blinked and refocused on Teiris. "Yes. I am in every nation of Poas and in Iecil, including my copies throughout this tower. I see, hear, and feel everything each of my simulacra experiences, though our moods change with the current activity. It's taken me centuries of slow practice to build the constitution to maintain so many at once."

"How many is that?"

"Fifteen," Siraas replied without hesitation. "Though five are in this tower."

Teiris gaped at the number. "Where is the real you?"

Siraas's narrowed her eyes at the question. "They are all me."

"Yes, but which is the first you? The original or core or whatever you might call it?"

Siraas chuckled. "I think you have a fundamental misunderstanding. I mean exactly that when I say all the simulacra are me."

"You exist equally over multiple bodies?"

"Essentially."

"And one of those was in Suanh's Chapel in Acrus, or at least nearby enough to hear the avaryll?"

Siraas nodded. "Yes."

"And another watched Queen Lilan die and be raised by Amer?"

"Sadly, yes."

Teiris took another step forward, feeling anger rise along with suspicion. She raised a hand to point accusingly at Siraas. "Are you a spy?"

The archmage laughed again and shook her head. "Not at all. A spy secretly collects information and reports back to an employer. I keep what I learn to myselves. Besides my dry status updates, I haven't reported back to the Dracon monarch since King Searcy. No offense to the regent king, but he's a child. Not to worry, Queen. All the secrets of Terswood are safe in this tower. I simply watch and observe, much like your daughter."

"I..." Teiris started and took a step backward. "I will need to revisit this conversation. How is my husband?"

"He's sleeping while I run a blood test, map his spinal nerves, and collect samples of mana pushed through his system."

"You have three of yourselves in the room?" Teiris exhaled. She could hardly imagine an ability like what Siraas possessed.

"Four. And I will join them if there is nothing else I can answer for you."

"I suppose not. I'll return to Terswood and begin my preparations there. Contact me at the slightest news."

Siraas nodded. "I have a simulacrum living in Terswood. I will have her come to you if needed."

Teiris shrugged. "What the hells, why not send her to the throne room right now? I'll have the Tersguard grant her — you — access to be with me at all times. You have the king's life in your hands. What harm could there be in having you beside me? Unless she's otherwise engaged."

"None of my selves are ever idle, Queen Teiris. That's an excellent plan. I'll meet you right away. Now, if you'll excuse me." Siraas stepped around Teiris and left for the stairs at the far side of the room.

Teiris rolled the ring on her forefinger for a moment, knowing that once she left this tower, only a handful of people in the world could return her here without traveling for days from Daelin's teleporting obelisk in Kornine. Teiris closed her eyes and let out a long breath. She knew her duty to the people of Terswood would not be satisfied by waiting in a tower for some progress to be made against Daelin's condition.

Without another glance at the slate boards around her, Teiris activated her ring and, with a pop and a jerk, stood in the warmth of her bedroom in Terswood.

6

Seeing him again broke me, but did act to reaffirm my role across the realms.

L one stepped to the prelen's side and touched her shoulder. As he closed his eyes and felt for Terswood, he hoped he had masked his annoyance at being asked this little task. He had teleported there a hundred or more times over the last decade. Feeling for it and the central courtyard beside his father's teleportation obelisk took almost no effort. Lone gently squeezed the prelen's shoulder and pulled from the ley lines to fuel his spell. With a feeling like being tugged forward, the oppressive heat of a Terswood afternoon replaced the stuffy room of chattering svarters. They both stood still for a moment to blink away the remnants of the teleport.

Not for the first time, Lone thought how nice it would be to teleport a person without him having to go as well, to touch someone and send them to a place of his choosing. The difference in the spell could not be that different, but it would take some amount of research. He heard his father's voice, spouting the trial of ethics that would come should some sinister person master such magic, but that was why Cazlandt's line had always closely guarded the secrets of teleportation.

"I thank you for your help, Regent King," Kaermys said in broken Common with a salute and bow.

"My pleasure, Prelen," Lone responded in Svarters.

The prelen smiled politely, bowed again, and fled toward the north side of the courtyard and into the city.

One down, a room full of svarters left to get later. Jazelyn can move a whole lot more at once, but she's worlds better at controlling ley energy than I. We need a better means of moving large groups across the continent.

Lone's eyes ran briefly across the manicured grass and hedges, over the central fountain shaded by a willow tree. Nothing remained of the battle months ago against daemon and his undead aunt. Teiris, or at least those she left in charge while she spent the time praying, did their jobs well cleaning and repairing the damage.

He looked at the dark obelisk, standing a foot taller than himself. His father created and installed these across the capitals of Poas when Lone was just an infant, perhaps in some early attempt to foster the peace Lone now strove toward. Only the rune for Dracon still glowed faintly. The single rune burned into Lone's mind as the conversation with Teiris echoed in his ears. Here, in this gaudy eyesore sitting among the natural architecture of Terswood, was the simple means Daelin had created for his son to visit anytime he wanted.

Lone breathed in the humid air of Terswood along with a refreshing amount of ley energy from the Gran Marc directly beneath his feet. Despite that, fatigue was edging into his senses as he traced his route across the ley lines back to Acrus. The location was becoming familiar and with a tug and pop, he again stood in the marble yard before the Gilded Basilica. He glanced around quickly to gain his bearings.

Guards cleared Suanh's Chapel, and those that remained of the summit's visitors milled around a few feet from the door. Lone took a deep breath and marched toward the man wearing a sandy-colored jerkin and breeches and a woman in a dark gray dress standing apart from the others.

"Sir!" Dehset Tekin snapped to attention and bowed.

"Regent King," Isold nodded respectfully.

"Dehset, let me see your device."

"Sir?"

"I saw you with a device that broke the avaryll's spell earlier. I'd like to see it, please." Lone held out a hand and waved to the pack slung over Dehset's shoulder.

"Device?" Dehset looked nervously between Lone and Isold. "Such a work of anti-magic would be strictly illegal under laws invoked by King Searcy in his three hundredth year of—"

"You're going to list laws to me?" Lone took a step closer. "Show me."

Dehset quickly shook his head. "I don't... That would be illegal."

Lone looked at the scribe. "Isold, please make note of a new law. Artifice General Dehset Tekin will show Regent King Lone the device he used to end the avaryll attack during the summit of nations, or he will be removed from his position and banned from learning anything related to magic again."

Isold finished writing in her notebook and smirked at Dehset.

With eyes wide, the young student from Evkasa set down his bag and fished out a ball of silver. Lone took it and turned it over in his fingers. Other than a dent on one side that seemed intentional and a small button opposite, it was a perfectly round sphere with no seams or obvious means of accessing the inner workings. Burns marked a ring around the middle, marring the otherwise pristine metal. Lone handed the device back, and Dehset quickly hid it away.

"You are a rare one," Lone said. "An indefensible magic assaulted all the leaders of Poas. Only Bard and the Archetype could fight it. We saw you use a device that ended the spell before the avaryll woman could do it herself. A device with that ability may make all the difference in a power struggle in this realm."

"I'm sorry, sir," Dehset whimpered. "I shouldn't have made it without your permission. I wasn't sure it would work."

Lone winced. "Maybe don't admit that part; that you used a device with unknown outcomes while in a room with all the most powerful people in the world." He slapped Dehset on the arm. "We don't know what the avaryll have in store for us, but that thing can neutralize at least one of their spells. I want you to focus on simplifying the design so we can produce it easily. For now, go to the house assigned to us, and I'll teleport us back to Dracon in a little while. I have someone else I need to talk to."

"Right away, sir," Dehset said quietly.

"I will see him there," said Isold, taking Dehset by the elbow.

Lone did not know where to find either Aiden or Dalbinth, but he would find someone who did. He crossed the white marble tile, quarried at some exorbitant expense two hundred miles south, and approached the steps of the Ascended. A regimen of halberd-wielding soldiers in gleaming golden armor covered the six tiers of six steps each.

Weapons crossed to stop him.

"Where is Archetype Dalbinth?" Lone said loudly to the twenty soldiers. "I must have words with him immediately."

As he expected, none of the men responded or even acknowledged hearing him. Lone approached the nearest.

"Soldier, what is your name?"

"Delphin Carter, Halberdier Second Class," the armored man replied. Lone could barely see his pale brown eyes through the visored helmet, and he moved to stand directly in the halberdier's line of sight.

Lone looked directly into Carter's eyes. "Where is the Archetype?"

Carter shifted in his armor and met Lone's emerald stare. He could feel the man's hatred as if it were a physical miasma pulsing from him.

"Regent King, good, come with me," said the casual voice of a man pushing through the soldiers. Still in the pristine white and gold weaved robes and stole, Aiden descended the stairs unescorted. Shocked soldiers parted for him.

Delphin Carter snapped aside with practiced precision as Aiden reached the bottom of the steps. The Archetype stand-in threw an arm over Lone's shoulder and pulled him away, leading them toward an ornately banded wooden door on the south side of the courtyard. Everything around here was ornate.

A shiver ran up Lone's spine, thinking of Carter's hateful eyes as he gave one more glance back at the golden soldiers. They had returned to their previous postures. The two passed into the cool dark of a small chapel, lit only by a few small leaded glass windows. The walls were stacked with pews protected under white cloth.

Without pausing, Aiden crossed to a sconce on the wall to their right to twist and pull some element near the base. With a barely audible click, Aiden heaved at the stone wall, pushing it back a foot before sliding it to the left. Even in the dim light, Lone could see the filigreed railing of a wrought iron staircase beyond spiraling downward.

"You go first. I will close up the door," Aiden said.

Lone gripped the railing and peered into the darkness, swallowing his growing sense of unease. "A few hours ago, you were worried about us talking privately at the summit for more than a few minutes. Now, twenty soldiers just watched us go into this tiny chapel."

Aiden rolled his amethyst eyes. "No one will think you kidnapped me. If anything, I just kidnapped you, and none of my soldiers will care about that. Get down there. Time is ticking."

Something in the total lack of professionalism got Lone on the steps and moving. He raised a palm and produced a small globe of light over it. He needed little in the near-complete darkness. Lone heard the grind of stone above as Aiden closed the secret passage.

Lone counted as he descended the wide iron steps, with only their bootfalls echoing in the well. When they reached the fiftieth step, Lone broke the silence. "Do you need a light?"

"I am fine," Aiden said somewhere above him. "I do not need light to see."

Once more about the spiral Lone caught a faint whiff of something acrid as they reached the bottom. Three rough-hewn paths were carved in the stone, all approximately equidistant. Lone's small light was quickly lost down any of them.

"I never expected the scragging avaryll to show up," Aiden said, picking the middle path. He walked ahead in complete darkness.

"How do you know them? We have over three thousand years of written history, and there is no mention of another race on Poas other than the svarters and fey." Lone again smelled the acrid scent. "Nothing of the kalvyr, either."

"That was sort of their intention," said the light shaper. "I met the avaryll ages ago, well before your history started. I am older than I look."

Lone barely noticed the rough walls making up the network of caves as Aiden led them through narrow passages. He noticed a dampness in the air, and all the tunnels continued with a slight decline. Lone was hopelessly lost but took solace in the sanctum stone on his left forefinger and his ability to teleport, should that fail. He would not be trapped down here.

"You're over three thousand years old?"

"Significantly. Hard to believe with a face this pretty, right?" Aiden looked over his shoulder with a wide grin, teeth flashing in Lone's meager light. "That was not my first trip to Poas, and I have been back to Isolis a few times since. I have seen a fair amount of this realm. I even helped set up the refugee population down in Iecil, which, thanks to your great-grandsire, are all dead now."

"Iecil..." Lone found he could only speak in sentence fragments. "Wait, my great-grandsire? You mean Cazlandt?"

"Of course. I guess you had four great-grandsires, but none as infamous as that one. Your sister would have known about what happened to those people, yet she never suggested I put them somewhere else. Imagine the weight of all knowledge, knowing you're setting up people, whole civilizations, to fail."

"Everything must have a solution. Even if it doesn't seem like the best one."

"So sage, Lone."

"Cazlandt wanted to subjugate the people of Iecil into slavery for the arch-mages. He gave his commander the Shadow Reaver, a featherr'ock steel blade, and disappeared for a year. Cazlandt came back and killed Lavin, but the genocide was done by then." Lone's shoulders slumped. He had learned horribly damning truths about his ancestor in the last few months.

"Thanks for the history lesson. So useful," Aiden said.

"Wait, you said they were a refugee population? What were they refugees from?"

"Try not to worry about that," Aiden grumbled.

They entered an area with smoother walls that still looked to be carved from natural earth. Another turn, and they were in a tunnel with light wooden doors spaced every few paces on alternating sides. Aiden stopped before one on the left, and Lone noticed the faint light peeking through the cracks in the ancient wood. The light shaper cleared his throat twice and pushed the door inward.

Inside was a square room of maybe a dozen feet on a side. Sitting at a small round table with two empty chairs was the kalvyr that had introduced himself to Lone as the true Archetype Dalbinth the Redeemer. At least, Lone thought it was. He had only met the one dragonman, but the copper scales, curving bronze horns, and coarse white hair were exactly what he remembered from that night in the gardens months ago. The Archetype wore a low-level priest's dark and unadorned robes, and a tube ran from his nostril to somewhere in his clothes, emitting puffs of acrid red smoke.

Dalbinth stood and bowed. Lone returned the gesture.

"Let us have a quick chat," Aiden said as he took off his stole and dropped it onto the table. He sat heavily in one of the other chairs.

Dalbinth reached for the stole and neatly folded it as he sat. "Please take care with the relics, Master."

"You seriously wear this stuff, Dalbinth? I have worn my fair share of full, traditional field armor, and these vestments feel so much heavier. I am glad I summon my armor when I need it."

Lone thumped a fist into the table. "I need answers," he said with more bite than intended. It had been a stressful few hours.

"That was why we brought you here, but ask away," said Aiden.

Lone licked his lips while he prioritized what he needed to know. What were the avaryll, and what did Aiden know of them? Who was Aiden, and what was his relationship with Alishia?

"Why this deception? You," he waved at the kalvyr, "introduced yourself to me in the gardens months ago, and you," another wave to the messy-haired man in heavy robes, "played the role in the summit. This is unnecessarily convoluted."

"Exactly to the point," said Dalbinth with a wheezing laugh.

Aiden scratched at his cheek. "Your sister told me long ago that you would suggest this summit of nations. She asked that I be present for it, but I did not know exactly when you would be born or when you would set the meeting. So I installed Dalbinth centuries ago, and he has been my proxy in Poas since. He told me when you were born and kept me up on things here. Then, when Quey brought him your plan, the plan to bring together all the nations of Poas, I came with all haste. It took me almost two months to get here."

Lone frowned and took the last open chair. That was not a bad answer. Dalbinth the kalvyr ran Acrus from behind the scenes, and Aiden came when he needed a public appearance. Did that mean Aiden would remain in Poas to keep playing the part? Or would he name the dragonman as his successor? What would Acrus, a nation still steeped in human supremacy, think about being led by a kalvyr? What would the rest of Poas think about this new race of people? Did any of that matter?

Lone remembered Delphin Carter's penetrating hate. "If you've led Acrus for so long, why is it still a nation of seething religious bigotry? When we sat outside the Redeemer's Labyrinth, Dalbinth, you said you've been tweaking the culture for two hundred years. Why is it still so terrible?"

Dalbinth glanced at Aiden before speaking. "Would you believe the people are moderate compared to when the Gilded Warrior placed me? Your Aunt Lilan, Elphame keep her, knew how close Acrus stood to a second Hallowed Campaign. I strive to weed out the worst and replace the blind hate with understanding and eventually love, but change must happen gradually."

"What about my sister, then? How do you know her?"

Aiden grinned. "Your sister is annoyingly cryptic, but I love her dearly. I first met her in my home realm. That was her first time moving through time, which is where, or when, she is right now, in Throk'tar, hiding from the storm in a haunted hunting lodge. Her skill is not yet good enough to return her to an exact moment, which is why she has been gone so long. Every time after, I met her as the Chronicler, having lived through the events that will take place here in Poas over the next couple of months. She always repeats how the role of the Chronicler is to observe and record, yet she has no problem with regularly getting involved with things. It is as if she works to ensure events happen as she knows they must."

"She really moved through time, then?"

"Mhmm. It was some combination of powers as Cazlandt tried to steal her away to help in his war. But she is smart and figured out how to do it herself after that."

Lone's jaw dropped. "Cazlandt? No, he's dead. Depending on how you count, he's dead three times over."

"Cazlandt comes up a lot, like a sour bowl of shrimp stew. Just when you think he is gone..." Aiden clapped a hand over his mouth and pretended to retch to his side. When he came back up, darkness washed away his grin as his hands balled into fists. "If it were not for Ali, I would have killed the bastard, and he would just have disappeared from your history long ago. Well, not *your* history since you would never have been born. But then, neither would your sister to take him to the past. Some events have to play out a certain way. It is best to not think so linearly about her." He shrugged.

"Fine then." Lone looked at the kalvyr, who remained quiet, breathing in his red mist. He looked back at Aiden. "Tell me about the avaryll."

Aiden huffed. "I am hardly one to say a single attribute can define an entire race. Not all gronyn are loud. Not all dwarves are greedy. Not all humans are handsome rogues." He flashed a bright smile and swept a hand through his hair. "But you can say all svarters are relatively short. And you can say all avaryll are relatively self-entitled asses. They claim to be Poas's first race and will tell anyone that, though I am not sure why anyone would care. They have been absent from the realm's history for probably ten thousand years. Their advanced and stagnant society will amaze you when you get to Isolis and Tidecrest. Their food? The worst."

Aiden pulled a handful of dried meat sticks from within his holy robes. He offered one to Dalbinth, then to Lone after the kalvyr refused with a shake of his head. Lone shook his head as well. Aiden shrugged, placed all but one on the table, and tore off a large bite.

"The avaryll have been cultivating a new world tree for thousands of years. With help, of course. They will try using it to control the realm by controlling the nexus of ley energy. I feel something grander will happen, or your sister would not have insisted so badly that I be here." Aiden took another big bite. "I thought she just wanted me around to witness your meeting of nations. She was always so proud of you. But then avaryll showed up."

"That's it?" Lone asked with disappointment.

"May I?" Dalbinth asked, and Aiden shrugged. The kalvyr continued. "Regent King, I am organizing a small military force to march on Isolis. We know that Queen Teiris is as well. Dracon does not have a standing military large in number, but you command the archmages of Poas, as well as the Royal Guard and a small army of crystal mages. We suggest you mobilize every force under your power. March them to Tidecrest or raise them to defend sensitive positions."

Lone looked between the two light shapers. "So you expect a fight?"

Dalbinth looked down at his folded, clawed hands. He had worn gloves when Lone met him outside The Redeemer's Labyrinth. "Have you viewed the remi-nisphere I returned to you? The one last owned by Kethry en Salo?"

Lone thought of last seeing the orb in Jazelyn's workshop. He had not noticed it when he was last in there after Dehset's tinkering wrecked the room. Surely, Jazelyn or Kiol would have said something had they viewed the memories stored in the relic.

"No, I left it for her mother to use privately."

No one spoke for several long breaths. Aiden chewed loudly.

Lone finally broke the silence. "Why is that important? Don't be coy. If you have some clue, say it."

Aiden reached for another meat stick and tapped it against his head. He laughed nervously. "You want to know what I expect? I..." He stopped himself, letting his mouth hang open. "No, I do not want to be the one to start the rumors and get you worked up. Keep those eyes and ears open. I have very little trust in the avaryll. Not even that they had done something to specifically cause distrust, but as long as I have known them, they have always been a shady lot."

"Assaulting the collected leaders of Poas with a severe magic field doesn't cause any distrust?" Lone asked, trying not to laugh.

"Well, yeah." Aiden took another bite. "There is that."

Lone looked between the quiet dragonman and the brash immortal chewing on jerky. He wanted to speak with Aiden and Dalbinth, but now that he sat between them, his mind moved to concerns of the realm's future. He had to return to Dracon and prepare the force Dalbinth suggested.

7

I've yet to figure out why the Piscinath, a people that spend over half their time in the water, use iron as currency. They end up with bags of rust.

Alishia laughed along with the brothers. Aiden's joke could barely be considered funny, but after a hard month on the road, almost anything was worth a chuckle so long as their feet were up and no kobolds were actively trying to kill them.

"What is the plan for tomorrow, then?" Aiden asked and pulled off his boots. They had rented a room on the second floor of the Muddy Ghost, a small roadside inn.

Ethan pulled a patched and ripped vellum map from his satchel and carefully pressed it flat on the room's single table.

"How about we go see the Quordath?" he asked, pointing to a dark smudge running north to south.

"Is that the bottomless pit?" Aiden asked nervously and sat at the edge of his bed covered in threadbare blankets.

Alishia chuckled again. Aiden hated heights.

Ethan frowned and studied the weathered map. "Well then, where do you want to go?"

A smile flickered across Aiden's lips. "I am surprised it was not your first pick when Elder Grimorc gave us leave: the world tree."

"Throkzil?" Ethan looked back to the map, but the details of the far south had been lost long ago. "We can probably find it. It is a giant tree, right?" He was grinning widely. "I do want to see it."

"Great, then we both win. You get to see a tree, and we also get to not see a pit to the seven hells." Aiden stood and slapped his brother on the back. "Sleep time."

"Color me surprised you are not going back downstairs to try anything with the waitress, the one in the green dress."

"You think I have a chance?" Aiden asked with excitement.

"No."

Aiden grumped to the side of his bed and pulled off his shirt. Alishia's mind flicked back to running into him at The Watching Wolf in Ragvurd. Those muscular arms, chiseled chest, rippling stomach... Aiden reached to unclasp his belt.

Alishia quickly ended her Sight.

While watching the boys across their years, she learned quickly that Aiden had no shame or modesty when he was around only his brother. She was glad he learned some of it later for their week-long trek across Throk'tar.

Alishia blinked a few times to take in the surroundings of the heart chamber of Throkzil. Uulthra's chrysalis hung in the space above her, wrapped in the vines and roots of the world tree.

In this chamber, a few years in their future, the Mraasil and the Captains Hauser would fight Cazlandt. Three were sent to the Lacuna Gap, and another was killed.

Ethan would not survive that encounter.

Stabbed through the heart a few yards in front of Alishia, and she could only watch. She fled with the murderer, who had been teaching her magic since. What if she scratched a warning message on the ground? Something that Ethan would see just in time to be saved?

"Focus," she told herself with a long breath. "You've been down this path."

"The Chronicler's role is to observe and record," she also told herself. "To gather all knowledge across all realms."

"To burden myself with the fates of all without being able to change anything. What is the purpose of such an existence?"

She asked herself this question a hundred times, out loud or not, and she had no answer.

This was the ninth time she had quietly slipped from The Stacks into Throk'tar's heart chamber. She told herself this was practice for moving to another realm and a time of her choosing. Watching the boys was to aid in training her Sight. She was not a creep for spying on them years before they met. She could now hear the scene while using her Sight, so it was valid training, though perhaps an invasion of privacy. She had visited a handful of realms other than Throk'tar and even spied on a young Etharis learning to shift into his bird form.

Alishia had yet to work up the courage or strength to visit Aiden after what would later happen in this heart chamber. While she wanted to know how one brother went on without the other, that was her Chronicler side thirsting for knowledge. Alishia, the half-human svarters princess, wanted to see and talk to a dear friend but blamed herself for what happened. She assumed Aiden would as well.

Alishia pinched her eyes tight around the tears and returned to The Stacks. With the barest thought, she sat in the wing-backed chair in front of the only desk on the balcony.

Cazlandt looked up from where he sat, reading a thin book by the balcony's railing.

"You look upset," he said in his harsh, ancient dialect. Alishia had yet to encounter another who spoke like him. "I assume you visited the boys again?"

Alishia leaned her elbows onto the desk and pressed her palms into her face.

"You have the entirety of existence to behold," the ancient archmage continued. "Why torture yourself?"

"Have you ever loved someone?" Alishia asked into her hands.

She had seen it enough to know Cazlandt would mark his place in the book and carefully set it aside before responding.

"No," he said.

Unprepared for the curt response, Alishia raised her head to consider her great-grandsire. He leaned into his low-backed chair with legs crossed under a bright yellow robe, the book resting on his knees. His hair and lengthy gray beard had long repaired themselves from the damage of Aiden's attack in the heart chamber. Cazlandt pulled off his peaked hat and touched the edges of the wide brim.

"I feel a kinship toward others of my kind. There are individuals I am fond of, including yourself, Alishia, but every time you come from watching Ethan Hauser and his brother, I know you have experienced something I never have. I almost envy you that, that sense of familiarity and friendship. Perhaps more."

Alishia studied him, seeing how his emerald eyes lost focus, and his face and shoulders fell slack. In all their time together, all their long talks, Alishia had never seen a display of emotion akin to what he seemed to be holding back now.

"Why have you not gone back to stop me?" Cazlandt asked. "You could leave yourself a note in Ragvurd warning of what would happen in the heart chamber. You could do any of a hundred things to better prepare for that battle against me and change the outcome."

Alishia bit her lip. There was precedent. Her future self had left a note for her in the very chair she now sat in. If she were to leave a message for her past self now, should she not remember finding that note? The mechanics of time travel were still beyond her understanding.

Cazlandt's words rang in Alishia's mind, *Why have you not gone back to stop me?* His tone was almost pleading, rather than the arrogant defiance, taunting her frail emotions she expected from him.

"Do you wish I had?" she asked. "Do you wish something had stopped you sooner in Throk'tar?"

"I admit to a feeling I wish I did not have."

"It's called guilt."

"Is that so?" He did not look up from the yellow hat in his hands.

"Are you ready to go home?" Alishia asked and reached to pick up Ethan's gift, the small bust of herself, from the desktop. She gently traced the rough edges of the sculpture with her thumb as she often did.

"Are you?" he asked with a raised eyebrow.

Alishia leaned back in the chair, unsure how to respond to the counter-question.

"Alishia," he started and tossed his hat to the floor. "I am sorry. I have endless excuses for what madnesses had taken me back in Throk'tar, but I know all are meaningless. Ultimately, my greatest failure was that I was too weak to overcome myself. Too blinded by my self-worth and righteousness. I should have done better, been a better person."

She opened her mouth to say something, though she was unsure what.

Cazlandt stopped her with a raised palm. He wiped the other hand across his eyes, pinching the nose of his bridge. It was the sly action of someone trying, poorly, to hide their tears.

"You are an excellent student," he said and picked at a piece of lint on his robes. "You are not an archmage, yet you do not have the same magics as a svarters. I think I may have taught you all I can. The boy was right when he told you much of magic is the product of confidence."

Is this just an act?

He spoke slowly, deliberately. "With the power I claim to possess, I could have ended the fight within Throkzil a hundred different ways, but I wanted to express my might. There need not have been a fight at all, but I provoked one. I killed so many gronyn while perfecting the spell that sent the Mraasil to the Lacuna Gap. I have killed so many others across so many realms. I killed Captain Ethan Hauser of the Imperial Gron Army, the boy that may have turned into your first love. Alishia, truly, I am sorry."

Alishia looked at Cazlandt's yellow hat on the ground. She wanted to believe his earnestness. When they first arrived in Throk'tar, she witnessed his ability to put on an act and manipulate emotions. This felt different.

"Tell me," he continued, drawing her attention back. "I am your great-grand-sire, yes? As tight-lipped as you are, I have gathered enough details on my own. My son will be the first king of Dracon. His son, your father, will marry the svarters queen to produce you. Tracing lineages and genealogy has always been a minor hobby of mine. The svarters claim to be descendants of their ancient first queen, Ters. If she held the power your people believe she did, that could explain your power. You should use your abilities to visit Ters and learn more about her and how the svarters people came to be.

"I have distracted myself," Cazlandt spoke without break. "Please tell me, did we meet before you came into The Stacks and I stole you away to Throk'tar? Do I still live in your time?"

Alishia chewed her lip again. "Your future leads to my past," she whispered. "I don't know how much I dare tell you that might change it."

"Tell me just one thing, then. Did my children love me?"

For a man who admitted to never experiencing love, Alishia found the question absurd.

"I don't know that, but I think your son respected you, as does my father. Though love and respect are not the same thing," she said. "I will tell you one thing, Cazlandt. When I return you to Poas, you will see the breadth of your mistakes and end the war campaign in Iecil. It may have been a spiral of guilt from that action that will eventually lead to your fall. Guilt can be a powerful tool to stop you from repeating mistakes."

"So my son is dead too then," Cazlandt heaved a deep sigh. "Funny that I do not know him, a boy yet to be born, yet I mourn him."

"Perhaps you will finally know love in your son."

Cazlandt set the book he had been reading precariously on the balcony's railing and pushed his palms on his knees to stand with a groan.

"To answer your other question," he said, "I am ready to go home. But I have one condition."

Alishia cocked her head.

"When a person has powerful muscles, strong magic, or political connections, it is easy to be strong-willed," Cazlandt said. "Your power is beyond anything else I have conceived. Do not let it consume you. Promise me you will not remain here alone. Promise me you will not continue spying on Ethan and his brother. You will want to spend forever to see across all realms and all times, but that acquisition and control of power has been my road. The gain of so much means little without an end goal. Learn from my mistake. Return to your family and loved ones."

Alishia nodded, marveling at the sincerity behind Cazlandt's tone. He would have never uttered such a sentiment when he first arrived, burned and scarred, in The Stacks. No matter what acting skill she had seen from him, this felt real. She waved to the heavy wood door to her right.

He took up his hat and strode by her, stopping to gently place a hand on her left shoulder. "Thank you," he whispered and leaned to kiss the top of her head. Alishia was still looking straight forward toward the balcony railing and the endless shelves beyond when she heard the door softly close behind her.

8

Witnessing firsthand the destruction caused by The Deluge was an early lesson in non-interference. I knew it would end, but couldn't tell the Mraasil.

E tharis and Ruvaal stood before the base of the new world tree. The archdruid had seen every one of the realms' Trees over his life. Some were straight and tall, others twisted and spread wide, but this one was unique. Thick aerial roots spread across the tiled floor of the Symposium, and tangled moss drooped to block out any clear view of where the tree broke through the ceiling high above.

Protectorate Alaraic reclined in his throne atop on a high dais before the tree. He swept his luxurious cobalt hair, as was the sign of all protectorates, over his right shoulder. "Such an honor to have two guardians present," he said in a voice that made the floor shiver.

Etharis touched a low root near him and heard the tree's voice. Her song was strong, but her words were unclear, like a child singing happy nothings. "This is beyond you and me, Ruvaal. Endanlegsil is born of the first Seed of Farsil. She is older than all others, save my own. Her birth cannot be witnessed by us, you and I, alone."

Alaraic stood and descended the tiered steps. His long cloak trailed behind. "The avaryll have done nothing but prepare for this moment for twenty moons, eight millennia. Our capital has been built and rebuilt to serve the tree."

The archdruid turned to Alaraic and glanced over his form as if seeing him for the first time. "You honestly believe your people could care for a world tree through her infancy? This isn't some house plant."

Ruvaal touched his brother's sleeve. "You can't be suggesting we call the others. There has never before been a congress of our kind."

Etharis turned from the protectorate toward Ruvaal. "I watched you be born, brother. I watched every single Mraasil be born." His glowing amber eyes were still, and his voice somber. "I watched as your trees created your bodies and split their life essence to give you breath. You were too young and weak to leave your realms to watch the next birth. So I watched you all. I alone watched. Before that, I tended your trees. Not all made it, but I did what I could to ensure those losses were few." He stopped to place his palm back on the exposed root. "Here is the first and only tree that has gone without my tending. Soon a new Mraasil will be born, which only I have witnessed. Our brethren must be given a chance to attend."

Ruvaal stepped around Etharis to stand between him and the tree's roots. He spoke in a hushed tone. "What of our other plans? What of the Ibaerite and undoing the Venatus? None of *this* means anything."

Alaraic cleared his throat to draw their attention. "My guests will be arriving soon. Perhaps you two could retire to a side room until announced?"

Ruvaal raised his arm, but Etharis was faster. A thick root of the world tree whipped from its place in the tiled floor to impact the protectorate in the chest, throwing him a dozen feet back. With fangs bared, the archdruid hovered over Alaraic. Partially in his cat form, he twisted a clawed hand in the protectorate's layered linen and satin robes and pulled him to his feet to hover an inch from the ground.

"You are not the one in command here, mortal," Etharis growled and threw the avaryll backward. "Can you begin to understand what has been done here? Seeing to the welfare of a young tree has been my sacred task alone since the beginning of creation. You would assume yourself worthy of taking that from me?"

Alaraic pulled himself to the first tier of his dais. "The World Tender cares for the tree," he said hoarsely.

The main door to the symposium opened with a crack, and nine avaryll entered in formation, wearing high-waisted hakamas and loose-fitting linen cross-tops. They seemed in no hurry as they passed the Mraasil to help Alaraic stand.

"The World Tender." Ruvaal turned to a stunned archdruid. "I suppose there would be no better substitute for yourself."

"He resides below, by the mana lake, when he is present." Protectorate Alaraic smoothed the front of his robes and turned to his guards. "I will leave you to your mediation while I walk through my gardens. Guards, attend me." He left the Symposium through a side exit with his guards close behind.

"What of the Venatus?" Ruvaal said to his brother's back.

"Enough of that, Ruvaal," Etharis said, returning to touch the tree's root with eyes downcast. "The World Tender? Here?"

Ruvaal crossed the few feet between them and pulled Etharis's shoulder to force him to turn. The archdruid would not look up to meet his eyes.

"So you're giving up?" Ruvaal could not hold back his anger and disappointment.

"I will not take away her life." Etharis looked up with a hint of a smile. "Verndari. That is her name. She would not be so close to birth without the Venatus."

Ruvaal pulled a small vial from his sleeve, containing a gem shard suspended in a milky solution. "We can use the Ibaerite to save Ters, Baris, your beloved Enzrok, and Milv. Verndari is not yet born. Why would you forsake our brothers and sisters that fell to the Gods of Naught for one we have never met?"

"Why do you still have the Ibaerite on your person? Destroy it, Ruvaal." Etharis returned to the tree and placed both hands on the exposed root. "She will be born soon. Return to Nethraanzil and await my summons."

Ruvaal scoffed and put the Ibaerite back in his sleeve. His form pulsed with purple energy, and a spark of light ran the length of his body. Then, he disappeared.

***

Ruvaal stood before his world tree in the heart of his sunless home realm most called The Afterlands. He had stopped correcting them centuries ago.

Nethraanzil was small compared to Farsil, but then everything was. Long, whip-like vines drifted in the breeze from branches a thousand or more yards overhead. Ruvaal leaned against the trunk and breathed in its power. He pulled the vial containing the Ibaerite from his sleeve and flicked off the stopper with his nail. He poured the milky solution into his palm along with the small gem of immeasurable power.

Ruvaal did as he and Etharis had done in the Deadloss, channeling their powers through the gem and attempting a teleport. As the last dozen times he had tried, nothing happened. Ruvaal lacked the power to activate the Ibaerite on his own. The power of Archdruid Etharis was required. With a grumble, he dropped the gem chip back into the vial and poured the suspending solution from his cupped palm.

The Ibaerite was useless to him, and Etharis was intent on seeing it destroyed. Ruvaal had one more final plan to sway his eldest brother. He pulled a glass orb from another pocket in his robes and rubbed the surface five times in one direction and three more in the other.

A small face resolved in the sphere: a human woman with pale skin and hair like fire. He opened his mouth to speak but choked on the words. So many centuries of planning. Seeing the Ibaerite get to Cazlandt's hands, capturing the floundering aether walker's spirit, and having Princess Alishia struck by an attack from the gem. Everything had floundered at the final moments. He had been too weak to grab Alishia from Terswood after she returned from Iecil, and now she was gone, traveling through time. The Ibaerite could mimic the Chronicler's power, but the process of awakening the gem was incomplete.

The face in the orb looked expectant.

"Come to Poas," he breathed. "The new tree must burn."

Ruvaal severed the connection and dropped the orb into the spongy moss at his slippered feet. He covered his face with his hands and sank back against the tree's base. He, the guardian of a realm, called for the death of another. Even if the threat of the continued daemon invasion might finally convince Etharis that the Venatus must be undone, he just called for horror to be unleashed on an otherwise innocent realm.

For the first time since the death of his sister Ters, Ruvaal wept.

9

The use of iron is symbolic of their abhorrence to wealth; that it weighs you down and is difficult to hold onto.

Lone teleported back to the marble yard before the Gilded Basilica just as Bard and Harnoon Ashta, owner of the Hungered Arena, were walking toward him. The two islanders did not look surprised by the regent king's sudden appearance.

"My king," Bard said first with a stiff bow. His tone held an unnatural attempt at formality. "Master Ashta has expressed a desire to return to the Western Isles immediately. He has requested—"

"Take me home," Ashta interrupted in a voice so heavily accented that the words were barely recognizable as Common. "I must immediately begin preparations for this invasion of avaryll."

Lone glanced up to the sky and the sun moving off the west. He had survived longer days of diplomacy but none so varied. After the avaryll, Teiris, then Aiden and Dalbinth, Lone was ready for either bed or some kind of action.

"Right now?" He directed the question to Bard. "I should get something to eat before going as far as the Western Isles." He thought of Aiden's offered meat sticks but was not yet so hungry to eat something stashed in a stranger's sweaty robes.

"Very well, Regent King. I am sure the other rulers of my islands will understand that we left them waiting for news because you needed a snack." Ashta bit off the words with a sneer.

"If I return you now, you say you will speak to the others about sending a delegation to Isolis?"

Ashta gave a curt nod.

Lone sighed in frustration. The Western Isles were the only nation that would not have yet already sent word home in some fashion. "Very well," he said. A feral glint in Ashta's eyes made Lone nervous. Raw anger in there made the regent king worry for his safety once they were off the mainland and away from the ley lines.

Bard laced his fingers through Lone's, pressing their palms together. "I'm right here," he spoke in Au quietly enough for only Lone's ear.

Lone grinned and squeezed his eyes closed before looking at Ashta. "Have you ever teleported before?"

"No," Ashta said with a laugh. "Do not concern yourself with my well-being."

Lone snapped his fingers and fumbled through his pockets for a scrap of parchment and a pen. He scrawled a quick note addressed to Isold asking that word get to General Jazelyn about ferrying the svarters back to Terswood. He made sure to include plenty of apologies for the imposition, especially after Jazelyn and Kiol's recent ordeal with the avaryll. Lone flagged a passing priest and asked him to deliver the note to the house assigned to Dracon. The priest accepted the parchment while trying to touch it as little as possible and left without a word.

"I certainly hope that all works out," he said to the priest's back.

Lone touched Ashta's right shoulder and closed his eyes again. He traced the ley lines west to the Gran Marc and continued. Lone edged his senses farther from the ley lines into the nothingness farther out to the ocean. He had a map months ago when he blindly teleported himself and Bard to Iecil. Now, he felt like he was dangling over the edge of a ship at sea, hoping to jump off and catch a piece of driftwood in impossibly dark water. There was a darker swirl out there that he only noticed as his senses slowly adjusted. Jazelyn had described Bard as a void when she did her ley walking. The other inhabitants of the islands would be similar, but that was not enough to risk a teleport.

Maybe I should take us to the coast of Eplear first, he thought, but distance did not really matter when the target was invisible.

He saw a flash of a pebbled beach and the grunts and squawks of gulls. Lone latched onto the location and pushed them toward it with a pop.

***

Lone appeared on the beach and collapsed to a knee, desperately gasping at the warm, humid air. He barely felt Bard's hand on his right shoulder as his body broke out in a cold sweat.

I overdid it, he thought and pressed a shaky hand on his knee to steady himself. *Taking two men with bodies that sap mana to an unfamiliar location essentially devoid of magic...* When he was ten, he had visited the Western Isles with his Aunt Lilan, but that hardly counted to help him target his teleportation magic.

Harnoon Ashta scoffed. "This is the power of the Archmage King?" he hissed, speaking in Au. "At least this is the correct island. Stand him up, Bartiado."

"My name is Bard," the islander replied with none of the anger Lone expected. Strong but gentle hands gripped the regent king by the elbow and helped him to his feet. "King Lone understands our language."

"I just brought you halfway across the damned world," Lone groaned as he stood on shaky legs and finally noticed his wet pants and the waves lapping over his boots. Had he brought them twenty more feet inland, he would not have salt water wicking up his cloak. But then, twenty feet in the other direction, and they would be swimming to shore. Lone was pretty sure he could not swim; he had never tried.

He felt some small amount of inner pride in bringing them to the correct island. Maps showed over a hundred in the chain, and he targeted the right one out of some stroke of luck.

Lone pulled at the mana crystal in his hip pouch to fill some of what was missing without ley lines. *When had I become so dependent on the constant stream of mana through my body?* he thought and stood a little taller as he followed the cries of gulls to the wide, blue sky dotted with thin white clouds. The sun, which was preparing to set in Ascalon, was high here. He strained to sense the closest ley line and barely felt the Gran Marc far to the east. By studying the maps in Jazelyn's workroom, Lone knew it was somewhere around two hundred miles away, but it may as well be in another realm for all he could pull from it. Lone felt like a handful of the stones from the beach were dropped into his gut, realizing the flaw in bringing Bard with him. *Can I teleport us both back out of here?* he thought with a groan. His sanctum stone would return him to Dracon, but he would not leave Bard here. *Maybe I can contact Jazelyn to rescue us if needed.*

Jazelyn.

Lone sent her and Kiol home but forgot to warn them about their wrecked workshop. The ancient archmage would be furious. Then she would get the note asking her to ferry a room full of svarters across the continent—nothing to do for that at the moment.

Lone stood straight and rolled his shoulders back. "I'm a busy man. Does this conclude our business?" he asked in Au.

Ashta cringed at Lone's words. "Hearing our sacred speech from the mouth of a foreigner. Grotesque."

"Can you walk, *menf?*" Bard asked softly.

Lone nodded and glanced along the shoreline. He noticed a group of men running from farther up the beach. He followed their trail back to a small group of huts with cooking fires wafting billowy lines of smoke. Even at a distance, Lone saw the men wore very little, and all looked as well built as Bard, with deeply tanned skin stretching over wide shoulders, thin waists, and— Lone averted his eyes with a deep breath. *Right, this island has only men.*

Ashta grinned, exposing his pointed teeth. "A welcoming party, good."

"I asked if this concludes our business. I have my affairs in Dracon."

"After I speak to the others, they will begin the work needed on the islands. I must return to my men abandoned in Acrus."

"So you want me to wait around and ferry you back?"

Ashta did not reply as the half dozen men came within twenty paces of Lone and the others before dropping to a knee with eyes downcast. "Master Ashta," said the one in the front. Where the other men were bare-chested, he wore a sash over his left shoulder and across his torso. "We were not prepared for your arrival." He spoke in an Au dialect so thick that Lone found it difficult to understand every word. The regent king reached for the pouch of mana crystal at his waist to work some minor spell of understanding but stopped himself. His supply was limited.

"Take me to Naiti," Ashta ordered.

Bard's fingers dug into Lone's forearm at the mention of his old master.

The man kneeling in front nodded. "He is in the arena this week. Come to our village and rest while we arrange an escort."

"Be quick of it," Ashta groaned. "I will find no relaxation in your shanties."

The men stood, and four were sent ahead. The others allowed Ashta, Lone, and Bard to pass before falling a few paces behind.

"You archmages are weak men," Ashta said while walking slowly over the beach's uneven pebbles and wide stones. "You rely solely on your magic and neglect the body's training."

Lone's hand balled into a fist. He opened his mouth, ready to challenge the man to a duel with sword or spear, but stopped himself. *Take this as a challenge,* he convinced himself. *If I can win over Harnoon Ashta as an ally, anyone on the mainland will be easy.* "Is that so?" he asked. "Have you met many archmages?"

Ashta scoffed and ran an eye over Lone. "You are the king of them, are you not? You must represent their core. Archmages pride themselves in their mastery of magic to defend and kill for them and make their lives easy. Yet you also wear such fine armor. Do you not trust in your magic to protect you?"

Lone considered an analogy in his man's line of thought. "If I were to throw a punch at your face, what would you do?"

Ashta looked at Lone again and laughed with a smirk. "I may just let you strike me."

"Fine then. What if Bard were to punch you in the face?"

He laughed again. "He would never dare strike a master."

Lone pinched the bridge of his nose. "Play along with me a little here, Ashta. Humor me. What would you do if someone strong punched you?"

"I would block or deflect the attack. Easily."

"And what if I were too close? Or somehow surprised you?"

"I would evade. Duck under or step aside."

"Why not both? Jump back *and* slap the attack away?" Lone waited a breath before continuing. "I can throw magic spells and create dazzling effects. I can create an aegis to protect me or teleport away. The armor I wear is the second layer of protection. I train my body to react without the aid of magic, which, as strong as it is, I won't rely on alone. It would be poor preparation to go to battle with only one sword if you may be disarmed."

"Are you expecting a battle, Regent King?"

"I try not to be disappointed when things happen completely different from my expectations and to have at least something prepared for any situation. I wanted a simple meeting of the nations of Poas, and we all ended up attacked by a race no one knew lived at our backdoor all these centuries."

Ashta's tone lightened. "You agree it was an attack by these avaryll?"

"It certainly felt that way as I was pinned to the cold floor of the Chapel."

"I will make sure they have time to regret that," Ashta growled.

"We should consider, Ashta, the avaryll have been cut off for thousands of years and never a part of our society. They will have different, ah..." Lone glanced at Bard, unsure how to say the word in Au.

"Etiquette," Bard offered.

"Thank you, etiquette," said Lone, wondering how that vocabulary never came up in a year of learning the language.

Ashta grunted. "I may dislike your station, Regent King, but I will not disrespect it. You will do likewise to me and call me *Master* Ashta."

Lone chewed at his lip. This was the culture of the island of Thrist. The Hungered Arena collected income from across Poas, putting that money into the few pockets that Harnoon Ashta chose. A few masters owned the villages and citizens to do with as they pleased. Lone could not imagine how Bard grew up in a village like the one they were now entering.

Rough shacks of mud, wood, and wide stones from the beach lined a narrow path. Lone saw men and boys, ranging from under five winters to well into their sixties, kneeling with eyes downcast in the open doorways as they walked by. He counted thirty when the group reached a wider area where six men hastily constructed a palanquin. Only wide enough to accommodate a single passenger, the carriage would hang from two long, wooden beams put over the shoulders men walking in front and rear.

"Why is this not already constructed?" Ashta asked without focusing on any one of the men.

"Master, it is my fault," said a man with gray hair hanging over his shoulders. "After the storm last month, we needed the wood for—"

A knife flashed in Ashta's grip as he crossed the few paces to the older man. "Turn around," he demanded.

Lone saw the tears in the man's eyes as he did as commanded. He moved to help the villager, but Bard stopped him with an arm across his chest.

Ashta snatched the man's hair, and after four quick swipes of the blade, he raised a fist of gray locks. He threw it to the ground, stalking past the man and into the hut behind him. Two villagers helped the weeping man to stand and led him away while another gathered what he could have the shorn hair.

"What in the seven hells did we just watch?" Lone hissed at Bard.

"Ashta removed the man as leader of this village."

Lone switched to speaking in Common so the villagers would be less likely to overhear them. "All for repurposing materials after a disaster?"

Bard pulled Lone away from the group. The villagers' eyes lingered on the two as the men dispersed back to their duties and completing the palanquin. "For not anticipating a master's will. These are the traditions of my island. I realize now that they are terrible, but this is not something to be dismantled overnight or without care."

"Will these men agree their lives are worth fighting for to change?" Lone waved vaguely to the surrounding village. "Would they ever lead a revolution?"

Bard followed Lone's gesture and frowned. "Not as they are. They see their lives of subjugation as an offering to Au."

Lone let out a deep breath. "That's for another day. Ashta said he wanted to see Naiti, your old master. Will that be a problem?"

Bard ran a hand through his short, silvered hair and clenched his fist, cracking the knuckles. "No." The single word carried the absolution of what he left unspoken.

"You lived near the Hungered Arena. Is there any family—" Lone forgot his words. Suddenly feeling lightheaded, he fell forward a step and into Bard's arms.

"*Menf?*" Bard led him around the corner of a shack, and Lone stumbled. Bard pushed him to sit on a tree stump used for a chopping block. "What happened?"

Lone took a few slow breaths, but everything felt slower, more labored. He reached for the ley lines and was again reminded how far away the closest one flowed.

"I'll be fine," Lone said, with deep breaths as the fog cleared from his mind. "Ashta may have been right about one little thing: archmages rely on magic. I'm used to a constant supply of ley energy. I think the lack of a line nearby is catching up with me."

"You've been without magic before." Bard placed a worried palm on Lone's cheek. "After healing me in Iecil."

"General Kiol told me the lines were drained, and some were shattered, but they still existed below our feet. Maybe I could still pull from them instinctually. I also wasn't surrounded by three dozen men that drain mana from their surroundings."

Bard flinched his hand away. "Sorry."

Lone snatched his partner's hand and pressed it to his chest. "Not you. Remember the avaryll said you're steeped with the magic of Iecil."

"They also called me a barbarian."

Lone kept Bard's hand pressed against his chest as he stood. "Yes, they did. You're an untamed beast of a man." He grinned and pressed his lips to the islander's. Lone's other hand slid around Bard's waist as someone coughed behind him. They broke the embrace and turned to see a young boy with a dark mop of hair waiting for their attention.

"They ready," he squeaked in fractured Common.

"Thank you," Lone replied. "How old are you, boy?" he added as the youngster was turning to return to the village.

The boy looked confused by the question until Bard repeated it in Au.

"Seven and four," the boy said, again trying Common.

"Thank you. We will be right there," Lone said slowly in his native tongue. The boy grinned, nodded, and left quickly.

"Eleven years old. I was that old when my father left." Lone frowned after the youth. "How long until he's fully indoctrinated into the culture of masters and their slaves and can no longer imagine a different life?"

Bard put a hand on Lone's shoulder. "I lived in a village just like this and it took only a few months away for me to see it could be better. Again, though, now is not the time for those thoughts."

As they rounded the shack, Harnoon Ashta stepped into the palanquin hastily constructed of driftwood and rope. Two barefoot men wearing only light loin-cloths and open vests hefted the carriage poles and took off at a jog. The owner of the Hungered Arena looked at Lone and Bard as he passed but said nothing. Three more men and one younger boy jogged after their master, carrying burlap sacks.

"Tribute," Bard explained at Lone's questioning eye on the unevenly filled bags. "As much as he imposed upon this village, he still takes more. Let's go."

10

The svarters thought themselves alone until the Mists rose. Then they and humans thought themselves alone in Poas.

L one was astounded by the stamina of the islanders hauling Harnoon Ashta without a break, though he should not have been after a year of witnessing Bard's capabilities. After almost an hour through the uneven paths of the island, through tight forests and steep inclines of loose stones, Lone's lungs burned as a stitch in his side begged him for a break. Rather than giving Ashta the satisfaction of showing weakness, Lone again pulled from the mana crystal at his belt to lend strength.

Bard noticed and frowned.

"You only have so much crystal, *menf*," he said in Common. Lone thought it a strange reversal that they now used his native language to speak secretly.

"It doesn't matter," Lone wheezed. "I can't use the crystal to teleport us away from here. You know what happened to my father when he tried that recently." Lone raised his left arm and wiggled the fingers.

Bard gestured to the sanctum stone Lone wore on that hand. The wide, silver band glistened in the dappled light filtering through the tall trees. "I am glad you wear that now."

Lone lowered his arm and idly turned the ring on his finger. "I wish you were wearing one as well. I should focus on reverse engineering how my father made these so I might make more. He was ten years younger than I am now when he made this one for my mother when she was pregnant with me."

"Or you could simply ask your father."

Lone waved away the suggestion.

"You could learn much from him. Your father was a genius with magic craft," Bard said.

"Yeah, 'was.' I hope Siraas can help him."

The group slowed as vines tangled the path, forcing one attendant to run ahead and hack at the overgrowth.

"Why isn't there a clear route?" Lone asked as they had the first moment to rest.

"Master Ashta decreed to take — to be taken — the most direct route. That leads us well off all roads."

Lone slapped at his neck and flicked the dead biting insect from his hand. "That guy's a real something."

"I have a request of you," Bard said.

Lone stood a little straighter, wary of Bard's serious tone. "Of course, anything."

"I would like you to attempt some reconciliation with your father."

Lone laughed but stopped short at Bard's unamused look. "You're serious? What is there to reconcile? He left when—"

"When you were eleven years old. He left his home because it was too painful to live there without your mother. He offered you to join him, and even if you declined at that moment, you could have gone to him at any time."

"Father abdicated all claims to the throne, and I was the crowned prince. I couldn't abandon that to live with the svarters. Aunt Lilan never would have allowed it."

"Your aunt would not have allowed your father to raise you? To observe another monarchy in action and widen your worldview?"

Lone shrugged and said nothing.

Bard continued. "When you were old enough to channel your powers as an archmage, your father taught you to teleport, a spell he allows no one else to learn. He gave you the means to visit him at any moment."

"And? He also could have seen me anytime."

"Have you ever asked him why he did not? Did you ever tell him what pain his absence caused in you?"

"No, but—"

"Please, I asked for a request, and you said anything." Bard raised his eyebrows.

Lone scrunched his face with a huff. "Fine, yes. I'll talk to my father when we get back." He swatted at another insect. "Unless we die of fever in this jungle. I'm not sure which I'd rather do."

"Thank you, *menf*." Bard squeezed Lone's hand and kissed him on the cheek.

Lone was deep in thoughts of how to broach the topic with his father as the man finished cutting the last of the vines and waved for the litter to proceed.

Harnoon Ashta peeked his head from the side of his carriage. "Explain this delay," he growled.

"There was a blockage, Master Ashta," said the man holding a long blade. "We are getting back underway."

Ashta scowled and looked back to Lone. "I am embarrassed for my people. This is your first time to our islands, Regent King, and this is the reception you receive."

"I've actually been here bef..." Lone trailed off as Ashta looked away, pulled his head back into the palanquin, and the men resumed their jog. Lone looked to Bard with a shrug and waved his hands dismissively.

The islander managed a half-smirk and rolled his eyes as they jogged after the others.

***

Lone visited the Western Isles, Thrist, and the Hungered Arena years ago with his Aunt Lilan. His memory of the arena was of a grand, oval building, five hundred feet across, with seating for sixty thousand or more. The excitement of travel obviously overwhelmed his young mind and greatly exaggerated the details.

They approached a wall of wooden spikes sunk into the ground and held together with stone and caked mud. Cheers of applause accompanied the clanging of metal from within.

Ashta jostled within his carriage until the men stopped and set him down. The island master stretched his neck and dug a single coin from a small pouch at his hip. He tossed it at the men, where it rolled in the dirt. None moved to collect it but kept their eyes downcast.

"That's more than you deserve, but I am a generous master. Take that and be gone. I'll find better transportation away from here."

"Thank you, Master," one man mumbled as he stooped to collect the coin. They backed away slowly, awkward with the palanquin until they were thirty paces away. They turned and ran, sticking to the road rather than cutting through the rough forest.

"The east gate," Ashta complained.

"What's wrong with the east gate?" Lone compartmentalized the man's behavior to address later. Ashta was already following the wall to the right, and Lone saw a gap in it with a trail leading away and through the trees.

"Nothing is *wrong* with it, but I prefer the west gate. Then, I may walk the circuit of my arena before taking my seat near this gate. That may be for the best, as Naiti is not expecting me."

Ashta continued alone as Lone looked back to Bard, trailing a few steps behind. He saw something he had never seen in the islander's eyes: fear.

"Do not worry for me," Bard said with a deep breath but stopped walking.

"You don't have to go inside. Hells, I don't want to go there. It's within my rights for us to return to that beach and I work on teleporting us out of here. We don't need the Western Isles against the avaryll, and I don't care if we left this island out of any new world order. Without magic, I don't even think they could get to Isolis within five weeks."

"I do not trust Ashta and will not leave your side."

"Then let's just leave. Go back to the beach, and I'll figure out how to teleport us out of here. Not to disrespect your birthplace but to all the hells with this place."

"No. We came with hopes of securing the aid of the Western Isles. We won't walk away from that now." Bard continued toward the gate, but Lone stopped him with hands on his shoulders.

"Bard, Naiti is in there. The man was a monster to you. You've told me stories of what he made you do: the murders, the beatings, the sexual humiliation. You walked away and owe that man nothing."

"He was my master. It was all within his right."

"And now you don't have a master. You have to agree that's better."

"The contract only ever loaned me to Dracon. Here, Naiti would still hold his claim over me. I find it surprising they have not taken me into custody yet for refusing the call from him months ago."

"We... we never talk about that. I thought it was settled."

Bard grinned without mirth and shook his head. "We sent a message. Words settle few things on this island."

Lone looked into Bard's pale blue eyes for a long moment and read the intention there. "Promise me you won't kill him."

"I promise I will try not to."

"Fair enough."

"*Menf...* Keep the magic you still carry within the crystals a secret. They think you are no more powerful than a fisherman right now."

They entered the Hungered Arena just as a beast of leathery wings, spiked scales, and ragged feathers knocked over the armored combatant in the pit below. The creature lunged on top of the fallen warrior, and even at the distance and over the crowd, Lone heard the crunch of armor or bones or both. The thing raised a jagged beak, dripping fresh blood and gore, and cawed into the air. Slaves of the arena were already circling the beast with nets to wrangle it and clear away the dead.

The inside of the arena was only a fraction of what Lone remembered, and the seating was only about a quarter full, with two or three hundred people in attendance. The onlookers sat in clusters around the bowl-shaped coliseum as an announcer barked in Au too rapidly and heavily accented for Lone to understand. Lone followed Ashta through a line of a dozen men with long daggers strapped to their thighs to a pavilion shrouded by sheer fabric that billowed in the slight breeze. Ashta snatched the fabric back, exposing a man seated on an ornate throne, drinking and being fanned by mostly nude young men.

"Master Naiti," Ashta said with a wide grin.

The other man jumped at his name, spilling his wine. "Master Ashta, what a pleasant surprise," he wheezed and stood, kicking away the boy rubbing his feet. Naiti wore dark leather shorts and the left half of a leather shirt, the right half being just straps to keep it in place. Lone thought it looked incredibly uncomfortable. His pale eyes looked past the other master to settle on Lone, then Bard. "You brought something that was once mine."

"You are in my seat," said Ashta, waving the servants to leave. They did so without having to be asked twice. Ashta shoved at Naiti as the other master slipped by him and took his throne to look down into the arena, where attendants raked sand over the last fighter's blood. Lone noticed from within that Ashta could see perfectly through the fabric, but looking from the other side revealed only faint shadows of his form.

When Lone last saw Naiti last year as the master pit Bard against the knife expert Whiar Fols in the Grand Hall, he was tall and powerfully built. Bard's former master was now little more than a husk of that man with dark bags under his eyes, sunken cheeks, and withered limbs. Naiti limped to Bard, picked at his fine shirt, and looked up at him. "My best boy is back. What a treat." He coughed and wiped blood from his mouth with the back of his hand.

Bard rolled his shoulders back and looked down at the master.

Lone recognized the symptoms but never thought the disease made it to the islands. "Naiti, how long have you been sick?"

The frail man turned to Lone and looked him over with milky, pale eyes. "Who are you?"

"Regent King Lone. We met when you brought Bard to Dracon."

"Hmm, yes," Naiti poked at Lone's stomach. "The fat boy at the queen's side." He twirled to Bard while Lone huffed. "I usually have a better mind for business, but I lost a lot of gold on you, Bartriado. I gave you a life, and you walked away from me."

Bard said nothing as he met his former master's gaze.

"You have advanced Red Bloom," Lone said. "I never thought your people would be susceptible to it, but then we thought the same for the svarters. Is this related to why you wanted Bard back those months ago?"

"Your concern for me is touching, boy."

"Do not mistake my questions for concern," said Lone. "You'll be dead in a month, but you won't see me lose a night's sleep."

"I will have to make it a month to remember. Your timing is impeccable, Master, if a little early," Naiti said to Ashta, and his breathing degraded into a coughing fit.

"Early for what?" said Lone.

Naiti stared at Lone for a hard moment before laughing, exposing chipped and red-stained teeth. "The champion returns."

Lone blinked and pushed past Naiti to stand in front of Ashta, blocking his view of the next combat being readied below. "What is going on, Ashta? You told me you would speak to the other masters and arrange matters to join us in Isolis."

"Did I?" Ashta sighed and craned his neck to see around Lone to the pit below.

Lone spread his arms to block the view further. "Is this the honor of the Western Isles?"

Ashta raised a hand and snapped his fingers. As one, the guards outside the pavilion turned to surround Bard. Two grabbed his arms, and another kicked out his knees. Long daggers were pulled and pressed against his chest and neck, drawing thin lines of blood. Bard struggled against them but quickly accepted the futility as a hand twisted in his short, silvered hair to hold his head in place.

"What is the meaning of this?" Lone's hand went to the hilt of his sword.

"Now, now, Regent King. Pulling your sword on a fellow ruler could cause issues. One you may not walk away from without your magic."

"Bard is a citizen of Dracon, you—"

"The slave is the property of Master Naiti, so by extension, my property as well," Ashta said calmly. "I loaned him to Dracon on contract. Not given to you to do with as you please. I received your missive claiming he is now a free man in Dracon, but that is not how the system operates, Regent King."

"Enlighten me," Lone growled.

"Bartriado's refusal to return when his master bade him supersedes any claim you have by contract. Further, through the relationship you two share, he has broken one of our highest laws. That he was not put to death as soon as we stepped foot upon the island is a mercy."

Lone's grip around his sword tightened, and Ashta continued. "Citizens of the islands must adhere to their masters' will. Those who do not must be made an example of, lest the greater population begin to feel this is acceptable. As a ruler, you must agree with that simple idea, Regent King. Without clear rule and law, there is anarchy."

Lone looked at Bard and the islander's clear body language of resignation: slumped shoulders, downcast eyes.

"You called him a citizen, yet you own him as property," said Lone, watching Bard. "Even within the ranks of masters, each is beholden to another, as Naiti is to you. How can he break from this?"

"I ask for the Challenge of Three," Bard said, raising his head, his eyes filled with a hate and rage Lone would never imagine from the man he loved.

Ashta waved a fly from the nearby fruit bowl before selecting one plump red berry. Without taking his eyes from Bard, he bit it and sucked the juice from within. "You wish to give up your island life to live in a frozen wasteland?"

"I do," Bard said quickly.

Ashta flicked the remains of the berry away and shrugged. "And if you should lose?"

Bard looked down at his former master with a clear look of disgust. "Should I live, I will return to Naiti's side."

Lone stepped forward with a gasp. "Bard, you can't—"

"I must do this."

Lone saw the fire of determination replace the hatred in Bard's sky-blue eyes.

"No," Ashta said and looked back at the combat happening in the pit. "You know the rules of the challenge, Bartiado. Upon your loss, your head will hang by the pit entrance below. None defy the masters." He selected another berry and waved Bard away. "I believe you know the way."

The guards roughly pulled Bard to his feet and dragged him away.

"No!" Lone reached for him, but four guards formed a wall of muscle and flesh. He drew his sword, but the men did not flinch or reach for their weapons.

"Regent King Lone, calm yourself."

Lone whirled on Ashta, bringing his steel within inches of the master's throat. "What is the meaning of this?" He nearly screamed.

"Lower your voice and your weapon. Unless you intend to use that thing, put it away and pull up a chair, Regent King." Ashta waved to the servant's stool beside him. "I suspect that, without your magic, you'll be here a while."

The battle below ended with the mixed approval of the crowd. A hulking man in armor Lone best thought of as "chitinous", all scales and spikes, was being dragged away while the victor, a much shorter, hunched creature waved a dagger to the small crowd and scurried to an entrance below where Lone now stood. As Lone watched, the stadium filled with a flow of new visitors through the far gate.

"Quite a turnout, Master Naiti," Ashta said and picked at another piece of fruit.

"I hoped to have everything in place for your return," said Naiti from where he stood awkwardly outside the tent. "Master Ashta, should Bartriado lose, yet survive..." His small voice dripped with a pleading tone.

"You cannot have him," Ashta said.

"I don't have much time left. Let me leave this world on a fond memory."

Ashta's gaze narrowed as his lip curled into a sneer. "One night."

Naiti clapped his hands and fell into another coughing fit.

Lone focused on controlling his breathing while imagining the joy he would feel when he tossed both of these men's heads into the arena.

A soft clearing of a throat made Lone turn to a young, underfed boy holding a simple wooden chair.

"Thank you," Lone said as he accepted it and set it down a few feet from Ashta. "This is all going to your plan, isn't it, Ashta? You never cared about a gathering of nations in Acrus. You only came to take back Bard."

Ashta dug through this pile of fruit, tossing out pieces at random. "I envy you, Regent King. May I call you Lone?"

"I really don't care."

"You don't care that I envy you, or you don't care that I call you by the name your father gave you?"

"My mother gave me my name. It was her father's. And I don't care about that or why you envy me."

"Your mother's father, is he still alive?"

"No. What is your goal here, Ashta?"

"You're about to see it play out." Ashta waved, and Lone's eyes fixed on the battlefield below. Weapons of indiscernible quality were placed on racks and in barrels around the edges of the oval of packed earth. Greatswords, axes, unstrung bows, and several others Lone had seen in his training room at the castle but had yet to practice with. "Bartriado's only route to freedom is the Challenge of Three."

"Which is?"

"Three consecutive fights without time to rest. I carefully curated what you are about to witness."

The stands were nearly full as the announcer rambled on in Au. Many newcomers wore finer robes with prominent jewelry that glinted in the afternoon sun, even from a distance.

"You knew he would call for this challenge. You traveled eight hundred miles across Eplear to be at the summit. You knew I would be there with Bard and that something would warrant you asking for a quick return to the islands. Only myself and two others present could perform the teleport, and you knew Bard would accompany me. This was all a very elaborate ruse to get him back in the ring."

Asha pushed away the fruit bowl and leaned back. "A master's orders must be respected. The avaryll cut the meeting shorter than I expected, or everything would have been ready when we arrived at the arena. The other variable was where you would bring us on the island."

"You're a monster, Ashta."

"There's no need to be so unpleasant, Lone. I may appear abrasive, but I am a pleasant man once one gets to know me."

"I'll work on changing my mind about you right away." Lone slid his chair a few inches farther from Ashta as the arena announcer spoke in Au far too fast. Lone caught something that, by context, thought meant "returning champion" and leaned closer to the fine silk curtain. Others in the audience perked up with the announcement, breaking from their private conversations to turn and watch the center.

Bard, now wearing only a white subligaculum and a single, flimsy shoulder guard, stepped from the entrance below Lone. Some in the audience cheered and clapped. Others hissed and threw whatever was at hand. Bard turned toward Lone, though he could not see through the curtain from the other side, and saluted with a fist to his chest.

Lone leaned forward. Despite his vast confidence in Bard's fighting ability, Lone could not help but think of the mana crystal at his hip. Though not enough to burn the stadium to the ground, it was more than sufficient to blast Ashta and make an escape.

Lone wrung his hands together between his knees.

11

Often, as a curse, people will remark about the seven hells. Much like the names and number of the Greater Ascended, the number of hells seems consistent across the teachings of other realms.

B ard lowered his arm and took a deep breath. He could faintly see the shadow of one figure behind the silk curtain, surely Lone, sitting literally on the edge of his seat. Stretching his neck to the side, Bard crossed to the nearest rack of swords, noting how quickly the arena had fallen into disrepair. The axes would have been polished to a mirror finish two years ago. Now, most of the weapons were rusted with dried blood. Unless they had stocked the racks with the worst choices specifically for his challenge.

"An old favorite of the arena has returned, Bartriado Hren! Place your bets now, gentlemen!" said the announcer. "This challenge will last only three rounds, or until the challenger is dead!"

Bard watched and participated in enough challenges within the Hungered Arena to know exactly what to expect. They would bring creatures and men up from the cages below in increasingly slanted odds, and Bard could freely change his weapons from the racks around the floor at any time. When Ashta had no more opponents to send against him, Bard would stand victorious.

He took a worn scimitar from the rack and moved to the center of the arena, where the iron gate opposite where he entered rattled open to the crowd's cheers. From the shadows stepped a lanky figure with features obscured beneath the raised cowl of a cloak.

"Our returned brother's first opponent," barked the announcer, "hails from the fey wilds of Nyphlym. The rising star of the Hungered Arena, Djarcar the Gnasher!" The crowd cheered as the gate lowered.

Djarcar raised his thin hands with sharp claws to pull back his hood and drop the cloak behind him, revealing a slender, furred face, thin ears, and enormous eyes. With the same smooth motion, the half-man, half-rat pulled a pair of segmented iron gloves from the back of his belt. He slid them on dramatically before settling into a low stance.

"Bartriado," he hissed. "I've heard the others speak of you, never kindly."

Bard looked from Djarcar to Ashta's shrouded pavilion and back. "A rat-man? I thought you were a feytale."

Djarcar dropped lower and was upon Bard within a breath. Surprised by the creature's speed, the islander barely raised his weapon to parry. The armored gauntlets flashed in the early evening sun. Bard felt their shallow bite across his bare forearms more than once as his weapon was too large and slow to meet every attack. Djarcar deftly hopped back as Bard found a single opening to slash the old scimitar.

"Not what I expected, Bartriado," Djarcar grinned, exposing long, yellowed teeth. "Have you gotten soft in your time with the mages?"

Bard glanced over the blood oozing from the many small cuts on his forearms and hands. They would be annoying but were nothing that would hinder his progress. He set his stance and said nothing.

Djarcar spat to the side and rushed forward with another slice aimed at Bard's gut. Rather than bringing this sword to parry, Bard moved forward and threw the scimitar at the wererat. Djarcar slashed at the flying weapon, leaving him open just long enough for Bard's fist to make direct contact with his pointy, whiskered nose.

Djarcar staggered back, one iron glove clattering to the ground as he raised a hand to a nose, pouring blood. He looked up with a grin as Bard drove a crippling sidekick into the wererat's chest. Djarcar crumbled as he was thrown a dozen feet back and lay still in the dirt.

Bard bent to retrieve the gauntlet, checking the claws for signs of poison and finding none. He turned his attention back to the wererat and wondered why the announcer had yet to call the match. *Am I meant to kill him?* Bard moved close to Djarcar and plucked two daggers strapped to the wererat's back, also checking them for poison.

The flesh along Djarcar's arms rippled as his back arched. His light cloth jerkin stretched and split as his body expanded and coated itself in a thin membrane. Bard scrambled away.

"We're about to see Djarcar's true form! Remember to tell your friends and associates about this day!" exclaimed the announcer.

Bard threw the dagger in his hand, sinking it to the hilt into Djarcar's enlarging form, ripping the membrane, and ran for the discarded scimitar. He bolted for the mound of bubbling flesh now fourfold the former size of the wererat. As he brought the sword down on the writhing mass, it burst open like a grotesque insect cocoon, and a thin tail slapped Bard in the stomach, easily flinging him away. By some luck, he held onto the scimitar as he raised to a knee and sucked at the air. A rat four or five feet tall and at least nine long wrestled free of its film to sit back on its hind legs.

Bard looked down at the little sword in his fist and scanned the arena's edges for something with more reach. He spotted a spear propped against the wall less than thirty feet away and ran for it. The crowd cheered again, but Bard would not look back with the spear now less than twenty feet away. Another two strides, and the rat slammed into his back, forcing him down. As he fell, Bard pivoted and blindly slashed out with the sword. He felt it bite into flesh, and the rat flinched away with a squeal. Rolling to his feet, Bard reached the spear, grabbed for it, and turned as the weight of Djarcar slammed against him again, ripping the spear from his hands.

Bard stared at the wide, vacant eyes of the giant rat only inches from his own, one with a fresh wound sliced across it. He followed the length of the spear through the beast's bloody maw to where it protruded from the top of Djarcar's head. Pain cut through Bard's side as the last shred of life left the wererat, and its mass slid over him.

***

Lone's heart skipped as the monster pounced on Bard. The islander pulled himself from under the rat's form seconds later, covered in blood that Lone prayed was not his own. "What in the seven hells was that, Ashta?" he raged without taking his eyes from his partner below.

"That was a shame," Ashta responded, sounding disinterested. "Djarcar came at no small expense to the arena. Few had seen his true form."

"He was a shifter of some kind? Magic shouldn't work here." Lone's words were more for himself.

"Djarcar was a feybeast. They come in many styles."

"Your healers should see to Bard before the next round," Lone said while watching the islander wipe blood from his face, chest, and arms.

"That is not how this is done, Regent King. The challenge carries through each round, and so must any harm. I knew Bartriado would perform well, but I expected him to go onto the next round with more than a handful of scratches and a broken rib."

Lone gripped his knees and watched as the main portcullis creaked open again.

***

Bard shook what he could of the gore from his hands as he bent to take up the dagger dropped by the wererat. As he did, a spike of pain flared from where Djarcar had hit him in the last strike, stealing his breath away. Bard growled at his ribs. *Broken or bruised?* With the scimitar in one hand, he tucked the dagger into the waist of his loincloth as a short, wide man, human this time, strode forward from the gate. Leaning heavily on a twisted obsidian staff, he wore a black jacket embroidered with red and purple flames at the bottom hem that dusted the ground. His long, snow-white hair flowed around a dark face, and the two thick horns rose from his crown.

"This is a rare treat, gentlemen!" The announcer's voice was as animated as ever. "From the White Ait, a long-time attendee of the Hungered Arena, first-time competitor, Master Scorhara!"

Bard stepped near Djarcar's body, ready to use it for cover.

"Few flee and return to challenge their masters, Hren." Scorhara's voice whistled in the air, barely heard. "I cannot fathom what you intend to accomplish here."

Bard recalled what he knew of the White Ait, the small, mountainous island farthest from the mainland of Poas. The inhabitants were said to possess a dark power that Bard assumed was just magic, but according to Lone, there were no ley lines nearby to make magic possible.

"Why does a master fight in the arena?" Bard asked. "Wouldn't you be more comfortable in the stands?"

Scorhara cocked his head, expressionless. "You mistake the meaning of my title. I am not a master of slaves but a master of my craft." He tapped his staff once, raised the other arm, and slowly gripped his gloved fingers into a fist.

Djarcar's corpse twitched beside Bard, and he jumped back with the scimitar raised. The sparsely-haired flesh undulated as if something were beneath, trying to push free. Bard backed away another step as the tissue split and white bone protruded. Djarcar deflated as more osseous matter ripped from the body, forming into a ball of bone hovering inches from his back. It shivered and compressed, bones breaking and reforming until they created a near-perfect sphere. Bard could not tear his eyes from it as the ball set onto the ground beside the mangled flesh of the giant rat.

Scorhara tapped his staff again, and the sphere unraveled. A bone-white monster stretched seven feet tall on legs bent backward like a cat's. Thin arms ended in claws, each as long as Bard's forearm. Twin points of pale blue light flickered from the sunken pits over a short muzzle of fangs as deadly as the claws.

"Behold but a trifle of the power of White Ait!" Scorhara's voice came again on the breeze, louder than before.

The air buzzed as the bone monster snapped chitinous wings from its back and hovered inches from the dirt.

Bard looked at the rusted scimitar in his hand as despair hit him hard. On a whim, he dropped the sword, took the dagger from his waist, and held it by the blade, ready to throw.

"Surely the challenger can't think he can hurt a bone devil with a dagger! What is he doing?" barked the announcer.

Bard pulled back to throw at the monster but released it at Master Scorhara. His aim was true as the dagger glimmered in the dying light, but, almost to draw out the drama, Scorhara shifted his staff to catch the dagger in the last instant. His laugh floated around Bard from every direction. The bone devil rushed forward, claws and teeth bared, unconcerned about any counterattack the islander may have against a direct assault.

It clattered to the ground around Bard, scattering bones and dust in lines behind him.

Master Scorhara stared forward, eyes wide, as he fell to his knees and forward onto his face. The hilt of a dagger blossomed from the back of his skull. Beyond him, a masked man stood by the iron gates with an arm still extended from the throw.

"No one could have seen this, gentlemen! The Dark Blade has entered the arena and killed Master Scorhara! An upset like this has never happened before! Is he working with our challenger? I'll have to hear from the judges if this counts as a win!"

The masked man, the Dark Blade, lowered his arm and strode forward. Though he wore a full suit of fitted leather armor, gloves, and a painted wooden mask, Bard knew the man's gait. They trained together for years and knew his body, his stance, the scars raked across his chest. The last he saw the man, he was bleeding from a score of gashes sliced by his own blade.

"Whiar Fols," Bard said and glanced at the debris of the bone devil one more time before focusing fully on the other man—his former training partner, brother, and more.

Fols tilted his head. The mask muffled his deep voice. "When you left me for your new master, I never thought I would have this opportunity, Hren. We can finish this between us."

Bard raised his hands in defense. "There is nothing between us, Fols."

"Nothing between us?" As he stepped to circle Bard, short blades flashed in Whiar Fols' hands. "You took the life that should have been mine."

"I did as Naiti instructed, to show speed and control."

"You humiliated me."

"I followed our master's order."

"Now you live an easy life with your new master." He paused his movement and fell into an offensive stance with muscles tensed. "Only one will walk away from this arena today." He nodded to a rack with javelins, staffs, and long swords. "I'll give you time to pick the weapon you will wield when you die."

Bard followed Fols' motion and looked back at the man. "No." He lowered his empty hands to his sides. "I won't fight you like this."

The announcer shouted behind Bard. "I'm being told the Hungered Arena will not be held responsible for the death of Master Scorhara, but the Dark Blade will face judgment, should he survive this encounter. The death of Master Scorhara does not count as a win for the challenger, but a battle against the Dark Blade will!" The crowd cheered around the announcer's words. "These two have a history. The true identity of the Dark Blade is a secret, but we can tell you he once trained with our challenger. Were they perhaps more?"

Fols threw two daggers as he closed the distance. Bard dodged them easily, but a third grazed the inside of his palm as he barely knocked it aside in time. The slashes came quickly from every angle. Bard met each one with force, aiming his blocks at the nerves just above Fols' wrist. It felt familiar as if the two were going through the practice they had done for hundreds of hours under Naiti's lingering eye.

Bard lunged to grapple, but Fols was faster. He spun and dropped, swinging high and low simultaneously with either knife. Bard would never imagine himself so hard-pressed against Whiar Fols. More wounds opened across his chest and biceps as Fols showed skill levels beyond the wererat Djarcar. Bard searched for an opening to attack but found none. His best defense was still insufficient to stop every attack, and he felt his stamina drain with every pained breath against his injured ribs.

Retreating another step, Bard was again too slow to stop the dagger that plunged into his left shoulder. With Fols' one weapon tied up for just an instant, Bard grabbed the man's wrist with his right hand and twisted as he drove a heel into Fol's knee. He knew the other man would never fight in the arena again by the feel of snapping tendons and how Fols screamed as he collapsed backward. With a spray of blood, Bard ripped the thin dagger from his shoulder. He kicked away the other dagger still near Fols' hand, knelt beside him, and pulled off the wooden mask with his free hand. Fols' teeth were grinding with pain, but his eyes were clear with murder.

"You're dead here, Fols," Bard said. "You killed a master."

"I've been dead for a year, Hren," Fols managed around clenched teeth. "Finish me now."

"Come back to Dracon with me. Regent King Lone will grant you asylum."

"You speak for your new master now? Is he collecting a harem of disgraced slaves?"

"Fols... Whiar... Please."

Fols closed his eyes, the same pale blue as Bard's, and blew out a long breath. His anger lessened when he opened them again. "Get me the herb in my left breast pocket. It will give me the strength to move on."

Bard did as asked and pulled a small flower with long, thin petals the color of rubies from the pocket. Bard was unfamiliar with the species but was never much of an herbal scholar. Fols opened his mouth, and Bard carefully placed the bloom on his tongue. He chewed it twice before his body visibly relaxed.

"Our challenger just fed the Dark Blade a blossom of devilweed! Another first for the arena, death by feeding your opponent poison! I hope this counts as a win."

Panic surged through Bard as a slow grin spread across Fols' mouth. "I'll have a lot to tell Au. I only wish I didn't know what it is to be betrayed by one I loved." Fols gently shook once, let out a long sigh, and was still.

Bard sat back on his heels, hands loose at his sides, staring unfocused at Fols. Memories he thought long forgotten flashed by unbidden. Bard was perhaps thirteen when they brought the new boy to his village. He raised him as a son and brother, a relationship later eroded by the influences and rigors of training under Naiti. Bard could only imagine what pain Fols felt or what injustices he blamed on Bard. He would never know now.

"Goodbye, Whiar," Bard whispered and gingerly reached to close the man's eyes. He took the wooden mask in his free arm and pushed to his feet.

The gates were already rising again. With obvious effort, four slaves pushed a metal crate forward, as tall as Bard and just as wide.

"This will be our final match, gentlemen! Our challenger is wounded and broken. How will he fare against the Shadow Imps?"

With the box positioned, three slaves fled back into the shadows beyond the gate while the unlucky fourth reached for the lever high on the side of the container. He pulled it and bolted for the gate that was already closing.

The front panel of the crate slammed open, stirring dust. Bard kept his distance as he squinted into the box containing nothing but shadows. With a soft hiss, those shadows flowed forward like a miasma and out stepped a Shadow Imp. It stood only just over five feet tall but felt imposing with dark skin stretched over limbs of muscle and sinew.

"A daemon? What other dregs do they have from the hells?" Bard crossed to take up a straight, long sword. He held it in a hand, still stinging from so many nicks from Fols, and turned to the imp. With nowhere to keep it on his person, he dropped Whiar's mask beside him.

The daemon splayed its left four-fingered hand, and a thin blade slid from his wrist. Perhaps it grew from the monster itself; Bard could not tell. The black blade looked slick with what was surely poison or acid.

Bard met the daemon's powerful backslash with his blade and grunted with the exertion. He had battled against left-handed swordsmen, but not with this sheer power. He was worried the cheap sword might snap in half. The daemon followed with a quick upward slash and a forward thrust. Bard leaned back to avoid the slash and spun to his right for the thrust. He brought his blade down around, aimed at the monster's neck.

The blade stopped inches from its throat, caught by the daemon's bare right hand. It grinned, showing so many dozens of teeth. Bard dodged backward from the black blade as it slashed at him. His sword hissed where it had cut into the daemon's palm. It grinned wider, head near to splitting in half.

Bard looked at his long sword, now nearly eaten through by the monster's blood, and tossed it to the ground. He stepped toward the daemon with bare hands raised to strike. His left shoulder screamed with the agony of the effort, as did his ribs, but that pain was not going anywhere—no need to give it attention now.

The daemon looked down at the sizzling sword and back to Bard, who covered the space to the creature in two strides. Bard caught it in the side with his right shoulder while pulling its legs out from under it, tackling it to the dust. The islander landed on top of the daemon and gave it a solid right cross to the top half of its head just as it hit the ground.

With a wet splat, the daemon's head exploded at the impact. The daemon's body hissed as it melted into the ground under Bard.

He knelt there, stunned, spattered with the gore of the creature he had just killed with a single punch. The daemon blood hissed at the ground but did not seem to affect Bard's flesh.

The arena was silent for what felt like minutes. Bard looked down at his hands in amazement. Daemon blood dyed his right arm purple to almost the elbow. The torture of his left shoulder faded. An invigoration shivered through him.

The announcer was speaking a rush of words Bard could not process.

The crowd erupted with excitement, and Bard remembered the introduction to this fight. The Shadow Imps. Plural.

Bard rolled away as a black blade barely missed his head. The second daemon looked identical to the other, with a thin blade held in its left hand.

It ran at Bard.

He dodged the first two swipes and ducked under the third. The pain in his ribs flared, slowing his next move just long enough for the daemon's right fist to catch him across the jaw. Bard spun and fell to his hands and knees. He pulled himself away from the daemon, trying to create a few more feet of space while he recovered from the blow. The daemon's blade dragged along the ground as it stalked forward, and a faint wisp of black smoke rose from the contact. It reached Bard and kicked him in the ribs, knocking him up and to his back. His vision narrowed as darkness pulsed at the edges, in time with his frantic heartbeat.

The daemon took another step forward and pulled back to kick Bard again, toying with him. Dredging from his final reserves of strength, Bard rolled forward into the kick and caught the daemon off balance. He leaned into its knees, toppling it backward. An odd sense of vigor washed over him as he made direct contact with the daemon. Bard pulled himself up to drive an elbow into the beast's head. Again and again, he pummeled the daemon with his free elbow, feeling that tiny burst of energy enter him with each hit. Every blow caused visible damage to the daemon's head until it, too, collapsed and melted into the earth.

Panting and with the brief surge of vitality fading, Bard staggered to his feet. He raised a fist in salute toward where Lone sat, heard the announcer verify his win, and collapsed.

***

Lone launched himself over the railing and pulled at the mana crystal at his hip to land gracefully on the arena floor thirty feet below. He sprinted to where Bard lay face down in a growing pool of deep violet. Heedless of the daemon blood burning where it touched him, Lone took Bard's right arm and dragged him from the puddle of ichor. He unhooked the pouch of mana crystal from his belt, poured a few into his left hand, and pressed his right against Bard's shoulder. As Etharis had taught him, Lone could not directly heal the tissue, only encourage it to mend itself.

Bard opened his eyes with a sharp breath. "How...?"

"Quiet, you're a wreck." Lone's hands quaked between labored breaths as he inspected Bard's wounds. "Bleeding from a dozen gashes I can see, a deep stab wound, broken ribs, and covered in poisoned daemon blood."

"How did I beat it?"

"Of course. I think the anti-magic of your body weakened them. I don't want to find another to test that right now. Lie still."

"Use your stone," Bard whispered.

Lone shook his head. "Don't be stupid. I won't leave you here." He looked down at the wide silver band and realized Bard did not mean for Lone to use the stone himself. All that fretting about how to return them both home, when the hardest half of that problem was solved easily, thanks to his father. Lone twisted off the ring, reached for Bard's left hand, and pushed his mother's sanctum stone onto his partner's finger. With that single motion, Lone's nerves settled, calming his shakes and centering his mental focus. "You were breathtaking to watch."

"Don't do anything stupid."

Lone bent to kiss Bard on the forehead. "I'll see you in Dracon. Home."

Bard was gone with a faint pop.

The announcer babbled excitedly in Au at such a rate that all the words slurred together in Lone's ear.

One good idea was followed by a terrible one as Lone stood and surveyed the arena. The deflated corpse of Djarcar the wererat slumped against one wall. His bones were scattered across the center. Ashta waved away Lone's questions about what magic made the bone construct possible. Perhaps a trip to the White Ait would be needed. Whiar Fols, the man Lone witnessed Bard carefully humiliate last year in the Grand Hall, lay dead with a trail of foamy spittle trickling from the corner of his mouth. Then, of course, the two daemon were beaten to a stomach-turning pulp. How had a slaver on Thrist acquired creatures the Mraasil claimed required a master?

This must end. Whatever magic awaits us in Isolis means nothing while this arena stands open.

Lone noticed the mask Whiar had worn and moved a few feet to pick it up. Bard had seemed interested in having it. He felt his passive cultivation slowly sap the energy from the mana crystal at his hip. Even if he cast no magic, that pouch would hold nothing but dust within a few hours. He imagined the bone devil constructed by Scorhara. Without magic, one does not rip the bones from a corpse and recombine them into something else. Yet as Lone watched the man with pure white hair tap his staff to create the creature, Lone sensed no use of ley energy by the strange islander.

He remembered watching Dalbinth work his light shaping outside the Redeemer's Labyrinth. That, too, used no ley energy. His eyes drifted to Scorhara's staff, still lying in the dirt, but he forced himself to focus on the present.

The regent king looked up to the master's silk curtain. He wanted to challenge Ashta to a direct duel to show he was not the weak ruler Ashta believed him to be. What little magic remained in his pouch would never see him through a fight, and while Bard had turned him into a decent fighter, he would be destroyed by whatever else the arena had in its underground cages.

"Master Harnoon Ashta, you have made clear your disinterest in the greater events of the realm. From his day, Dracon will no longer consider the wishes of the Western Isles when addressing the nations of Poas."

Ashta's laugh reverberated across the basin. "Foolishness. Do you think the Western Isles are in any way dependent upon the mainland? Your threats are meaningless."

Lone waved at the racks of tarnished weapons. "I see the state of your arena. We'll see how long your status remains when you no longer have the wealthy underbelly of the continent coming to bet on your matches."

Ashta laughed again. "You come to my island and think to impose your misguided sense of morals? Begone, little regent king."

The crowd laughed and jeered. They threw things at Lone, but none with the force to reach him. He stared at the master's curtain as it shifted in the slight breeze. The announcer spoke in his rapid Au, and Lone only understood enough to know he was being mocked. Lone flicked his gaze to one of the iron gates at the sides of the arena. Perhaps it was the pride of the line of Cazlandt, but he would not be rejected, to walk out alone as the crowd jeered around him.

Lone tore the pouch from his hip and clenched it in his right fist. Though most of the crystals were dull from his drain upon them, Lone still felt the bite of their edges through the thin hide bag. "You're a coward, Ashta."

He prepared for a snide retort, but the silence was worse.

"Go home, little king," the announcer said in broken Common.

Daelin's words rang in Lone's head as a memory from fourteen or fifteen years ago flashed by. *You can not teleport using mana crystal. The crystal structure contains the potential ley energy required for a teleport, but it is a matter of throughput. No matter the purity of the crystal or the quality of the cuts, one simply can not draw quickly enough and hold enough of the energy to complete the spell.*

Rage and embarrassment wrested for control. A sharp pain ran from his right shoulder and down his arm as Lone inhaled sharply. With a flash of pale green light, the mana crystal in his pouch was crushed to dust as he drew out all their power. Mana surged through his veins, and he felt himself pulled toward a dark obelisk in a colorful yard. Someone screamed as the cobblestone rushed to meet him.

12

The realm locals call The Glory is relatively tiny. The world tree is barely taller than me. I didn't stay long, for fear of stepping on someone.

Jazelyn watched the smoke rings expand and disperse from the heat of the blazing hearth. She lay on the floor before her favorite wing-backed chair and flicked the thin black cigar into the fire before reaching for another from the case beside her head. Boots scraped as Kiol stepped beside and squatted close.

"Since when do you lie on the floor, Lyn?" He forced a smile.

"Since when are we completely humiliated by overwhelming magic?" She lit the cigar with a flick of her thumb and took a deep drag.

Kiol sat back and waved away the plume of smoke from his wife. "It was actually a little refreshing, don't you think? To know the avaryll are so advanced means we could strive to their level. You and I could be so much more, love."

"Glorious, my heart swells with your enthusiasm." She looked away from him into the dancing flames. "Do you honestly believe that we humans can match the avaryll? Not only did they teleport us away to hold us helpless for days, but they completely obscured their presence from me for centuries. Not even Cazlandt was aware of them. We will never be their equals."

Kiol picked at the straps of the leather bracer on his left wrist. "At least they can inspire us to refine our skills and become the most powerful humans."

Jazelyn rolled her head to face him. "Queen Lilan was almost a thousand years my junior, and she controlled me for days to create a magic codex for her. I have shoes ten times older than Regent King Lone, and he grasps concepts of enchanting or Breaking faster than I ever could. General Miech, a mere crystal mage, showed more ingenuity, and now this child Dehset, barely more than an infant, is shaping up to be similar."

Kiol looked back to Jazelyn's workshop, where he just finished sweeping up the last of the disaster. When they entered after returning from Acrus, Jazelyn grumbled the young student's name but only sighed and continued to their personal sitting room.

"I must come to terms with it, dear." Jazelyn took another long draw of her cigar and expelled the smoke in a shapeless plume. "I am a relic. Stagnant and unchanging."

"You were so excited by discovering the purple ley lines months ago, Lyn. What other secrets lay within the aether?"

"The purple ley line represented a connection between realms I overlooked for over a thousand years."

"When did you and I last do some real training together? We don't have to be anywhere right now. Let's go throw around some magic."

Jazelyn took another slow pull on her cigar and kept her glazed stare cast to the ceiling.

Without a word, Kiol pushed back to his heels, stood, and disappeared around the wide base of the chair. Jazelyn returned her gaze to the fire until her husband returned a moment later. She looked at him and away again with a sneer of disgust at what he held between his hands. He sat cross-legged and opened the hinged lid of the small wooden box.

"I assure you I am not in the mood for that, Kiol."

Careful not to activate the orb, Kiol pulled it from the plush interior and set it on the floor, pushing the box aside. "Enough moping. It's time to do something productive. We've waited long enough, Lyn. Tonight is the night we look into your daughter's past."

General Jazelyn only looked into the flames.

Kiol rolled the glass orb on the stone floor, very aware of the dull, hollow sound it made. "So Acrus tried to kill you when Kethry was a baby. Then they stole her reminisphere only days after she was lost to her aether walking. Now, six centuries later, a daemon mistress is using her body for who knows what terrible deeds. But sure, none of that matters because other people are more powerful than you. A race of magically infused beings we know almost nothing about? So what? What about Cazlandt? He was far more powerful than you, than Lilan, than anyone, but he was also an enormous dick. I may be fast with my spells, but you would completely crush me in an actual fight, and I'm the combat general of all archmages. Now, stop wasting our time wallowing and watch Kethry's reminisphere with me."

Jazelyn flicked the remains of her cigar into the fire, pushed to a seated position across from her husband, and scowled at him. "You really piss me off sometimes."

"If I didn't, we wouldn't have been married this long. It's part of my charm." He leaned forward to kiss her cheek.

Taking a deep breath, Jazelyn placed her right hand against the orb while Kiol put his on the other side.

***

Jazelyn looked around the room that was destroyed centuries ago to make space for her two-story workshop. A four-poster bed with a flowing canopy of midnight velvet sat against one wall. The bedside tables were stacked with books that Jazelyn would not have to approach to know were mindless works of fiction. Oil paintings of sweeping landscapes, mysterious dark forests, and castles perched precariously on mountaintops covered the walls. A large rug with a vaguely floral design covered most of the only wood plank floor ever installed in Castle Dracon. Opposite the bed was a dressing table with a tarnished silvered mirror. Another stack of books threatened to topple from the edge of the table.

Jazelyn looked around and found she was alone. Kiol must be viewing the memories in his own mind. She saw the box that would contain the reminisphere on a small table beside two empty teacups and stepped toward it. She stopped at the sound of music.

Wearing a plush dressing robe, Kethry burst from the door beside the bed and strode to the dressing table. She sat, brushed her long, red curls with the short-bristled brush in her palm, and hummed fragments of a tune Jazelyn once sang to her nightly.

Jazelyn knew there was no preparing for this moment, which is why she had left the orb untouched for months. Her knees felt suddenly weak, and she reached for the table with the box and cups to steady herself. Jazelyn breathed the words as Kethry hummed.

> My sweetest girl
> Upon those quiet tomorrow twilights
> Lost the last moon
> And left the world to the darkest of
> nights

Her hair aflame
With eyes that saw more than any of ours
Sought the lost moon
To return the best friend of all the stars'

Jazelyn could remember no more. A song she had sung to her daughter every night for a century was lost, and Kethry suddenly stopped her humming.

"It's open," Kethry softly said without breaking stride with her hair brushing.

General Jazelyn balked as her younger self pushed the door open and entered. She wore the same sort of gossamer blue dress she still wore today and looked unchanged from her current self. Expect perhaps the eyes. Jazelyn could not place the difference, but they felt somehow foreign.

"You should be in bed, dear. Tomorrow will be a long day," said the younger Jazelyn.

"I haven't needed sleep in centuries, Ma."

Jazelyn stepped into the room and behind her daughter. "You know what I mean. You should rest." She offered a hand to take the brush. Kethry sighed and relinquished it for her mother to brush her hair. "Please, just do not stay up all night Walking. Read your silly stories or practice your needlework."

"I haven't touched my stitching in years."

"Kethry, please do not be difficult. I worry about your Walking until we work out the magic of using an anchor."

"I don't need an anchor. I've never had a problem finding my way back."

"You have never had a problem *yet*," Jazelyn corrected.

With a tightness in her gut, the older Jazelyn knew when this scene occurred. This was the last night before Kethry was lost to the aether. Jazelyn could not remember what grandly important event was planned for the next day because she never attended it. She tried to convince Kethry not to Aether Walk until they could develop safety measures. Kethry argued her mother was being overprotective. They both ended up shouting, and the silver mirror would crack as Jazelyn slammed the door on her way out.

When Kethry did not come down the next morning, a servant went to fetch her and returned screaming.

Jazelyn broke from her reverie as the door slammed, and a fine line split the mirror. Kethry threw a book at the closed door and spat a curse at her mother. With a frustrated fluting sound, she stormed to the table with the reminisphere, snatched it from the box, and crossed to the bed, throwing herself across the pile of down-filled blankets.

With Kethry holding the orb, Jazelyn felt her vision pull closer to her daughter as she heard her thoughts.

"This is my magic," Kethry said. "Uncle Caz may have helped me initially, but this is mine. I developed Aether Walking. Ma can't tell me how to do something she herself doesn't understand."

Jazelyn frowned at the petulant thoughts unbecoming of a woman starting her seventh century of life.

Her vision suddenly pulled into Kethry as she began her Aether Walk. The ley lines blazed with vivid light and colors Jazelyn could barely comprehend. Kethry seemed uninterested as she rushed along the Gran Marc toward Terswood at speeds Jazelyn never imagined. She pushed deeper, tracing a faint purple ley line into the world. Jazelyn had followed such a line months ago, moving slowly and carefully, terrified of losing her direction or becoming disentangled from the only path back to her body. Kethry surged forward with recklessness. Total darkness surrounded them for a period impossible to determine, and just as the line was beginning to resolve itself again, to drop them to the realm below, to Senguosh, Kethry leaped from the purple ley line into the nothing. Jazelyn's heart jumped into her throat.

This is how she does it, Jazelyn thought. *This is how she was lost. She was angry with me and threw herself into the expanse of nothing between realms, gone beyond the aether.* Her mind churned, unconvinced. *No, she must return from this to record the reminisphere.*

Out of the darkness, Jazelyn saw they rushed toward a small cottage floating in the dark, just like the one they shared in Eplear before Dracon was founded. They flew through the space, and Kethry's body, or at least an image of it, again formed to alight just inside the open door. She now wore a blue satin dress, strapless and sweeping the ground as she stepped toward the other occupant of the cottage.

"I'm back," Kethry greeted.

The short girl with dark skin and green eyes grinned. "Kethryane, you have returned so soon." Despite her innocent look, her voice was smooth and deep, layered with a steady lupine growl. "Have you come to accept my offer?"

"Almost. I don't know what else I can learn in Poas. I've been to dozens of realms with my Unc— my mentor, and each only offers the barest additional understanding."

"I will grant you power and knowledge. You will easily understand concepts beyond what you can now barely imagine. Why have you returned if not to take what I offered you?"

Kethry paced around the other. "You never told me your name. I want to know who I'm dealing with."

The grin widened. "They called me Baris."

"No, that was once your name, or perhaps the name of the one whose power you've absorbed. What are you called now? And you can drop this facade." Kethry gestured at the girl's body.

The girl called Baris cocked her head with a grin, exposing sharp canines. "You are a clever one." She hunched forward, and her body hissed black steam. Her limbs lengthened as her skin turned a pale magenta. Long-tipped ears poked from lanky, light green hair as she stood to tower over Kethry and consider her with eyes like smoking coals.

Jazelyn screamed for her daughter to flee but was helpless in the memory.

Kethry showed no fear, disgust, or even surprise at the transformation. "I bet that feels better."

Baris nodded from where she hunkered under the relatively low ceiling of the cottage.

"Again, I ask you, what is your name? Your *true* name?" Kethry asked.

"I have never been asked that, but it is only fitting I no longer call myself Baris." The creature paused to think until a grin exposed those terrible fangs. "Morna. You may call me Morna Dey."

Jazelyn's phantom jaw dropped at hearing the name pass those twisted lips.

"Explain how you can grant me this power," Kethry demanded. "Tell me your true story."

Morna raised her lip in a sneer. "You will understand all after you accept it. You only waste your own time."

"I will have all the time in the world afterward. Perhaps I wish to relish what time I have left in this form."

Morna let out a ragged breath. "I was once the guardian of my realm, caring for my tree and the creatures living under my protection. One day, the daemon, harbingers of the Gods of Naught, came. They corrupted my tree, turning me into what you see now. Most of my kind were imprisoned ages ago, but I escaped here, hiding for a time I cannot guess. I only survived by feeding upon another guardian banished here."

"Baris," Kethry hummed.

"Yes, that was his name. I do not recall mine before arriving here. I offer you the power of a realm guardian, the power I once possessed. You will be as a god in Poas."

Jazelyn could hear no more over her raging thoughts. *Guardians of a realm, the Mraasil. The daemon masters are corrupted Mraasil. One from another realm is now controlling my daughter's body and has been holding her captive for centuries.*

"It's a tempting offer," Kethry said but looked unconvinced. "Though if I had this power like what you once had, what good would it do me? The realm guardian was defeated. The minions of the Gods of Naught were defeated. Couldn't I be defeated as easily? I'm not looking to take over or rule, but I want to learn all I can without anyone stopping me."

"Do not confuse my words, child. I was not banished to his place; I escaped by my will. I was limited to my realm, to my tree, and was captured. You are unfettered and possess the power to stride through the aether and between the Wheres. You can evade the essence of Nothing, should you choose, and it would ignore you. Had I your freedom with my power, nothing would stop me."

"Sounds too easy," said Kethry, turning toward where Jazelyn stood in the corner. She seemed to look directly at her mother with a knowing intensity before looking back to the corrupted Mraasil. "I accept. But—" she said quickly as Morna's grin spread, "—I must return home to leave a message. I'll only be a moment."

Morna Dey's look of disappointment withdrew to a point as Kethry rushed back to her body. In an instant, Jazelyn was thrown against the stone outer wall of her daughter's room. Kethry jumped from her bed and returned the sphere to its small box. Her gaze focused on her mother, and Jazelyn saw flecks of amber in her daughter's dark irises, which she had never seen before. "I'm leaving this for you, Ma," she said, touching the reminisphere. "If you're watching this, something must have gone wrong with the deal with Morna Dey. Hopefully, you will watch this in the next few days and can help me. Directions to that cottage in the aether are in the sphere and, from there, find some clue about what happened. I'm sorry to put you through this, Ma. I'll explain when you find me."

Kethry returned to her bed and spread herself comfortably over the blankets.

The memory fizzled into darkness.

Jazelyn gasped and pulled her hand from the orb as though it had shocked her. She looked across to Kiol.

"That was weird," he frowned. "She just brushed her hair for about two hours and read in bed until the memory ended. I was expecting a lot more. I'm sorry,

Lyn." He reached to touch her hand before recognizing her blank expression. "Lyn?"

"You..." She blinked rapidly. "You saw nothing else? Nothing of the Aether Walk and Morna Dey? Of her needing me?"

"No, I—"

The words poured from Jazelyn, and Kiol's expression softened as his jaw hung slack.

"She needed a rescue..." Kiol gasped.

"I never once thought to check the reminisphere. I thought it was a silly bauble Cazlandt brought her from Terswood. I kept it in my room for almost a year until the Acrus invasion, when it was stolen. Six hundred years ago. I..." The words caught in her throat. Kiol fell forward to wrap her in his arms, but she shoved him back. Jazelyn took the smooth reminisphere in both hands and stared into its murky depths. She took a deep breath, thinking of how the answer to saving her daughter was lying less than twenty feet from her body. Jazelyn took another deep breath, faster, faster. She screamed and threw the orb across the room. It hit the far wall with a dull thud.

Kiol was crying enough for them both, wiping his eyes and nose on his tunic sleeve. "You couldn't have known, Lyn. The message telling you to watch the sphere was inside the sphere. If she had left a physical note saying—"

"A note..." Jazelyn snapped her attention to him and slowed her breathing. "Is that what Alishia's note from The Stacks meant? About being wary of the Mraasil? That the corrupted ones control the daemon?"

Kiol thought about it and shrugged. "I can't say I've met enough daemon masters to know. If Morna Dey was a Mraasil, I'd say yes, they do."

"You fought beside Ruvaal against the daemon in Terswood. Do you think he can be trusted?"

"He and Etharis cultivate an air of enigmatic mystery with their ancient powers and knowledge beyond our mortal ken. Do I trust them? No. But you described Morna Dey's form as twisted and corrupt. Maybe our two purple-skinned pals are still good."

Jazelyn frowned while considering. "Examine the timing of this. Archetype Dalbinth sounded sure that the avaryll would reveal a world tree in Isolis. Does that mean a new Mraasil? Etharis and Ruvaal were already in Isolis when the avaryll captured us. They surely are at this tree by now. Morna Dey fled the battle months ago, and no one has seen her since. I could not land the final blow while she wore my daughter's face. She is still out there. What will it mean for Poas if

Morna Dey returns and takes the power of this new world tree? If she corrupts the new Mraasil?"

"That's an excellent bunch of questions, Lyn. Sounds like things to ask our green-haired friends when next we see them."

13

Wererats imply the existence of other were-things. Maybe weresvarters.

L one quietly excused the healer and his assistants and closed the door behind them. "I'm glad they knew to bring you here rather than your old rooms in the north barracks," he whispered, crossing the cold stone floor to where Bard lay propped up in their bed. His left hand was the only part of the islander's top half not shrouded in linen bandages. The sanctum stone reflected the light of the hearth.

Bard's pale blue eyes drifted open, and a smile slid across his lips. "I knew you would have no trouble returning home, *menf.*" His strained voice was little more than a whisper.

Lone's right hand tingled as he sat on the bed and leaned to kiss Bard on the bandaged forehead. "You saw his entire plan from the moment Ashta approached you in Acrus. You knew he only plotted to get you into the arena."

Bard closed his eyes with a slow breath. "Yes."

"Yet you went along with everything. I don't know if that's bravery or suicide."

"It was the only way to secure my freedom." Bard frowned and raised his hand to a scratch on Lone's cheek. "What happened after you sent me away?"

"I... I made an ass of myself before crushing a small fortune's worth of mana crystal to teleport into a gutter in Vanna. I woke to people stepping over me like I was a common drunk."

"You used mana crystal to teleport? I thought that was impossible."

"Not impossible, just really stupid. At least I didn't blow my hand off doing it like my father almost did. I..." He paused and adjusted himself beside Bard. "I brought Whiar's mask."

Bard closed his eyes for a long breath and spoke without opening them. "Thank you."

"Who was he?"

Bard opened his eyes, and Lone saw the deep grief in them. "Later."

Lone put a hand flat on Bard's chest and closed his eyes to extend his senses into the man. Broken ribs and fractures in his right elbow and hand. Grievous injuries to his shoulders and knees. Below the white linen, Bard's skin was probably purple and black rather than his deep tan. Lone pulled his hand away when he felt a frightening amount of internal bleeding. "I can heal this." He put his left hand on Bard's chest and a tingling right hand on the islander's stomach. He pulled it away with a twinge and shook it.

"What's wrong with your hand?" Bard asked.

"Nothing. It's felt weird since the teleport is all."

"Perhaps you leave it to the professionals." Bard coughed and winced with the fresh shot of pain. "Remember what happened last time you tried to heal me?"

The image of his hands soaked in blood came to mind. "That was different. You were basically dead. You're up and talking this time. Also, Kiol was pulling the ley energy for me. I only directed it. I can do this."

Lone's first thought was to focus on each wound and pour healing mana into them, one after another, but he again remembered Archdruid Etharis's words. "See the body as you wish it to be." Lone did not know what Bard's inside should look like, but he envisioned the islander's soft smile and the light patchwork of old scars over the rough skin of his chest. His hands glowed green as he pulled from the abundant ley nexus under the castle to fuel his workings.

Lone felt the simple guided regeneration could do more with just a little additional mana, so he fed it. As he did, something new blossomed. He began to understand a sort of magic inherent to Bard's body. Not *magic*, but also a simple lack of it. His body held a distinct void that would devour and annihilate magic. Lone poured more ley energy from the nexus into it, hoping to understand how it worked.

"Lone!" Bard shouted.

Lone's eyes snapped open to a room full of blinding chartreuse. The green light was so bright that it hurt to look at, all glaring from the tattoos down his right arm. His ears ached with an odd pressure while a sharp tang burned his throat with every quickened breath. Bard's left hand pulled at Lone's on his chest.

"Lone!" he shouted again, and the archmage fell back. The light faded, and the room returned to the oranges and reds lit by the hearth.

There was a faint popping sound, and two figures stood over him: a tall woman with jet-black hair tied back loosely wearing a simple green dress and a shorter blond man in a white tunic and matching trousers.

"Regent King!" Jazelyn stepped back for Kiol to offer a hand. "What in the seven hells happened here? I last felt such strain on the ley line when Cazlandt raised the castle from the hoarfrost."

Lone dusted himself off. "I was healing Bard."

The two generals looked at the weaponmaster in bed as the green light faded from him.

"Maybe you should leave the healing for the professionals," Kiol said. "Remember what happened last time? By the gods, Lone, you were pulling so much mana."

Lone considered his spell and gasped at his stupidity. He had linked the ley nexus to Bard's void, essentially eradicating mana at an alarming rate.

Jazelyn finished her slow examination of the room. "I was unaware you were returning to the castle, Your Grace. Are your matters complete in Acrus?"

Lone thought of speaking with Teiris, Dehset, and Aiden before the coerced trip to the Western Isles. "Far from it. Teiris took my father for treatment, but I have to get back there."

"Per your note, I ferried the svarters home with a series of teleports," said Jazelyn. "Isold, Tekin, and Lieutenant Dreyma are home as well."

"Thank you, I nearly forgot. That got me thinking about ways to teleport a larger group at once. Maybe a portal or gateway connecting two points." Lone paused, noticing the redness in Kiol's puffy eyes. "What's happened?"

The generals shared a glance, and Jazelyn spoke quickly. "We viewed Kethry's reminisphere. We have learned details pertaining to the origin of the daemon masters and perhaps the daemon themselves."

Lone raised an eyebrow and gestured for her to go on.

Jazelyn licked her lips, seeming uncharacteristically unwilling to launch into a lecture.

"The daemon masters are fallen Mraasil. Morna Dey is, was, a Mraasil," Kiol said quickly.

Lone held up his hands for Kiol to pause his rapid speech. "The daemon are controlled by former Mraasil. The Archetype said he thinks a new Mraasil will soon be born in Isolis. What's keeping a new Mraasil from falling as Morna Dey and I assume others have?"

Kiol shrugged. "We thought that too. No clue. But knowing there's a connection between our purple friends and the daemon is helpful. We should prepare for more than uppity mages in Isolis."

"Anyone worry the avaryll aren't on our side?" said Lone.

"They have given no reason to trust them in any manner," said Jazelyn.

"Maybe I don't need to get back to Acrus," Lone said and paused to consider who else he might speak with there. "I want the royal guard to double their training. Everyone needs to be in top fighting form within five weeks. Call in the reserves from Winstadt and Culem. Bring—" He looked down at Bard's wrappings and touched a palm to the islander's cheek. "Kiol, that's your task. Appoint someone to the physical training until Bard is well enough."

Kiol cleared his throat. "One problem, Lone. Daemon are essentially immune to physical weapons. Even if we call in all the archmages across Poas, most of whom aren't trained in combat magic, assuming they all show up, that's a pretty small fighting force."

"What about crystal mages?"

Kiol shook his head. "They're a good reserve, but there aren't many more than archmages with any fighting ability. Be glad we don't have the wars across Poas to require we train everyone to kill."

Lone looked back at Bard, who looked to have dozed off. "There is one more weapon. I've seen it firsthand. Daemon are not unlike us archmages in their dependency upon ley energy. They are only immune to swords while they have a constant flow of it. Disrupt that and bash their heads in."

"And how do you intend to accomplish that?" Kiol asked with a smirk. "Are you going to heal someone before the fight and shatter all the ley lines?"

"Bard nullifies their power, and General Tekin is working on a device."

Jazelyn and Kiol looked at each other. "General?"

14

Long live the Mushroom Overlord!

Etharis expected few to heed his call, but he could not hide his disappointment from the mere four who stood or sat around him at the base of Farsil. He paced before the ruined entrance to Elogoh'an while waiting for the last to arrive.

"Who else is coming?" Shundaii asked from where she lay reclined in the soft grass. Her knees were crossed, and her floral-print dress was spread around her like a picnic blanket.

"Ruvaal, the brooding one," said Bireal from the edge of the clearing. One of the few unique Mraasil, with horns and a thickly muscled tail, leaned to smell the pungent flowers that bloomed around this small space. The many small skulls strung from their waist clattered together.

As if summoned by speaking his name, the air quivered with a flow of purple mist, and Ruvaal appeared with a spark of light.

"You took long enough," Etharis glared at this brother.

"Let's get on with this," Ruvaal said and looked around at the collected Mraasil, nodding a greeting to each.

Five pairs of glowing amber eyes turned to Etharis. "I knew few would come. Our kind have grown weary over the eons, and many choose to rest while their realms carry on without them. While my heart is heavy upon seeing so few, it is nice to see those I haven't laid eyes upon in an age. We are about to encounter a unique opportunity in Poas, the realm of our sister Ters, Elphame hold her. The details of the events leading to the present state there are unimportant, but know that Poas has a new world tree that is about to birth its Mraasil."

"The events are unimportant?" said Aymaa, and eyes turned to where he leaned against the statue of Elphame at the entrance to the clearing. He wore only loose, asymmetric shorts to expose a deep purple bare chest and arms networked with scars and tattoos. "There's suddenly a new world tree, and you just hand wave the details of how that happened."

"Yes, yes, I want to know more of this, Ethy," Tesoti said quickly as their eyes flitted between the others.

Etharis sighed. "We can find this out together. For thousands of years, Poas has secretly cultivated the growth of their new tree, Endanlegsil. She sprouted from the first Seed of Farsil."

"The one you were born holding. The one that was lost," Tesoti clarified with a shake of their head while biting a nail. "I guess this means it's found now."

Aymaa pushed from the statue to pad forward and circle the group. "The mortals of Poas would hide the existence of a new tree? How were they even capable of such a thing? How do they know how one tends for a sapling world tree? How would anyone know how to care for one in an existing realm?"

Etharis slowly turned to keep pace with his stalking brother. "The World Tender has ministered to Endanlegsil."

"Your old student?" Aymaa asked.

Etharis set his jaw and took a deep breath. "Yes. My old student has been caring for the tree while maintaining that secret from me. All that matters is a new Mraasil will be born soon. We must be there for her."

"As you were for us?" Shundaii asked from the ground.

"Yes," said Etharis. "This birth will be the first and only Mraasil birth any of you will witness."

The others exchanged confused glances.

"Are you quite right, Etharis?" Shundaii asked. "We and two dozen more witnessed Celium's birth. You presided over it and made a tremendous fuss."

Etharis flinched. That was not true. Felen was the last Mraasil born. He alone had witnessed it. He had a full and clear memory of easing the Mraasil to the rocky ground beside his world tree. Etharis had never heard of a Celium.

He opened his mouth to vocalize his confusion but was interrupted by a sound like a gasping wheeze, and a seventh Mraasil appeared in the clearing. They stood hunched, shorter than the others at barely six feet. Ragged clothes hung from an emaciated frame.

"Sorry I'm late," they said with a cough.

Four of the other six greeted the newcomer with "Hello, Celium." Etharis and Ruvaal shared a glance. The archdruid knew all of his brethren but not this one. He moved closer, looking down at the unknown Mraasil, and took a deep breath.

"The Deadloss," said the archdruid, identifying the scents of their realm. It had changed dramatically since he and Ruvaal had last visited, but there was no mistaking it.

"The what?" Celium looked unsure and clutched at their scraps of clothes. "I said I'm sorry."

Etharis looked back to Ruvaal. They had never returned to the Deadloss after their experiment using the Ibaerite to move through time. The archdruid knew a tree was now connected there but had not considered that meant a Mraasil as well. A Mraasil he had never met. One that the others knew and said he should know as well.

Etharis looked at each of those gathered and his eyes lingered on Celium. In that simple act of pushing a drop of life into the Deadloss, they had altered a grand series of events with an unknown scope. The archdruid bit his lip and continued speaking. "The native race of Poas, the avaryll, used the disruptions caused by the destruction of Tersil to create a protective barrier around their lands. No one thought much of it until..." he and Ruvaal had altered time. Etharis had thought it was just a world tree and some mushroom people in a sickly realm, but here was a Mraasil that the others, those he had known their entire existence, all knew. The flow of time had been altered, realms and other Mraasil, yet Etharis and Ruvaal were unchanged.

"Until what?" Aymaa asked, narrowing his eyes with suspicion.

Etharis shook from his reverie. "Until Ruvaal and I went to see the avaryll on our wanderings."

Bireal stood from where they still sniffed at the flowers and leaned backward, stretching their back. "Is that so, Ruvaal? You and Etharis still do that Flaying Brothers thing?"

"Scions of Flayme," Tesoti corrected. "Strange name."

Ruvaal narrowed his amber eyes with a smirk. "You're not going to tell them, Etharis? The reason we knew to go to Isolis?"

"Ruvaal..." Etharis hissed a warning, but that only piqued the interest of the others gathered.

Ruvaal grinned darkly and spread his arms, speaking loudly. "We traveled through and altered time. Etharis and I remember a wholly different reality. We harnessed the power of the Chronicler herself." He crossed to Celium and looked down at the hunkered creature. "You shouldn't exist. Your realm's tree was dead, and you were never born. We undid that."

"Ruvaal! Enough!" Etharis roared.

Ruvaal turned to his brother and laughed. "We could do more, but our arch-druid brother is too afraid. He cares more for a Mraasil yet to be born than he does for the countless others that fell to the Gods of Naught and their daemon pets."

Etharis advanced on Ruvaal, but Aymaa stopped him with an outstretched arm.

Shundaii stood smoothly. "You don't deny this, Etharis? So it's true? You moved through and altered time? What did you do?"

The archdruid grunted his frustration. "We planted a handful of spores in Celium's realm long after it was abandoned and severed from the Trees."

"My realm was never cut off," squeaked Celium. "The Ascended were about to have you prune it, but new life sprouted. It's different from other realms, but it's home."

Was that true? Etharis thought. *Did we go back so far that the Deadloss was still in the grand line of Trees?*

Aymaa lowered his arm. "What does Ruvaal mean you could do more? How did you access the Chronicler's power and move through time?"

The gathered Mraasil leaned closer to Etharis.

"Go ahead, Ruvaal. Since you obviously want to turn them against me, you tell them."

Gazes pivoted.

Ruvaal touched his chest with a hurtful look. "I would never mean to sow dissension among our people, brother. I don't want to mislead them with half-truths." He cleared his throat dramatically as he pulled the vial from his sleeve. The other Mraasil craned nearer to see it. "The Ibaerite. A shard of the Lacuna Gap, the expanse between the Wheres, a physical manifestation of the Chronicler's power. Etharis and I channeled our energies through it to travel to a place and time of our desire. We went to the Deadloss and ended up reviving Celium's tree."

The ragged Mraasil shrank at the mention of them.

"We did it once and can do it again. We can do something even grander," Ruvaal continued. "We are the guardians of our realms, set to our sacred duty by the Ascended at the very beginning of time as we can comprehend it. What would you do differently with all that you know now? How many tragedies have we seen too late to stop? What great harm could you stop from happening?"

Ruvaal looked at each of the others before setting his gaze on Etharis. The impassive archdruid slowly crossed his arms.

"We've thought of one. You would all think of the same as well," Ruvaal said. "The Venatus. Imagine if the humans never called the Gods of Naught."

Shundaii and Bireal gasped while Tesoti scratched at their cheek, and Aymaa chewed his lip.

"Exactly, imagine," said Etharis, pulling the attention of the others. "It's nothing but an idle exercise for an under-burdened mind. I planted one handful of spores, and now the Deadloss has life, and Celium was born. We defeated the Gods of Naught in Poas ages ago. Are you sure things would be better? That something worse wouldn't happen instead? There is no means of imagining the impact of undoing an event with the scope of Venatus. An event that directly touched dozens of realms and impacted hundreds more. Thousands or millions of millions of lives."

"The dangers are obvious," Shundaii said thoughtfully. "No one can deny that. It is a question of risk versus reward."

Aymaa nodded and grumbled, "I still regularly have to clean up daemon skulking around Hoari."

"We failed as guardians," Shundaii continued. "Looking back, it's clear Baris's humans would eventually attempt what they did. They thought they were so clever. Our inaction is as much to blame."

Bireal nodded slowly. "If you stop them once, those humans would just try again. Perhaps they should have been completely cleansed."

"No," Etharis snapped. "It is not our place to dictate the lives of those living in our realms, only to guide and encourage them away from dangerous paths. Yes, the Venatus was a clear failure, but we all learned a powerful lesson, one that will never be repeated." He stopped himself and pinched the bridge of his nose. "This banter is over. If you don't wish to be there for the birth of our new sister, so be it."

"So sayeth the archdruid," said Tesoti.

"Etharis," Ruvaal said in a near whisper and stepped closer to his brother. "I've spent as much of life in your company as not. We ran with the Hauser boys for how long and if that wasn't overstepping our bounds as passive guardians, what is? We have a real opportun—"

"No." The archdruid's voice was as clear as a dead bell.

Ruvaal growled, baring his teeth. "Aymaa said he's still fighting daemon in his realm. Tempus Fa has hordes of them across its infinite landscape. We thought all the daemon masters and the Gods of Naught were sealed away, yet how do you explain Morna Dey? She fled the battle and is unaccounted for. If one daemon mistress is unsealed, how long until more return to power and call their pets to action that are now just idly roaming across a hundred realms?"

"A daemon mistress is loose?" Shundaii jerked to full attention. "No, they were all sealed with the defeat of the Gods of Naught. Why is this the first we've heard of this, Etharis?"

The archdruid grumbled under his breath. "Come with me to Poas while we await the birth of Verndari. There is much to discuss."

15

The swamp hag's look and smell brought me close to retching, but I couldn't imagine a sweeter voice.

Queen Teiris bent over the wide map of Poas before her. Three carved ships represented Captain Hihowl's flagship and the svarters fleet well past Gurrim'Nosh and the borders of Nyphlym. They would move farther to sea to avoid coming too near to those enchanted fey wilds. Another week would bring the ships to the eastern border of Isolis, and an estimated four-day march across unknown terrain would be made to Tidecrest, arriving days before the deadline. Teiris hated the number of unknown variables, but there was little to be done.

"Are we certain the barriers around Isolis are completely down?" Prelen Kaermys asked. "Our scryers have seen into the lands and glimpsed the city of spires, but magic can be fooled. Has King Daelin or another of the archmages teleported there yet to confirm?"

Teiris shook her head as she pulled back her auburn hair and quickly tied it with a leather strap. "General Jazelyn confirmed with her magic that the barrier around Isolis is down, but she spoke against teleporting there yet. She requested as much time as possible to study the ley lines and currents that are now accessible without the barriers. We have almost two weeks until the next rising of Ersha when we are all due at Tidecrest. If the archmages cannot confirm the safety of Isolis, the svarters will. If the avaryll hold the power of a new world tree in Poas, the svarters will be there to share in that power."

"What does that mean, the power of a world tree?" asked Sion. Teiris flinched, forgetting that her young brother was standing so close to her left.

Teiris thought of standing before Farsil, the world tree of Tempus Fa. The impossible scale of that tree made the base look like a solid wall of bark as far as her eye could see. Ruvaal had teased the knowledge that her ancestors built

Terswood on the husk of Poas's long-dead world tree, Tersil. Teiris had not spread that information out of fear of starting a holy civil war in her city.

"We can't know for sure, Sion," she said, staring at the map with eyes unfocused.

"Isolis has shrouded itself for all of history," said Matron Wynlen, the shriveled crone who led the Sisters of the Moons, Teiris's great-aunt. "Perhaps it was by a force akin to The Mists, cloaking them from the world like a mother's safe embrace."

"Or a cloak to hide beneath while they gather the power to overtake the rest of Poas," Kaermys countered.

Wynlen frowned. "Our queen described the avaryll as similar in physical nature to the divine Mraasil, but pale-skinned. You should have more faith than to assume all strangers harbor ill will, Prelen."

Teiris chuckled to herself at the term "divine Mraasil," and waved down the conversation. "This does us no good. We can theorize the avaryll's intentions until we're as purple in the face as the Mraasil. All we know is they implied they would attempt to assert a ruling force over the other nations. They did call the humans a child race, which was fun."

A small sound of a throat clearing pulled the eyes of the svarters around the central map table to the silver and white-haired human woman sitting by the door. Siraas vass Soss wore a tight bodice and a flowing dress of cream and brown hues, common in Terswood.

"Apologies. Present company excluded," Teiris said with a grin.

Siraas shook her head. "Not that. I could not care less about the opinions you or the avaryll have for my race. No, I have news to share about King Daelin."

"Already?" Teiris rushed to the archmage's side. "It's barely been two weeks."

Siraas nodded. "My time following you has given me brilliant insight. Over a week ago, I developed a new cultivation technique for the king, the first new technique of its kind in over a thousand years. He has been learning and testing it since. My tests indicate sufficiently positive results to allow him to return home."

Prelen Kaermys stepped beside Teiris. "You had the king use untested magic techniques upon himself? Why not on another of your copies?" Her lip curled into a sneer.

"Of course, the king tested upon himself. My cultivation works perfectly well. Testing something on myself would be meaningless."

Teiris put a hand on the prelen's forearm, and she backed away a step. "When can the king return?"

In response, Siraas glanced to the open doorway beside her. King Daelin entered, wearing his quilted armor bearing the Terswood seal, and beside him, another Siraas vass Soss in the same white and red trimmed dress as when Teiris met her. Teiris looked up at her husband's emerald eyes and the clear lucidity that had been so fleeting these last months. His gray beard parted in a wide smile, and she rushed to wrap her arms around him.

"I feel better than I have in years, Teiris," said Daelin. "Siraas is a true miracle worker."

Teiris pushed back to examine her husband at arm's length. "And you're still cultivating mana?"

"Yes, I—"

"Could we have the room?" Teiris said, dismissing the others to file past them and out the door. Sion lingered where he stood by the map. "You too, Sion. I'll see you in a few hours."

Sion huffed, pushed past her, and was gone.

"I'll see myself to the obelisk and Dracon," said the Siraas in a white dress and turned to leave.

The other Siraas moved farther into the room to lean against the map table. "Carry on as if I weren't here," she said, pulling a small notebook and pen from her bodice.

Teiris sighed but turned back to Daelin. "Is it a lasting cure?" She again looked her husband over. Other than the glimmer in his eye, he seemed no different, but that was enough.

"This new technique differs from what archmages have been using for over a thousand years, but I do already feel the effects of it," he said. "Cazlandt's technique pulls mana through the body and expels it, almost like a digestive system. Siraas thought we may equate my issue to..." Daelin took a deep breath. "To not having a *movement* these last twenty years, creating a blockage in my system."

Teiris bit her lip to stop laughing. "I'm glad I'm not human, and my body does all this naturally. So what's different now?"

"Using the same analogy of bodily systems, the new cultivation is like holding my breath. I hold ley energy within myself, like a svarters, rather than allowing it to pass through me."

"That gives the same benefits? Siraas said you had an allergy to mana. You know how I get when I eat ground nuts." She gripped her throat with both hands and stuck out her tongue. "It doesn't matter how you prepare them. An allergy is an allergy. How is this different?"

"I have never shirked from an understanding of complex theory, but when there are six simulacra of Siraas speaking over each other and drawing out mathematical equations and biological formulae, each doing a different portion of one line of numbers and symbols... I found myself overwhelmed. Especially in the beginning. I had not realized my state was at such a point."

"You were real bad, my love." Teiris patted his hand and turned to the other archmage. "Siraas, why do you have to talk to your other selves if you share one mind?"

Siraas shrugged without looking up from her notebook.

Teiris shook her head and returned her attention to her husband. "Lone will want to see you immediately, to know you're well. His new artifice general has something to give us an edge against the avaryll."

Daelin looked past her to the map table strewn with wood-carved units. "You do not require me here to coordinate troop movements?"

"No, by last reports, everything is moving on schedule. We will need you when Hihowl gets close to Tidecrest. I'd like you to teleport us, Prelen Kaermys, and as many Tersguard as you can to her as we approach the city."

Daelin grunted. "They could have taken an obelisk to teleport from the one in the courtyard."

"That thing weighs how many tons?" Teiris asked with a chuckle.

Daelin did not share in the mirth. "I set one in Iecil months ago to aid in the efforts at the ruins. The core component could fit in a hip pouch. It is really no different from your sanctum stone. I designed them large and heavy simply for aesthetics and so no one would move them once in place."

Teiris touched the wide band on her left forefinger with a pang of guilt and maybe a touch of sadness. Had Daelin been well, he could have saved the fleet weeks at sea. "Can you take one with us, then? So more aid can come to Tidecrest as needed?"

Daelin nodded with a grunt.

Teiris was glad her husband was back and seemingly well but did not miss those grunted replies.

16

Siraas vass Soss, fabled archmage healer, was accused of creating diseases just to cure them.

Numbing cold blasted across Lone's cheeks and whistled past his ears. He struggled to pull himself from the snow and ice that buried him to the waist. Twice the size as what attacked him months ago, the remorhaz unhinged its jaw and snatched up one of the explorers. The man's scream cut short as the beast snapped down and dove into the snow. Lone pulled at the ley lines to cast something, anything, to free himself to help the other men, but the magic fizzled away.

"Distract it, Lone!" General Miech yelled from somewhere, but Lone could not turn to see the late artificer.

This is a dream. Wake up, wake up.

Lone clawed to the surface, driving away the nightmare by sheer force of will. He opened his eyes and exhaled a ragged breath to the chill air of his bedroom. A weight pressed on his legs from a blanket Bard must have tossed off him some hours ago, lending physical fuel to the dream. He measured his breath, but his skin prickled from the sheen of sweat and the cool breeze from the open window. Careful not to disturb Bard beside him, Lone pulled back the covers to swing his legs off the bed and sit up with his head resting in his palms.

He knew it was a simple nightmare. Everyone had bad dreams. Yet every time he had one, it reminded Lone of his father's affliction. Described as twenty-five years of the most vivid and horrible dreams, Daelin said they abruptly ended with the recent defeat of Amer.

Lone's right arm and shoulder tingled like he had been sleeping awkwardly. He flexed his hand and rubbed at the arm where his runic tattoos glowed a faint green.

He caught a brief flash of light around the edges of the closed door leading to the antechamber before the tower's stairs. He thought it a trick of his senses, something brought on by his sleepy brain's reaction to the dream.

Still...

Lone glanced back to Bard, snoring lightly before grabbing his dressing robe and crossing the room. As he walked the dozen paces, he extended his senses ahead and could feel something strange on the other side of the door. Something disrupted the mana, someone he was not familiar with. Lone cast a protective aegis in front of himself and waited for the interlocking blue hexagons to settle before reaching for the door handle and pulling it open.

Lone sucked in a breath of surprise. A masked man stood at the far end of the hallway. Faintly glowing marks across his chest and one arm lit a lithe body of packed muscle.

"Regent King," breathed the stranger in a deep bass, speaking heavily accented Svarters. "I bear you no ill tidings."

Lone redoubled his aegis and cast a Light spell. By his pointed ears and height — more than a head taller than himself — Lone assumed the man to be an avaryll. His brown and white robes were cinched at the waist with a wrap of crimson cloth. Above his trim waist, the robe was only pulled over his right shoulder, showing golden tattoos that arced across his exposed chest and left arm. Knots of muscle rippled under his tan skin, bulkier than even Bard, as the markings emitted a soft haze of light that drifted from him like smoke. His hair, as pure white as clean linen, flowed as if touched by some otherwise unfelt breeze. Lone's eyes fell on the man's mask. Deep etching in the wood matched the design of tattoos across his chest with only two small holes for the avaryll's pale eyes.

"No ill tidings?" Lone pulled his robe tighter, feeling exposed without armor or sword. "What is the meaning of coming here in the middle of the night? Who are you?"

The avaryll slowly raised his hand to pull off his mask, revealing an unlined face with a trimmed, white beard. "Tanathil. Tanathil Neridove. I represent the Einingu, a faction of avaryll that wish to have your ear for a short while."

Despite the situation, or perhaps because of it, Lone chuckled. "I don't suppose you could come back during regular court hours?" He attempted to probe the avaryll using magic, but the stranger emitted a suppressive aura. He could feel his aegis wearing down.

Tanathil shook his head. "I am sorry, Regent King. I do not come with the support of the protectorate. It would not end well for me if he learned of this visit. I'm sure you can sense obscuring measures I have in place to give us more time."

Lone debated between running back to wake Bard and attempting to teleport across the castle to recruit the help of Jazelyn or Kiol. He settled on relaxing his shoulders and mentally switching to diplomacy. Besides, even discounting Tanathil's obvious physical strength, the magical prowess required to teleport into Castle Dracon undetected was a testament to his skill. "Tanathil of the Einingu, you say? I regret my ignorance of any faction of your people. What do you represent?"

"We stand for reason and unity. Though few would think otherwise of themselves. The Einingu have lobbied against our isolation, wishing the avaryll to dispel the barriers around Isolis, to join the others of Poas, and to share Endanlegsil's growth with them. The protectorate is to blame for our people being strangers."

"And what is the Einingu's interest in me?" Lone asked.

"You gathered the first council of nations in Poas, though ill-fated as it was. You represent a unifying force, Regent King. We believe our goals align with your own, which also means your goals do *not* align with those of the protectorate."

Lone had only guesses at the avaryll leader's plans for this celebration of the "rebirth of mana."

"I know essentially nothing about the protectorate. You think he will make some move for power?"

"Undoubtedly. Protectorate Alaraic has removed all advisers and scaled his guard back to the barest force. He is gathering and hoarding magical artifacts and has smiths working endlessly to create more. He is preparing to seize power over Poas when Endanlegsil matures."

"So because I gathered the nations of Poas, you think they might rally behind me to stand against the protectorate, should that need arise?"

"That is our hope, yes. The Einingu will fight at your side."

"You would fight for the freedom of those you know nothing about? Maybe even against your people?"

"We would. We wish to live in peace beside the humans and svarters. We will not follow a protectorate who wishes to use the tree's power to hold dominion over the rest of Poas."

"I certainly hope nothing comes to combat, but Dracon, nor any of the other nations, will bend the knee to the protectorate." Lone licked his dry lips and felt the tingle return to his right arm, or maybe he only again noticed it. "At least, I hope they wouldn't. Are you visiting the other leaders as a warning, then?"

Tanathil shook his head once. "I cannot risk leaving the city again. I have already stayed too long. This was not a call to action, Regent King, merely a warning to be alert within Tidecrest and with your dealings with the protectorate. I'm sorry, I must return." He raised his left hand to his chest in what might have been a salute or farewell gesture.

"Wait, Tanathil, can we speak again once I'm in the city?"

"Certainly, Regent King. I will find you." The avaryll raised his mask to his face and disappeared with a burst of golden light.

Pain shot down Lone's right arm, stealing his breath. He yanked up the robe's sleeve to see his tattoos glowing with an intensity far beyond what they had before Bard entered his life and dulled them. He sensed no excess mana in the ink, no reason for it to behave in any manner. Lone gripped the throbbing forearm on his way back to bed, pushing regenerative magic into it without effect. He dropped the robe, and by the time he sat on the edge of his bed, the pain had dulled to an ache. He flexed his hand again before pushing under the covers.

"Everything well?" Bard mumbled in a drowsy Au.

"Just had to piss. Go back to sleep."

Bard sighed and rolled toward him, throwing an arm over Lone's chest. Lone tensed at the touch that felt colder than the nightmare. It lasted only a heartbeat and was again the familiar warmth and weight he was used to. The pain vanished with Bard's touch. Lone peeked under the covers, and the blazing light was again just a faint green glow.

I'll worry about it all in the morning.

Lone rolled away and pushed his back into Bard, earning a squeeze. Despite his mind churning over what had just happened, sleep retook him within moments.

17

Archmages swear fealty to the Dracon crown in exchange for learning the mana cultivation technique to make them immortal. They live forever to then also serve forever.

L one pulled off his thick fur gloves and placed a hand on the black granite of his father's obelisk in the Castle Dracon courtyard. General Jazelyn stood beside him in a long, dark coat lightly trimmed with fur. The frozen wind tugged at her loose braid.

"It'll be nice to use this for more than for me getting to Terswood when I'm feeling lazy," Lone said, tracing the dark runes across the smooth stone. He took a small chisel from his pocket and opened a notebook from another. Using short and careful strokes, he carved a new rune to match the one on the parchment. It only took a minute before he was holding the page next to the work to check for errors. "Looks good to me."

Jazelyn said nothing as she took the notebook from Lone and performed her own inspection.

"Not that I would doubt your work," said Lone, "but this is a little nerve-wracking. We've created a new type of magic and rely on it to get our group to Isolis. I wish we had a means of testing it more thoroughly."

Jazelyn handed the book back.

Lone tucked it away with a sigh. "You've been quiet for weeks, General. Was it something the avaryll did while they held you?"

Jazelyn traced a finger along the new rune, leaving a trail of red light as she did. "Other than starving us of mana, the avaryll did not mistreat us."

"Then what is it? Something more to Kethry's reminisphere?"

Jazelyn took her finger from the obelisk, and the soft glow settled into the stone. "All is prepared. I have tied the rune to the location I curated in Isolis.

We are done here for the moment." She bent to pick up the heavy canvas pack between their feet.

Lone put a hand on Jazelyn's wrist as she raised it to perform her teleport. "General, stop. We are preparing to ferry an army of almost two hundred across the continent using untested magic. Talk to me. Convince me that your mind is fully on this task."

Jazelyn glared at the gloved hand on her arm, but Lone refused to move. "I have been distracted, but do not doubt my discipline of mind. I have performed and repeated the calculations and models and have no doubt this portal will operate as designed."

"Fine then, convince me on a personal level, Jazelyn. You're a powerful arch-mage from the first histories of our kind. No one else alive comes close to your level of knowledge and experience. I was terrified of you my entire childhood because…" He let the sentence hang, unsure how to finish it. "You're more than that now. You're a friend. I want to understand what's happening." He pulled his hand away.

"I will not add my burdens to you." A gust of chill air almost ripped her words away.

"Please. Even if I can't help, telling me may ease you some."

Jazelyn kept her gaze where Lone's hand had been for a long breath, then looked to him, her dark eyes edged with tears.

Lone gasped and backed away a step.

"Kethry spoke to me," she said, her voice barely audible in the snowy courtyard. "She addressed the reminisphere directly to me with instructions on how to find her within the aether. I never thought of viewing it. Her body lay without her mind for centuries because of my incompetence. Had I done the obvious six hundred years ago, Morna Dey would not be controlling my daughter's body. How many would still be alive? Queen Lilan? All those svarters that died when the daemon attacked? General Miech?"

"I… But the orb was stolen, you—"

"I had it long enough before Acrus sieged the castle. I have no explanation for why I did not view her reminisphere immediately."

"I'm sure you tried everything else, Jazelyn. I had never heard of a reminisphere until we found Cazlandt's in The Stacks. Why would you think—"

"Enough, Your Grace. I appreciate the attempts to comfort my injured emotions by deflecting my guilt in this matter but know there is nothing more you can add of value. I have spent many long hours over these weeks."

"I'm sorry."

Jazelyn gently touched Lone's shoulder. "I appreciate the attempt. Over the last twelve centuries, many terrible losses have fractured my mind. I long ago learned to compartmentalize the hurt lest they compound and destroy me. Such is the curse of immortality that you will learn in the years to come. I hope you can do as I have and find a way to overcome life, unlike so many others of our kind."

Lone frowned at the thought. Jazelyn seemed to deal with all the painful things in life by being cold and emotionless. *Is that what I'll be like in a few hundred years?* He found comfort in knowing Kiol was hundreds of years old and nothing like his wife.

"Worry not for now, Your Grace," Jazelyn said. "You will either succeed or not. There is little sense in fretting over your future at this moment."

"Kethry, is her mind still within the aether?"

Jazelyn slowly shook her head. "I, of course, followed her instructions immediately, using Kiol as an anchor. There was the image of a cottage like the one we shared for years in Eplear. I have never seen a construction anything akin to that within the aether. The place is otherwise a background of white noise, of incoherent ley energy."

"Then Kethry...?"

"I believe her to dwell within her body in some manner. I take some minor consolation in knowing how the passage of time varies wildly between individual realms, as well as the space between them. I lost my daughter six centuries ago, but to her, perhaps it has been hours."

Or so much longer, Lone thought and turned again to the obelisk. "We'll save her, General. Return to that cottage in the void as you can; perhaps some clue will present itself. Knowing the connection between the Mraasil and daemon is a good lead. I'm pretty sure at least Etharis will be at the world tree, and we can force him to answer our questions."

"Your Grace!"

Lone turned to the near-hysteric voice of Isold running from the doors leading back into the castle.

Jazelyn intercepted her junior assistant and put her hands on her shoulders. "What is it?"

"It's Master Arvil. You're needed in the north tower immediately."

***

"Master Arvil Rees," said the priest of Suanh, "will be remembered for his quick wit and keen mind."

The priest droned on in his sermon. Lone pulled the collar of his long wool coat tighter and gazed at the form shrouded in violet cloth atop the pyre. Where he thought should be the sadness of loss was instead a dull hollow pit. At somewhere well over eighty years, Master Arvil was one of the oldest humans without the longevity of an archmage, and Lone knew this moment would come eventually. Now that it had, he wondered why he felt nothing.

"I commit his body to the flame as his soul rests with Lady Elphame." The priest took the torch offered to him and lit it with a wave of his hand. After setting the pyre alight, he backed away and handed the brand to Lone. Lone watched the dance of flame for a moment before pushing it into the dry kindling and offering it next to General Jazelyn. Few were in attendance, just the castle staff and Daelin. Master Arvil never had a family and when one gets as old as he, any friends left Poas long before him.

Lone thought of Master Arvil's office as he watched the flames lick at the gray sky. In contrast to the chaotic energy of the pyre, Arvil's desk was a model of organization, stacked with the memos, schedules, and accounting work of one perfectly suited for his life task. One might think the man intended to drift away peacefully in his sleep that night with his affairs ready, but that was how he lived every moment of his life: in perfect order and preparation.

Lone touched his breast pocket and felt the crinkle of the envelope within. He had found the folded square of red parchment on top of all that paperwork; his name was scrawled with white ink in Master Arvil's easily recognizable writing of embellished, flowing loops. Lone had tucked it away to read later.

Jazelyn stepped to Lone's side as the flames licked into the gray sky above. "Take your time, Your Grace, but we have matters to attend to regarding the portal to Isolis."

Lone blinked, realizing he had been staring at Kiol and Isold, standing beside each other, dabbing at their eyes. "It will take a while to sort out all the duties Master Arvil attended to these last six decades, but Dracon will need a new scribe immediately. I want to offer the position to your assistant."

Jazelyn looked at her husband and Isold with a nod. "If it pleases you, Your Grace. I underutilize her as it is. She spends more hours seeing to the needs of General Tekin these days. I will speak to her."

"Thank you. She will join us in Isolis then."

18

*I'm happy to report I was able to continue my study of feybeasts outside of Poas.
Those native to other realms have a much milder reaction to wheat.*

Dehset Tekin adjusted the steel bracer on his left wrist as he bent over the
crate of spare materials. He hefted the container, weighing almost thirty
stone, onto the sturdy table at hip height. Dehset grinned at the bracelet, pleased
with himself and the enchantments he built into it. He put his hands on his hips
and stepped back, letting out a small breath of contentment for the order he
was slowly bringing to the late General Miech's workshop. What had once been
endless rows of unlabeled devices and scrap was slowly becoming endless rows
with a hint of sense. Two third-year acolytes from the Royal Arcane Academy
toiled somewhere near the back, carefully sorting through a box of cubes.

Dehset grinned again. He, the son of a poor blacksmith and a lame tanner
with only a single full year of Academy instruction to his name, was now one of
the three generals of Dracon. Regent King Lone stressed that the promotion was
provisional, but that was weeks ago, and no one had taken away the title. Now, he
had apprentices working under him: two bright-eyed boys younger than himself
from wealthy families and with more formal education.

"Tekin."

Dehset jumped at the sudden, deep voice behind him. He turned to the fine
quilted cloth armor and looked up into the gray beard and emerald eyes. "King
Daelin!" He slid back and bowed.

"I have need to speak with my son, but those that control his schedule cannot
seem to find time for me, but it is you I ultimately must see. I have come for your
design of the so-called 'mana bomb,'" Daelin said flatly.

Dehset nodded, jaw slack. "It's right over here, Your Grace." He bowed again and moved to the main workbench at the front of the shop. He took up the small sphere and handed it to the king.

Daelin's eyes passed over the sphere to Dehset's bracer. "Did you make that as well?" he sighed.

Any confidence in his post in Dracon bled away with that question and the disinterested tone in which the king asked it. Dehset pulled his arm back and covered the bracer with this other hand. "Y-yes, Your Grace. I was casting strength enhancement spells on myself so often while cleaning up the workshop. I made this to keep a spell active."

"Show me," Daelin said in a voice that would not be challenged as he set the mana bomb on the workbench and extended a hand clad in light leather gloves dyed to match his armor.

Dehset slipped the bracelet from his wrist and passed it to Daelin. His limbs immediately dropped, and he felt heavy and exhausted without the enchantment.

Daelin grunted and lifted the steel close to his face, examining the runes etched into the inner edges. "A very simple spell," he said, more to himself. "It pulls energy from nearby mana crystal. Is..." he turned the bracer and squinted. "There are no limiting runes."

"No, Your Grace. I couldn't get the shape right, so I left them out. Were..." He tapped his thigh and shifted weight from his left to right leg. "Were those really necessary?"

Daelin unceremoniously tossed the bracelet onto the table beside the mana bomb sphere and glared at Dehset. "We must construct all devices under strict safety measures. If you wore that bracer inside a mana crystal cave, it would overpower and rip your body apart. Were a svarters to wear it, it would drain their very essence and kill them. Were I to wear it with my new cultiva—" He stopped himself with a quick shake of the head. "Deadly consequences aside, the enchantment is always active, even if the bracer is not worn, meaning it is a constant drain on nearby mana sources. I will admit to underestimating your skill level before, but creating items akin to this is foolish and irresponsible."

Dehset glanced at his two devices on the table and down to his shoes.

"What have you to say for yourself?" Daelin asked with less anger than Dehset expected.

"I lack training, Your Grace," Dehset said to his shoes. "I tinker with the works of men greater than myself and create what minor items I can. I might never have realized the issues with my bracer if not for your skilled eye."

Daelin put a heavy hand on Dehset's shoulder and squeezed. The young general looked up to the ever-stoic eyes of the king.

"How old are you, Tekin?"

"Eighteen, sir."

Daelin grunted though it may have been a chuckle. "I was your age when I married Aaislin. She enjoyed long walks through Perith and the frozen forests beyond, even while pregnant with Lone and after his birth. She always insisted on going alone, without me or the royal guard. I spent those hours alone in my workshop in the north tower. I created minor trinkets there for years: pens with endless ink, self refilling decanters, parchment that can be wiped clear for temporary notes, a dozen other minor items of convenience. For my wife, I created a ring to return her home, the first sanctum stone. I made the heatless lamp so she might stay up late reading. I drafted the blueprints for the teleportation obelisks scattered across Poas, now mostly inactive, that she might travel at her whim."

Daelin paused long enough for Dehset to worry about what to say to fill the silence. Luckily, the king eventually continued. "I cannot fault your desire to explore the craft, but these so-called 'better men' than you — myself and General Miech — had only the benefit of greater resources at our disposal. You have those resources now, and I expect you to use them."

"Resources, Your Grace? Isold gathered and brought me whatever materials I asked for, and the mana crystal supplies are seemingly endless here in the castle. General Miech left no legible notes. Even after months, I can barely make out his handwriting in the few books he left. I got a fifth-year Academy book about runecraft, but it had no useful examples or applications. It's just history and theory. The seventh-year book is all labs and worthless without an instructor and specific materials."

Daelin finally took his hand from Dehset's shoulder. "What do you need more than anything to improve your skill as an artificer and runecrafter, Tekin?"

The answer was obvious to Dehset. "Instruction. A mentor." He remembered that terrible crash from below as he activated his first mana disruption device, wrecking General Jazelyn's workroom below his own. "Someone to guide me from the worst of my mistakes."

"Do you not worry that an instructor would stifle your creativity?"

"Not if they looked over my work and gave feedback and suggestions while leaving me to make what I want to."

Daelin grunted again. "Such are the resources of Dracon. My grandsire gave me initial instruction even before my powers as an archmage surfaced. I later assisted General Miech in the infancy of his career. It should be the general that passes that knowledge on to you, but regrettably..." He drifted off and shook his head before scooping up the mana bomb and steel bracer. "I will return these tomorrow with notes and improved designs. Comparing what you created against my version and reasons for alterations will be more than enough to guide your first steps toward safer and more robust items in the future." Daelin turned and left through Miech's — Dehset's — living space and the tower stairs beyond.

Dehset lightly slapped himself on the cheek and jogged after the king, catching him on the landing outside his door. "Your Grace!"

Daelin lowered his hand as he prepared a teleportation spell. He looked at Dehset expectantly.

"Thank you."

Daelin slowly nodded and waved his right hand in an oval pattern. With a soft popping sound and a gentle breeze, he was gone.

Is King Daelin, legendary archmage, artificer, rune crafter, and war hero, now my mentor? The man who the guards and servants of Castle Dracon whisper to be emotionless and gloomy wants to help me? Dehset thought gleefully. His first encounter with King Daelin weeks ago left Dehset doubting everything about his life's decisions. The man that just left seemed a completely different person, sharing personal stories and displaying some tiny amount of what might have been emotion. King Daelin was now combating Generals Miech and Kiol for persons Dehset most admired.

Not caring if he was grinning like an idiot, he returned to the workroom to look across the countless unidentified objects left by his predecessor.

"This is my workshop," he whispered. His rank of general may have been given provisionally, but he would prove his merit. Through the mentorship of King Daelin — maybe he could call him just "Daelin" after a little while — Dehset would create one grand design after another, leaving a trail across Poas for future generations to praise him. Those unborn children would read whole chapters about Dehset in their history books. Instructors would craft lesson plans in his honor.

Dehset sat at the workbench. His workbench, no longer belonging to the late, but great and significant, General Miech. This was General Tekin's workbench now. With King Daelin — just Daelin — critiquing his only functioning designs, Dehset opened his notebook to a fresh page and wrote the header "Future Works."

His pen hovered over the crisp parchment, as blank as his mind.

He created his first device to locate mana sources out of a need, as was his strength-enhancing bracer. The mana bomb was an accident made by combining random bits from other schematics he did not understand.

Dehset tapped the pen on the blank page, leaving behind splotches of ink—the endless pen, owned by Miech, one of a half dozen made by Daelin. Every literate person in Poas would want one of their own if only they knew of their existence. He looked beyond to the heatless lamp, giving off a steady, adjustable light that would never tip and burn down your house. Why were these items never manufactured for the masses?

Dehset's mouth twisted into another grin as his road to fame became clear.

19

Knowing that something terrible will happen rarely prepares you for it.
Sometimes the knowing only acts to drag out the grief.

Daelin jerked awake from his own snoring. He picked up the square glass, tipped it to his lips, and set it down with a frown. It was as empty as the bottle of Mountain Oracle whiskey beside it. He scratched at his beard while debating between fetching a fresh bottle, going to bed, or continuing the projects before him on his workbench.

He blinked, realizing he was swaying slowly on his stool. He was drunk but aware enough to know his work would be inferior in his current state. The venture to Isolis was only days away, and the many defensive devices he intended to construct were yet unfinished. There was still so much to be done. A simple Purge spell would cleanse the whiskey from his system, but that would be a waste of rare alcohol aged since before his father was born.

But then I could drink more, he thought with a smirk that quickly soured. Mountain Oracle for not for the pleasure of drinking, only for getting especially drunk.

Daelin used the work table to push himself to stand and let out a labored breath as he resigned himself to bed. Sirass's new cultivation worked to mimic the results of Cazlandt's technique, but he was still not fully acclimated to it. He rubbed at the pain still lingering in his left hand and wondered if that ache would ever go away.

The king turned and stumbled back when he saw he was not alone in the room.

A woman of perhaps thirty winters stepped from the shadows. Long-tipped ears poked from her sandy hair streaked with black, and her sleeveless, floor-length dress was a dark blue to match her eyes. A wide belt cinched her at the waist, where her hands were quietly folded before her. In contrast to the fine dress, she wore a dark leather bracer on her right forearm.

Daelin squinted in the light of the heatless lamp behind him. This was impossible.

"Alishia?" he asked and took a shaky step toward her. It was clearly his daughter, yet aged into a woman. She was not much taller, but her presence seemed somehow larger than before.

"Hello, father," she smiled.

Daelin glanced back at the empty bottle on his workbench and at his daughter. "Alishia? Is that you? You look so different."

"Yes, it's me. I've just come to visit a moment."

"Your brother has been worried sick about you. Well, we all have. I see you found my bracer." He gestured to the adornment standing out on her right arm. "I hope it fits you well."

Alishia laughed, sounding nervous, and touched the bracer. "Yes, Father. It's been very useful." She laughed again and looked at her feet. Her laugh choked with a sob.

He stepped closer and reached for her hand. "Is something wrong?"

With a deep, shaky breath and eyes streaming with tears, Alishia looked up at her father. "I'm sorry, I shouldn't have come. I just wanted to see you."

Daelin frowned as his hazy mind worked to process the scenario. *My mind has been clouded for months. Why am I drinking?* "Your mother would like to see you. She is probably still in the map chamber." He stepped toward the door with an arm raised to escort his daughter.

"No."

The punctuation of her single word stopped Daelin with more power than one of his wife's Stun spells.

"No, Father. I'll see them all soon enough. I'd just like a few extra moments with you, please."

Daelin met his daughter's gaze again, and she broke. Alishia rushed forward and silently sobbed into her father's chest. Her body spasmed with the weeping. Unprepared, he stroked her hair with quiet shushing and placations that everything would be alright.

His mind was starting to cut through the mists of centuries-old whiskey, putting together all the questions that should be obvious to ask. Mostly, where had she been these last months? Daelin left those unsaid as he comforted his child.

Alishia abruptly pushed herself away and wiped her cheeks and nose with both hands. "I'm sorry. I shouldn't, I'm just really... Can I watch you work for a while?"

All questions and excuses about being tired or drunk left him, and Daelin could only respond with, "Of course."

The king sat back at this workbench, and Alishia set a stool beside him. He quickly got back into the rhythm of carving runes and connecting segments of inscribed spells using threads of mana.

"Tell me about what you're working on," she said.

"Are you interested in runecraft and artifice now?" he asked.

"I may be." Alishia smiled, put a hand on her father's forearm, and plucked a small sphere from the table with the other. "What does this one do?"

He took the device from her and set it down gingerly. "That is a design of Tekin's, the young boy working in General Miech's workshop. It disrupts local ley energy, effectively disabling any spell work in a six-yard radius by repelling the mana fueling it. It feels odd to create devices of war that could be used against me, but we are preparing a defense against the avaryll."

Alishia's dark blue eyes moved over the scattered parts of the disassembled device. "Are you building more of them?"

"I am. I have been analyzing Tekin's craftsmanship and making notes to guide him in the future." He pointed to the piece of parchment crammed with his thin scribblings.

"You're mentoring him, that's nice. You seem better, Father. Your new cultivation method must be going well."

Daelin set down the tool in his hand and turned to his daughter. "You know about that? I am ashamed that my grandsire's technique caused such damage to my body, but Siraas found a brilliant workaround inspired by your mother's people."

"That's good." She patted his arm again. "Keep working. I won't bother you again. I just want to watch."

"You are never a bother, my dear."

Hours must have passed as the first light of dawn brightened the gardens outside the workshop's single window. He glanced to his right, seeing the stool Alishia had watched him from against the far wall. Daelin leaned back, wondering if it was all a dream, a hallucination brought on by a night of imbibing too many ancient spirits.

No, Amer's nightmares and occasional waking vision were gone. His daughter's tear-filled eyes and wracking sobs were real. No sane father could imagine that raw hurt and anguish in their child.

The dried tear stains on his tunic's chest were also very real.

Part Two

20

The realm locals call The Glory is relatively tiny. The world tree is barely taller than ... Wait ... Did I already write this down somewhere?

A lishia held the wrought-iron railing and looked out over The Stacks. The shelves that had always been a chaotic, twisting maze now stretched into the distance as tidy rows. A soft ambient light, like in the heart chamber of Throkzil, replaced the darkness in the library. Yet this place was not just an endless depository of tomes, scrolls, and loose parchment. This was The Stacks, The Eternal Library of Sundered Knowledge. A realm that touched all other realms at all times, yet time did not exist here. The concepts were still wild and confusing, yet she felt she always knew these truths.

As a child of mortal parents, Alishia imposed her concept of linear existence here. It was a concept all mortals required for every function of their bodies. They exist between breaths and heartbeats; measure their lives by days and moons.

Alishia gripped the rail and leaned back at her hips to stretch her shoulders. She remembered the design of the barrier being a series of irregular circles, and now the iron was twisted to resemble the branches of trees reaching to meet the smooth bar at hip height. So much was gradually changing around her in The Stacks, yet there was some memory of it always being this way. She turned and leaned back. The single steel-banded wooden door leading from the library looked innocent enough, but she could visit anywhere and anywhen through it. Alishia had witnessed the very beginning of realms and the birth of the first Mraasil. She had laid against the roots inside Throkzil and watched the Hauser boys, almost feeling as if she were beside them on their travels. She had watched her father unleash the power of Cazlandt to destroy Amer and understood why it had failed, causing a magic-born plague to spread across the world. There was still so much to see and learn. She could step through the door to visit the First High Queen

Ters, guardian Mraasil of Poas, creator of the svarters race. She could witness the events that led to the destruction of the world tree Tersil. Or perhaps go to the first human world and learn of the Venatus. Or the origin of Cazlandt.

Just the same, she could move forward to the end of all realms, when the exchange of mana and life grew too thin to sustain themselves, and all of existence winked into the nothing from which it came.

But since the days or months since Cazlandt had departed for his own place and time, Alishia's mind hung on one thing. She absently ran her thumb over the stone-carved gift from Ethan and stepped toward the door. Cazlandt's words rang in her head as clearly as if he were speaking into her left ear.

"Why have you not gone back to stop me?" he had asked.

In her other hand, she squeezed a short, handwritten note, crumpling the parchment. That did not matter; her younger self could read it all the same. As Alishia opened the door, she held firm the image of that room in The Filthy Shield Hawker. She would leave the note for herself, altering her past, but Ethan would be alive. Whatever damage such an action caused, be damned. Why have the power to move through time if she could not undo past mistakes?

As Alishia stepped through the doorway, she felt herself gently pushed aside. She slipped around her intended destination like a leaf on a light breeze, water around a mossy river rock.

"The Chronicler has come," said a droning voice. Alishia's senses quickly adjusted to the room's blinding light. She had no eyes, no body. Her awareness floated, suspended in a featureless space before a semicircle of featureless entities like specks of lightning—six large and a thousand smaller.

"The Chronicler, what an honor," said another with a slow, breathy voice.

Alishia recognized the voice of Enid, and the beings resolved into the known forms of the Greater Ascended.

"Does this mean our plan will work?" said Khizreus, stroking his long black goatee. "She only comes to witness significant events."

"Or glorious failures," said Dhumjir.

Alishia saw her body take shape until her vision seamlessly pulled into it. She stood on the wood plank floor of some large meeting room, like the Senate chamber of Eplear. The Greater Ascended sat around a circular table with a thousand others floating formless beyond them in the higher tiers of seating. Alishia looked down at the silk gown she now wore, masterfully embroidered with the curving branches of a majestic tree along the neckline. The delicate gloves reaching to her elbows were more glamorous than she was accustomed to, even considering the extravagant national balls she had attended as the princess of Terswood and Dracon.

"Elphame, what success have you met?" asked Thexses from the center of the six. The king of the gods' form was still nebulous and abstract.

The goddess of death said nothing from behind her jawless skull mask but raised a limp arm toward the center of the table. A pinpoint of violet energy formed and grew into the shape of a person. It stood tall, wearing a tan duster jacket and matching slacks, leaving his violet chest bare and long, green hair untamed. His outlines were still hazy, as if viewed through old glass, as he glanced at Alishia before turning to face the Ascended.

"Baris," Enid named the Mraasil. "Do you know where you are?"

Baris looked across those gathered and, when recognition dawned, dropped to a knee with his head lowered. "The Ascended, it is my greatest honor to be in your presence."

Baris. I know that name. Alishia thought. *Was it Ruvaal that mentioned it?*

"An honor you do not deserve," said Khizreus.

"What do you last remember, Baris?" Suanh asked quickly.

The Mraasil opened his mouth to speak but looked suddenly confused. "I'm not sure. I was at the Leystrider Industries headquarters, but then it gets strange. It makes little sense. There were monsters and an impossible darkness. Am... Am I dead?" He wrung his hands as his glowing amber eyes flitted between the Ascended before settling on Alishia. He jumped to his feet and reached to grab her shoulders. "Chronicler, that's what you were warning me about. Something went wrong that day. You—"

"Enough." Thexses' command reverberated in the chamber, making Baris let go. "You have failed your realm, Guardian. Those you watched bridged the gap between the Gods of Naught and the Trees. They bring our creation to ruin."

Cliffside! Alishia suddenly remembered. *Governor Safare, the leader at Cliffside, said Baris was the Mraasil of the human realm where the Venatus started.*

"What can I do? I'll do anything!" he pleaded. "I only ever wanted to help the humans reach their goals. I love them. I care for them as my dearest children."

"You loved them? I'll show you how they ended," said Khizreus, waving at Baris. The Mraasil's eyes stretched wide with horror as his breath caught in his throat. He collapsed, weeping.

Enid frowned at the realm guardian curled on the floor. "I'm sorry you pulled him from the aether for nothing, Sister. He doesn't seem to know anything."

"It is done. We now need someone who can stop the daemon," said Dhumjir slowly. "Someone we can forge into a force strong enough to fight these monsters and their masters. Someone that can stand against the Gods of Naught."

A chill tickled Alishia's spine as Elphame exhaled like the final breath of a dying man. The goddess of death again pointed as two motes of light took form. They swirled and orbited each other, one pale yellow and the other a ruddier brown.

Enid looked down at the Mraasil as he tried to push himself to his hands and knees while wiping at his face. "Do you recognize these two, Baris? My sister thinks they may have some use."

Baris took a deep breath and looked up. Clear joy spread across his continence. "The Taigh brothers! Two warrior mages with power only surpassed by their virtue. They're unstoppable!"

"Apparently not," said Khizreus with a smirk, "because they're dead."

Enid waved down the wailing outburst from Baris. "At least they died uncorrupted, as you did, Baris. Elphame pulled them from the aether before they moved on to the next realm in the great chain."

"Do it yourselves," Alishia said and stepped forward to stand beside Baris. "Why do you need agents to stop the Gods of Naught? Why do you not fight them yourselves?"

All eyes turned to her and widened as if noticing her again for the first time.

"Foolishness," boomed Thexses. "No realm would survive such a conflict."

The other Greater Ascended nodded as though that explanation was more than adequate.

Alishia jumped at the piercing laugh at her side. She looked up at Meave, Sundered Chaos, standing beside her, and Minerva, Sundered Chaos, beyond.

"You think the Ascended have that power?" Meave's laughter trilled again.

"They're nothing but creatures of a singular purpose. They have no original ideas outside of their aspects," Minerva said as she swept her cloak over a shoulder and cocked her head at Alishia. "Funny to find you here, Chronicler. Though I suppose you're everywhere, eventually."

"Cute dress." Meave traced a finger along Alishia's embroidered neckline, causing her to shy a step backward with a shiver. "Do you still have that seed?"

Alishia ignored the question. "What are you two doing here?" She glanced back to where the Ascended debated what to do with the two souls plucked from death.

"We can't send them fully formed," said Enid. "They must grow up in the culture to form their desire to save their realm. They must be loved and nurtured by their kind. We can grant them our boons and enhance what natural gifts these two had to bring them something closer to our perfection."

Minerva stepped forward and poked at the souls dancing in the air. "Why are we here, you ask? Do we need a reason to be anywhere? We introduced ourselves as agents of Chaos, right?"

Meave laughed again. "If the Ascended are like our children, planned or not, and the trees are their children, that would make these two cuties our great-grand-sons."

Minerva turned back and waggled her hand back and forth. "Eh, not really, but I guess close enough. They are cute, though."

Enid dramatically clasped her hands together and slowly spread them apart. As she did, the two souls grew into human men. With a beam of crackling, red lightning, Dhumjir channeled his power into one figure, wrapping him in gleaming plate mail. Thexses expelled a nebulous cloud of mist to clad the other in long, leather armor. Suanh sent forth a mist that soaked into their heads, and Khizreus tossed just a speck of energy at them.

Alishia looked at Elphame as the goddess of death raised a long, thin finger. She curled it once, beckoning the two souls. A thin smoke like the wavering of air over a campfire pulled from the men to collect around Elphame's hand.

The men's faces remained indistinct, but the Chronicler still recognized them.

"Ethan... Aiden..." Alishia whispered. She felt a flash of heat on her cheeks as she turned to the Chaos Sisters. "Whatever you're planning, you two need to leave."

Minerva, hands on her hips, stepped directly in front of Alishia. "We have to leave? But we only just got here."

"These two are too important," said Alishia. "I won't have you sowing your-selves into what's about to happen."

"Maybe we should leave," said Meave, pouting with her lower lip. "We could do the Chronicler a favor, and perhaps she'd repay us someday. Maybe she would give us some trinket in exchange."

A toothy grin spread across Minerva's face. "Do you want us to do you the favor of leaving, sweet sister?"

"Sister?" Alishia recoiled.

"You must know something more of your nature by now," said Minerva. "Know that you're a fragment like us. Sundered Knowledge."

Alishia looked between them and the two men beyond. Ever since one of the Sundered Law brothers' confusing comment about her being something like them, another Sundered, Alishia tried not to dwell on something she knew nothing about. *Since I first heard mention of the Chronicler,* she thought, *I was told my role was to observe and record. My future self probably set that in legend so others would repeat it to me. Everything is cyclical without an origin.* Her shoulders slumped as she shook her head with a heavy sigh.

"Humans have spread over several realms now," said Suanh. "Where will we send them?"

"What good is there in saving one realm?" Dhumjir intoned. "The daemon spread quickly."

"It will take them time to destroy all the daemon, but they have to start somewhere. How about the Gasping Seas? It's the most developed of the human realms," said Enid. "Or rather the realm where humans have the most development of their own."

"What about him?" Suanh asked and nodded to Baris.

Enid shrugged. "Return him to the aether, and his life force will feed the next realm."

"Excise the Mraasil," Thexses boomed.

"Isn't that a waste?" Khizreus asked. "Yes, he allowed the Gods of Naught to come into our—"

"No. Excise him. Banish him to the expanse between the Wheres. Let his essence languish for all time."

The expanse... The Lacuna Gap? Alishia thought. *Are they about to punish a Mraasil's soul by sending it to The Stacks?*

Elphame pointed again. Baris's scream cut off as his form shattered like glass that dissolved into nothing. It took less than a heartbeat.

The Ascended looked unimpressed and turned back to the two men.

"This bores me," said Thexses, and their form blurred. "Send them and be done with the matter." They faded away.

Enid looked at the vacant space and sighed. "Dhumjir? I think it should be you. We built these men for war. Though please be gentle."

The god of strength and conflict nodded, spilling long, red locks over his shoulders. "You will be our agents in the mortal realms. Return to life in the Gasping Seas, noble Taigh brothers, now Forged. Fulfill your destiny and push back the Gods of Naught."

Dhumjir raised his fists as arcs of red lightning gathered around them. Opening his hands, the power shot forward, enveloping the men.

Meave sneezed.

The brothers were gone with a crash of thunder.

Alishia looked between Minerva, smirking as she examined her nails, and Meave, casually stretching her arms over her head.

"What did you do?" she hissed.

"It is done," Dhumjir pronounced. "We have done all we can. It is up to the mortals to save the Trees." He reverted to a spark of energy and faded.

"Thank you for being here, Chronicler." Enid smiled and was gone along with the other Greater and the thousand lesser Ascended.

Alishia stood alone in the meeting chamber with Meave and Minerva.

"What did you do?" she repeated louder, turning on Meave.

She brought the back of her hand to her lips and laughed. "Just making things interesting. Bye now!" Alishia blinked, and Meave was gone.

"She has a point," said Minerva. "Growing up with your own sounds boring. I'm sure we'll run into each other plenty more." She smiled, tapped Alishia on the nose, and disappeared.

Alishia realized the simple truth of what had just happened and stood without seeing for minutes. History would have veered in a drastically different direction with her intervention.

I wanted the Chaos Sisters to let this moment go without their involvement, but that would have altered the course of everything: my own past. My experience with the boys required this to happen as it did, for them not to be sent to the Gasping Seas. Any minor change can have the most unexpected outcomes.

She suddenly became very aware of the texture of the note in her hand, even through the silk gloves. She turned it over to read one last time.

"Cazlandt has attacked Rirzil. He will see through Aiden's illusions and..." she let the paper fall from her hand rather than read the last words. It vanished before hitting the floor.

21

I visited the realms in reverse order in the chain along the Trees and noticed some very interesting things.

Jazelyn dropped into the aether, and Poas' ley lines fell away to distant scratches in a field of wild static. There was one obvious location in this field of nothing, and it took her only a thought to arrive at the cottage identical to the one where she raised Kethry after fleeing her home village. It floated in a backdrop of inky black with the fragments of the front porch drifting before it, tethered only by the fact that they belonged nowhere else here. Since first coming here weeks ago, Jazelyn wondered what other physical structures may impossibly exist within this chaos between realms, but now was not the time to explore that. A candle was lit in the single window. Someone was at home.

Jazelyn floated to the door and pushed it open. Everything from the curtains around the kitchen window to the old table and chairs to her right looked exactly as she remembered them. A Mraasil with dark green hair halfway down their back stood and faced her with a smile. He wore only loose pants and an open jacket that reached almost to his knees, leaving his chest bare.

"Baris?" Jazelyn guessed from the Mraasil identified the last time she had seen this cabin.

"In the flesh, as it were," he swept a low bow. "You must be her mother."

"Kethry, where is she?"

"Not here. Not right now."

Jazelyn looked over the Mraasil, searching for a hint of the twisted creature he would become. "Are you Morna Dey, as well?"

Baris took a deep breath and sat in another chair facing Jazelyn. "That's a complex question. How much time have you got?"

"For my daughter, I have until the end of everything." Jazelyn took the chair across from Baris and crossed her arms as she leaned across the table.

"Very well. My memory has gaps, but I've filled them the best I could. Maybe you'd like some tea?"

"Why would I want tea in an astral form? Tell me what you know."

"Right. The mortals of my realm, humans like you, were always so inventive in new ways to utilize ley energy. They built breathtaking cities that spanned continents, airships, and devices that created food at your command. The problem, as you might expect, was in fueling all that at once. Even in the healthiest realm, the ley lines can only move mana at a given rate. With their newest advancements, they overstressed the ley lines and shattered some. The results were disastrous, as you might imagine. Entire cities reliant on a steady flow of ley energy fell to anarchy overnight."

"I can imagine. How does your story apply to my daughter and Morna Dey?"

"Yes, yes. I was working with the mortals of my realm on fascinating new technology that would power their magic needs for a dozen or a hundred generations. Things went poorly, and the seams between realms were frayed. It unleashed an evil force into the realm."

"The beginning of the Venatus," said Jazelyn. "I have read fragments of this tale of humans fleeing between realms with daemon at their heels."

"If that's what it was called. The daemon killed me in Diyar, and the Ascended sought to punish me by sending me here to live out eternity alone, completely alone. Except I wasn't alone."

Jazelyn raised her eyebrows and waited for the Mraasil to continue.

"The beings that killed me left a seed of malevolence deep within my being. So deep, even the Ascended couldn't sense it when I stood before them in judgment. That seed sprouted and festered in this timeless sink until it had a voice and a presence. It was a parasite, feeding off what I was as a realm guardian but never fully consuming me."

Jazelyn tapped a nail on her lips. "That corruption spread to other realms and was in each of the other Mraasil lost during the Venatus. You were an exception, banished here, rather than your energies being scattered to the next realm."

"At least, that's how I think I remember it. I sometimes wonder if they sent me here without corruption and something came later." He scoffed and tossed his hands in the air. "Time means nothing here, so who knows? Kethry found me after that corruption had taken control of my being. It offered her power in exchange for a route from the aether back to the mortal realms. It named itself Morna Dey and, with that name, crushed what was left of my resistance."

"I viewed Kethry's memories of that, but she was lost after returning to Morna Dey to accept the offer."

Baris nodded. "Even after Morna Dey spent ages devouring my soul, I have difficulty calling her evil. Her masters, the Gods of Naught, drove her will. She is compelled to return existence to how it began, before the realms or Ascended or Primes were formed. She also has some fleck of hesitation about that, since she knows she will no longer exist if she succeeds, and she does want to exist. I think I'm partly responsible for that after she spent so much time feeding upon me."

"What happened when Kethry returned to Morna Dey?"

"Right, sorry. She uncoupled herself from me to attach to Kethry instead. I'm sure Morna Dey planned to simply take over and return to Kethry's body, but your daughter was ridiculously powerful. She created traps and mazes for the daemon mistress. I sat right here without the strength to stand and watched Kethry siphon from the thing's essence, all planning to subdue Morna and gain access to her power, my power. I like to think she would have returned that to me afterward. I can't guess how long they fought, but Kethry won. She was about to seal away the being that is Morna Dey and obliterate her from the cosmos. Kethry saw it too late, how Morna feigned that last weakness and how it lulled your daughter into premature victory." Baris paused and rubbed at his face with both hands. "A battle with fireballs and spears is far simpler than one fought completely in the mind. The more power she held, the more she could lose at any instant. I watched it all, but I can not explain exactly how Kethry lost in the end. Morna Dey left here to take control of Kethry's physical body."

Jazelyn's shoulders fell. "Almost six hundred years passed in Poas between when Kethry was lost to the aether and when her body disappeared. Are you saying she continuously battled with Morna Dey that entire time?"

"It was a lengthy battle."

"Neither have returned since?"

Baris opened his mouth to respond but considered his words. "Not exactly? I haven't seen anyone in this cottage with me since they left, but I sometimes feel a presence. A murmured word or a density in the air. That sort of thing."

"This cottage. How did you come to be here? This is pulled from Kethry's memory, but it sounds as though you and Morna Dey existed here before my daughter first came."

"That's a wobbly memory for me. I vaguely remember the Chronicler being here, creating this space, and giving form to my essence. Sometimes a little girl would draw on the walls, but I don't clearly remember. After all, I've been dead a while, existing in this place like a dream."

"The Chronicler was here," Jazelyn started and shook off her line of thought. "Since she fed off you for so long, do you believe there is enough of my daughter remaining to save her from the daemon mistress?"

Baris frowned. "Even at the end, when I was completely under Morna's heel, and she controlled every ounce of my being, I was still there. When she left me, she left completely." He sighed. "Obviously, for your sake, I hope the answer's yes. From what I witnessed of Kethry's battle with Morna, your daughter is by far the strongest mortal I've seen or heard of regarding raw will and discipline.

"Kethry is the tree the daemon mistress is coiled about like a choking ivy. You might destroy both with enough force, but you must unravel Morna Dey first if you hope to save your daughter, which I assume you do."

Jazelyn nodded but kept her gaze downcast. "I assume the only way to pry Morna Dey from my daughter is to offer her another tree."

"Good luck finding another more enticing than what she has now."

***

Jazelyn's eyes flew wide to her husband's worried face a few feet away and her bedroom's stone ceiling beyond.

"Did you find the cottage, Lyn?"

She sat up and took a long drink of cool water from the glass Kiol offered before speaking. "Yes, and I spoke with the Mraasil Baris." She left out no detail as she repeated the conversation verbatim.

Kiol squeezed her hand. "I hope you don't intend to be this new tree, to try some show of motherly love and offer yourself as a sacrifice to Morna Dey."

"I considered it but quickly dashed that thought. What could I offer the daemon mistress that she does not already have in my daughter?"

"You'd be a willing host. If Kethry is in there, actively fighting back, even to some small degree, that must hold back Morna's power."

Jazelyn shook her head. "Knowledge and experience are the source of my power. In Iecil, I unleashed the full might of my combat prowess against Morna Dey and barely scratched her."

"But you did scratch her. You forced her to retreat. Even Teiris summoning the fifth moon and calling down the full wrath of Enid didn't manage that. You need to stop selling yourself short. Just because others in the world excel over you in some area doesn't mean that your abilities are worthless."

Jazelyn took a deep breath and released it as a drawn-out sigh. "Lone should be made aware of what we have learned, though maybe not everything."

Kiol raised an eyebrow and scratched at his blond head. "You don't trust him? Think he'll run off to offer himself as a tribute to Morna Dey?"

Jazelyn considered that for a moment. "It is more that I worry it will distract him from his duties in Isolis. I do trust Lone, but I also trusted his aunt. I find it difficult to trust anyone I have known for fewer than four hundred years."

"Glad that doesn't discount me." Kiol grinned and leaned to kiss her nose.

A smile twitched on Jazelyn's lips. "I must think more on this, but we have a portal to finish."

22

Ancient magic isn't innately more powerful, but it is often simpler. A spell meant to do a single thing will always have a more powerful result than one more complex.

Regent King Lone touched the black stone obelisk's new rune, surrounded by his generals, weaponmaster, chief scribe, and three dozen of the most highly trained members of the royal guard. Three times as many more martial experts, crystal mages, and a handful of archmages waited just inside the castle rather than standing in the biting wind. Lone linked the rune with a thread of mana to the ley lines running below his feet, and the carving responded with a dark glow that leeched some of the natural gray gloom from the courtyard. The murky power rippled in the air, and Lone stepped back as an oval of darkness formed between him and the obelisk, gradually gaining a sense of solidity until it was almost seven feet tall and four wide. Motes of deep purple energy drifted from the edges of the gate.

Kiol chuckled nervously while tugging at his pale blue quilted armor. "I didn't expect it to look like a portal to the fourth hell. Should we run some more tests?"

"My calculations are precise," Jazelyn said without looking at her husband.

Lone turned to the surrounding crowd, realizing that some may expect a rousing, rallying speech. Lieutenant Dreyma opened her eyes a little wider as if expecting exactly that. Lone blew a long, misty breath out into the frigid air.

"The avaryll came to us veiled in threat. We are now going to Isolis to accept their invitation, hoping they were misunderstood but prepared for otherwise. We will not be caught off guard again." He unclipped the small copper ball from his belt and held it up. "We hope not to need it, but give thanks to the genius of General Tekin for providing us a means to combat the avaryll's superior magic."

Dehset withered when all eyes turned on him. He fidgeted with the straps of the heavy pack on his back.

After a single word of thanks, expectant eyes returned to Lone. The regent king cleared his throat. "It goes without saying, but stick to your training, and we'll see about the birth of this new world tree."

Lieutenant Dreyma stepped forward. "I will secure the area, regent king." She passed through the portal without hesitation, followed by a dozen of her guards in light blue leather armor. Each seemed to fade and dissolve as they crossed the boundaries of the spell.

Kiol approached and put a hand on Lone's shoulder. "Impressive speech, Lone. I still have chills."

Lone glared back at his old friend. "My grandsire may have given you your title, but I could take it away."

Kiol raised his hands defensively and laughed as he walked into the portal behind Jazelyn, Isold, and a jumpy Dehset.

Soldiers, crystal mages, and the few, very few, archmages that heeded the call of their king streamed from the castle to enter the portal. Lone met the eyes of each that passed.

"Words are unnecessary," Bard said softly in Au beside him.

"We should bring the twins and their nurses as well; then truly, everyone in the castle will be going."

"And the chefs," said Bard with the hint of a smile.

"Good idea. We'll want for some good food while we're there." Lone nodded at the last soldier through and turned fully to Bard. "You're next, my love. Are you sure you're well enough?" He put a palm on Bard's side, where wraps of oiled linen protected bruised ribs under the light cloth armor.

"I won't leave your side."

"Well, you have to for a moment. I need to disable the portal from this side before going through."

The weaponmaster slipped a hand behind Lone's neck and pulled him close for a kiss. It could have lasted until the next thaw and still felt too short. Bard pulled away and was gone through the black portal. Lone sighed into the cold and looked up at the castle around him. Not for the first time, a seed of worry festered in his chest for the twin princes in the eastern tower. Rarely had anyone committed so much raw power to a single purpose, leaving the seat of Dracon so very alone.

Lone stood alone in the courtyard, letting the icy wind tug at the hem of his calf-length jacket. He traced a finger along the edges of his mother's brooch pinned to his baldric. He recognized it as the clumsy work of a very patient eight-year-old and perhaps not an appropriate accessory for a king, regent or not. Tears threatened at the thought of his lost sister.

Before he could dwell on it too long, Lone blew out a cloudy breath and touched the shimmering rune on the obelisk, severing the thread tying it to the ley lines. The portal immediately lost some of the sharpness at its edges. Lone ducked through before it was gone.

His body exploded into a thousand shards of agony that were gone before he could appreciate it. Strong hands took him by the biceps to help him to his feet, and fresh pain erupted across his eyes. He squeezed them tight against the blinding light.

"*Menf,*" Bard breathed beside him, and Lone smelled the man's familiar musk.

"I..." Lone gingerly opened his eyes again and blinked away the stars.

A blurry shape in the proportions of Jazelyn approached him. "Apologies, Your Grace. I realized too late that there would be complications in entering an unpowered portal. I should have remained behind to end the spell and teleported myself here."

"But it worked?" Lone tried to ask, but even he could hear how slurred the words came out.

"Yes. My calculations were precise, bringing us exactly two miles southwest of Tidecrest. Give yourself a moment, Your Grace. Lieutenant Dreyma is securing a perimeter."

Lone leaned forward between his knees, not remembering having sat down, and focused all his energy on not retching.

Bard whispered at this side. "Even I, who has never had an interest in grand cities or the building of one, am awestruck by it."

"Tell me about it," Lone said, finding Au's gentle phonemes easier to speak and hear at the moment.

"We sit among tall grasses on a hillside that slopes toward the city. A sheer, white cliff rises behind Tidecrest, shielding it from the north. The city itself looks like an island, ringed by a moat or pit with only two bridges spanning it."

Lone grinned. "Impressive defenses. What of the city itself?"

"It fills half my view. Hundreds of alabaster spires reach to the sky, but the tree shadows all. Lone, I could never conceive of a tree that looks as large as an entire forest. Its trunk grows from the city's center, and its branches spread wide over the tallest and farthest towers."

Lone pressed the heels of his palms into his eyes. He blinked away the last of the dizziness and accepted Bard's arm to help him back to his feet.

"You good?" Kiol asked, but Lone turned to Jazelyn.

"I know you didn't rush yourself designing the portal, General, but perhaps an extra moment to test and explain everything in advance next time."

"Apologies, Your Grace." Jazelyn bowed stiffly at the waist.

Lone met her cold, dark eyes when she straightened. He could never be truly upset with the ancient archmage. He trusted she did everything in her power to ensure the magic worked as expected, so he only grinned and shrugged. "Nothing to worry about now. Your modification to the obelisk worked perfectly. Though it still feels like my head's on sideways. Let's get on with it. How do we approach the city?"

Lone turned to view Tidecrest for the first time, and the breath caught in his throat. The sprawling metropolis of Vanna in Eplear was the largest city in Poas, so densely populated that it was estimated one in twenty of all humans on the continent lived in that single city of high, brightly colored, and claustrophobically packed homes. Lone could fathom nothing larger until today. Bard's description of towers, fortifications, and the tree above it all had been accurate but did little to prepare Lone for the scale of what lay below. For how tightly packed those towers were, it would be a waste of space if the avaryll numbered under a million residents in Tidecrest.

The armies of Barbarles and Jaiketh were visible in the fields south of the city, each numbering many multiples of the barely two hundred that Dracon brought. The two military camps were neatly arrayed with tents, cooking fires, and patrolling guards, keeping a wary distance from each other. Queen Teiris's contingent of svarters was marching in from the east, flying their flags of green and cream, but still miles away.

"Well, there's four out of seven. What of the other nations?" Lone asked aloud. "Evkasa and Eplear? I don't see the Holy Seat's banner down there, either."

Isold cleared her throat before answering. "Ersha will not rise until overmorrow. We are still two days early, per the invitation. By reports, the army of Eplear is due here early tomorrow, but Evkasa was bringing a group smaller than ourselves and should be here already. Maybe they're within the city?"

"Maybe. Maybe it's the same for Acrus, and Archetype Dalbinth is touring those pearly streets as we speak."

"Come on, Lone, let's get down there and get a drink," Kiol said, clapping him on the shoulder.

Lone hushed his friend and turned to the group he had followed through the portal, a mix of Dracon soldiers in blue leather, crystal mages in far more casual attire, and archmages wearing whatever outlandish blend of colors and fabrics they saw fit. He addressed the commander of his guard. "Lieutenant Dreyma, you and five of your choice will accompany me to the city. The rest can set up near the host from Barbarles. They can entertain the Serpent King's forces and be a better buffer between them and Jaiketh."

***

A half-hour later, with most of their forces unpacking bags and pitching tents between the two major forces already in place, the delegation from Dracon approached one of the polished stone bridges spanning the gap into the city. Peeking over the edge, Lone could make out shadows of the crevasse's bottom, some fatal drop below, and the sides mottled with handholds. A person with any climbing skill could easily scale their way up or down either side. The bridge was wide enough for his twelve to walk comfortably in two rows. Lone took the lead in crossing, followed by his generals and scribe. Bard fell in with the guards at the rear.

"How did this all exist under our noses?" Kiol asked as he craned his neck at the soaring towers and boughs of the world tree beyond. Meticulously manicured gardens spilled over the edges of most balconies along the spires, giving an impression that nature tried to reclaim this ageless city but settled for a stalemate.

Ahead, three avaryll stood in the center of the bridge. The middle one wore long, deep green robes that pooled around her feet. She casually clasped her pale hands in front of her, and a massive, leather-bound tome hung from a strap at her hip. The others on either side were a half-head shorter, with faces obscured behind white plate helms. None of them had weapons in hand or anywhere else obvious on their persons.

"Regent King Lone of Dracon and associates," she called. "I am Seventh Celestial Mage Prashek, here to welcome you to Tidecrest and to bear you to your accommodations."

"Thank you." Lone stopped a few paces away and tapped his breastplate twice in salute. "Would it be appropriate for me to call you Prashek?"

"Of course, that is my name." The avaryll fell into step beside Lone with the hint of a smile. Her guards made way for the group to pass and followed behind Dreyma and Bard. "Welcome to Tidecrest, regent king. My people have been preparing for this moment for so many generations. It is my true honor to be alive for it."

Lone was not ready for the mage's light, almost bubbly, tone. When Sren and Fors burst into the convention in Acrus weeks ago, Lone assumed all avaryll would be equally nasty. Aiden's feelings about their race, which he was eager to voice, added to those premature prejudices. "Thank you. Could you tell me more about what we are here to witness?"

Prashek laughed again. "I worry I won't give it justice, regent king. I'll leave that to the protectorate to explain when you meet with him."

Lone frowned but carried on. "Your city is grand beyond my very imagining. Perhaps I could see more of it once we're settled?"

"Of course. It would be my honor to show you everything about Tidecrest." Prashek ran her eyes down Lone in a way that made him uncomfortable.

He cleared his throat. "Have the contingents from Acrus and Evkasa arrived?"

"Archetype Dalbinth has been in and out of the city for weeks."

Lone suppressed a groan. Of course Aiden had some means of quickly traveling to and from Isolis.

Prashek continued. "Sultana Bayram of Evkasa arrived yesterday and has remained in her quarters with her handmaidens. I dare say I know not which of the dozen women is the Sultana herself."

"If any of them are. I guess everyone is accounted for, then. What can you tell me about the tree?" Lone asked as he stared up at the great loops of moss that hung from the thick branches of the world tree hundreds of feet over his head.

"Endanlegsil," Prashek cooed with careful pronunciation. "In her infancy, she grew so quickly that the entire city had to be razed and redesigned twice to accommodate. Entire reservoirs were created and destroyed to quench her thirst. I've seen the old city maps when Tidecrest lay on the edge of a vast inland sea. Lucky for us all, she drinks the mana of other realms now. We no longer must remake Poas to sustain her." She chuckled to herself.

Lone thought of the scope of such projects and again found it hard to fathom. "How is it that the tree has been a secret if such work was needed to sustain it?"

"'Her,' not 'it,'" Prashek corrected. "How old are you, regent king?"

"I'll soon be thirty."

Prashek laughed and quickly caught herself with a hand over her mouth. "So sorry! As much as I've studied humans and your life cycle, it's still hard to believe any species can get anything done living less than a few hundred years."

"And how old are you?" Lone asked, estimating by the lines across her forehead and at the corners of her eyes that the avaryll was in her early fifties.

"Just shy of three hundred, in the later two-thirds of my life." Prashek pushed back her glossy, topaz-colored hair. "We avaryll live on average a little longer than svarters."

Lone gaped at the number but threw an eye to Jazelyn at his side, knowing the archmage was several times that. "How was asking my age relevant?"

"Oh yes. Endanlegsil's seed was gifted to us some eight millennia ago. Her explosive growth wrecked the city of Tidecrest for ages but settled at a slower rate after four or five thousand years, still well before humans came to Poas. Your mere thirty years, regent king, is the barest wisp of mana in the aether. By the time humans arrived and the Mists rose, we were already well-adhered to our goal of focusing all energy on the tree and the moment that is so soon upon us. We had generations to seal and protect our borders to reduce distractions from the outside."

They were off the bridge now and moving through the smooth, gently winding streets of Tidecrest. No building stood shorter than ten levels, giving a sense of the towers looming overhead, ready to crash down on them.

"The Mists, Teiris has mentioned that, but the svarters have almost no record of what it actually meant."

Prashek sighed. "Yes, any avaryll worth anything knows the full history of Poas and her people, but is that the question you want me to spend time answering?"

Lone wanted to reply "yes" but knew a full history lesson would not be relevant at the moment. "I suppose not. Tell me of your people, then. It must have been not easy, sealing yourselves away while knowing a world awaits just outside your borders. Are all avaryll in agreement about that decision?" He winced at his clumsy wording.

Prashek made a thoughtful humming noise. "The avaryll are a varied people, and naturally, few decisions are made unanimously. Some factions exist, little more than social fraternities. The Unfallen Ranks, Celestial Prism, and Celestial Undersight, for example."

"Lots of celestial themes in Tidecrest."

A smile flickered across Prashek's lips.

Lone watched her expression closely. "The Einingu?"

Prashek's grin faded with her gaze focused ahead. "Luckily, we have the protectorate to settle all disputes and set the final decree."

Lone understood the response as a confirmation of her knowledge about Tanathil's group, as well as a disdain for them. He moved on. "What about you? What does it mean to be Seventh Celestial Mage?"

Prashek's grin returned. "The protectorate arrays himself with the best examples of our people. In other nations, that usually means military strength, decorated war heroes, and the like. We avaryll have never fought a war, not since Tersil burned, though don't assume that doesn't mean we can't fight. I'd wager your greatest mage against any citizen of Tidecrest. No, we value knowledge and wisdom. Protectorate Gair, Protectorate Alaraic's predecessor, chose me as a celestial mage because of my passion for foreign cultures. I have studied every minor facet of human and svarters life from afar for hundreds of years. I might know your people better than you!" She beamed.

"Is that so? You should have come with the invitation, Prashek. High Inquisitor Shaman Sren and Third Celestial Mage Fors were... I'll call them intense."

"They were? I selected them personally. I thought they best reflected the average mindset of humans and svarters. Your people so often require a firm hand to be taken seriously."

Lone thought of how the avaryll literally brought the room of delegates to their knees. The sweat beading from his nose and brow as he fought against their superior magic forcing him to the marble tile. He shook away the reverie. "There is a gulf between study and experience. Your knowledge of foreign cultures will grow exponentially when you walk amongst my people."

"Is that an invitation?" Her gaze ran over him again, predatory.

"Once our people have an understanding, sure."

Prashek clapped her hands. "Delightful! I really am looking forward to it. Imagine being an expert in people you could only ever view from carefully timed and positioned scrying magic, never able to ask them a question or taste their food."

"Speaking of being amongst a people, where are yours?" Lone craned his neck to look down another empty street at the next intersection.

"We avaryll are too busy to mill about the streets, not when our greatest accomplishment is about to come to fruition."

"You expect to welcome the birth of a new Mraasil," Lone said, more than asked.

Prashek nodded enthusiastically. "And with it will come the resurgence of mana to Poas. I am told the ley lines are thin threads here compared to when Tersil was at her height. Have you been to other realms?"

Lone started at the topic switch. "No. Not unless a demi-realm counts."

"A realm within a realm?" Prashek laughed. "No. Impressive as that may be, it doesn't count. I ask because I have read other realms have mana in quantities manyfold that of Poas. I hope our realm will be like that soon."

"Have any of the avaryll been outside..." Lone started to ask but lost his words as they entered a wide plaza. Directly ahead, a building larger than any other he had seen soared into the sky. The main trunk of Endanlegsil stretched like a solid wall of bark from its roof.

"The Symposium," Prashek announced.

Despite the overwhelming size of the structure and the titanic tree sprouting from the center, Lone's eye glided down and focused on the three figures in conversation by the Symposium's grand, arched doors. He recognized Archdruid Etharis and Ruvaal from their clothes, but the third Mraasil looked wrapped in thick leaves. Lone gasped as he became sure it was not a trick of the light. The third Mraasil had curved horns and a thick tail.

"What an honor!" Prashek gasped and sped forward. The Mraasil turned to face the group. Ruvaal's lip curled downward while the horned one looked wholly disinterested. "Honored Mraasil, please allow me to introduce—"

"Regent King Lone, Archmage Jazelyn, and... others. Welcome to Tidecrest," said Etharis and followed Lone's eye to the third Mraasil. "You know my brother Ruvaal, of course. This is another of my siblings, Bireal, guardian of Muertsil of Urbus."

Lone cleared his throat and inclined his head in a bow. "A pleasure, Guardian Bireal, Ruvaal."

Bireal inhaled deeply, and a hint of a smile crossed their lips, exposing one sharp fang. "Regent King Lone, yes? How is it you know Cazlandt? I sense his power within you." Their voice was a cool whisper.

Lone's knees felt weak at hearing the name, and he stumbled back a step. "Cazlandt is, was, my great-grandsire. He, uh, he died when I was young. Too young to remember. I never knew him."

Bireal took another long breath. "That must be what I sense in you. He's dead, you say?"

"Assumed dead, yes."

"Cazlandt is dead." Bireal paused to lick their lips as if physically tasting the words. "I'm unsure how I feel hearing that." They flicked their lavender tail. "I owed him a debt and would not see it go unpaid. Perhaps being his progeny, you would accept it in his stead?"

"I think all debts owed to Cazlandt can be called off, honestly. What did he do for you?"

"Simply put, Cazlandt brought my realm back from the precipice of extinction and saved me from complete madness."

"Wow." Lone nodded in amazement. "That must be some story."

"A thrilling story, for sure," Ruvaal said, cutting off Bireal's response. "Something for another time." His gaze lingered on Lone for a breath before turning back to Etharis. "This only adds to the point I was trying to make, dear brother."

"It's their realm, too," said Etharis. "One might argue they have more right to be here than you."

"That's rich since you were the one to beg the Mraasil to come here," Ruvaal said, leaning back with a huff.

"What's this about?" Lone asked, forcing himself to pull his eyes from the hypnotic undulation of Bireal's tail.

Etharis cleared his throat. "After seeing the amassing forces outside Tidecrest, Ruvaal would like to rescind the avaryll's invitation and send everyone back to their respective nations."

Lone frowned. "We're here at the behest of our new neighbors, the avaryll of Tidecrest, not you, Ruvaal."

Ruvaal narrowed his amber eyes with clear anger, but Etharis spoke before he could. "I would have agreed with him not long ago. The birth of a Mraasil, ushering new life to a realm, has been my sacred duty alone since the literal beginning of time. I would have kept it that way, tossing everyone from the city while Verndari is born, even the avaryll. Seeing the collected standards of Poas in the hills south of the city changed my mind. The young Mraasil, so close to birth, will have a power that belongs to all of Poas."

"We won't be inviting thousands of their troops into the room," Ruvaal said. "Send the armies away, at least."

"Our armies are here," said Lone, "because the invitation wasn't the most... cordial."

Etharis snickered with a hint of an underlying purr and winked as Ruvaal. "Have you never met a human, dear brother? They feel naked without a sword on their hip and a battalion at their back. The svarters aren't much better after so many centuries around them. The armies on the hills are harmless so long as they don't start bickering amongst each other."

"And if they do?" said Ruvaal. "When did they last have so many forces in one place? What if they all turn on each other? I'd hate to see those green hills see bloodshed."

"Stop it, Ruvaal. We're done with this," Etharis snapped.

Ruvaal turned on a heel and left in a swirl of his red and blue robes. Lone watched him go for a moment before the Mraasil turned down a side street away from the Symposium.

Etharis waved at his brother dismissively. "Leave him. He always pouts when he doesn't get his way. Lone, I'm sure I know the answer to this, but your sister isn't back yet, is she?"

While he knew the question was probably harmless, Lone sensed suspicion in hearing it. What separated Etharis and Ruvaal from being daemon masters? What about this quiet, horned Mraasil standing beside them? "No, she has not returned."

Etharis took a deep breath and frowned. "That's a shame. I expected her to be here for this, but there's still time. Let's step inside and have some tea while we wait for your parents to get here." He grimaced as he looked across the gathering of twelve humans and three avaryll. "Maybe not all of you. Maybe like four."

Lone chose against correcting Etharis on the relations, calling Teiris a parent. "I saw the Terswood contingent arriving. They shouldn't be long." He turned to scan the retinue behind and around him. "Jazelyn, Kiol, and Bard with me. Seventh Celestial Mage Prashek, could I impose upon you to see Lieutenant Dreyma and the others to a comfortable place to rest?"

"Of course, Regent King," the avaryll said with a grin and slow incline of her head.

"Care to join us, Bireal?" Etharis asked.

"No thank you, archdruid."

General Tekin focused on the straps of his backpack and kept his eyes down as he followed the group. Lone reached to tap Isold on the shoulder. "Keep an eye on him for me, would you?"

23

*To contrast The Glory, everything in Groos is huge. I could barely see over a
sprig of clover and the people — a feathered and furred people with wings to
fly — tower over sixty feet tall. Yet the Mraasil is a normal size.*

T hough his father described Farsil in Tempus Fa as ten times as large, Lone
could stare at Endanlegsil for a year and still be astounded by its size. Aerial
roots so thick, six men with arms outstretched could not wrap around one arced
high before sinking into the floor of the Symposium. The ground itself sloped
gently upward as if the entire structure were built on a hill, to a silver throne
nestled among those sheets of roots and moss. A pale avaryll with radiant cobalt
hair and resplendent blue-scaled armor perched upon that throne. A stoic guard
in white plate stood to either side of him.

"I forgot he might be in here," Etharis sighed.

The avaryll rose and took one step toward Lone and his group. "Regent King
Lone of Dracon, I presume?"

"Yes, and may I introduce—"

"I am Protectorate Alaraic, Keeper of the Silven Rings of Anshamot, Master
of the Nine Circles, Chief of the Ways, Exarch of—"

"This will take a while," said Etharis as the avaryll continued droning on with
an endless stream of meaningless titles.

"—welcome you to Tidecrest," he finished at last.

"Thank you." Lone attempted to recall half the titles, but settled for remembering the protectorate's name. Tanathil's warning about the protectorate rang
in Lone's ears as much as the archdruid's belittling words.

Etharis stepped forward. "Save your breath, Alaraic. We're just passing through
to get a cup of tea. Send Teiris and Daelin this way when you see them, would

you?" The archdruid continued towards a simple door along the Symposium's outside wall.

Lone looked between Etharis's back as he walked away and the expectant leader of the avaryll. The regent king quickly decided and turned from the archdruid to approach the protectorate's throne.

"Protectorate Alaraic," Lone said, tapping his leather cuirass in salute. This close, he could see the throne appeared to be made of rough tree bark wrapped and coated in silver. Bark not unlike that of the world tree around them. "Your throne is stunning, Protectorate."

The avaryll smiled and stepped aside to provide Lone an unobstructed view. "My predecessor fashioned it from a discarded limb of Endanlegsil. I could hardly imagine a more fitting seat for a leader. Your crown of ice is a stunning work of art."

Lone automatically raised a hand to touch the heavy crown. As uncomfortable as it had been when first wearing it, he must have become used to the weight without noticing. "Thank you, Protectorate."

"Please, call me Alaraic, if I may call you Lone."

"I would like that."

"Come for a closer look at my throne."

Lone approached the silvered throne. Even after his litany of hobbies over the last twenty years, he knew virtually nothing of carpentry or what it might take to craft something out of wood and do it well. As he lingered, touching the throne's joints and application of the silver, he could tell it was well done, even without a proper basis for comparison. "Exquisite. The avaryll artists must be exceptional. Let me introduce General Jazelyn, overseer of the archmages, General Kiol, strategic liaison to the study of magic, and Weaponmaster Bard, head instructor of non-magical practices within the Dracon Royal Guard."

Alaraic adjusted his scale armor before taking his seat on the throne again. "A pleasure to meet you all." His cobalt eyes, matching his hair, flicked across the four, and he chuckled as he pushed farther into his seat. "Each group coming to Poas speaks volumes by who they choose to bring before me. The Serpent King came with a small battalion of faceless guards. Sultana Bayram offered me a gift of incense from her home, though I don't know which of the six women was the leader, obscuring that simple truth from me. Dracon now stands before me with one of the oldest living archmages and two trained for war. What meaning of force am I meant to glean from this, Lone?"

Lone swallowed hard and fought to keep his expression even. "I have no hidden meaning, Alaraic. I come beside my most trusted advisers. If you wish to talk about hidden threats, how about how you captured and imprisoned my generals for days when they entered Isolis weeks ago?" Lone gestured at Jazelyn and Kiol.

Alaraic shrugged and shook his head. "Yes, I think I remember something about that, but as you say, they were trespassing in my lands. Such a punishment was light." He gripped the armrests of his throne. "You brought your artificer to Tidecrest but had enough sense to leave him outside these doors."

"General Tekin is—"

"I am told he is talented, someone to watch. Runecraft and artifice were never things I had a mind for, and having a natural talent for such an art is rare even among my people." Alaraic glared at Lone.

Lone cleared his throat. "Protectorate... Alaraic, as I'm sure you were told, a summit of the nations of Poas was just coming underway when your emissaries arrived. They mentioned their annoyance at not being invited, but I'm sure you appreciate that our ignorance of your people resulted from your centuries of applied skill. I hope to resume these summits to foster a greater understanding of people across our realm. Little would delight me more than your presence."

"Thank you, Regent King, but we shall see if any of that is necessary. Our world is about to change. In two days, you will see this throne in the shade of Endanlegsil is not for just a leader of the avaryll, but of all Poas."

Lone could not stop himself from glancing at Jazelyn at his side. Even her ever-stoic face showed shock at hearing the intent spoken so plainly. "Are you saying you intend to take singular command of Poas?"

"For eight thousand years, the avaryll have fostered the tree that grows around us, that will be the revival of mana and life to this realm. Would you not agree it is fair and fitting that the avaryll stand over the new world we have created?"

Lone bit down on his tongue, hoping the pain of it would keep him from speaking the words crashing through his mind. *They've done nothing in my lifetime, much less eight thousand years! They sat behind their barrier as Amer slaughtered thousands in Iecil. Red Bloom ravaged the innocent. Daemon attacked Terswood.* All the time spent at his aunt's right hand had done little to prepare him for this moment. He counted six slow breaths before speaking. "So much is still to be decided. It was a pleasure to meet you, Protectorate. I look forward to our future conversations." Lone turned in the direction Etharis had gone before Alaraic could say anything more. With every step toward the single door before him, Lone expected the protectorate to yell some echoed words, another passive-aggressive threat, or something offensive. As the door closed behind him, the silence, the statement that nothing more need be said, was worse.

***

"Took you long enough," said Etharis, waving for the group to sit while he moved to a gaudy brass tea set.

"I didn't want to be rude to the protectorate," Lone said as he stepped into the small sitting room. A half dozen couches upholstered with thick, red velvet lined the walls.

"He just intends to take over the world in two days," said Kiol. "How did you resist putting a fist across his face, Lone?"

Etharis waved dismissively at the spellslinger. "Don't worry about Alaraic. Compliment his shoes next time you see him, and he'll forget about past injustices. What do you take in your tea?"

"Past injustices?" Lone scoffed. "He was nothing but clear about how he plans to use the tree's power to rule over the realm."

Etharis poured out cups from a kettle. "Don't worry about him. He's a lot of talk. The power of a world tree is for the realm, not for an individual or single race. Now, sit. And again, how do you take your tea?"

Lone chose a couch facing the door, and Bard sat beside him. Jazelyn and Kiol took another beside them.

"Just a little sugar and milk," said Lone.

Etharis nodded and handed a steaming cup to Lone, adding nothing to the brew. "This way's better, trust me. Don't let the additives spoil the herb."

"Sometimes a lump of sugar can make the bitterest root palatable," Jazelyn said while accepting the offered cup of plain tea.

Etharis handed cups to Bard and Kiol before settling across the couch beside the door with a grin. "Very clever, archmage. I feel like there's some joke in there about sugarcoating things."

"That was not my intention," said Jazelyn.

"What's going on here, Etharis? Why are we sitting in this little room with a world tree to look at on the other side of that door?"

Etharis inhaled the steam of his tea. "World trees are kind of my thing. You may not know, but mine was the first. I saw every one of them in every realm to maturity. Did anyone in this room know that world trees were a thing a year ago? That surprises me because of how closely you worked with Cazlandt, Jazelyn. Didn't you used to travel the realms with him?"

The archmage set her cup back in the saucer and nodded slowly. "For a while, yes. The difference in ley energies between the realms upset my cultivation, and

I was forced to remain in Poas. We never encountered a world tree; he never mentioned them to me. I only ever read accounts of them in The Stacks."

"Cazlandt was a tight-lipped little son of a daemon," said Etharis. "Why do you care so much about seeing the world tree when you didn't know they existed until recently? With the experience and knowledge that comes with my age, whatever room I'm in must be the most interesting place in all the realms. Why else would I be there, right?"

Lone had found it all too easy to forget the archdruid's grand role across the realms after he had served tea to him. He sipped, resisting the urge to wince at the bitter bite. "Please accept my most sincere apologies, Etharis. Archdruid Etharis. Was there a particular topic you wished to discuss?"

Etharis grinned and nodded as he took another slow sip of tea. "Thank you, young king. Yes, I have something of dire importance, but I don't want my other siblings involved." He swiveled his legs to the ground and leaned forward. "We have to find your sister immediately."

Someone knocked at the door and pushed it open. Teiris and Daelin entered with another avaryll attendant behind them. Etharis waved the avaryll away and gestured for the newcomers to be seated without rising to offer them tea. "Queen and King of the svarters, where is your daughter?" he asked as they sat.

"Archdruid, why are you so intent on finding Ali now?" Lone asked before Teiris exploded.

An uncharacteristic darkness entered his glowing amber eyes as Etharis glowered and raised an arm to the door. His whispered words came quickly, manic. "It was she that got the Seed of Farsil into the hands of those that would plant it here. She commanded them to keep it secret even from me and provided them the magic to shield all of Isolis. Alishia has orchestrated a line of events involving a world tree, and, as I said, they're kind of my thing. My patience is vast beyond mortal measure, but this situation has me wearing very thin. I would know her intention here."

"If she walked through the door right now," said Lone, "I don't think she'd have your answers, Etharis. Aiden implied that Alishia will return, not the Chronicler. I mean, Ali is the Chronicler, but not quite yet. You know what I mean. Ali's future self would set all this in motion."

"Madllyn said much the same," said Teiris.

Etharis coughed into his cup, and his amber gaze slowly shifted to the queen. "Madllyn is your maid in waiting or something, I hope. Or are you casually telling me you spoke to a Sundered?"

"She came to me months ago, and we have spoken a few times since."

Etharis laughed and leaned back into his couch, downing the last of his tea. "If I hadn't come to your aid after Daelin blew up the entrance to Elogah'an, my life would be much simpler now. I wouldn't have ended up in Poas and mixed up with the business around the Ibaerite. Ruvaal would be a lot less grumpy, that's for sure."

Silence shrouded the room for a moment, broken only by Kiol sipping at his hot tea.

"It is best to not dwell on past actions, Archdruid," said Bard. "My people accept they are a sum of their past choices. Undo one, and our lives would unravel like a weaving."

"The tapestry of life," Etharis mumbled, leaning back to stare at the ceiling. "Your life wouldn't unravel. It would just look different as other paths were taken." The room darkened as the archdruid closed his eyes for a moment. "When I first met Alishia, she was the young girl who left Poas just a little while ago. Years later, when I next met her, that girl was gone, replaced by the Chronicler. You are right, Lone. When your sister returns, she won't be the one that sets all this in motion. She must go through some trial or hardship that steels her resolve as the Chronicler, converting into one that observes and records but does not interfere beyond ensuring events happen as they must."

Etharis took a deep breath and snapped his eyes open, some of the gentle joy returning to his face. "I'm sorry, Teiris, Daelin. Would you like some tea? Daelin, maybe something a little stronger?" He jumped to his feet.

Daelin's emerald eyes flew wide as he avoided looking at this wife. "No thank you, Archdruid. I gave up the drink."

"That's a shame to hear," Etharis said with a wink, handing them each a cup and saucer. He refilled his own before taking his seat again with legs over the arm of the couch. "My concern here is with the wellbeing of the tree and the Mraasil that will be born soon. The tree is being cared for as we speak by one I have absolute trust in, though that trust was stretched after learning what he's been doing these last eight thousand years behind my back. That's mine to deal with. The lot of you care about the politics of this situation. How will the avaryll, the world tree, and a new source of mana fit into the worldview of Poas?"

"Exactly," Teiris said, setting the empty cup on the marble floor before her. "There's more. I would learn if the avaryll share a common ancestor with the svarters. Ruvaal told me—"

"Oh, you do," Etharis said with a long draw of tea. "And I think that connection will give the svarters a leg up here."

Teiris sucked in a breath between her teeth. "Would you care to elaborate, Archdruid?"

Lone could feel the exasperation dripping from her words.

Etharis finished his second cup. "Ters attempted something no other Mraasil ever imagined doing. She tied her people to her tree to make them immortal. Not literally tied them to a tree, magically intermingled them with it. She weaved a population of avaryll with Tersil, hence..." He raised his empty cup to Teiris.

Teiris brought a hand to her throat. "First High Queen Ters created my people herself?"

Etharis nodded. "I was upset when I found out, but by then, you had been breeding for a few generations, and the Venatus was running rampant across a hundred realms. We had the insane idea to burn Tersil to trap the Gods of Naught. We sacrificed one realm to save countless others. The svarters lost their immortality when the tree died, of course."

Lone saw the quiet conflict across his stepmother's emotions and could only guess at the storm within. He spoke in her silence. "Considering that, Etharis, please tell us how we may aid in your goals of safeguarding the tree so that we may return to the avaryll and see what bonds may be forged there."

Etharis looked at Lone with a raised eyebrow. "That might be the most suffocating sentence I've heard from you, young king. Are you spending time with my brother?"

Lone shook his head and sank back into the couch.

"Any other lingering questions before I return to the tree's care?" Etharis asked.

Lone waited for Teiris, but she seemed more interested in her hands. "What about Bireal?" he asked. "You and Ruvaal look so alike. I assumed that other Mraasil would be similar. Why does Bireal have horns and a tail?"

"How surprisingly racist of you, Lone, thinking we all should look alike," Etharis said with a wry smile. "Most Mraasil come from a single mold, my mold, but with so many of us, there are exceptions." He swung his feet back to the floor and stood. "This was a lovely chat, but I'm sure you all understand my tight schedule. I'll leave you to it and go check on the tree." The archdruid was out the door in a swirl of his long leather and fur jacket.

Teiris sank forward with her hands cupping her head, and Kiol was immediately at her side with a comforting hand on her shoulder.

A somber chill settled in the room as Lone placed his and Bard's cups back on the service. "I can't imagine what is going through your mind, Teiris. I know how highly your people regard Ters, and now to hear she created the svarters from the avaryll. I—"

"Thank you, Lone." Teiris stood and left the room in a rush.

Kiol stood and clapped a hand on Lone's shoulder. "I thought you were better at the talking part."

"I should see to her," Daelin said and left after his wife.

Lone watched his father leave and fell back into the seat Etharis had been occupying. "What now?"

"I have one question for everyone," said Kiol, waiting for all eyes to be on him. "Can we all agree that tea was gross?"

Bard smirked, and Jazelyn rolled her eyes away from her husband. "Might I suggest we return to Seventh Celestial Mage Prashek? She mentioned accommodations and a tour of the city."

***

Back in the Symposium, Alaraic sat on his throne, flanked by his guards. Two other figures stood before him wearing light traveling clothes and gesturing wildly.

"Is that the Bismats?" Kiol asked.

Lone used a speck of ley energy to enhance his vision, intending to see what artifice items the leaders of Jaiketh had on their persons. Magic crashed over him like a physical wave as the sheer quantity of it temporarily blinded him in the space before the world tree. He quickly negated the work and turned to Jazelyn while blinking away the afterimage of mana.

"General, have you viewed the ley lines from here? It's unbelievable."

"Naturally, Your Grace. Monitoring the ley lines is my primary duty. I have hardly taken my mind from studying them since stepping through the portal from Dracon."

"And?"

"I can confirm the power of a before unknown ley nexus under this very spot. It is similar in the number of lines crossing under Castle Dracon or Terswood, but an influx of new mana outshines the other great reservoirs of mana in Poas tenfold."

"Tenfold?" Lone choked on the words. "How can Dracon compete against the avaryll?"

"With careful words and no small amount of luck, we will not have to."

The Bismats turned toward the group from Dracon and waved. "Regent King and generals! We look forward to catching up with you!" Lady Bismat yelled, and the pair moved toward the main entrance of the Symposium.

Lone returned the wave. "I hope they just mean to catch up and talk about recent social events," he whispered to Kiol beside him.

"I'm sure they mean to catch up with, meet, and exceed the magic and political clout of Dracon."

"Do we have clout?" Lone smirked.

"I like to think I do," Kiol flashed a smile.

"Maintain your poise," Jazelyn warned them both and gestured to the double doors out of the Symposium.

Lone inclined his head respectfully and saluted the protectorate before leading his small group from the cavernous building.

24

The first thing I noticed was a distinct increase in the quality, where sentient life and civilization existed, of baked goods. The closer to Tempus Fa, the better the pies.

S eventh Celestial Mage Prashek met Lone outside the Symposium and led him and his group to a low building sitting oddly among the soaring alabaster towers. Within, a circular space was obviously designed as a central gathering point. Thirty doors were spaced evenly around a walkway overlooking the small, groomed trees and overstuffed chairs. Dehset and Isold conversed beside each other as Dreyma and her chosen guards stood at parade rest across the room. They approached when Lone entered.

"Dracon has those four," Prashek said, gesturing to the doors to their left. "All rooms have identical accommodations and comfortably sleep two each. As I have already described to your scrivener, there are other hostels within Tidecrest that can accommodate many of your remaining retinue."

"Thank you, Prashek. The soldiers may be comfortable with the Serpent King's troops, but I imagine the other archmages will want to stay in the city."

"The pleasure is mine, Regent King. I'll leave you to settle in and check back in a few hours. Dinner and entertainment are planned but call for anything you need before then. I would be delighted to give you that city tour in the morning."

"Well, isn't she a delight," Kiol said from beside Lone as the avaryll left the hotel with her guards in tow.

"Right." Lone turned to his group. "Ersha rises overmorrow in the early afternoon. That gives us almost two full days to explore Tidecrest and learn what we can about the avaryll and the world tree, to prepare for what threat posed or boon offered after the Mraasil is born."

Isold opened her small notebook to a page showing a crude, hastily sketched map. "From what I have already gathered," she said, "the avaryll are isolationists, even amongst themselves. There are hints of some minor factions, but they live solitary lives. The Symposium seems to be their only major gathering place. There are only a few pubs and no theaters. Their libraries are similarly decentralized, kept in private collections. Tidecrest is enormous but sparsely populated."

"Few pubs?" Kiol asked with raised eyebrows. "Good luck getting Brarlyh and Blessed in here."

Lone raised his gaze to the vaulted, unadorned ceiling. "Any guess how many of them there are? The city could hold a million."

"I would estimate fewer than fifty thousand," said Isold as she swiped through her notebook.

"What a waste." Kiol scratched at his dark beard. "And we're assuming all the avaryll in Isolis live within Tidecrest? Why does this hotel exist? Why are there others within the city if no one visits?"

"We are currently visiting," said Jazelyn. "Prashek stated they have rebuilt the city several times. They knew this day would come, and it is not beyond reasoning the last city planners intentionally left space. Similarly, as isolationists, their population may have dwindled over their years of cultural stagnation."

"There's nothing we can answer standing here," said Lone. "Let's take a quick moment to freshen up in the rooms and come back with a plan for how to spend the next two days."

"Neither Kiol nor I will require the beds to sleep, but there may be desks or tables in the rooms that would be useful," Jazelyn said.

"You assume the avaryll sleep in beds," Kiol wrapped a hand around her waist with a wink. "They might sleep in slings or upside-down like bats."

Jazelyn looked down at her husband with a gentle roll of her eye and a hint of a smirk. "The avaryll claim they have watched humans and svarters for centuries. I think it safe to assume they constructed lodgings with our customs in consideration."

Kiol released his wife and threw the arm over Dehset's shoulder. "Come on, roomie. You're not staying with Isold, so it's you and me."

Dehset nodded quickly and let the combat general lead him to the stairs, Jazelyn and Isold following close behind. Lone looked at a frowning Lieutenant Dreyma. "What's the matter?"

"I will secure your room, Your Grace. I assume and hope that won't be necessary, but we are in unfamiliar territory. The last time any of us were in Isolis, they held the generals captive for days."

"Thank you. Take the last room so you're near, please."

"Of course, Your Grace." She bowed and moved to ascend the steps with two of her five royal guards.

Bard's eyes were in constant movement around the hotel's interior, searching for threats.

"What's the..." Lone paused, realizing he had started the question in Au. It had become their default language when they were alone or wanted to remain private. He switched to Common so as not to be rude around the remaining guards. "What's the matter, love?"

Bard sighed and squeezed his eyes tight. "I know I am being silly, but I find it hard not to search the shadows for one of Ashta's agents. It's yet to sink in that I might be free from that life." He rubbed at his left shoulder, the one Fols had stabbed.

Lone shook his head. "What you had there wasn't a life."

"Am I a bad person to find relief knowing Naiti will soon be dead of a wasting disease?"

Lone rubbed at his chin while he considered a response. "I mean, we should never be glad for the death of another, but Naiti is an exception. The man was horrible to you and is complicit in a system that maintains slavery over an entire island. He deserves the gruesome death that is coming soon to him, if he hasn't already met it. Another part of me, sounding like my Aunt Lilan, would ask if Naiti knew better. He was born and raised as part of that world. Did he ever experience anything different that made him doubt his path? Is he perhaps worth some small helping of pity?"

Bard shrugged. "That has always been the way on the island of Thrist. We have always offered that way of life to Au."

Lone shook his head. "To say Naiti is complicit in slavery, what does that say about me? The notice I sent to the Western Isles asked for a weapons trainer, knowing they would bring slaves. I advised my aunt to sign your contract, knowing you were not a free man. I told myself we were hiring you, but I knew we were paying your master for your time and expertise. It makes me sick to say it aloud, Bard. To admit I traded gold for you." He wiped at his eyes with the heel of his hand and cast an eye over the guards scattered across the room. None seemed to react to his words.

"You visited the islands years ago when you were too young to understand what you saw there," Bard said. "You know now and project that guilt back to an earlier you that did not know better. Do you have experience being a slave?"

"I... no." Lone stumbled over what he was sure was rhetorical.

"Before this last year, as I told you of my life, you did not know what being a slave meant. Before you witnessed me fight Whiar in the Grand Hall, you never might have guessed they mistreated me as one."

"I never see you reading the *Ansh var Shavra* anymore," Lone said to break the topic. "I know you carry a copy with you, but for months, you always had it open in every spare moment."

Bard touched his empty breast pocket. "I haven't touched it since we returned from the isles. I think my support of Au has been... shaken."

Lone glanced at the guards again and noticed more than one quickly looking away. "Let's continue this in private."

"Your Grace, the room is secure."

Lone looked up at Dreyma on the balcony above with relief. "Thank you, Lieutenant."

"I will be next door. Please do not leave the hotel without an escort."

Lone took a deep breath, feeling the surge of pure mana below his feet. So close to the world tree, he felt powerful, more invigorated than ever. What threat might stand against him, feeling as he did now? He also recognized the avaryll would be similarly empowered, with thousands of years of breeding and training here. "As you wish," he relented, and Dreyma's shoulders visibly relaxed.

***

The room was not as extravagant as Lone had stayed in elsewhere when visiting the nations of Poas. He was thankful for only needing a few hours of sleep a night, as they would not come easily on the low, long, narrow beds. Bard laid on one, and Lone laughed at seeing the islander wider than the mattress. "I thought she said the rooms *comfortably* slept two." Bard grinned and rolled a foot to the floor's smooth, cold stone. "Long and thin, just like the avaryll."

"I see what Aiden said about the stagnant culture here," Lone said, looking across the barren stone walls and narrow window that looked out to the side of the next tower over. Other than the two beds, the room held a cramped, upright wardrobe, a matching writing desk, and a door leading to a smaller room with a privy and a washtub set into the floor. Lone played with the knobs around the tub's faucet and was delighted by the instant hot water. "The tubs in Dracon either have to maintain the temperature or take a moment to heat," he commented to a less interested Bard. "Is it wrong that I want to pull this apart to see how it works?"

"I feel there are more pressing matters than the operation of a bathtub."

Lone continued to play with the bath controls. "An understanding of their runecraft may prove invaluable. You're right, though. That's a task for Dehset."

***

Returning to the central common room, Lone saw Dehset and Kiol sitting huddled on a couch in an animated discussion with, of all people, his father. Shenraafi, the Serpent King of Barbarles, stood in his flowing feathered cloak beside Teiris. A mix of a dozen humans and svarters milled around in small clumps under the ever-present eye of the guards of each nation.

Teiris, Shenraafi, and myself. Leaders of three of the eight... minus the Western Isles, seven... plus Isolis, eight... nations of Poas. What if what the avaryll interrupted five weeks ago could begin again here and now? Lone mused and glanced around the other closed doors overlooking the space. Which one was Sultana Bayrum of Evkasa hiding behind with her gaggle of handmaidens? Were the Bismats of Jaiketh napping a stone's throw away?

As they passed his father, Kiol, and Dehset, Lone heard enough of their conversation to know the three were excitedly talking about the bathtubs in their rooms. Lone kept moving to Teiris and Shenraafi.

When he was a few paces away, the Serpent King turned to face Lone and spread his arms to reveal the blue iridescent scale armor under his heavy cloak. Lone smirked, thinking of the bard's tale that Shenraafi's armor was crafted of merman flesh when he was the Crowned Pirate of the Farfathom Deeps. Not true, but the tune that went along with the story was catchy.

"King Lone, so good to see you," said Shenraafi in his odd accent that drew out the vowels. No one else in Barbarles spoke like their king, and Lone wondered where the affectation derived. "Greetings, Weaponmaster Bard."

Lone smiled at the older man. "It's good to see you as well, Shenraafi. I'm sorry we didn't have a chance to talk in Acrus. Hello, Teiris. How are you feeling?"

Teiris waved away the question and took a deep bite of the red fruit in her hand. "I was about to lie down for a bit before whatever dinner the avaryll have planned for us. I must admit, I have low expectations based on their design aesthetic."

"I won't keep you too long, then," said Lone. "I realized all the leaders of Poas will again be in one place. I'd like to make another attempt at the interrupted summit of nations, especially after the protectorate's thinly veiled threat to me."

"Threat?" Teiris asked around her fruit.

Lone told them how Alaraic intended to sit over the whole of Poas once the world tree came into bloom.

Shenraafi's snicker grew into a booming laugh. He wiped at his eyes. "I'd like to see them try. Even if I ordered my people to follow the avaryll, every citizen down to the seven-year-old stable hand would fight to the death before they submitted to an outside power."

"Their mastery of magic seems formidable," said Lone.

"And they sit atop the world tree," said Teiris. "I don't know how the avaryll actually use their magic, like a svarters, like an archmage, or some other option, but living and breeding on a nexus of power will automatically enhance them."

"Right," said Lone. "I'd like to speak with the other nations to ensure we're all on the same foot about the avaryll. We can include them in future meetings, but I'd like to finish the one interrupted last month."

"And the isles are out, I hear?" Shenraafi's sun-bleached eyes fixed on Bard.

"Due to the inhumane practices of the islands," said Bard, "Dracon no longer recognizes the Western Isles as a sovereign nation."

Shenraafi hummed thoughtfully. "I suppose it's no difference to me. They couldn't be farther away geographically. In all my travels, I've only met a few from there, and you, Bard, are the only one I've liked."

"Good riddance," said Teiris. "I think we were all expecting threats here in Isolis. After kidnapping Jazelyn and her husband and that entrance they made in Arcus, with that show of force, we would have an uphill battle integrating the avaryll into the rest of Poas. Integrating them or adjusting to their presence. But if you'll excuse me, I marched ten miles with my army today before getting emotionally draining information dumped on me. I'm going to retire until dinner."

"Pleasant sleep," said Shenraafi, and the three men bowed. One of the Tersguard broke from her station to follow her queen up the stairs and into the room close to Lone's.

Three women wrapped in traditional tan garments of Evkasa came down the steps. Lone and Shenraafi watched as the representatives of Sultana Bayram, or perhaps one was the sultana herself, approached Kiol, Daelin, and Dehset.

"Dehset Tekin," said one woman in a clear voice that pierced the room, interrupting the animated conversation. "Sultana Bayram wishes to express her disappointment that one of her citizens has accepted a military title with a foreign nation." The three women turned and left the hotel through the main doors.

Dehset's eyes bugged, his jaw dropped, and his shoulders slumped forward. Before Lone could approach his artifice general, Dehset fled his company and ran up the stairs, disappearing into his room on the upper level.

Lone watched him flee, realizing for the first time that he offered a coveted position of power in his country to a foreigner with essentially zero proven skill or moral references. Was his first official decision as regent king of Dracon to promote a child student to one of the three top positions of his government all because he destroyed a room in the castle? He made a mental note to speak with Deshet soon.

Lone turned his attention and watched the Serpent King in profile for a moment, remembering the long hours by the fire, clutching a favored stuffed toy and listening to the man's ridiculous stories that he swore were the honest truth. He always thought of Shenraafi as that odd uncle who used to be an adventurer until he one day settled down and was named king of a nation. *When did I last see him for a personal visit? I must have been fifteen or sixteen. Aunt Lilan stopped taking me because Lium was born later that year.* Shenraafi turned to him, smiling with eyes that, in the right light and were they darker, looked just like his late cousin's. *Aunt Lilan never disclosed the father of her boys...*

"I'd rather not get too far ahead on theorizing how to protect ourselves from unknown threats," said Shenraafi. "Enough of that. What news of your life? Why have I not yet seen the official notice of courtship here?" He waved a finger between Lone and Bard. "I thought that was the custom in Dracon. Or are you going more on the route of Evkasa's practices?"

Lone's back stiffened, and he could feel his eyes bulging. "I..."

"There has been significant political upheaval in Dracon this last year," said Bard in his best statesman's voice.

"That's right," said Lone. "We're waiting for things to settle down a bit."

"Well, don't wait too long," said Shenraafi. "Trust my experience. If you wait for the right moment, there will always be the next thing that makes you delay. Especially in positions like what we're in, my boy. Being a leader of men is a journey from one crisis to the next."

"Thank you," Lone said, running a hand through his hair.

Shenraafi sighed. "I'm sorry, but I need to see to my soldiers outside the city. You're welcome to join me. We can talk more on the way."

Lone's first reaction was to decline, but he had to see to his own soldiers and mages. They would want and need instruction on how to spend the next two days. He looked back at his father and general, still in huddled conversation, and wondered why Jazelyn and Isold were not in the central room along with everyone else. "Yes, I'll join you. Bard? Care to come as well?"

"Thank you, but if you don't mind, I must follow Queen Teiris's lead and lie down."

Lone closed the distance with a pang of worry. "What's wrong?"

"I..." Bard rubbed at his forehead. "Perhaps a migraine. Perhaps the glut of mana here is causing me stress."

Lone bit his lip and nodded. "Go lie down. See my father or Jazelyn if, wait, never mind. Just use your stone if you want to return to the castle." He took Bard's left hand and ran a thumb over the wide silver band on the islander's forefinger.

"Assuming I don't nullify the power after wearing it this long," said Bard with a quick smirk.

Lone ran his hand up Bard's arm to rest on his cheek before leaning for a kiss and to press his forehead against the other man's. "Go rest. I'll be back before dinner."

Bard returned the kiss before leaving for the stairs on the far side of the room.

As he watched Bard's graceful gait, anxiety crept into Lone's mind like a growing mold. Nothing bothered the weaponmaster's constitution, but now a slight increase in mana saturation did?

"I miss young love," Shenraafi sighed. "Come, let's keep your promise. See to the troops and get you back to your man."

Lieutenant Dreyma and two guards from Barbarles fell in step behind the kings as they left the hotel.

25

To counter the quality of baked goods, jams and jellies get worse. There's a sweet spot right in the center.

Now that the idea had wormed its way into his brain, Lone could not help but see more of his cousins as he watched King Shenraafi walking beside him. His hair and beard were more salt than pepper, but Lone could imagine how dark it and his eyes were when Shenraafi was the feared Crowned Pirate before they both faded in sun and salt spray. His prominent cheekbones were just like Lium's. Something about the shape of his eyebrows and nose was the same as the twins, Eylas and Gael.

Was he at Lium's pyre? Lone could not remember either way, but that day had been a flurry of emotion. King Garriet from Eplear had been there, so surely the king of Barbarles, Dracon's strongest ally, had also been present.

"Seeing you with Bard reminds me of when Rosalia and I first met," Shenraafi was saying. Lone shook from his inner reverie. "We couldn't keep our hands off each other until my seventh daughter was born."

Lone tried to remember the names and order of the princesses and princes of the Barbarles court. "But don't you have four sons older than Elnora and two of each younger?"

"With another on the way!" Shenraafi clapped Lone on the back.

"Congratulations," Lone said with a quiet sigh, thrilled that his memory came through.

"Rosalia says she's done after this, but she said that after having Fulke. Four months later, she's telling me she wants another."

Is this when I ask if my cousins are his bastards?

"What of the archmage king?" said Shenraafi. "Yes, I know, you're the regent king, holding the title for the twins, and don't need your own heirs, but what are your plans for children?"

Lone stumbled forward on a loose pebble. "I have no plans for children. You might guess that Bard and I will have a harder time conceiving."

Shenraafi laughed and again slapped Lone on the back, sending him forward a step this time. "There are always options. Your aunt, Elphame hold her near, wanted children but not a husband. She made it work. If you and Bard wanted one or six, there are ways."

"Hmm, yes, about my cousins. I wish I knew who their father was. Or fathers. Now that Aunt Lilan is gone, I wonder what sort of contract she had with those men and if they would be interested in being a part of their sons' lives."

"I wish you good luck in that endeavor, Lone, but I doubt you will learn anything. The matter of royal concubines has always been a closely guarded and secure process, akin to a business transaction, really."

"Is that so? It sounds like you know a lot about this."

Shenraafi stroked his beard while they walked. "I admit they have approached me. That's how they operate, like some secret society of matchmakers lurking in the courts around Poas. I obviously do not need more heirs of my own."

Lone worried about pressing too directly, so he diverted the topic again. "It might have to be Bard's child or children since archmages have difficulty procreating. To my discomfort, General Jazelyn commented recently about my father's virility to have two children." Lone watched the other man for a twitch or some little tell but noticed nothing.

"I'm sure, yours or Bard's, you'll love her just the same. Castle Dracon could do with some more children living there. They would return life to those dusty corridors."

"There is the concern of them not being archmages."

"Yes, Lilan spoke to me often about that," said Shenraafi with a long sigh. "I don't envy you that. I couldn't stand the thought of outliving my children by centuries."

They crossed the bridge out of Tidecrest. The Serpent King excused himself to see to his people, leaving Lone and Lieutenant Dreyma to approach the few tents flying the light blue flag of Dracon. Mage Varon, wearing his finest yet still rumpled robes, led the other half dozen archmages to meet their king.

"Regent King, what news of the city?" Mage Varon's voice was a strained whisper. Every time he heard the ancient man speak, Lone wondered how anyone could hear him in the back of the lecture halls at the Academy.

Lone looked over his fellow archmages. He had called the six dozen of his kind across Poas, but only these cared to attend. Even so, Hawk Stouthelm and Angaret looked bored and annoyed, having to abandon their card game to see what their king wanted. The three soldiers they played against stood at attention around the cards on a low table. Blessed Aubreda and Brarlyh Eldn stood together, but their glassy stares and wavering stance made Lone sure they were sharing flasks of something strong. Rusl, master of illusory magics, sulked apart from the others with arms crossed and his dark hood shrouding his face.

"The avaryll have promised lodgings within the city for any that care to stay within," said Lone. "We have less than two days until Ersha rises, and I would like to spend that time wisely."

"What've you got in mind?" Hawk Stouthelm asked and pushed his round glasses up the bridge of his nose. Though weak of limb, his masterpieces of brush and chisel graced the Grand Hall in Castle Dracon.

Lone rubbed at his cheek while collecting his thoughts. "The avaryll have existed in our backyards, unknown, for all human history in Poas. I'd like to know how. Learn their history. I've had it confirmed they are ancestors of the svarters, so how do they use magic? Like the svarters or like human mages? What are their strengths and weaknesses as a species and a society?"

"I'm not much of an investigator." Angaret tossed thick, blond curls over his shoulder with a flick of his wrist.

"Well," said Lone, "find what you can. It's an enormous city. Aubreda and Eldn, I've been told there is at least one tavern. Maybe the avaryll are willing to share a story over a pint."

The bleary-eyed archmages looked up with a grin.

"Varon, search out a library, of course. Stouthelm, work with General Jazelyn to draw a detailed city map. Rusl, search out for focuses of power. Protective and illusion runecraft, that sort of thing."

"What should I do?" asked Angaret.

Lone considered the young-looking man with a perfectly symmetrical face. After a few hundred years, Angaret developed the magics to reshape his body, usually to the current standard of beauty, but the process took months. The regent king tried not to frown at the six archmages that came at his call. Two drunks, a brooding spy, an ancient scholar, a frail artist, and a vain shapeshifter. They would be worthless in a fight.

"You're good at reading people, Angaret," Lone guessed. "Go with Aubreda and Eldn."

Angaret grinned and shook back his curls. "Of course, my king."

Lone dismissed himself from the archmages to move with Lieutenant Dreyma toward a group of royal guards and crystal mages sharpening swords. Another two dozen practiced a spear kata beyond.

"Attention!" Dreyma barked. Those seated shot to their feet, and the kata paused mid-thrust for the soldiers to snap to a ready stance, standing tall with their shoulders rolled back. Lone wanted to clap but forced his approval to manifest as a slow nod. He rarely found reason to see the guard before Bard came to train them, so he had little comparison for how the islander had transformed their training.

Lone cleared his throat. "Thank you. I won't take too much of your time. The avaryll have invited us to station within their city, but first impressions leave me hesitant. I intend to learn more about their motivations and may reassess that decision this evening. Carry on here, and we will adjust as needed." He tapped his chest twice in salute, and the lines of soldiers before him repeated the gesture.

He looked back to the spindly towers dappled by the tree that shaded the entire city. Moss hung from those wide boughs, swaying gently in whatever wind it might find up there. Lone started back toward Tidecrest with Lieutenant Dreyma a few paces behind. He paused and gestured for her to walk beside him. "Lieutenant, I'm going to check on Bard, then would like some time alone to roam the city."

"No, Your Grace. Your safety is my only priority here. I can keep my distance but will not be negligent in my duty."

Lone chuckled. "I appreciate that. I really do, but we are the avaryll's guests. Surely they won't attack me."

"We know nothing of these people, Your Grace. The protectorate invited you, but that does not mean other factions do not exist within the population of this city."

"Between my magic, my sword, Dehset's mana bombs," Lone patted the cloth pouch on his hip, "and my sanctum stone, I could take care of myself and let you see to other matters, Lieutenant."

Dreyma curtly shook her head. "There is no matter of importance here except for you, Your Grace."

Lone nodded with a sigh. "Your commitment to duty is admirable, Lieutenant."

As they crossed the bridge back into the city, he wondered if Jazelyn and Kiol would have fared better against capture by the avaryll had they a protector like Dreyma. Surely, it would have ended the same way. The two were beside Etharis and Ruvaal and still overwhelmed by the avaryll's magic. If a rogue faction of avaryll within Tidecrest wanted to act against him or one of his party, there was little Lone or Lieutenant Dryema could do to stop them.

***

After a few minutes of passing through the sterile, empty streets of Tidecrest, Lone saw a small group loitering before the hotel. Bard and Kiol stood close as if they had been in conversation, making Lone wonder what they might have to discuss.

Lone slipped a hand around Bard's waist for a quick kiss. "Feeling better?" Some of the islander's color had returned, but he still looked pale and clammy.

Bard rubbed a hand across his abdomen. "Not entirely, but I cannot stay in bed here."

Lone slipped his hand into Bard's and turned to Kiol. "The archmages are going to do their things to find out what they can across the city."

Kiol smiled wide. "Great to hear! I'm sure they'll do an amazing job."

His smile lingered, and Lone rolled his eyes. "I'm just glad any of them came at my call."

Kiol snapped his smile into a frown. "Each archmage swore fealty to the crown of Dracon before we taught them Cazlandt's cultivation technique. We granted them immortality in exchange for aiding an underpopulated, frozen nation. That all but a few drunks and loners ignored their king's call is shameful. Did you see that Siraas vass Soss is here but came with the svarters?"

Lone had not noticed the famed healer archmage but had not yet fully seen the Terswood contingent. "Maybe she's here to monitor my father after his treatment."

"She could place a simulacrum with each nation here, but she's only with Terswood. Read into that as you like."

She wants to watch my father and has no interest in what else happens here.

Lone took a deep breath and dismissed that conversation. "Where's Jazelyn?"

"She is resting," Kiol said slowly, unsure of his words. "She's planning to scry and aetherwalk all evening after the dinner, so she's rallying her strength. Her words."

Lone grunted thoughtfully. "It's not like her to rest. Ever."

"Between us and the wall, I think she's feeling the same upset of humors as Bard. Something about the quantity or quality of mana this close to the tree is slowing her down. She's just far more sensitive than you or I. She told me to go on with you and leave Isold to tend to her."

"You think she'll be fine?"

"Of course," Kiol scoffed. "She wouldn't send me away if she thought there was a real danger."

Lone started to laugh but stopped himself. He witnessed enough of the relationship between the two archmages to know they had complete honesty and confidence with each other. "Prashek said she'd show us around the city tomorrow, so does that mean we're free to roam until this dinner with the protectorate?"

Kiol pointed down the street north toward the mountains. "That way."

"What's that way?" Lone glanced down the empty street in both directions.

Kiol flung his arms up in a shrug.

"Solid case, general." Lone waved to Bard. "Let's see what's this way."

Spear in hand, Lieutenant Dreyma fell in behind the three men as they wandered randomly into the foreign city.

26

A few other natives of the Western Isles perished of Red Bloom, but few with the resources to drag out the disease like Master Naiti did.

B ard's fingers pressed at the soft linen at his left shoulder.

"Maybe we should ask Etharis to look at that," Lone said.

Bard dropped his hand. "You forget the archdruid's place. He describes himself as the first being across all realms, the immortal guardian of all creation. Not someone to treat a simple stab wound."

"It's hard to reconcile that with the eccentric tea lover. I've talked with Jazelyn a few times on a similar topic, on how to handle longevity and..." His mind revisited the conversation with his father and the general over breakfast pastries not long ago. His hand clenched to a fist.

"Wow," Kiol hummed. "Au really is eloquent."

Lone cringed, not realizing he and Bard had slipped into the island language. "Sorry, Kiol. You speak Au?"

"Just the basics. Hello, thank you. Where's the privy? I've been practicing the translation spells for it, eavesdropping on you two when I can. Purely for scholastic advancement, of course."

"We can speak in Common."

Kiol flashed a smile and dismissed the offer with a wave. "I could use the practice. It's impressive that you picked that up in under a year. Lyn relied on magic for understanding for over five years when she lived on the islands. You speak three languages, are handy with artifice, spell-breaking, and swordplay, have a solid understanding of magic theory, and can creatively come up with something new as needed. You are a true jack of all trades, Lone."

He shrugged. "Only because I haven't focused on anything yet."

"Eh, you're thirty. Don't rush it. Did your aunt ever tell you the rumors about Siraas? That the first few diseases she cured were ones she created?"

"Siraas vass Soss? The archmage healer that just saved my father's life? No way."

"No, some other random person named Siraas. Yes, of course her. They're just rumors, but it shows what a person will do to make a name for themselves and prove to the world what they're good at. I mean, it was never confirmed, but... Whoops, dead end."

Lone looked up at the alabaster towers that closed around them without an exit. "You know how to get back, right?"

Kiol scoffed. "Are you doubting my sense of direction? We just... Oh."

They turned to see a single, hulking avaryll standing in the alley leading from the inlet, blocking their only path. His brown and white calf-length robes fluttered in the slight breeze, as did the golden power from his tattoos. Bard stepped forward, but Lone held him back with an arm across his chest. "Tanathil."

The avaryll pulled off his mask and nodded, speaking in his heavily accented Svarters. "Regent King, I hope you might have a moment."

"You know this guy?" Kiol hissed.

Tanathil raised his left hand to his chest. "Tanathil Neridove, representative of the Einingu."

"He visited me a few weeks ago with a warning about the protectorate. A warning that seems perfectly valid now." Lone looked beyond the avaryll to Lieutenant Dreyma creeping near with her spear ready. "It's safe enough, Lieutenant. Please, join us."

"He *visited* you?" Kiol asked with eyebrows raised. "Where?"

"While Bard was still recovering. Tanathil teleported into our antechamber to deliver a warning."

Dreyma kept her spear ready as Tanathil stepped aside for her to pass. He showed no sign of surprise, clear that he knew she had been within striking distance of his back.

Kiol reached up to put a hand on Lone's shoulder, gripping it tight. "Lone, you need to get better at being someone of importance. The three of us take the responsibility for your safety seriously. You can't work against us just because a tall decanter of Evkasa winter wine with a body chiseled by Dhumjir himself comes to your bedchambers one night. Bard, I'm guessing by your face, this is news to you, too?"

Bard nodded slowly, his jaw tight.

Lone saw the hurt in the islander's pale blue eyes. "I'm sorry. I should have gotten someone immediately but wouldn't leave Bard with a stranger. I was dealing with so many little details and working with Jazelyn on the portal, and then Master Arvil..." He closed his eyes and took a deep breath.

"I might not know what you should have done differently at the moment," said Kiol, "but we shouldn't be hearing about this for the first time weeks later."

"I am sorry. I'll do better."

Despite everything else about the situation, Lone looked across the three others and could not stop wondering what odds they may have against an avaryll such as Tanathil. Lone had felt the man's suppressive mana aura, hinting at a wildly powerful control with magic and those arms... Even if he was worthless with a weapon, he could surely do a lot of damage with a solid punch. "Apologies, Tanathil. You would like to talk? I'm feeling vulnerable with our backs literally to a wall."

Tanathil raised the mask to his face and gestured to a side of the dead end. Lone squinted to make out the fine lines of a door set in the smooth stone. "Please, let's take this conversation off the streets."

"Your Grace..." Dreyma warned.

"If he meant us harm, we would be dead already," Kiol said and nodded his chin to the five shadows on balconies around the alley. The other avaryll wore masks like Tanathil's.

As they followed Tanathil to the disguised door, Lone tried to grant the avaryll some measure of trust. Clearly, they meant no physical harm to the four, but Lone wondered what political game he may be walking into.

***

Lone expected to be led down twisting corridors to the den of some secret cabal deep in the underbelly of Tidecrest. Instead, he felt a mix of disappointment and relief upon entering a rather plain square room with high walls lit by oil lamps. A dozen doors lined the floor level, with another six at the top of sets of stairs cut into the stone. The other masked avaryll, each with long hair the color and luster of precious gems, descended those steps to join Tanathil and the group from Dracon at a high, round table in the center of the room. Lone held back a smirk when he saw Kiol staying back with Dreyma. The tall table only came to the short spellslinger's shoulder.

"I would imagine," Lone began, "that a faction opposing the protectorate would have difficulty existing under his nose. I barely know the man, but he seems confident in what he feels is his birthright. As enormous as Tidecrest is, we're a stone's throw from the Symposium right now. Is it safe here?"

Tanathil removed his mask and set it on the table before him. The other gathered avaryll kept theirs on. "You needn't worry yourself with our hardships."

"Well, you have my ear."

Tanathil touched his white, neatly trimmed beard. "As I told you before, but for the benefit of the others—"

"Apologies," Lone stopped Tanathil with a raised hand. "Lieutenant Dreyma only knows a bit of Svarters and Weaponmaster Bard even less. Can you speak the human language?"

"Regretfully, no. Human languages are only taught to a few and are tightly controlled. I was never in a position to learn."

"Well, this is a hassle," Kiol grumbled and turned to Dreyma. He asked her consent before touching two glowing fingers to her forehead and repeating it all with Bard. "It won't last that long on him."

Tanathil cleared his throat. "The protectorate is stripping away those around him, removing others from positions of power and replacing them with those most vocally supportive of him."

"That sounds like the behavior of someone preparing for something big," Lone said.

"Who normally advises the protectorate?" Kiol asked. "And on what matters does he need advisement in an isolated city?"

"There are still the matters of internal security, city planning, distribution of resources, and so forth. For matters directly regarding Endanlegsil, the throne has followed the instruction of three outsiders."

Lone considered the last word for a moment, wondering if he mistranslated it. "Outsiders? But no one has known of your presence. Who are they?"

"We know them only by title. The Gilded Warrior, the World Tender, and the Chronicler."

Lone gripped the table's edge as his knees threatened to give out.

Tanathil narrowed his pale gaze. "You've heard of them."

Lone shook his head and took a deep breath. He hoped to see the first at dinner, and his heart ached at hearing the mention of the last one. He could not guess who the World Tender might be, but everyone seemed to love their titles. "I've heard of two but don't know exactly what their titles mean. This is your story to tell. The world tree will be vital in the protectorate's plans or, for the rest of us, our defense. Tell me more about these three that know so much about it."

Tanathil drummed his fingers on the table before continuing with a quick nod. "The three have skipped through avaryll history, guiding our path. I have met none of them that I know."

"Can you describe them?" Lone asked.

Tanathil's eyes glazed as they lost focus for a moment. "The Gilded Warrior wears golden armor and wields a hammer of purest light. The World Tender can change his body into the elements, becoming the incarnation of fire or wind. The Chronicler will look at you with silver eyes that bore into your soul and sear away all but your simplest truths."

Lone blinked at the intense descriptions. From his few interactions with Aiden, the messy-haired immortal seemed like a goof with a fixation on snack foods, not a being worthy of all that. That was also certainly not about his sister, either. Sweet, quiet Alishia who loved to tease Lone about his slight issue with focusing on a task. No, surely not. *Boring into peoples' souls?*

"We'll keep an eye out for them," said Kiol. The general knew Alishia was the Chronicler, but Lone only shared with Teiris and Bard about Aiden going by the Gilded Warrior.

Lone's eyes paused on his short friend for a moment, regretting not telling him everything. As a ruler of a nation, as much as he loathed it, Lone knew keeping secrets was a part of the game—secrets to manipulate those in other countries or within the court. Here, Lone just forgot to share what he knew, unintentionally holding onto critically important details. He hated the deception of politics but knew he had to play by the same rules as everyone else.

Tanathil tapped his mask. "I have practiced my words, but looking at you now, I'm unsure how much more must be said. As I told you when we met, should it become necessary, we would join the camps outside the city to fight for your freedom. The protectorate will not sit in dominion over the realm."

Lone glanced over the five masked avaryll around the table, each with golden markings like Tanathil's, though with unique elements to the swirls of glowing ink. He settled his gaze back on the leader. "How many members does the Einingu have?"

"Only a few dozen possess conviction enough to wear the mask."

"I... wow, so few. Has the protectorate hunted you?"

"It's not that. The avaryll as a people have spent so long obscured by our magics that we have grown lethargic and apathetic. It is easier to follow the arbitrary laws of a leader than to question him and his right to rule. The Einingu formed three moons ago upon witnessing the genocide among your people. We petitioned the protectorate then to allow us to intervene and were denied."

"Three moons, twelve hundred years. Do you mean the Hallowed Campaign? That shaped the role of mages in our world. My great-grandsire founded Dracon as a refuge from it."

"I know you mean well, Regent King, but a lesson in history from you is not required."

Lone felt the heat on his cheeks. "Sorry."

"The protectorate then denied us the opportunity to stop that atrocity, but it was hardly the first time we, the avaryll, looked the other way from the rest of Poas. Even before the days of Protectorate Gundil, when the Seed of Farsil came to my people, the avaryll began to close off from the rest of Poas. The settlements far to the north and west drifted apart, and we collapsed to Tidecrest."

The image of a frozen, mummified couple in bed flashed in Lone's mind. How many avaryll lay under the hoarfrost far north of Dracon? A younger part of his mind, a part that rarely had a voice lately, thrilled at the prospect of exploring ancient subterranean avaryll cities deep in the world.

"How did you get the Seed?" Kiol asked. "Maybe we could get another and grow our own world tree. The protectorate can keep this one."

A smile flicked across Tanathil's thin lips. "I can show you a mural of the story. It is one of the few pieces of art from that era that remains and passed into the Einingu's protection when we were founded. Come, it's less than twenty minutes from here."

***

The other masked Einingu dispersed through the doors around the room without a word, and Lone followed Tanathil through the last. Kiol stayed a few steps behind, followed by Bard and Dreyma in the rear. After a few of the twisting, downward-sloping corridors and steps that Lone expected earlier, they passed through a series of dark chambers lit by murky sunlight filtering through slits in the ceiling. The walls showed signs of an earlier architecture, of rougher stone blocks fitted together smoothly without mortar.

The group was silent, save for the clink of Dreyma's armor and their heavy bootfalls.

Kiol pushed past Lone. "Talk to your man."

Lone flinched at the general's words, and his pace slowed until the weapon-master strode beside him.

"Not now, Lone," Bard said in Common while focusing his eyes straight ahead.

Lone had heard that tone from the islander before but never directed at him. "Just let me explain or apologize or something," he said in Au.

"'Or something?'" Bard still spoke in Common. "What is worst for you, that you think I'm upset or that you think you made me upset?"

Lone floundered, considering the differences and implications of Bard's question. "I mean, I know both are true."

"Do you understand why I'm upset?"

"I didn't tell you about Tanathil. I should have woken you immediately, but it all felt surreal. You were sound asleep and, don't forget, severely injured. I was up early to test the portal, and then Master Arvil and my arm—" Lone tripped forward and grabbed his right forearm. *How did I completely forget about that?*

"What about your arm?"

Lone pulled up the sleeve to see a hint of the softly glowing ink on his wrist. "My tattoos were blazing with power. It hurt so much, but I got back in bed, hoping to ignore it and go back to sleep beside you. You touched me, and all the pain went away."

Bard inhaled deeply and let it out in an inaudible sigh. "That has not happened before or since?"

"No."

Bard ran a hand through his silvered hair and finally switched to speaking Au. "I didn't understand all of Tanathil's words, but there was something about the Chronicler stripping away all but your barest truths. What is your truth, Lone?"

"I'm forgetful. I recall names and events well enough but don't remember to share information with those who need to know it. I'm impatient and impulsive."

Bard twirled his finger for Lone to continue.

"Jazelyn told me I should delegate tasks more often and ask for help from those around me. That's the hallmark of a good ruler."

"Close. General Kiol called you a jack of all trades. Not because you lack focus but because you want to do it all yourself. You choose to take on every burden personally. Designing the portal that got us here, searching for the Shadow Reaver, investigating your aunt. It might be selfish, or it might be protective. Neither are strictly good or bad qualities, and it's yours to decide where that balance lays."

"So..." Lone touched Bard's arm. "You're not mad at me?"

"I am a bit. We can work it out tonight. I think we've arrived."

Tanathil stopped in the middle of a small circular room and turned to face them. Light filtered down along the walls, and after walking through dim passages, it was enough for Lone to make out a faint relief around the room.

"This room is from the original construction of Tidecrest," Tanathil explained. "In fact, the stone of this chamber was laid perhaps ten millennia ago, though the relief is half that. Few chambers such as this remain under the city. The story begins here." He pointed to a panel beside the door they had entered through. A massive tree stood with flame licking from its highest boughs. Some hints of brown paint still clung to the stone, but otherwise, only the whites and lighter tones remained. "The burning of Tersil is always the first event in the history of Poas. We know almost nothing from before then, including how and why Ters created the svarters from my people."

Moving to the right, the next panel showed a figure laid to rest and covered with a shroud. Judging by their heights and long-tipped ears, two avaryll and a svarters stood behind her, heads bowed in mourning. "Without her tree, Ters withered. Upon her death, the svarters absconded with her body, with the help of Archdruid Etharis, and the Mists rose to cover Poas."

Lone looked at the panel again and wondered if what he assumed were avaryll were actually two Mraasil. He glanced around and counted six panels as they moved to the third, a nebulous cloud with little detail.

"The Mists," said Tanathil. "A dark age for Poas that lasted a dozen genera-tions. Travel to Terswood became near-impossible with the terrible creatures that roamed the world. Populations shrank as food became scarce. But then..."

He moved to the next panel. An avaryll with flowing hair held something over his head, with two others standing before him. Gold paint still clung to the person's armor on the left and around lines of radiance from the held object.

"The World Tender and Gilded Warrior gifted the Seed of Farsil to Protectorate Gundil. Many have wondered how they came upon the Seed and why they gave it up, but these are not questions we may ever answer."

The next panel showed an avaryll kneeling before a mound of dirt with a sapling growing from it, and the last was one sitting on a throne before an immense tree in the background.

"What happened to the Mist?" Kiol asked. "It's not in human history."

"Though we can't know for sure, the accepted answer is Endanlegsil burned it away in her infancy. She pulled strength from the old roots of Tersil, and one day, it was gone. It was then that the avaryll first detected humans to the west and on the southern continent."

Lone returned to the panel of Protectorate Gundil holding aloft the Seed of Farsil. The seed hovered in the space between the protectorate's upheld hands. His eyes lingered on the figure to the left, the Gilded Warrior. Messy-haired, jerky-eating Aiden. At the second panel with Ters in repose, he wondered if the darker paints had faded a few thousand years ago, if the two taller ones were Etharis and Ruvaal and the short one the Chronicler, Alishia. Once his mind produced that idea, he had no doubt of it.

My little sister, immortalized in stone five thousand years ago for something that happened just as long before that.

Lone felt suddenly cramped and claustrophobic. He tugged at his collar to blow air down his shirt.

"We should get back," he said. "I'd like to play along with Alaraic's game for the moment, which means putting on a pleasant face at his dinner."

"Fair idea." Tanathil nodded his approval. "The protectorate will offer hospitality, but I recommend against stationing your troops within the city; keep them on the fields to the south. Alaraic holds enough control of Tidecrest that you will be hard-pressed to keep yourselves safe from his will, much less hundreds of others with far less magical inclination."

"Thank you, Tanathil Neridove." Lone tapped his chest in salute. "I wish we could stay longer."

"With luck, we will see much more of each other in the future." The avaryll smiled an easy, asymmetrical grin that Lone could not help but return.

Lone faced the center of the room, held out his hand, and closed his eyes. The others' hands piled onto his as he traced back across Tidecrest, searching for the mana beacon he had left in his and Bard's room in the hotel. Despite the glaring energy pulsing from the young world tree, the beacon's pull was clear. Lone pulled in more ley energy than he needed to compensate for Bard's added requirement, and with a pop and tugging sensation, the four stood exactly where he intended between the two awkwardly long and narrow beds.

"That took a lot longer than planned," said Kiol. "We'll have to rush to get ready for dinner. But on the bright side," he tapped the bracer on his wrist, "I recorded that entire conversation and our path through the tunnels."

Lone had not thought to do anything like that and nodded his admiration for his friend. "Smart, very smart. That's the bracer Miech made you?"

"Yes. Now, if you'll excuse me," Kiol cleared his throat and locked wide eyes on Lone. "I'm going to share this with my wife immediately because she will value knowing what we did and learned." He turned to leave.

Dreyma followed him and turned with a salute before reaching the door. "I will check on the others and wait for you downstairs, Your Grace." She bowed and left.

The door closed with a click, and Lone became instantly aware of the silence in the room.

After only a few breaths, he could take it no longer. "Are we good?"

Bard sat on the long, thin bed, and Lone wondered how Tanathil, with shoulders so wide, might fit in such a thing.

"Yes, *menf*," said Bard, pulling Lone from his thoughts of the avaryll all being side sleepers. "We are both now aware of your recurring behavior and have been vocal about it. We can work together to correct the habit."

Lone heard an unspoken "or else" after that. Realizing and admitting a destructive behavior was always the first step to eradicating it. Bard taught that in his martial classes as he highlighted the little extra movements in a stance or sword stroke that became a tell to your opponent if not done intentionally.

Lone wrapped a hand to the back of Bard's neck and bent to kiss him. "Thank you. Now, we should get changed into our nice things for dinner."

Bard frowned down at his pale blue linen shirt and dark trousers. "I am wearing my nice things."

Lone bit back his smile. Being forgetful had paid off for once; he was usually never able to delay giving a present. He picked up the satchel on the other bed and set it beside Bard. After his father returned from treatment, Lone asked him to create the bag as a near duplicate of what he had made for Teiris years ago, a bag much larger than the outside measurements implied. Lone reached deep into the small bag and started pulling out pieces of the new armor he had crafted and tailored for Bard. "I can't wait to see you in this," he nearly giggled with excitement as his fingers sank into the cloak's thick fur.

27

It would go against my self-imposed rules of non-interference, but I really want to swap a few bread and jam makers from the far ends of the chain.

Lone adjusted his leather bracer and straightened his icy crown in the silvered mirror. He smiled to himself at the perfect fit of his new armor. A chainmail shirt separated blue quilted cloth from a hard leather cuirass and segmented steel shoulder plates. He carefully pinned the ruby and silver brooch to the baldric and counted the six mana bombs in pouches at his hip before taking his sword belt from where it lay on the bed. Though not one of the rare featherr'ock steel pieces, the short sword would hold up well in a fight. Lone tightened the belt as the bathroom door opened.

A coat of white dire bear fur with a high collar and silver buttons swept past Bard's knees. He wore it open to show his leather armor underneath, also crafted of dire bear and belted with snow shark hide—two of the most powerful and iconic beasts of the north in one stunning armor set. The hilt of Bard's great swords poked over his shoulder, and he rested a palm on the longsword at his hip. He shifted uneasily under the new armor.

Lone was warm enough in his attire but knew he would sweat profusely in Bard's heavy gear. Luckily, the islander rarely noticed heat or cold.

"I'm not used to wearing this much," said Bard. "I worry it would encumber me in a fight." He stepped beside Lone by the mirror.

"We're not here for a fight." Lone admired their reflections for a moment. "You won't have to wear it too long. We'll have dinner with the protectorate and hear more about how he plans to take over the realm. You can come back and strip all that off. Though, as much as I enjoy seeing you in what little you usually wear, I think this suits you perfectly."

Bard pivoted in front of the mirror, viewing himself in profile.

Two sharp raps at the door. "It's time, Your Grace," came Kiol's muffled voice.

Lone felt the burn of gazes upon him as he and Bard descended the steps to the hotel's main level. In addition to his father, Teiris, Shenraafi, and Queen Rosalia, almost every leader of Poas stood within thirty feet of each other. The Bismats and Sultana Bayram with her handmaidens. Even Aiden, in the guise of the Archetype, dressed in starched white and gold. A single, sufficiently powerful fireball spell could rewrite the dynamics of power for the realm. Only King Garriet of Eplear would remain to rule. Lone shook off the grim thoughts.

"You took my advice," said Daelin as Lone stepped off the stairs. "This is an excellent look for you."

Lone's brow pinched with confusion for a moment as he remembered what his father was talking about. After having his own green and cream armor tailored, Daelin suggested Lone create a signature look for himself. Apparently, he thought this was it. "Thank you. It's my first time wearing this all at once. I love all the pouches."

Daelin grunted with a nod. "Pouches are useful."

"Good evening, everyone," called a voice by the entrance, and Lone turned to Seventh Celestial Mage Prashek, standing with a guard to either side of her. "Protectorate Alaraic has granted me the honor of escorting you, our most esteemed guests, to the dining hall adjacent to the Symposium. We have prepared a meal of local delicacies while respecting the dietary restrictions of those in attendance. As I have communicated to each of your parties, we are limited to two from each nation to dine with the protectorate. Rest assured, equally delightful dishes will be provided for everyone here."

Lone glanced at the sandy-cloaked figures from Evkasa and wondered if the true sultana would be in attendance. He left his father's side, and Bard followed close behind as they cut through the gathering, aiming for Aiden and the hulking, cowled priest at his side.

Shenraafi took his queen's hand as the group filed after Prashek.

Once they left the hotel, Lone pulled Bard to catch up with Aiden. "Find any good seeds lately?" Lone whispered. He nodded to the huge priest. "Greetings, Dalbinth."

The cloaked kalvyr inclined his head in response.

"Had some history lessons, have you?" Aiden responded, speaking in hushed Au.

"An interesting lesson, yes. You brought the Seed to the avaryll. I keep realizing you're more than I had imagined. What's going on here, Aiden?"

"I feel I should take that as a compliment." Aiden grinned and waved his wrist at Lone. "What's going on is that you are about to have some of the blandest food in your life. I hope you have some spices or a sauce hidden in one of those many pouches."

"Would you *please* give me a straight answer? What are we walking into here?"

Aiden slowed their pace to let the Bismats gain a few paces and glanced back at Teiris and Daelin behind them, deep in their own discussion. "I seriously wish I could, Lone. I act at your sister's will, accepting that she is a force far more powerful than I, with a view far wider than mine. Since I saw the Seed delivered to these people, I have had little to do with them."

Lone considered the words, unsure if he trusted Aiden's claimed ignorance. "Who is the World Tender?"

"Scragging hells, Lone, you really have done your research." He scratched at his mess of dark hair and sighed. "You will meet him before this is over. Leave it at that. I never trusted the avaryll, but I doubt they are the big worry here. Your sister would not have taken me from my other tasks for intra-realm politics, even if it is her home realm."

The Symposium came into view, and Lone knew the dining hall must be close; his time with Aiden grew short. "What are your other tasks?"

"The same I have been doing for most of my life. I scour the realms in search of humans. Hopefully, our people will have a realm to call home again."

"*Our* people?" Lone repeated, again unsure of a mistranslation. "You aren't an archmage, so you can't be human by how old you are. You must be something greater to live so long."

"Flattery again?" Aiden grinned at Bard and lightly slapped Lone on the arm. "Whatever differences there may be between us, I am still human. We three are of one blood. You may think the population in Poas is of note, but it was nothing compared to the grand cities and cultures our people have lost to the daemon that stalked us across the realms. You may think Poas is your home, but you are the descendants of refugees. This is only the home your forebears have made it."

Lone imagined Poas without the svarters, avaryll, or whatever creatures lurked in the forests of Nyphlym or the far shores of D'Kreti. A realm just for humans sounded like a xenophobic nightmare.

They entered the dining hall before Lone could respond, and avaryll, in white jackets and matching cloth gloves, ushered him to the last seat at the long, wide table with Queen Teiris at his side. They assigned Bard to sit across from him next to Lone's father.

Plates of pale, steamed vegetables lined the center of the dining table, alternating with the seven-wick candelabras, which provided the only illumination in the room.

Teiris leaned over to whisper, "It's like your council of nations all over again, Lone, but with less religious persecution."

"The night is young."

The queen snorted and snatched a linen napkin to cover her mouth.

"Do you trust them? The avaryll?" she asked.

"That's a very common question. Have you spoken with Alaraic yet?"

"No. We were going to speak with him when we arrived, but the guards waved us to join you with Etharis."

"I'll let you form your own opinion, then. Here he comes."

The protectorate entered through a wide door behind the head of the table. Lone and the leaders stood as their host approached.

"Thank you all for attending, and I hope our missing representatives arrive safely and soon." Alaraic's deep voice rattled the flatware. "Please, be seated." Lone expected Alaraic to seat himself first, based on the avaryll's feelings of his own importance, but he waited for each of the dozen to be seated before sweeping back his blue cloak and settling himself in the ornate, high-backed chair.

The door behind Alaraic burst open, and a row of servants marched in bearing golden platters of puddings and pale mush. They ladled a loose soup into the bowl in front of Lone. The murky broth separated after only a few breaths until he stirred it to poke at the soft floating bits. He leaned close and sniffed at the soup, but it only smelled of salt. Lone glanced at Teiris as she shot him a look to show she was equally unimpressed before she lifted a spoon to sip.

Servants cleared the soup to bring out the next course.

"Honored guests," Alaraic began and rose to lean forward with palms flat on the table. "Five weeks ago, Acrus hosted a council of nations at the suggestion of Regent King Lone." He gestured down the long table, and heads turned to face Lone. "The goal, I was told, was to bring unity and strengthen alliances between the peoples of Poas. I applaud the regent king's efforts but will take this further. Unity requires more than conversation. It requires a clear hierarchy where orders may be carried out swiftly. Imagine a drought ruining the harvests in Jaiketh." He spread his arms to wave at the Bismats. "There would not be time for a council to decide what aid to send. Response must needs be immediate. A storm on the shores of Barbarles leaves hundreds homeless. The other nations should send immediate assistance."

King Shenraafi tossed his napkin over the plate of shredded leaves and brushed his hands together over it. "What've you got in mind for this *clear hierarchy*, Alaraic?"

"Poas requires a single entity to see over all others. One that may bring together our fractured parts. On the overmorrow, Tidecrest will sit on the most powerful nexus of ley energy in the realm and be home to our new realm guardian."

"That's fine and all for the mages," said Shenraafi, "but nexuses mean nothing to the rest of us."

"You don't speak for us all," said Lady Bismat. "We in Jaiketh would relish the opportunity to practice artifice in a region so steeped in magic. If the protectorate offers access to the ley nexus and greater security and communication, we would listen. Pray know that Dracon has hoarded the wealth of magic long enough. It's only fair it's time to share." She smirked and shrugged at Lone. His fists clenched under the table. All of Jaiketh's treaties with Dracon had been negotiated by his grandsire, all well over a hundred years ago. Lone knew Jaiketh disliked Dracon, but to his knowledge, they never reached out to smooth over relations.

"We have all we need in Terswood," Teiris said as she covered her plate with a napkin. "The svarters have lived in quiet harmony for countless generations. If accepting the power from the new tree means bending the knee to you, Protectorate, I decline in the name of my people. We will return to our forests and let the rest of Poas go on without us."

"What if another invasion of daemon and undead invades your city?" Alaraic spread his arms, palms up. "It took the might of Mraasil and northern mages to fight them off last time."

"Yes, the attack came from without, brought on by northern mages." She turned to Lone and patted his fist. "Elphame hold your aunt near."

Alaraic stood a little taller and rolled his shoulders back. "Does anyone else wish to deny the wisdom and unity I offer?"

Shenraafi scoffed and shoved back from the table. "I do in the name of Barbarles. My people will never bow to strangers." He stood and gestured across the table to his queen. "Come, dear. We're done here."

Lone slapped his hands on the table to repeat Shenraafi's declaration, but the protectorate's booming response froze him in place.

"Insolence. Get out of my city," he growled. "Flee back to your ports of putrid fish and rotten whores."

The candles flared high for a breath before nearly extinguishing. Lone blinked away the sudden brilliance. He saw Alaraic seated again, looking paler, with a sheen of sweat on his brow visible even at a distance. The Gilded Warrior stood near him.

"I think you mean to say, Protectorate," Aiden said in his easy drawl, "is that everyone is welcome to attend the birth of our Mraasil, and they are welcome to enjoy the facilities of your grand city until then."

Alaraic stood, and Lone could feel the glamor the protectorate cast to restore a hint of color to his cheeks. "Of course, Archetype. I promised hospitality within Tidecrest until the birth of the Mraasil. An avaryll, and certainly the protectorate, keeps their word." He stood before the silent group for a moment before swiftly turning to leave through the door he entered through.

"Well, he's a bit of a hothead," Teiris chuckled when the protectorate's cobalt hair disappeared behind a slammed door.

Shenraafi slipped his hand around his wife's waist as she stepped beside him. "Barbarles and Terswood are a hard no, then. Jaiketh is a yes. What about you, Archetype? Will Acrus join what Alaraic is offering?"

Aiden smoothed his thick robes. "The official stance of Acrus is to reject the use of magic, so we will decline."

"Sultana?" Shenraafi asked with eyebrows raised.

The two women in bulky, sandy robes, more appropriate for a mountain-dwelling monk, looked at each other before looking back at the Serpent King. "We will consider the matter in more detail before deciding."

Chairs scraped across the stone floor as everyone pushed from the table. Bard and Daelin stepped around, as did Dalbinth on the far end. Lady Bismat joined her husband on the other side. The room naturally divided itself on the topic.

Shenraafi nodded. "And you're out too, right, Lone?"

"Of course. I want to see Poas united, not ruled over."

"Ha!" Lord Bismat scoffed. "You refuse because Dracon won't hold all the power? You can't stand that another may be allowed to rise and rival the monopoly of magic you've held so long."

"No, Lord Bismat," said Lone. "If you think Dracon is so terrible in our power hoarding, what might you expect from the avaryll? Specifically the protectorate. You see by his outburst to King Shenraafi that the protectorate will be moody and rescind an offer whenever he feels slighted. You would rather take his scraps than work together to create a world of true equity?"

"We've picked at the leavings dropped by Dracon for too long," said Lord Bismat. "You require all archmages to remain beholden to you. You hold the world's supply of mana crystal. The only magic academy of worth is on your desolate, blighted shores."

"You assume a lot, Regent King," Lady Bismat sneered. "Protectorate Alaraic described one to rule over the realm, then described the coming realm guardian. He might mean she would hold that power."

"Don't be naïve," said Teiris. "He described the ley line nexus and realm guardian as part of Tidecrest. Alaraic *is* Tidecrest. He's not just keeping that throne warm for the Mraasil."

Lord Bismat rolled his eyes and shook his head. "Why are we debating each other here? When King Garriet arrives tomorrow, I'm sure he'll side with you, but so what? It gives Jaiketh a stronger, less crowded route to the future the protectorate offers. The rest of you will come around, or you won't. It's no matter to us."

Lady Bismat slipped her hand into her husband's. "Come, my sweet. There's no need to get yourself riled up here."

"Well spoken, both of you," Daelin said with an approving grunt as the door closed behind the Bismats. The sultana and possible-servant were close behind.

Teiris heaved a deep breath. "I guess that answers the question, Lone. No, I don't trust the avaryll." She cast an eye to the discarded meal laid out behind her. "Come on, Daelin. I'm glad I packed my own food."

"Right?" said Aiden from Lone's side. "I told you the food would be terrible."

"We could always teleport home to eat," Daelin offered.

"What happens now?" asked Shenraafi. "I think it's clear we've made an enemy of Alaraic, or at least I have."

"I don't think anyone is in immediate danger," said Teiris. "Etharis and others," her gaze drifted to Aiden, "are here. I think the archdruid would be upset if blood were spilled on the eve of something so important to him."

Daelin nodded. "Were anyone to flee the city now, it would appear as an act of cowardice or aggression."

"No matter how it looks," said Shenraafi, "we're not sleeping in that hostel tonight. We will stay with the troops outside the city and see you in the morning. Pleasant sleep to you all."

They exchanged farewells, and the Serpent King left with Queen Rosalia, leaving those from Dracon, Terswood, and Acrus alone in the dining hall.

"So," Aiden started with a whistle. "I guessed by your glances that Lone told you some about me?"

"That you're an immortal light shaper that's known my daughter for years, and he's," Teiris pointed at the cloaked priest standing behind Aiden, "the dragonman from the poisoned lands across the seas that has led Acrus the last few hundred years?"

Aiden shrugged and nodded.

"There's more, Teiris," said Lone. "So much more."

28

Poas became an unofficial dumping ground for the realms' refugees: humans, kalvyr, all the strange things in Nyphlym.

Alishia let out a long breath with one hand on the door's brass handle. She had hidden in The Stacks for too long. She shared the space with Cazlandt for what felt like a decade, or perhaps one very long afternoon, but, despite her nodded promise otherwise, she had spent more time alone since he returned to his place in history.

It was time to go back.

Back to being Princess Alishia, sister, daughter, and devout follower of Enid.

She had spent so long, too long, alone tracing the lines of the small sculpture Ethan made for her while idly rolling the bracelet of wooden beads from Throk'tar.

With another deep breath, she pulled the door open and stepped onto unadorned marble.

This was not Castle Dracon, not where she should have exited the library.

A dozen pairs of eyes stared at her, wide with surprise, in the circular room dotted with groups of couches and tables.

A man wearing a navy blue, thigh-length jacket crossed with an icy baldric rushed to embrace her.

"Ali!" yelled the familiar voice as he crushed her face into his chest.

Unsure, she returned the hug as recognition slowly returned to her. "Lone?"

He pushed her away to arm's length, smiled at her, and squeezed her close again. After a heartbeat, Lone pushed her away again with a frown. "Ali, you've grown."

She quickly thought of all the long hours or days spent in other realms and the time spent in The Stacks with Cazlandt and after he left. She could not recall last seeing herself in a mirror, but she supposed she must look different. "I've been gone a while."

"Three and a half months, but the change in you is more than that. We've all been worried sick. Well, I have been worried sick. Your mother's been in contact with someone above the Ascended, telling her everything is fine."

"Meave or Minerva?"

"Ah, neither? She called herself Madllyn."

Alishia looked over at the others present. Bard, Jazelyn, Kiol, a confused-looking young man with darker skin sporting the pin of a Dracon general, a few archmages whose names she could not remember wearing flashy garb, and a handful of Dracon guards standing at attention.

"Princess Alishia," said Jazelyn. "I was the last to see you as I suggested you use your power of Sight within The Stacks. Did that pan out?"

"I remember that," said Alishia. "That felt like a lifetime ago with you and Uncle Sion in my room. I did as you said, General, but was delayed. Cazlandt attacked me and pulled me to another realm in the distant past and—"

"Cazlandt?" Lone interrupted. "But he's dead."

"I know, but it was out of time." She glanced around the room again, not recognizing the plain architecture. Stairs to either side of her lead to a second-level balcony lined with doors. "Where is this?"

Kiol cleared his throat. "We're in a hotel in the avaryll city of Tidecrest in Isolis."

She blinked. "Isolis?" She had missed much in the last few months. "And why are we here?"

Kiol answered again. "The avaryll invited the nations of Poas to watch the new world tree mature and give birth to its Mraasil tomorrow."

"Mraasil? Is Etharis here?" The image of a glowing acorn flashed through her mind, of watching the Ascended ease the newly born archdruid to the ground, of Enid so lovingly feeding him. That Seed was still safe in her desk within The Stacks beside the mementos from Throk'tar.

"He is," Lone nodded. "Along with Ruvaal and a horned one with a tail. Ali, I can't say enough how happy I am that you're back. Come on, our father and Teiris will want to see you immediately. They went to see to their troops a while ago; we could probably catch up."

Lone took her by the hand and pulled her toward the door, but she resisted. "Wait, I want to try something first." She practiced her Sight across a half dozen realms over months or maybe years since last being in Poas. Maybe much longer, but did time really matter? She remembered how it felt to first test her power here, which gave her a direct means of comparison for how her ability had matured.

She blinked, and Lone gasped.

Her vision expanded and filled with the new tree. She knew its name, En-danlegsil, and she sensed the new Mraasil's energy near her surface. Information flooded her mind as her Sight washed over the landscapes with control beyond what she thought possible when she last used her ability in Terswood. She saw Tidecrest, a gleaming city of a thousand spires, shaded in dappled shadows by the tree, surrounded by the banners of a half dozen nations. Her vision expanded across the fey wilds of Nyphlym and the odd beasts native to that region to the south. West over the jungles in Jaiketh and the sands of Evkasa. She willed her Sight to focus on the world tree, to absorb what knowledge she could from it. Her Sight dove deep under the tree to a crimson lake, but rather than focusing there, she saw a glimpse of a scene that did not belong to the present. She saw herself taking the glowing Seed from The Stacks and handing it to a faceless pair, one of which radiated sunlight. The one not glowing accepted the Seed in gloved hands.

The scene burned in her mind, and she breathed the name "Ethan."

"Ali," said a familiar and impossible voice.

Alishia ended her Sight and blinked back to the hotel. He stood right there with a messy mop of dark hair, a mischievous little smirk, and bright amethyst eyes. "Aiden." Lone caught her by the elbow as her knees almost gave out. "This can't be real."

Aiden stepped forward slowly, as one might approach a frightened animal. Alishia looked over his garb of heavily starched whites laced with spun gold, so out of place with what she always saw him wearing in Throk'tar. This had to be a dream or some illusion. Everything felt so real, from her brother's easy, familiar smile to the potent smell of Bard's aftershave.

"Lone, is this the present?" Alishia winced at hearing her question's inanity.

He looked confused and shrugged. "I'm not sure how to answer that."

"Convince me this isn't some illusion. Tell me something only we would know."

"You're sounding slightly like a crazy person, Ali. Fine, ah..." He looked down at the silver and ruby brooch on the breast of his armor, unpinned it, and handed it to Alishia. Her eyes widened with a wash of relief at seeing it.

"I thought I lost it in Throk'tar!" She cradled her brother's hand in both of hers.

"I found it in The Stacks while searching for you. When I gave this to you, I told you about when I gave it to my mother. She told me it was the most beautiful piece of jewelry on the continent. She wore it every day for the rest of her life." His voice cracked as he spoke.

If this was an illusion, it was too convincing, too cruel.

Alishia pinned the brooch on her vest and turned. "Aiden, how are you here? How long ago were we in Throk'tar?"

"Time gets a little weird between realms, but it was close to eighteen thousand years on the Poas calendar," he said in his slow drawl, and his grin widened. He was close enough now and reached to hug her. The embrace felt somehow familiar, though they had never touched for this long during the week in Throk'tar. "You and I obviously have much to catch up on, Ali." He pushed a loose strand of hair behind her long-tipped ear and brought his hand back, holding a flower made of light. She took it and bit back a grin as she felt a weight and solidity the construct lacked last time. Alishia looked across the people staring at her, thinking it was a little strange to see so many humans in one place after only being around Aiden, Ethan, and Cazlandt for months. In her travels, she had seen a dozen other sorts of people in a half dozen other realms but no others from her father's race.

All those eyes on her also triggered her years of etiquette training and made her conscious of the state of her hair. Her gaze lingered over the unknown young man with the general's pin before focusing on her brother again. "Is there a place I can freshen up before we look for my parents?"

"You look great, Ali, but of course. My room is just up this way." Lone started leading her to the stairs, but General Jazelyn stepped in front of them.

"Your room is full of men's things," she said to Lone, and as she looked down at Alishia with a gentle smile, she replaced Lone's hand on her arm with her own. "Come, child."

Alishia paused on the third step to look back down at her brother and Aiden, both smiling widely.

***

Sixteen years of a princess's life left Alishia quite experienced in being seen to by handmaidens. She expected General Jazelyn to be cold and exact in her ministration, but the ancient archmage hummed an unknown melody while brushing Alishia's hair. She sat on a small stool and looked at herself in the mirror, barely recognizing the person staring back at her, seeing what Lone meant about her looking grown. Alishia touched her cheeks, once soft and plump, now with defined cheekbones and jaw. She leaned a little closer and noticed thin lines of silver running through the dark blue of her irises.

Alishia looked down at her garb. When she left The Stacks, she had been wearing a comfortable cloth tunic, pants, and high leather boots, but now she wore a stunning midnight blue gown with a sweeping neckline and silver embroidery of a complex pattern down the left side.

"Your brother had quite the tale for us last night," said Jazelyn. "There is a mural less than an hour's walk from here showing you with Ters as she lies in repose."

A single knock rapped on the door, and it pushed in without waiting for a response. Jazelyn's assistant, Isold, entered, holding a silver platter with a carafe and three goblets.

"Good, thank you, Isold. You are free to stay with us."

"I thought to see Ters," said Alishia. "I almost did several times." She accepted a goblet from Isold and sniffed the weak wine before taking a sip. *When did I last eat or drink?*

Jazelyn paused the brushing. "I can empathize, but I cannot understand or appreciate how your life has changed, Princess. Perhaps it would be appropriate that I call you Chronicler, now?"

"No, I'm still Alishia. I've been through and seen a lot, but I'm still me." She laid a hand on Jazelyn's. "Thank you for this moment, General. The truth is, I've been gone so long, at least I think I have, that I feared coming back. The more time I spent in other realms, the more distant I felt from it all. Like reading a dull book, everyone's lives blended together. I knew their names and stories but just didn't care. The only thing that kept me sane was watching the boys."

"Boys?"

"Aiden and Ethan. I hid in the heart chamber of the world tree to watch their adventures. I imagined myself walking beside them and joining them by the campfire." She laughed and covered her face with her hands. "Praise Enid, I sound like a voyeur when I hear that out loud."

"You suddenly came into a unique power after a series of traumas, Alishia," said Jazelyn. "I offered to assist you, but truth be said, no one could give you real guidance."

"Aiden did. He told me magic is mostly about confidence and intent. That gave me a hint on how to control my Sight."

Jazelyn hummed thoughtfully. "I suppose some may say that. I certainly would not."

Alishia noted how the general did not ask more about Aiden and their relationship. Maybe she already knew everything or was putting it together at this moment. Maybe she did not ask out of respect for Alishia. "The boys were the first people I've met that didn't know me as a princess. We traveled for days before they knew, and other than a few awkward comments, it changed nothing between us. In many ways, though I only knew them a week, they were more real to me than most I've known my whole life. Whenever I felt lost, I'd go to Throk'tar and check on them."

Isold refilled their goblets and set the carafe on the dresser. "Aiden is downstairs right now. Where is Ethan?" she asked.

"He died," Alishia said quickly. "Cazlandt murdered him." She expected the words to sting, but they left her with a strangely hollow sensation.

Jazelyn's hands flew to her necklace with a gasp. "I am so sorry, my child. That man was a visionary, an inspiration to thousands, but I knew him better than most. He held a darkness close to his heart. For him, there was no moral boundary. He would do anything to achieve his goals. We uphold his name to keep his legacy of archmages in high regard, but... I am sorry."

"It was a long time ago. I never forgave Cazlandt, but I grew to understand him for what he was. It became less about *him* and more about what I learned by observing him. Like watching the boys gave me hope in goodness, Cazlandt showed me how it might sour."

"They'll be waiting for us downstairs," Isold said, setting the empty wine cups on her tray.

Alishia stood and faced Jazelyn. Looking up into the archmage's dark eyes, a sudden urge overtook Alishia, and she wrapped her arms around the general. "Thank you again." Jazelyn stiffened at the touch but softened and put her arms around Alishia's shoulders after a breath.

Alishia pushed back and smoothed the front of her dress. "Who's that wearing a general's pin down there?"

"General Dehset Tekin," Jazelyn said with a soft groan. "To summarize, his incompetence and negligence wrecked my workroom. Regent King Lone rewarded Tekin with a promotion to monitor him better. The boy shows some promise but requires more supervision than we currently have the capacity for. Luckily, your father has shown an interest in mentoring him. He idolizes your father."

Alishia looked at the door but made no move toward it.

Jazelyn took Alishia's hand and squeezed gently. "I see your hesitance. In my younger days, I joined Cazlandt on a few journeys to other realms. I know the exhaustion that comes with it. We are touring the city today, but you can rest here and have Isold curate your visitors."

Alishia looked down at the chunk of mana crystal on the end of Jazelyn's necklace and back to the door. "No, I've been away long enough."

***

Lone grabbed and hugged her at the bottom of the steps.

"I can't wait to sit in that old oak with you to talk about everything that's happened," Lone said beside her. "And to hear what you've been doing even more. I mean, we'll talk as soon as whatever is about to happen settles, and it doesn't have to be in that oak tree, but that's our spot. Aiden has been annoyingly cryptic about everything for weeks. It's taken a concerted effort not to strangle him for answers, though I'm pretty sure he's leagues more powerful than me."

Alishia looked across the mix of faces in the room, familiar and not. "Where is Aiden?"

"I—" Lone spun, whipping his gaze over the room. "Thrice damned daemon snuck out."

Or he's just invisible, Alishia thought with a smirk.

"Yes, of course we'll catch up," she said. "I'd like to see mother and father first."

"Sure, sure." Lone reached a hand to her forearm and closed his eyes. They moved rapidly under his lids, and Alishia knew he was searching for their father's signature to teleport directly to them. His lips curled down into a frown. "I can't find him. They're probably within the city again and too close to the tree. I haven't yet figured out how to see through the interference it gives off."

"Maybe I can."

Alishia blinked, and the world expanded. Rather than the tree and Tidecrest, the image of the faceless pair that took the Seed returned to her. She knew of only one individual who might blaze with the light of a sun, and if that guess proved correct, the other individual would be obvious but also impossible. Ethan died with a sword through his heart in another realm eighteen thousand years ago.

Yet...

His twin brother hugged her just a few moments ago. Alishia tried to silence that spark of hope. *I'm sure a thousand or a hundred thousand people have had power like Aiden's since the beginning of time. I could have seen any of them. Yet, would I trust the Seed of Farsil to anyone but the Hauser boys? Then again, I knew them for a week. As deeply as I cared for them, would I entrust the Seed to two boys*

I just met? I... She knew it was only that doubting voice trying to convince her what she knew was true. She witnessed the Ascended forge Aiden and Ethan's souls. Those two boys she stomped around with through the damp forests of Throk'tar held more power than any other mortal. The gods tempered them for a purpose. A purpose which, after eighteen thousand years, Alishia guessed, was yet unfulfilled.

Magic is confidence and intent, she reminded herself and focused on finding her parents. Her Sight slid away from the cryptic scene and moved south to the armies camped in the hills. She saw the Tersguard and Sisters of the Moons, but no sign of her parents.

Alishia floated in nothing with a simple cabin drifting askew before her.

"Not this again," she groaned and stepped through the front door. Rather than walls covered with charcoal line drawings, everything looked and smelled freshly painted in a neutral purple-brown color.

A gaunt, nearly skeletal woman wearing a slip that highlighted her frailty stumbled from the bedroom. Alishia rushed to catch her as she tripped forward. "Kethry," Alishia named the woman as she eased her to the plank floor.

"I tried to stop her," Kethry said around cracked lips. "I've tried to stop her for so long. The harder I pushed, the stronger she became, and the weaker I got."

"Morna Dey."

"She left, called by her master in the orb."

"Ruvaal." Alishia was uncertain why she felt so sure. Still, she could easily imagine Ruvaal sitting under the shade of Nethraanzil, holding a glass ball and issuing commands to the daemon mistress. *Perhaps that's not just my imagination.*

"Where has she gone?" Alishia asked. Kethry's weight in her arms diminished with every breath.

"To gather her children, then to Poas. Stop her, Chronicler."

"How?"

"If I knew that, I wouldn't be where I am. I tried to fight her with strength. Maybe you can do something clever."

Lone's wide emerald eyes and slack, horrified face filled her vision. She sat reclined on one of the many cushions around the hostel's main floor, with those from Dracon clustered around her. She pushed her brother aside to sit up.

"Morna Dey is coming. We have to warn the protectorate and the troops outside."

"Morna Dey? When?"

The front doors to the hotel burst open with a bang, interrupting her response. Queen Teiris entered, wearing a stiff, forest green gown trimmed with cream, with King Daelin at her side. Behind them strode Alishia's Uncle Sion, Prelen Kaermys, Matron Wynlen, and a handful of other prominent svarters. Sisters of the Moons and Tersguard choked the entry.

"Ali!" Sion shrieked and broke rank to run and wrap his arms around her. He seemed smaller than she remembered.

"Hello, Sion," she laughed and pushed her uncle away. Teiris tossed the boy aside to move in and embrace Alishia. Her mother said nothing, but her grip was strong with a faint tremble, holding Alishia close.

"I'm home," she said and clung to her mother.

Teiris sharply inhaled and stepped back, grinning widely and dabbing at her eyes with a handkerchief. "Praise Enid, my love, and you're just in time."

Her father was next with a squeeze far more gentle than her mother. "Is this a new dress? I like how it complements your eyes," he said after releasing her to arm's length.

"Thank you, father. Yes, it's new."

"It's stunning, my love," said her mother.

"Was there a problem with your bracer?" Daelin asked and gestured to her right forearm.

"My what?" She imagined her father toiling in his workshop for days on some new bit of runecraft for her. She waved down her own question. "Never mind, there's no time! Daemon will attack the city soon!"

Her mother hesitated for only a breath. "Where are they coming from?"

"I think south of the city."

Teiris turned to her husband. "Daelin, Prelen Kaermys, return to the troops and make all preparations. Pull us closer to the city. I will speak to the protectorate."

Alishia barely saw her parents for three minutes before they were leaving again.

"I'll get to our forces and spread the word to the other nations," said Kiol. "King Garriet just arrived with Eplear. He hasn't even been in the city yet."

"Go with him, Lieutenant Dreyma," said Lone. "I'll be along as soon as I can."

The lieutenant nodded, and Jazelyn slipped a hand onto Kiol's and her shoulders. They disappeared with a pop.

"We have to tell Etharis and find Tanathil," said Lone.

"I'll go to Etharis," someone squeaked. Alishia looked at the young man with the general's pin, Dehset Tekin. He was older than she, based on her years in Poas, but now Lone, even Bard, looked like "young men" in her eyes.

"You think you can find him?" Lone asked.

Dehset dug through his rucksack and pulled out an oblong metal device with lots of exposed wires. "Yes, sir, Your Grace."

Lone stared at Dehset for a long moment. "Well, go then, find him. Tell him Morna Dey is returning, and he'll know what to do." He watched Dehset scurry off and grumbled, "I have to do better about him. I keep forgetting he's here."

"Ali, Lone!" They and Bard all jumped at Aiden's sudden words. "There is someone you have to meet."

"Not a good time, Aiden," Lone warned. "Daemon will attack the city soon."

"Then we really have little time. Come on, come with me."

He turned to leave, but Alishia caught him by the arm. Her nails dug into the thick vestments. "Aiden, who is the World Tender?"

Aiden bit his lip and sighed. "I will explain real soon, I promise. Come on."

She released and followed him out of the hotel at a pace that kept her near to running. Lone and Bard followed.

Dalbinth, the role Aiden adopted to have a place in Poas, the thoughts streamed into her like reading from a book. She knew that fact, but not how Aiden came to be here or how he survived the eighteen thousand years since she last saw him. *Will I pull him across time as I did Cazlandt? Does some magic hold him in stasis for the time?* She did not know enough about magic to know if that was possible, but it felt unlikely that any spell could leave a person completely untouched by age after so long. Even the Mraasil had a few extra creases on their foreheads since then.

She knew the route through Tidecrest, knew which turns Aiden would take next, and was not at all impressed by the Symposium's scale as the immense building came into full sight.

I gleaned everything about this city when I used my Sight.

Rather than entering the Symposium, they cut to the left and entered a building with steep, narrow stairs leading down.

Beyond it, the ever-narrowing tunnels increasingly reminded her of the warrens beyond the House of Enid in Terswood. Within a few turns, the world tree's roots were bursting through the walls, closing off paths and making others impossible to pass without turning sideways.

After a few sharp turns and steep drops, Alishia became hopelessly lost, yet she also knew the route in perfect clarity. She stopped thinking about it too much and gave up trying to estimate how far down they had traveled, especially as they skidded sideways down a ramp of collapsed marble that may once have served as a wall to some massive underground structure.

"Almost there," Aiden said and dropped to his hands and knees to squeeze on his belly under a thick root that left barely a foot of space between it and the smooth stone floor. Alishia shimmied under and watched Lone consider the gap for a long moment. He pulled off his leather cuirass and handed it to Bard as they exchanged quiet words and a kiss.

"What's going on back there?" Alishia said through the gap.

"Bard won't fit. He's going to go back up to find Tanathil."

Lone grunted and groaned as he pulled himself through the tight crack, pushing his scabbard ahead of him as he went. He looked over at Aiden when he stood up on the other side. "How did you get through that?"

Aiden shrugged. "I can fit through tight places when I need to."

"We'll be back as soon as we can, love," Lone called back to Bard.

After another turn, Lone barely squeezed through another vertical gap. They followed Aiden down a steep decline until the floor suddenly dropped away before them. Lit by the iridescent, ruby lake far below, a thousand roots formed the cavern's roof, larger than the Symposium overhead. Thin strands of red dripped like blood from the roots into the water below.

Aiden stopped to spread his arms over the view. "The mana lake of Poas. It is rare to be this close to the surface."

"Mana lake? What is this place, Aiden?" Lone closed his eyes to focus and immediately winced and blinked rapidly. "This is more mana in one place than I have ever felt, even deep within a mana crystal excavation."

"Yeah, what do you think mana crystal is?" Aiden waved at the lake again.

"Mana is pulled from other realms through the tree and spread along the ley lines, where it pools into these mana lakes. They used to be all across Poas," said Alishia, surprising herself with the flood of knowledge. "After Tersil was lost, they dried up as the energy fed into the ley lines and was consumed. Where it was cold, the far north and thousands of years ago, what is now Iecil, the liquid mana froze into crystal as it flowed into the ley networks."

"How do you know that, Ali?" Lone asked.

Alishia shrugged.

"Your sister is the Chronicler, Lone. Get used to the random spouting of facts. Come on, and be careful not to touch the water."

They followed as Aiden picked his way down the steep basin, and within a minute, they strode across the soft, flat soil toward a figure kneeling by the water's edge. As the man wearing a calf-length leather jacket rose and turned, a wide smile broke over his face, creasing the edges of his green eyes.

"The World Tender," said Aiden.

29

King Gerold XII was buried with the greatest respect, but a tremor collapsed his section of the catacombs.

Alishia's knees shook, and she took a single step backward. "No," she whispered around quick breaths. She spent months, perhaps years, grieving for the loss of her first love, or at least her first potential love. Ethan Hauser, Captain in the Imperial Gron Army, gentle elementalist, savvy diplomat, and fierce warrior. She had sat in the heart chamber of Throkzil beside Uulthra's chrysalis, using her Sight to watch the boys on their adventures, almost feeling like she was a part of them. She held close her hatred of Cazlandt for the murder while she learned to accept the man and his wealth of flaws. Alishia mourned Ethan's death and the bright future he would have had if only she had never entered Throk'tar beside her great-grandsire.

If not for her.

Confusion and shock overwhelmed her as she stared at the impossible, at the one standing a dozen feet away.

Ethan hid a smile behind a hand smeared with fresh dirt.

Her legs numbly crossed the span as she stepped close enough to see the tears streaming down his cheeks. Alishia last saw Ethan in Throk'tar with a sword of pure mana piercing his heart. She looked into his vibrant green eyes.

Ethan reached a dirt-stained hand toward hers. "Hello my—"

Her hand was a dark blur across his face with an echoing slap.

Before Ethan could raise a hand to his cheek, Alishia wrapped both arms around his shoulders, pulling herself up to her toes to press her lips against his.

"They do that a lot," Aiden groaned behind her. "You get used to it, I suppose."

Ethan touched his reddened cheek with a gentle smile as Alishia stepped back. "You did not warn me that would happen," he said.

Alishia shook her head. "How are you two here? Ethan, you... At least I thought you..."

"I was," he nodded slowly.

"But that was eighteen thousand years ago." She looked at him with blurry eyes as he wiped a thumb across her cheek. Like a dream, his face had the same smile she remembered, untouched by the years. "This can't be real."

"It is very real," Aiden chuckled. "Ethan was dead by Cazlandt's blade, and I followed him not much longer after." Aiden stuck out his tongue and drew a finger across his neck. "But we got better. When the Ascended made us, they left out one ingredient."

"When they forged you," Alishia murmured, remembering the term Dhumjir used. "You can't die?" She fought back a chuckle at hearing her own words.

"We can. It is just less permanent," said Aiden.

Alishia took a long breath to remember each of the Ascended, granting power to the souls that would become these two. "Elphame took something from you."

"She denied us Her gift," said Ethan.

"Death is a gift?" Lone scoffed and crossed his arms.

"Most certainly, Lone," said Ethan. "It creates a sense of urgency to know everything has a deadline. It creates that drive to forge a legacy that will continue after you. I have no doubt you noticed amongst the archmages how listless they become after only a few hundred years, how distant and uncaring they are. You begin to see the lives of mortals like sand draining between your fingers, and you struggle, wondering why you would bother grabbing for more sand."

"Well... Try not to be so scragging gloomy," Aiden said, slapping his brother on the arm.

"And you've been wandering the realms all this time?" Alishia asked.

"Not wandering," said Ethan. "We trained with Etharis and Ruvaal, calling ourselves the Scions of Flayme. You joined us for a long while, Ali. We, you and I, grew close." He reached a finger to trace along her arm, shyly biting back a smile. "We fought to end the daemon and Gods of Naught here in Poas, as was our destiny in life, to stop the Venatus. Then you gave us the Seed of Farsil and set us on the mission here."

"Well," Aiden added, "you have been here. I have had my own tasks in other realms."

Lone's attention perked up. "The daemon. Morna Dey will attack the city soon."

"That is probably why you are here," said Ethan to his brother. "It must be something big if the Chronicler insisted on us being present."

Alishia brushed her hand against Ethan's fingers and spoke as if not hearing their words. "I hid in The Stacks for so long. A dozen times, I thought to see the last days of Tersil. I probably would have seen you there. Perhaps it's better I didn't." She laced her fingers in Ethan's and turned to the other brother. "Aiden, I wanted so badly to see you after... after I left with Cazlandt. I couldn't bear the thought of seeing your pain without Ethan. I wasn't strong enough. I'm sorry."

"There is nothing to be sorry about, love," Ethan said, raising her hand to kiss it.

"All that time I spent mourning you, I could have just visited later, and you'd both be fine?"

Aiden pulled a string of wooden beads from his robes that looked identical to what the boys purchased for Alishia from Shroaker the Broker. He thumbed through them and paused at a bead carved from dark, almost black wood. "Want to see?" he asked, raising the beads between Alishia and Lone.

Lone squinted. "I can sense the enchantments on those. Are they like a reminisphere?"

"Close enough, yeah," Aiden nodded. "Each bead has a particular memory I want to remain pure. Suanh may have specifically blessed us, but our minds are not completely infallible after enough time. Immortality, true immortality far beyond what an archmage or even Mraasil experiences, comes with a complete lack of humility. This bead reminds me of how I felt before we knew."

Lone pinched his brow with confusion and opened his mouth to speak.

Aiden held up his other hand. "Hold all questions for the end. I know, daemon. You will experience about four days in only a few seconds."

Alishia reached with shaky fingers for the bead Aiden offered. She toyed with her ability to drift through time enough to watch the boys in happier days before they met her, and she brought Cazlandt to their realm. This bead held a memory she could have witnessed herself if not for her guilt, founded or not.

Lone took her extended hand, squeezed it, and guided it so they touched the bead simultaneously.

Alishia's vision compressed to nothing but that black bead as it expanded to fill her world in a heartbeat. She was falling but with no sense of motion. An instant later, she floated in the dimly lit space of Throkzil's heart chamber. She gasped at the sudden flood of utter despair that threatened to devour her being.

30

The direbears of the north can sense a coming thaw and will come from their caves a few days in advance.

Aiden clutched trembling fingers into the shoulder of his brother's soft leather jacket and pressed his forehead against Ethan's. The tears and gasping sobs were fewer now as exhaustion compressed his world into nothing beyond the two of them.

"Aiden," Etharis said softly in that smooth voice and placed a lavender hand on the boy's shoulder. "Aiden, we should leave. Let us take you home."

"Home," Aiden mumbled and leaned back on his heels, leaving his right hand on his brother's chest. He wiped at his face with as emotion numbed him, creating an odd sense of clarity. "The humans at Cliffside, we must go to the Ebon Blockade about them. Ethan was always the talker."

Ruvaal nodded. "I can handle that. I'm sure I can figure out what to say." He turned to leave the heart chamber.

"The inn at Ragvurd," Aiden continued, quiet and hollow. "We need to settle up the bill. It would have taken most of the steel we had left, and Ethan never wanted to be left with an empty pouch. He always had to keep enough for emergencies."

"Anything else?" asked Ruvaal.

Aiden put his left hand gently on the crown of Ethan's head as the tears threatened again. "If you see Shroaker and Sump, thank them. Alishia liked the present."

"I don't know who or what that is, but I'll keep an eye out," said Ruvaal, again turning to leave.

"No," Aiden called after the Mraasil. "No, wait. These are our tasks. My tasks. Ethan would want me to see them through."

"Are you certain?" Ruvaal asked from across the chamber.

Aiden nodded and looked back at his brother.

"He cannot stay here," said Uulthra, guardian of Throk'tar. Aiden blinked away tears and looked up at her as she stepped toward him with an unnatural grace. Her glowing amber eyes fixed on the archdruid.

"Uulthra," Etharis said gently, "give him a moment."

"The heart chamber is no place for a mortal and especially no place for a corpse. It cannot stay here," she said coldly, reaching for Ethan.

"Don't touch him!" Aiden spat and slapped away Uulthra's violet hand. He felt his armor lock into place. The gleaming plate swirled with clouds of shadow, but the surge of power was familiar in his exhausted limbs. It shattered and fell away within another breath.

Etharis stepped between Aiden and the native Mraasil. "They saved your realm. Ethan gave his life defending your tree. You owe them both a great debt that can never be repaid."

Aiden looked down at his brother again. For an instant, he saw his own light-summoned armor, made of pure white energy, faintly covering Ethan. He blinked, and it was gone.

"I owe them nothing," Uulthra hissed. "Humans are to blame for all of this. *They* are to blame. I owe no thanks or boons to a people that solves a problem they create."

Etharis stepped around Ethan's body to place a hand on Aiden's shoulder. "Let's go. It seems the venerated guardian of your realm has no interest in decency. Ruvaal and I will walk with you."

Aiden carefully pushed his arms under his brother and barely noticed the weight as he lifted him with numb arms. He left the heart chamber by some secret path, trailed by the two Mraasil. They must have discretely fueled Aiden with magics, because he never paused as the world faded from black to red, blue, red, and back to black again, but the weariness in his limbs never grew enough to force him to stop. As the sky lightened to red on the third day, Aiden made out the dark spires of the Blockade and hurried his pace up the steep hill. He almost made it to the entrance formed by the rib cage of the Great Beast Kelngarn when his strength finally failed. Gron warriors ran forward as he dropped to his knees, then backward.

***

Aiden awoke shirtless on a cot, covered with a scratchy blanket. He lifted his head to look around the small hospital room. Clean bottles and vials containing anything an experienced shaman needed for healing covered the few tables and shelves in the corners. A figure covered in a canvas sheet occupied the cot beside him: Ethan. Aiden tossed his blanket aside, swung his legs over the edge of the bed, and reached to touch his brother's hand through the tarpaulin. Tears threatened, but he felt a dull void where he knew the raw hurt should still be.

"You're up, good," said a nasal voice at the door. Aiden turned to the short gronyn woman wearing a deep red smock and a necklace of bone and tusks, which showed her to be a shaman healer.

"How long was I out?"

"Only a few hours," she said, handing him his shirt. "I am sorry for your loss, Captain. Chancellor Koughat has asked to speak with you immediately. The Mraasil already explained the situation."

"Thank you. I know the way. My brother..."

"He walks with our honored ancestors, but I will care for what he leaves behind."

The interior of the Ebon Blockade housed all the greatest trophies of gronyn dominance over the magnificent beasts of Throk'tar. Skins of snakes that could swallow a warrior whole, talons and skulls from winged monsters larger than a home, taxidermied bodies of a dozen different creatures that once plagued the hills and valleys of the world. Now, the gronyn ruled and cultivated the land in relative peace. Hopefully, they could now share it with a settlement of human refugees. Aiden saw nothing but the ground a few paces before him as he traveled the halls, passing marching and stationed warriors who snapped to salute him.

For a gronyn so near in influence to the emperor, Chancellor Koughat kept a modest office in a quiet corner of the Blockade. There was no door, but Aiden cleared his throat and stepped onto the plush furs marking the threshold. Through the thick haze of incense clinging in the air, the chancellor sat beside a table stacked with parchment and ledgers.

"Come," said the gronyn war chief as he stood. His leather and bone armor creaked as muscles flexed, but Aiden knew it was not just for show. Koughat earned his place through efficient and exact military maneuvers over his many decades of service to the Empire.

"Chancellor," said Aiden and pounded a fist to his chest in salute.

"My mother used to tell me stories of Uulthra, the world guardian, but to think I just stood here talking to two others... I wish she were still alive for me to tell her. Captain Hauser, I express my sympathies for your loss."

Aiden opened his mouth to speak but only nodded.

"Archdruid Etharis explained to me about the humans, others like yourself, east of here. You and your brother placed them under your banner, hoping the Council of Tribes will grant them asylum. Is my understanding correct?"

"Yes, sir."

Koughat crossed to a narrow table of incense and used one dwindling stick to light another. "You argue the humans are unaware of our laws, that they are not beholden to the blood oaths. I tell you, the Council will not care. Our laws, our oaths, need not be accepted by each member of society, yet we are all bound by them. If we discovered an island of before-unknown gronyn tomorrow, the Emperor, the Council, and I would hold them to the codes of the Empire. These humans have savagely killed many of our people and must be held accountable."

"Sir, let me make my case to the Council of Tribes," Aiden pleaded.

"Make your case to me first." Koughat crossed his thick arms. "My advisers are raging for this human settlement to be razed, but I have stayed their blades for now."

Aiden breathed in the cloying incense and stared at Koughat's wide leather bracers studded with the skulls of small animals. His entire case hinged on the humans being unaware of the laws of the gronyn when they arrived. Such a defense now seemed laughable. Ethan would surely have some silver-tongued way around this.

"The humans did not know gronyn were an intelligent people," Aiden said and coughed in the haze. "They thought us only advanced animals."

"You say *us*, but you are not gronyn, Captain. You are like them. Do you think like they do? Or did? Do you think gronyn are savage beasts?"

"N—no, sir. Of course not."

"Then the problem is not with the entire race, but with *these* humans." Chancellor Koughat sighed. "You walked by the trophies of many creatures and monsters coming here. Many of those beings were ancient, with their own vast intelligence. But they threatened the safety of the gronyn people and were put down. The Council will not see the humans as any more than a threat. I am sorry, Captain, they will not hear your case."

Aiden's first mission without his brother was a failure. "Please, Chancellor. There must be something I can do."

"I am truly sorry, young captain."

"I offer *Kren'dushaakt*," Aiden said before his mind could fight the idea.

The chancellor's shoulders slumped with a heavy sigh. "That they would listen to."

***

Much like the walk to the Ebon Blockade, Aiden remembered little of the following day. The Council of Tribes convened, and Aiden stood before them. The three wizened tribe elders sat on plush cushions beside Chancellor Koughat with three dozen high-ranking gronyn crowded into the room's edges.

Aiden focused on the smoldering coals of the brazier in front of him, breathing in their meager glow to sustain his waning strength. He tried his best to remember the story Elder Grimorc told him a dozen times. "When our empire first formed," he said in a clear voice as his knees threatened to give out, "the twin brothers Ralfit and Kren held strongholds high in the hills on opposite banks of the Boccercur. When their father, the emperor, became ill, the brothers argued over who would inherit the throne. Ralfit gathered a thousand gron soldiers and marched to the river's edge. Kren stood alone on the other side. 'Where are your troops?' laughed Ralfit. 'No gron will fall in my stead,' replied Kren. Sure of a victory, Ralfit's army surged across the shallow water. The Boccercur ran red for days, and Kren's hammer arm never grew weary as he stood alone against hundreds, knowing he must do what the army he was unwilling to sacrifice would have.

"In the end, Kren stood surrounded by the bodies of a thousand of Ralfit's best. Exhaustion finally took him, and Kren fell to his brother's hammer, just as shamans cured the emperor's illness. The emperor banished Ralfit and named Kren's eldest the next emperor."

"Captain Hauser," said one councilor. "You have come to face judgment, not to tell a story poorly."

"As with ancient Kren, rather than risk my tribe, I will bear their burden. I, Captain Aiden Hauser, stand before you to give voice and offer penance for the colony of humans, others of my race, east of here. I offer *Kren'dushaakt*. I accept full penance for the crimes committed by the humans at Cliffside Canton."

The room collectively gasped and broke into a buzz of whispers.

"The humans have killed dozens," said one elder.

"This will mean your death," said another.

"A public execution," said the last.

"If you accept the terms, the Council will hold by the blood oaths and bring these humans into our society," said the second.

Aiden had no breath to speak but nodded. He accepted this task beside his brother and now, without Ethan's quick mind, he would complete it as best he could. If his death saved a small city, it was a price he would pay.

Chancellor Koughat stood, drawing the eyes of all in the room. "Your honor and courage outshine even your light-forged armor, Captain Aiden Hauser. This council accepts your offer, and with the greatest sadness, I sentence you to death. By all honor, we will spare the humans of Cliffside Canton for your sacrifice." The chatter in the room rose quickly. Aiden heard "pale skin" more than once.

"But," Koughat continued, causing immediate silence. "The method of execution will be left to my discretion. An honorable fall of the ax at first blood."

First blood, evening. I will join you in a few hours, Ethan, just without my head. Or without my body, whichever way that goes. Despite everything, Aiden grinned to himself. *Hopefully, Ruvaal settled the tab at the inn.*

***

Chancellor Koughat held an ornate, double-bladed ax beside Aiden. They stood alone in a small, private room in the back of the Ebon Blockade with only an old, stained tree stump.

"You honor us all with your commitment, Captain," the chancellor said. "They will sing of your bravery for many generations."

Aiden could not help but notice the single wedge cut deep into the stump's center. "Thank you for making this quick," he said and sank to his knees.

"A hero's pyre has been built, awaiting you and your brother."

A voice screamed for Aiden to flee, to summon his armor and punch the chancellor through the wall. To run to... to where? Maybe if Alishia returned, he would have some means of escaping Throk'tar. He shivered, thinking he would even accept Cazlandt's help at that moment. Where had the Mraasil gone? No... at least this minor act would do good. Running would only get people killed.

He leaned forward, looking over that deep groove with an old stain. He heard the ax whistle, then darkness.

***

Alishia woke, shivering, on the rocky ground. She reached for her brother, looking just as pale as she felt. His fingers were ice in hers, but she gripped them just as tightly.

"They killed you," he mumbled as they pushed to a seated position. "Killed you for wanting to save a group of humans you didn't even know."

"It was my choice," said Aiden. "I knew what price I would pay, but allowing the Gron Army to slaughter that town was never an option. When Ethan and I were later reborn, we assumed it was for our selfless acts, a one-time gift granted by Lady Elphame. Maybe a divine clerical error."

"But?" Lone urged.

Aiden glanced at his brother, and Ethan said, "But we should say no more. It was you who told us everything, Ali. If you learned our truth from us, then later tell our younger selves, it gets messy."

"You try to avoid time travel paradoxes as much as possible," Aiden added.

"I'm so lost," Lone said as he stood on shaky legs and offered a hand to Alishia.

Aiden laughed and put an arm around Lone's shoulder. "There is a lot of catching up to be done here, I am sure. Ali, you have orchestrated a great number of events culminating right now. You gave us the first Seed of Farsil to give to the avaryll. You told Ethan to secretly tend the tree for thousands of years, not even telling Etharis. You wanted me present for Lone's summit of nations."

"The daemon are about to attack," she said. "That must be why I wanted you here. You can fight them. The Ascended forged you for that purpose."

"Well, it was hardly for my singing ability." Aiden flashed a toothy grin.

Ethan dug an elbow into his ribs. "Be serious."

Aiden groaned. "Time travel is a mess. We leave it at that."

Lone gasped and clutched at his right arm. All eyes turned to him as he sank to his knees.

"Lone!" Alishia dropped beside him.

Tears streamed down Lone's cheeks as he clenched his teeth and groaned.

"What's happening to him?" Alishia sobbed, afraid to touch her brother. Wisps of green energy wafted through his sleeve and leather bracer.

"Something is pushing too much mana into the runes in his tattoos. Lone," Ethan knelt and put both hands on Lone's shoulders, "Bard is not here to bleed away the excess. Lone, find the source of the influx and sever it as you would any Breaking technique."

Alishia could only watch as Lone sucked in ragged gasps of air. His emerald gaze stretched wide, and lost focus. He clawed at the leather straps binding his bracer in place. Sweat beaded across his brow and clung to the tip of his nose. As quickly as it started, he exhaled a breath of relief and fell into Alishia. Unprepared for the weight, she nearly fell backward.

"What was that?" Alishia hissed as Ethan pulled Lone's weight off her.

Lone sat upright by himself, breathing slowly and clutching his arm.

Ethan shook his head with a frown. "The beginning of the Entanglement, as you called it."

Alishia cringed. "I don't like the implication of a name like that."

"Lone may be good at many things, but unique to him is how he can channel energy through his tattoos."

"What's unique about it?" she asked.

"He can draw a great deal of ley energy into himself, specifically his right arm, and store it. I guess he cannot control it yet. What just happened was a random filament of energy from the mana lake attaching to his runes." Ethan sucked in a breath between his teeth and ran a hand through his hair. "I am sorry. I do not think I should say much more. You were the one to tell me all this, Ali. In my past, your future."

Alishia looked at the thick roots weaving through the ceiling of the chamber and the ruby lake before them. "Time travel is lousy."

"It has been utter hell on our relationship," said Ethan.

"Our..."

Ethan smiled and kissed her again.

"Remember, dear brother," Aiden said with a mischievous grin, "she is basically a sixteen-year-old girl right now. What do you estimate the age gap to be?"

Ethan coughed and stood.

Alishia still felt the pressure and texture of Ethan's lips against her own, mixed with the heat of her cheeks and neck as she looked up at him. She waited so long to see those green eyes again. He was no longer the awkward boy from Throk'tar, but she could still see it in how he averted his eyes now. Alishia looked back to her brother, staring down at his hand as he flexed it in his lap. "Something is wrong," she said and blinked.

Her vision blasted from the mana lake to view the tree from far above. The towers of Tidecrest barely glistened through the thick canopy of Endanlegsil. She felt a small comfort as she was not taken to the cabin or another vision.

Something dark pulsed in the hills to the south. She watched as nebulous, inky shapes flowed from a score of portals, slithering and writhing into a mass that covered the landscape. To her Sight, the portals were as clear as a window through which she viewed a space that had never known light. Not just the expanse between the Wheres, but touching something beyond. Something that poured despair and futility into her. Something so unknowably vast that her own existence, the existence of all realms, all that was or would ever be, seemed laughably insignificant.

Another portal formed, as large as the others combined. A many-faced creature of impossible girth pulled its serpentine body from the nothing into Poas.

The daemon looked to their mistress with flaming locks, Morna Dey, as she waved them toward the city.

Alishia snapped her vision back to the mana lake.

Aiden and Ethan both had hands clapped over their ears. "I can hear them!" Aiden shouted with a wince.

"Hear what?" Lone asked as he looked frantically between the others.

"Daemon." Alishia felt cold, with sweat prickling at her back. "Endless daemon. One as tall as the clouds."

"The Exalted," Aiden said in little more than a hushed whisper.

She felt a deep, booming resonance in her chest. It vibrated the marrow of her bones and pushed the last breath from her lungs. Lone clapped his hands over his ears while the boys winced and cringed.

Ethan lowered his hands with eyes wide. "The Toll," he gasped, still shouting over sounds Alishia could not hear. "Tidecrest is under attack."

31

The monk who founded Whiteherst Den is rumored to have fallen in love with a dryad from Nyphlym. The rumor continues to say they are both still alive to this day.

Morna Dey pulled back the hood of her cloak and looked up to the clear blue sky. The sun warmed her face as she smiled and breathed deeply. The mild breeze rustled at her clothes and curly red hair. Across the gently flowing sea of grass and yellow flowers, miles to the north lay the city. Towers of alabaster and opalescent marble thrust into the sky, glinting brightly in the light of day. In the center stood the tallest spire of them all. From the top sprouted the canopy of a tree — *the* tree — that cast its shade over much of the city, the shining city of Tidecrest.

What a shame.

Army encampments dotted the fields of grass. Four, possibly five, distinct camps churned with the tasks of a late morning.

Morna grinned. This may take more effort, but that meant more fun.

She reached forward with both hands, and with gripping motions, phantasmal fists appeared in the air before her. They ripped apart the space to form a portal of blackness lined with arcing violet energies. Two greater daemon with bodies of smoke stepped forth, followed by a dozen lesser winged imps and slithering hounds. Morna grinned as another six portals opened around her, and similar beasts stepped forward. The gateways closed as the last daemon stepped through.

Morna's smile faded at the edges at seeing the small force; possibly enough to wipe out the human and svarters armies, but also possibly an even match. She repeated the gesture, feeling the rush of energy flow from the void outside the Wheres, flowing from within her stolen body to her fingertips. Morna repeated the gesture and looked to her right, then to her left. A score more sets of seven portals opened in a line to either side of her, spewing daemon into the clear morning air. She stumbled forward a step. *Maybe too much.* She took a slow breath and looked at the world tree in the distance. *No, never too much.*

"My beautiful pets," she said, looking over the creatures, "this is our last order until I am set free again. Then we can have some real fun."

The daemon shifted but said nothing, not that any could speak. They existed only to serve Morna.

The daemon mistress raised a finger toward Tidecrest. "Destroy the city and kill everyone within. Corrupt the tree so our true masters may retake this realm. Once the tree is under my control, do as you please."

The daemon showed no emotion, but Morna felt pleased, excited even.

She looked up to the nearest greater daemon and snapped her fingers with sudden realization. "I nearly forgot! Come, Exalted." As before, she summoned spectral hands, but they formed a portal three dozen feet across the grass rather than in the air.

Sinewy clawed hands reached upward from the gateway to grasp the edge. Two, three, six. The Exalted's five heads with wide, gaping eyes and rictus grins came next as it pulled itself from the portal. Its eyes smoked with a foul, black mist. It pushed at the portal, widening the black opening and heaving its hunched, spined back into the sunlight. It kept pulling, extracting its spiked, serpentine body, and stood to its full height, a mountain among ants.

The gateway closed, and Morna reached toward the Exalted, towering to the clouds above her.

"You will have the greatest fun. I am sorry you so rarely get to come to the mortal realms." She smiled at it as it looked down to consider her—a spark of intelligence glinted from within the mist of its eyes.

Morna could hear the low tone of alarm broadcasted from Tidecrest as its citizens scrambled to defensive positions.

"If you find any with purple skin and glowing eyes, save them for me," she told her subjects. "Now, go. Do what you were meant to do."

With only the sound of beating wings and scurrying feet, the silent daemon army turned and surged toward the alabaster city and the new world tree in Poas.

As her daemon slithered and loped toward the waiting armies, a name suddenly came to Morna; a name she heard her master in the orb say, but had fled her mind and memory as quickly as it was said.

"Etharis," she hissed with a grin. "I will have fun with you."

***

Shenraafi, the Serpent King of Barbarles, strode through his troops. The men and women formed perfect rows, wearing serpent hide armor and holding a mix of polished bardiches and pikes. Behind them, lines of archers wore lighter cloth armor. The king paused before a pikeman at random. "Your sword."

Without hesitation, the soldier pulled the short sword from his hip sheath, flipped the grip, and bowed as he placed it in Shenraafi's waiting hand. The king ran a thumb down the blade and tested the weight and balance with a few quick arcs before handing it back to the soldier. He walked to the front of the company and looked to his right to give Tidecrest one more glance.

Looking back at his troops, Shenraafi saw King Garriet strolling through his soldiers a hundred yards away. Having arrived less than an hour ago, Eplear's army numbered more than the others combined.

The Serpent King adjusted his long, feathered cloak and focused on the men and women before him. "While I am glad the avaryll did not mean for war, my chest swells with pride looking at this pinnacle of Barbarles might. Each of—"

"My king!"

Shenraafi turned to the breathless shout and followed his soldiers' gazes and pointed arms. To the south, darkness flowed over the hills like a rolling fog. Points like burning coals flowed through it, freezing the Serpent King in place. "Bring my spyglass," he whispered to whoever was near, and a lieutenant rushed away. Shenraafi squinted at the shapes gaining resolution as they neared, but he needed no enhancement to see the creature that stretched to the clouds. It spread six spindly arms, and a mist flowed from it like wings as wide as the horizon. It arched back like issuing a screamed challenge but made no sound as it slithered forward on a serpentine lower half. Shenraafi had seen a host of sea monsters as the Crowned Pirate of the Farfathom Deeps, but nothing looked so foreign to this world, nothing so...

"Daemon," his lieutenant breathed while holding out the spyglass.

Shenraafi tore his eyes from the slowly encroaching mass to frown at the shorter man. "Fey tales," he grumbled, not convincing himself.

"They attacked Terswood months ago, my king. They are real."

Shenraafi's bones quaked, and his breath was suddenly short. What he thought was nerves and fear, he quickly realized was some tone of alarm raised from Tidecrest. The Serpent King looked to the other armies of svarters and archmages. Both appeared to still be in shock at the sight.

"Company! About face! We defend the tree!" Shenraafi accepted his long, double-bladed polearm from the lieutenant and raised it high overhead. The soldiers raised their own weapons and roared.

***

Queen Teiris stared at the group of a dozen priests wearing long white robes laced with gold. The hand with three raised fingers embroidered across their chests marked them as acolytes of the Holy Seat of Acrus. They arrived only moments ago and stood in formation, facing southward.

"Must they be so close?" she grumbled.

"Is something wrong with them?" Daelin asked from her side.

"They're just... staring. It... It just..." Teiris paused to shiver. "I'll never understand how a people can be so dedicated to the Ascended, yet get the message so incredibly wrong."

Daelin grunted thoughtfully. "They would argue your focused commitment to Enid is wrong. You cannot both be correct."

Teiris curled her lip. "Yeah, well, if they're right, I'm fine being wrong. Why are they even out here and not in the city with Aiden or Dalbinth? Why only a few priests and not any of those halberdiers in gold armor we saw in Ascalon?"

Teiris winced at the sudden onslaught of sound and clapped her hands over her ears, but the sound, like a thousand distant screams, faded as quickly as it came.

"Is something wrong?" Daelin asked.

Teiris looked up at her husband. "Something..." She turned to look south as a dark form reached for the clouds, and black mist poured across the hills and fields approaching the city at her back.

"Daemon," she whispered. They stretched across the horizon, a hundred times what decimated Terswood months ago. A primal, instinctual dread grew within Teiris, telling her rational mind the obvious.

This force will end the world.

Prelen Kaermys, leader of the Tersguard, was already shouting orders when Teiris first felt the deep resonance in her bones as if some force was shaking her soul. The Tersguard adjusted ranks to face south. "What are your orders, my queen?" Kaermys asked with only a trace of fear in her voice.

"There is no option, Teiris." Daelin said on her other side with a grunt. "I see no way the combined armies of Poas can win against such a force, but neither is retreat an option."

Teiris glanced at the Barbarles army nearby and how they rallied for battle, as well. "We must protect the tree, but you're right, Daelin. We're dead standing out here in the open. We will fight a defensive retreat into the city in the hopes the avaryll have a means of protection."

***

Lone opened his mind to the ley lines, only for the brilliance of the ley nexus below to momentarily blind him. He shoved his senses south, away from the tree, before he recovered from the glare and felt it. To his astral eye, the daemon force appeared as a flowing miasma, pulsing and undulating. They were a dark blemish on the otherwise ordinary paths of the ley lines. The daemon he fought in Terswood were a mere distraction. This was a force to wash over Poas and leave nothing in its wake.

He blinked and was back in the heart chamber of Endanlegsil.

Aiden still had a hand covering his right ear. "They have never been this loud before," he shouted.

"I can't hear anything except the Toll," said Lone. "And I feel that more than hear."

"You've fought them before," Alishia said rather than asked. "On a scale like what stands outside. The Ascended designed you for this very purpose: to be daemon hunters. I watched as they forged the two of you and sent you to stop the Venatus before it spread too far, but the Chaos sisters interfered and sent you instead to Throk'tar."

"Aye," said Ethan, casting a worried eye toward the ceiling and what growing horrors were coming nearer on the surface. "We fought skirmishes with them until we went against the full might of the Gods of Naught here in Poas, standing beside your First High Queen Ters. We trapped and scattered them while Tersil burned."

"We can talk about all that if we survive," said Lone.

"Right," Aiden said and turned to his brother. "Will you join me, or does the tree still need your attention?"

"Someone has to guard the mana lake," said Ethan. "But you cannot fight the Exalted alone. I wish Etharis were here."

"Great!" Aiden slapped his brother on the shoulder. "Lone and I will go find Etharis and send him down to take your place. Then you can join us for some daemon stomping fun."

"He's here," said Alishia, as a million scintillating butterflies manifested in the chamber. They gathered and coalesced into the form of the archdruid.

Etharis cast his glowing amber eyes over the group and smiled. "Ali, you're back, wonderful. It's a joyous family reunion here, save for what's happening outside. I'm sure you're aware by the droning of the Toll, but there is a force to the south that needs your special attention, boys. Go, and I'll guard the lake."

Aiden nodded and rushed from the room, stripping the heavy regalia of the Archetype as he did.

Ethan paused beside Alishia. "We will, of course, talk about everything when this is over." He kissed her again, just a peck on the cheek, and she grabbed his hand as he tried to flee after his brother.

"I can't lose you again," she said.

He turned and raised her hand to his lips, kissing her knuckles. "I must, Ali. They literally made my brother and I for this. Even if we die out there, maybe we can take out a chunk of daemon when we return."

She blinked up at him and held his hand tighter.

"I promise to tell you everything when things are safe, my love. Or, maybe I will not. I know a much older you. I... Time travel. It makes things awkward."

Alishia loosened her grip. Ethan kissed her again and was gone.

"You as well, Lone," said Etharis. "There are other Mraasil in the Symposium right now, in the room where we had our tea yesterday. Go to them and have Aymaa join you, the one with the sword. Leave Celium and Bireal to protect the tree at the main level."

Lone nodded and reached to squeeze his sister by the shoulders. He kissed her on the forehead and, not trusting a teleport in this place of overwhelming ley energy, ran after where the brothers had left.

***

"What about me?" Alishia asked as she lost sight of her brother.

Etharis narrowed his eyes. "You will be exactly where you need to be."

"That's hardly helpful."

The archdruid shrugged and knelt beside the crimson mana lake. The palm of his right hand hovered inches from the calm surface. "She'll come early because of this."

"The Mraasil?" A name floated to the front of her mind: *Verndari.* She dared not say it out loud as she had after Etharis was born. "Why aren't you worried about the daemon at the gates?"

"This won't end like the fiction books I know you're a fan of, where someone makes the ultimate sacrifice at the last moment at the base of Endanlegsil to save the world. If the daemon get by the armies, they're getting into the city. If they get into the city, they're probably getting here, or at least into the Symposium above us. If they get here, it won't be one stray hound loping in, bleeding a trail of smoke. I'm not discounting my power, but I saw the forces stretched across the horizon and would stand little chance against them."

"So you'll just stay down here and carry on like nothing's different?"

"That's my intention. My lot in life has been to care for the Trees and their guardians. I will see to it until the very end."

32

That something is old or original doesn't mean it's good. Ley Slip, also called Shadow Step by some, was the first means of teleportation, but... ick.

L one again removed his sword to wiggle through the space Bard was too muscled to fit through. He would have been lost in the warrens below the Symposium if not for the trail of Aiden's discarded vestments. By the time he stepped back into the wide street before the enormous building, he wondered how Aiden might still be wearing anything at all, but also how so many layers of heavy cloth could fit on his frame. *Perhaps he's actually a very slender build.* Very *slender.*

A worried-looking weaponmaster ran from a side street to meet Lone as he reached for the Symposium's door.

"There you are. I've been worried half to death." Bard gasped and clutched Lone by the forearms. "The city is chaos. I haven't found Tanathil but had little hope."

They fell into step beside each other across the wide marble floor, aiming for the simple-looking door at the side.

"Hopefully, he finds us or gathers the Einingu to battle the daemon outside." The vines and greenery of the cavernous room devoured any echo of Lone's words.

"Daemon?" Bard asked without breaking his pace. "The avaryll cried out about the attack and scattered when they rang the alarm."

"Aiden and his brother went to..." Lone stumbled as pain returned to his right arm. He undid the straps of his bracer and pulled up his cloth sleeve. Pale green energy pulsed from his tattoos, bringing with it an agony that threatened to drop him to the smooth marble floor. Bard gripped both hands around Lone's forearm, feeling like claws of icy pain digging and twisting into his flesh. Within a few breaths, all physical torment ended, leaving Lone sweaty and shaking.

"What is happening, *menf*?"

Lone took a few slow breaths to calm his nerves. "Ethan called it the Entanglement. I didn't have the chance to ask for more detail."

"Ethan?"

"Aiden's brother, the World Tender we've been hearing about. He seems less annoying, but apparently is in a long-term relationship with my sister's older self, which immediately makes me not like him."

They reached the door, and Bard opened it for Lone to enter first. Inside, three Mraasil stood around the central table, deep in their animated discussion. Aymaa's sword rattled in its scabbard as he gripped the hilt, but the powerfully built guardian relaxed as recognition crossed his face.

"You are the young king the archdruid told us about," he said in a deep and raspy voice.

Lone nodded, not caring to correct his title. Horned Bireal stood beside him, making the withered-looking one Celium.

"The archdruid sent me for you, Aymaa, to fight against the daemon."

Another lavender-skinned Mraasil, blocked behind the others, stood and faced him. Lone suppressed a gasp.

"Ruvaal," Lone said, letting his hand rest on the pommel of his sword. "I didn't think you'd be here."

"I wouldn't dare miss the birth of my new sister." The Mraasil flashed the hint of a feral grin.

"King Lone," Celium said in a quavering voice. "Is it that bad outside?"

"One must never underestimate a daemon threat," Bireal growled.

"What are the archdruid's commands for the rest of us? Are we to remain here?" Ruvaal asked.

Lone scanned across the amber eyes on him. "He wishes Aymaa to join the fight outside and Celium and Bireal to remain to protect the tree. Ruvaal, come away as well. I saw how you fought in Terswood. We will need your might."

"As you say, young king." Ruvaal nodded.

Aymaa moved to usher Lone and Bard from the room. "Our place is with our sister when she is born. Not in the battles of your realm."

"This is an invasion of daemon," said Lone. "Not some squabble between nations. Men and women will die on the field soon if they aren't already. My sister said one was as tall as the clouds—"

"The Exalted? I must see this." The sword at Aymaa's hip flashed with deep blue energy as the Mraasil unsheathed it. "Lead onward, archmage king."

Lone nodded and turned to walk a fast pace toward the main doors of the Symposium, with Bard beside him and a Mraasil on either side of the pair. He briefly opened his mind to trace a ley line out of the city, again thinking of attempting a teleport, but the intense energy beside Endanlegsil overwhelmed him. Lone quickened his pace.

"Halt!" Protectorate Alaraic's voice reverberated through the marble under Lone's feet. He twisted to face the cobalt-haired avaryll rushing toward him. Aymaa edged a pace toward the protectorate with his hand on his sword as if he might defend Lone and the others from the avaryll leader.

"Daemon at my gates!" Alaraic shouted as he pulled to a stop with two armored guards flanking him. Lone rested a hand on the pommel of his sword. "I should have never accepted the tales that the Venatus ended. Now daemon threaten my city and my tree because of your stinking kind."

Lone tilted his head, unsure of Alaraic's meaning.

"The daemon, historically, hunt humans," said Ruvaal. "It's as though they imprinted your race as their target all those ages ago."

Lone tightened the grip on his sword. "Send out your forces, Alaraic. We must defend the tree."

"The tree was delivered here by humans. This was all a long grift by your people. You've been in league with the daemon since the start." Alaraic spat on the tiled floor and turned to leave with a flourish of his cloak.

Aymaa stepped in front of Lone, blocking his view of the protectorate's back. "Deal with him later, young king. We have the Exalted and a horde to deal with." He hurried them toward the massive arched doors just behind them.

"What is the Exalted? Alish—" Lone stopped as he glanced southward. Through the gaps in the towers, he saw it. Rising on a serpentine body, the five human faces were hazy through the afternoon clouds. A half dozen clawed arms stretched from the side of a spiked, hunched back. "In Enid's name..." His knees weakened at the sight of the distant daemon.

"No..." Ruvaal brought a hand to cover his mouth. "This should be a flood of lesser daemon, maybe a few greaters. This is too much. No one has the power to call the Exalted."

"I can hardly believe what I'm seeing," Aymaa said to Lone's other side, lowering his blade that still pulsed with faint blue light. "The Exalted, Cleaver of Worlds, Mother of Daemon. We defeated her at the beginning of time."

"Before the Venatus?" Lone asked.

"Yes," said Aymaa. "When the realms were populated with only their Mraasil. She could never be fully destroyed, so we disassembled and scattered her across the aether."

An odd sense of lucidity washed over him as Lone stood mesmerized by the slow movement of the daemon. It, she, must have been miles away but looked so close due to her sheer size. "How is she the Mother of Daemon?"

"She existed, lurking, within the aether," said Ruvaal. "Her presence is imprinted deep in every filament of ley energy. Every so long, a fragment of her would slither out and gain physical form. Bireal told us they just had a hive of them to put down recently."

Lone finally tore his eyes from the impending doom. "Ruvaal, what did you mean this should only have been some minor attack?"

Ruvaal whirled on Lone in a flash of his red and blue robes. "I have been fighting daemon longer than your human brain can comprehend. I know how they organize and move. Unless you are suggesting I had some role in bringing the daemon here?" He stepped toward Lone with his brow pinched over blazing amber eyes.

"What? No," Lone stammered and raised his arms defensively. "I... No, I mean, it sounded like you thought this was an attack on an impossible scale." Bard slipped his hand onto Lone's shoulder and squeezed gently.

Aymaa frowned and traced a finger along a deep scar across his chest. "It took the combined strength of a hundred Mraasil to defeat the Exalted. We have five here. Poor Celium lacks the constitution, though they would want to help anyway, and the new Mraasil will be weak for months if she even has the chance to be born. Our only hope lies in the Forged."

"Aiden and Ethan?" said Lone. He knew strength could hide itself within a deceptive frame but could not imagine those two young men standing against the colossus he watched.

"There's no sense in trying to flee, Ruvaal," said Aymaa, narrowing his glowing, amber gaze at the other Mraasil. "I'm sure you want to run back to the Afterlands and skulk, but no place will be safe if the Exalted is born again into the mortal realms. We don't have a fraction of the strength required against that."

Ruvaal's scowl exposed sharp canines. "Where were you when I stood with Etharis, Ters, and the Forged all those millennia ago as we sacrificed Tersil to seal away the Gods of Naught?"

"Please!" Lone stepped between and pushed apart the Mraasil, each a foot taller than himself. "Whatever apocalypses you each were or weren't present for in the past doesn't matter now. The end of my world is literally just outside this city." He moved past them and took off to the closest bridge at a run, Bard at his side.

After a few long strides, a sudden burst of wind surged from behind, knocking them both forward and off their feet. A buffer of air held him and Bard aloft as Ruvaal floated up beside them. Lone's stomach clenched as the three shot upward and south. From the height, he saw the darkness flow across the green hills and the armies preparing to face it. A small clump of pale avaryll marched from the city while a thin line gathered around the city's edge.

Ruvaal slowed their movement as they neared the armies of Poas and gestured toward the Exalted, the daemon the size of a mountain. "The Forged take the field."

Lone squinted to make out the two figures running toward the horde of daemon. Aiden looked to be without armor. Ethan only wore his leather duster. Neither had a weapon in hand. A breath before they collided with the oncoming daemon, they flashed with a burst of light brighter than a dozen suns. Lone winced and shielded his eyes with an upraised arm. He rubbed them, blinked away the stars, and rubbed again, not believing what he saw. Aiden now stood at least thirty feet tall in shining armor, blazing with a light that was painful to look at directly, and his brother was gone. Aiden, the Gilded Warrior, cut through the daemon without pause, aiming for the Exalted.

"There!" Lone pointed to the front of Terswood's line, where a flash of cream-colored armor stood out against the darker greens and browns of Ters-guard armor.

"Your father," said Ruvaal.

"Yes, of course, get me down there!" He looked back at Ruvaal, whose amber eyes drifted over the scene below them.

"Your father, not your own people? The forces of Terswood and Dracon are at least a half mile apart."

Lone opened his mouth to reply but had nothing to say. He could not be in both places, but who would need his sword arm most in the battle? Would it even matter?

Ruvaal groaned. "There is no point to it, Lone. There is no stopping a force of this magnitude. Your father, every human and svarters down there, every living being on Poas, will be dead soon enough. The new tree will burn."

Lone awkwardly shifted in the cocoon of air the Mraasil held around him and Bard. "I won't float up here and watch that happen. Put me down."

"You go to your death." Ruvaal sighed.

"What do you suggest, then? Flee back to your tree in the Afterlands? Hope the daemon get bored with killing everyone I know and love and just leave? I see what Aymaa means about you. You're a coward."

Ruvaal's glowing eyes narrowed to slits. "You would speak so to one so far above your station?"

"I don't give a single damn about what you are right now, Ruvaal. I only care that you're stopping me from defending my home, those I love."

"Your sister is the only one that can stop this."

"Speak plainly, Mraasil," Lone spat through clenched teeth and struggled against the cushion of air holding him and Bard in place some deadly fall over the city's edge.

"She alone can skip through time. One little event would unmake this all." Ruvaal spread his arms across the field, and Lone's breath quickened at seeing the daemon only yards from engaging the armies of Poas. "She alone can stop this."

Lone gave a glance to the battleground and back to the Mraasil. "You go speak to her, then. Send us down." He stopped his physical struggle to examine the matrix of Ruvaal's spell. He found it quickly enough, a single filament of magic that ran through it, holding it together. Lone reached for that strand, holding on with a firm mental grip, ready to Break it and send them hurtling to the ground if the Mraasil did not release them.

Ruvaal sighed again. "Very well, though no one will be left to light your pyre."

With the same sudden acceleration, the three shot over the armies of Poas, toward the head of the Dracon force wearing light blue. General Kiol shouted orders from the front as he organized a line of archmages. Lone knew each of those archmages had less combat experience than he did at fifteen. The crystal mages mixed among them would perform better but were limited by the mana crystal in the pouches at their hips.

A sharp breath later, Lone and Bard were falling forward before Kiol and Jazelyn, trying to stay on their feet from the sudden deceleration.

"Your Grace!" Jazelyn said, looking over at Ruvaal and turning to the daemon.

"Farewell, Regent King," Ruvaal said, disappearing with a blazing spark running up his body.

Lone waved off the Mraasil and turned to Kiol. "There are too many. We should fight a retreat to the city and take no risks."

Kiol nodded and shouted the order across the troops. A wave of visible relief spread over the mages and guards. Kiol's hand flashed a pale yellow. He raised it and shot a quick burst of energy, hitting and obliterating a hound that broke from the pack. The other archmages unleashed their displays of magical prowess but to a lesser impact. Blasts glanced off the thick hides of imps, and Lone could not decide which was more disturbing: the unhurried pace of the daemon or the fact that they paid no attention as one beside them fell.

Lone pulled his sword, wishing it were a work of featherr'ock steel, but there was no time to return to the Vault at the castle.

The closest daemon were only a hundred yards away. A force ten times what attacked Terswood months ago faced off against each nation of Poas. Even if the imps, hounds, and fliers could be dealt with by magic, it was the greater daemon that terrified Lone. They walked among the more mundane beasts, thrice as tall, massive creatures of mist and sinew. After General Miech gave his life to destroy the one in Terswood, Kiol said it would have taken razing half the city to bring it down by force. Lone counted twenty lumbering over the battlefield.

"We could run," Lone whispered with a chuckle, slipping his fingers into Bard's.

The islander squeezed his hand and raised to kiss Lone's fingers before letting go to draw the greatsword on his back.

Dracon took a collective step back, and Lone glanced at the Serpent King's armies, which were not far away. With a mighty bellow, Shenraafi's forces surged toward, as did those from Eplear beyond them.

Lone strung together a muttered curse that referenced each of the Greater Six and a few honored saints. General Kiol glanced at him with a mix of incredulity, worry, and determination. Lone took a deep breath and nodded.

"Find strength in our allies!" Kiol shouted. "Send these daemon back to the seven hells!"

The cheers that followed conveyed more enthusiasm than Lone expected, but it was still a pitiful response to their combat general's rallying cry. Kiol raised both hands and fired rapid blasts from both. Every hit found a target and disabled, if not destroyed, a daemon, but others stepped over their fallen comrades. Other archmages attempted to emulate Kiol's performance, but he was the only spell-slinger. Lone felt the tug of ley energy that the general pulled into his body to throw the spells at such a rate. The mana flowed to Kiol, feeling to Lone like he stood in a shallow but swift river.

Lone held his blade horizontally before him and set his left palm on the flat of it. Before he could perform an enchantment on the sword, he again felt the growing discomfort in his right arm. Grabbing his sleeve at the shoulder, he pulled at the seam, hearing the stitches rip, and a breath later, took his sword in his left hand to shake the sleeve to the ground. Green energy rippled over the runes of his tattoos, swirling with eddies of darker hues, growing more uncomfortable with every heartbeat.

"*Menf...*" Bard reached for Lone's arm as he had beside the world tree. Lone stopped him with a warding palm and, despite the urgency, let his mind dive into the energy to identify it. He quickly found the tendril that bound the energy to him and knew he could sever it as he had beside the mana lake, but he held off. By the green color, he expected regenerative or healing power, but the color had no meaning beyond what he chose as a dye all those years ago, the one that closest matched his eyes. This was nothing but a glut of mana that pulsed with his own rapid heartbeat, completely in synch with him. Lone licked his dry lips and moved his sword back to his right hand. He directed the energy to flow down his wrist and follow the sword. As he exhaled, his blade pulsed with personal magic.

Lone snapped his attention back to the battlefield. Barbarles and Eplear clashed swords and spears with the daemon, but the latter were endless. Directly ahead, a greater daemon charged a dark orb of energy between the long horns shooting up from its head. Stealing a page from Ruvaal's spell book, Lone threw his free hand behind him and focused a blast of air to propel him forward. The greater daemon drew up on its hind legs and fired the orb of black power at the front of the Dracon army, directly at Kiol and Jazelyn.

Lone had only an instant to regret his decision as he twisted in the air to slash at the orb with both hands on his sword's grip. The spell Broke cleanly in half, and each side fizzled in a wink. Twin volleys of magic from Kiol pelted the confused greater daemon, but to no effect. With no idea where the influx of mana, the Entanglement, came from or how long it would last, Lone again propelled himself forward, aiming his sword at the smoke that made up the greater daemon's neck. He felt the drag of the blade and almost lost hold of his sword before landing and rolling into a crouch. The greater daemon stumbled once and dissolved to ash as it collapsed.

Lone panted and wiped the sweat from his brow. He looked down at his arm and sword, expecting the green light to dim after felling such a foe, but they were doubly bright, the swirling eddies even darker. He watched for a breath, hypnotized, his mind trying and failing to understand this new thing and how he might control it. Lone looked back to the last bits of the greater daemon blowing away in the wind, realizing he had killed it in a single swing.

Impossible...

Lone snapped back in time to parry an imp's slash and countered with a stab. The daemon fell back and dissolved as the greater one had.

Go to Terswood!, came Jazelyn's words in his mind. Not caring how she had managed that, Lone fell into a defensive stance, knocking away the daemon that came too close while mentally searching the battle for his father. He slashed a hound and, as the monster exploded, saw a greater daemon beyond charging its dark orb attack. At the same moment, he sensed his father a short distance east. Lone spread his hand behind him, preparing to launch at this second greater daemon, but stopped himself. In the moment of battle, General Kiol and General Jazelyn coordinated the effort. They were the commanders here. If they directed Lone to Terswood, he would go. He parried another imp and cast his teleport with a tug and pop.

***

"Lone!" Teiris shouted from where she held out both hands, trembling and breathing through a clenched jaw. Lone followed her gaze to the greater daemon she held in a Stun thirty feet away.

He was already running forward. The daemon saw him and moved in slow motion in some attempt to defend. Lone's sword dragged along its smoky underbody, feeling to him like double the resistance of the last one. The beast shook once and dissipated to nothing.

"How did—"

Lone heard nothing more of Teiris's question as senseless agony throbbed from his shoulder to wrist. His mind blanked for a dozen quick breaths. No thought was possible with such absurd torture. On the thirteenth breath, he imagined himself removed from his body, looking down on it from above. Teiris rushed to his side as he knelt in the grass, arm and sword ablaze with power, screaming into the sky.

Why is this growing as I use it?
Only Bard can pull this from me.
He caught the glint of light off the palm-sized orbs on his belt.

If my arm holds this glut of ley energy, would a mana bomb dispel it? The tinkerer within Lone pondered the question as Daelin ran and slid to a stop beside him. Teiris was telling him what happened as Tersguard engaged in fierce combat all around. Lone screamed, literally out of his mind from the pain, when his father reached for that glint. He tugged one of Tekin's devices from Lone's hip, thumbed open the safety, and pressed the button.

The surrounding combat froze for an instant as the green flames along Lone's arm and sword swirled into the bomb in Daelin's left hand and extinguished. With the source of pain gone, Lone's mind returned with the sensation of falling. He met his father's emerald eyes, mirroring his worry, as his stomach lurched with waves of force from the bomb that washed over him with soft, green light. With every pulse from it, Lone knew something was wrong with its operation. Every wave took from him some core of his essence, stripping every cell of his body of what defined him, of the ley energy that made him an archmage. His father pressed his eyes closed and held his head in both hands. Teiris and the closest svarters reacted the same way.

The daemon around them staggered and fell. Well-trained Tersguard seized their opportunity and slaughtered the monsters as they tried to recover. Despite his stomach lurching, Lone saw how mundane swords and spears sliced through the normally impervious hide to slay the smaller daemon.

With the pulse of the mana bomb abating, Lone pushed to his feet and offered his free hand first to Teiris, then his father. Each felt like lifting dead weight with an awkward strain on his wrist as he helped them.

Lone started asking his father what went wrong with the mana bomb, but the daemon were recovering. Daelin clasped his hands and spread them apart in a motion Lone knew meant to create a summoned sword. Nothing happened. In unison, father and son reached for the leather pouches at their hips and dumped out the dust that was mana crystal just a moment before. Daelin frowned and pulled a steel short sword from his hip.

"We can't beat them without magic," Lone said to his father and glanced at Teiris beside Prelen Kaermys, each with a sword in hand and engaged with a daemon hound.

"We must," said Daelin and gripped his son's shoulder. "Take this moment while they are weakened." His eyes lingered on Lone for a breath longer before running to his wife's side.

Lone faced the bulk of the daemon horde and the Exalted looming in the haze beyond. It now wielded a scythe in each arm and flailed them at targets too small or fast for Lone to see. With no access to ley energy, he was trapped, unable to teleport back to the Dracon forces and Bard. Taking a deep breath, he raised his short sword and ran to fight beside the nearest Tersguard.

33

Kalvyr do share a common ancestor with dragons and wyrms, but do not descend from them. It would be more accurate to call them second or third cousins.

"We throw everything at the Exalted," Ethan yelled at his brother's side as they ran by an army of confused humans trying to muster and organize against the wall of daemon.

Aiden's eye ran up the twisted form of the Mother of Daemon, known only to him by myth. Those stories got the description of the monster's form correct, from the many human faces, six gnarled arms, and the rotted look of its scaled hide. What those old tales lacked was a sense of the Exalted's motion. Rather than a smooth slink of a serpent that he would expect from the thing's body, it twitched forward as if scuttling on a million tiny legs slightly off beat with each other.

"It will be weaker than when the Mraasil fought it, I hope? From being imprisoned for so long?" Aiden asked.

"Do not think about how it was then. Focus on its present form."

The lesser daemon were only a hundred yards away, a wall of smoke and fangs shrouding the hills for a half mile in either direction.

With each stride, Aiden pulled at the sunlight on his back, filtered through the clouds but no less vital to him. Each step felt lighter, each leaving a deeper impact in the soft grass. The Light swelled within him as the daemon grew ever nearer. He could see their individual forms: imps, hounds, and fliers. *How could the armies behind us stand against so many?*

They were only a dozen yards from the closest daemon when Ethan sprinted past him. A pale light shimmered across his brother's form, and he sank, still running, into the ground and continued as a hump below the daemon toward the Exalted.

Light burst from Aiden as he called his armor, eradicating the nearest daemon, shredding the next row, and blinding others. He gathered more, projecting his size and power to loom over himself, daemon faltering at the sight of him. Aiden reached out and grabbed the golden war hammer that formed as he closed his gauntleted hands around the shaft and cleaved it through the daemon, sending a half dozen flying without effort. Five swings later, he was through the lesser daemon. Aiden focused on his left palm and called down a shaft of light, swimming with thin, iridescent fishes, that dispelled a great daemon on contact. He waved his arm, directing the light to destroy another.

"Aiden, our focus is the Exalted," said Ethan, sounding as clear as if he stood beside his brother.

"We can stop these. They are no threat to us but will roll over the human and svarters armies."

"Focus, Aiden."

Ethan burst from the ground as a construct of earth, fragments of rock circling his stone form and slicing through the air to impact against the Exalted. Bands of earth rose to entwine its serpentine form while the ground sank below it. As it shifted against the bonds, Ethan's body glowed red from an inner heat at the joints until the rock exploded outward, pelting the beast and leaving Ethan as a swirl of red and orange flame floating a dozen feet from the ground.

Aiden gave the back side of the daemon horde another glance, saw the hole he had cut through it closing, and turned to the Exalted. They could fight the horde, but Ethan was right. It would drain their stamina, giving them no chance against the Mother of Daemon.

What chance do we have, anyway? he thought as he craned his neck upward.

The colossus halted its jerking movement with a groan like the last breath of a dying man. Dark mist swirled before it, and the Exalted reached to form a scythe with a handle like a human spine that snapped into existence.

"Copycat," Aiden grumbled.

"Weaknesses?"

"Daemon are usually smoky or vulnerable to my Light." Aiden craned his neck to look over the obscene size of the Exalted. "Toss me," he said.

The swirl of fire raced toward him, and the red flames gave way to pure, rippling air. Aiden braced himself as his brother wrapped around him and threw him at the Exalted, aiming for just below the faces. The bone scythe arced through the air but passed harmlessly over Aiden's head through the massive projection of himself. He was almost to the creature's chest, which looked more like rotted meat the closer he got. His war hammer flashed to the shape of a comically large sword, and he jammed it forward as he impacted.

The blade pierced deep, and Aiden slid down the length of the Exalted, opening a wound as his Light sword dragged through its flesh and slowed his descent. Smoke and acrid blood hissed against the Light projection over him, and the monster groaned as Aiden reached the ground and rolled away. He dodged another swing of the scythe and looked up at the long gash still leaking smoke... and closing as it did.

"It heals too quickly," he heard his brother say from the other side of the monster. Back in his blazing form, Ethan channeled a stream of fire into the monster that dragged lines of smoke, but did not seem to bother it. He dropped into the ground and erupted again as stone to ensnare the Exalted with vines and rock.

Aiden reached up and called down another pillar of Light and fish to crash onto the Exalted's hunched back. It flinched and groaned but suffered no noticeable damage.

Shadow swirled before the Exalted again, and it pulled another scythe from the air, then another, until all six arms held a weapon. It focused attacks on Ethan's stone form, swinging and crashing strikes that sparked against his rocky surface. More whips of thorny tendrils shot from the ground, ensnaring two of the monster's arms. "Try something else!" Ethan yelled. "I can only hold it a moment longer."

Aiden heard the strain in his brother's voice and dropped to a knee. *This is just stupid. What manner of daemon or anything is unaffected by my Light?* He tried to draw a deep breath but choked on the foulness of the beast's dead flesh. If the Light — the power of purification and the direct antithesis of what force fueled the daemon — did not work against the Exalted, he would give it a taste of its own medicine.

Shadows cracked across Aiden's thirty feet of solid Light armor, seeping into the joints and carving away at the sharper edges. He looked up to that space before the Exalted, where it summoned the shadow to form its weapons. Though the day was still bright with the haze of an overcast afternoon, Aiden saw only the darkness as his golden armor shattered and motes of light drifted away on the unfelt breeze.

The inky cracks remained, forming a ghost outline where his armor had been. It shrank and pulled around him, forming a solid, unadorned protective layer. When Aiden called the Light, it sang his praises, and he would admit that feeding his ego played no small part in his decision to pursue the practice of light shaping.

Shadow whispered of what greatness he could achieve through it, if only he would reject the limitations he placed on himself, things that constrained his power, things like mortality and his connection to his brother. Light sang of past deeds, Shadow of a possible future.

Gritting his teeth, Aiden called upon that force that only wanted to be used and was unjustly vilified. He pulled Shadow from the horde of daemon now engaged with the armies before the city, adding density to his form. From that same place just beyond the boundary of realms, from where the Exalted pulled its scythes, Aiden called more. Under each blade of grass that blocked the sun's muted rays, more. He raised both hands overhead, forcing the Shadow to shape itself into a dozen blades around him, each thrice his height.

The Shadow sang in his veins, gleeful, promising. *This is nothing*, it would whisper. *This beast would be nothing before you, wielding my power without regret.*

Aiden lowered his arms, and the blades flicked from his sides, impaling through the bulk of the Exalted without crossing the space between, dissipating in the light on the far side. Shadow would not slice flesh, but Aiden felt it cut far deeper. The Mother of Daemon roared and turned on Aiden, dropping him to a knee with the force of its screech, hands clapping over his ears. Vines ensnared three of its arms, but another swung its scythe in a clean arc. Aiden resummoned his Light armor just as the blade struck him, tossing him away. The air blasted from his lungs when he landed in a heap. He gasped for breath and pushed to his hands and knees.

Stone erupted from the ground, again throwing an arch over the Exalted's length, keeping it from moving forward with bands over its dark form. It shook and writhed, shattering the bonds as fast as they were formed.

"Any more ideas?" Aiden said, spitting out the metallic taste, frowning at the red splattered across the grass.

"You can pierce it, cut off an arm!" Stone Ethan slid around the bulk of the beast, stopping between it and Aiden. "Hells, cut off more than one!" It broke free of the vines to swing a scythe in a low, horizontal sweep. A column of rock shot from the ground, but the scythe cut through the stone like cheap parchment to impact against Ethan's stone form, shattering a chunk of him with the impact. Aiden heard his brother's pained grunt.

Aiden sucked in the Light and pushed to his feet with a groan. He wiped blood from his mouth and watched his brother explode back into fire to fly around the Exalted's head. It dropped a scythe that dissipated into misty shadows to attempt to grab at him.

"Distract it a moment," said Aiden.

"What in the seven hells do you think I am doing?"

Aiden looked down at his left palm, at the tiny spark of light forming there. It looked innocent, barely more than a mote cast from a campfire. He focused on it, seeing deeper into the layers of the speck, connecting each layer to the next, creating a chain of Light that fed upon and fueled itself. He dove deeper into the minuscule point, each layer a thousand times the size and intensity as the one above it. Finally, he could go no further. The next would contain more Light than existed in all of Poas. Snapping out of the spark, Aiden closed his fist over it and breathed in its power. His vision dimmed as his armor blazed and grew, fueled by the Light of that single point. His avatar, sixty feet tall, was still dwarfed by the Exalted. It mimicked his movements as he reached forward and formed a long sword from the air.

The Exalted turned on him and raised five scythes in defense as he swung the sword with both hands. Aiden felt the resistance in his own limbs as the blades crashed far over his head. He screamed, and his armor flashed brighter. Somewhere in the back of his mind, he heard the tormented moans of daemon from the horde fighting with the humans, but that felt like a realm away, in another time. The Exalted hissed and groaned, and the blade of one scythe shattered.

"Watch out!" Ethan shouted, too late.

The Exalted swung a scythe at Aiden's Light construct from the other side. Unlike his flimsy projection when Ethan had tossed him at the monster, Aiden's form was now as solid as living flesh. When the Exalted's blade hit him from the other angle, Aiden felt it in his own body like a crack against the ribs. He faltered for just an instant, more than enough time for the Exalted to shred the Light with efficient slices.

Aiden again dropped to a knee and tried to call the Light to bolster him, but he had put too much into that single attack. He attempted to push to his feet but fell with a huff. He looked up to the Exalted as it reformed its shattered weapon and raised them all to bring down at him at once. The air blurred around him, and the scythes bounced off an invisible shield only inches from his head. Aiden saw his brother as a shimmer in the air beside him.

"They forged us to fight daemon," Aiden said. "This thing is no daemon." He paused to click his tongue. "I think that means we can leave it for someone else, yeah?"

He winced as the scythes came down again against Ethan's air shield.

"Physical and fire do nothing. It heals immediately from Light and Shadow. We have to kill it in a single attack. Give it no time to recover."

"And I know we are considering the same thing," Aiden groaned.

"I see no other way."

Aiden shut his eyes with a sigh. "This is going to hurt."

"It always does."

34

Snow sharks hunt in packs of three to eight, but a herd can have up to thirty members.

The battle raged too intensely for Alishia to follow it all at once. The armies of Barbarles and Eplear fought with sword and spear, but mundane weapons did little against the protections of the daemon. Hounds and imps picked off soldiers while fliers harried their back ranks.

A line of avaryll stood at the edge of the city, well behind the human and svarters armies, picking off flying daemon with efficient spell attacks. Oddly, the flying daemon seemed more content to attack the troops than advance into Tidecrest.

She called too many daemon. They're held here by her will but aren't following her orders.

Jaiketh and Terswood fared better, with artifice and innate magic, respectively. She watched her parents fighting hip to hip, throwing spells between the ranks of the Tersguard surrounding them. Her father's summoned sword floated behind him and flashed a gold arc across the flying daemon that came too near.

General Kiol rarely paused his constant stream of spells. The color of his magic varied as each found a target, and he alone kept the daemon at bay before the line of Dracon troops. She saw green fire and focused on her brother. Bard stood beside him as Lone's sword erupted with the same energy that assaulted him by the mana lake just a few moments ago. He focused on it and gained some control as he charged at a greater daemon. Lone slashed the beast's dark energy attack in half before slicing through the thing's neck. His power surged, and he struggled to maintain it. He looked up at the next greater daemon.

Her focus was on her brother, but she also saw the greater daemon pushing toward her parents' forces. *Go to Terswood!* she screamed at her brother, knowing he could never hear him. Other greaters shot blasts of dark power into the Eplear and Barbarles forces, leaving craters where soldiers had been, creating space for lesser daemon to spill through the careful formations.

The last group of only a dozen priests wearing white vestments stood on the far side of Terswood. A hand with three fingers raised was embroidered across their chest, and they called down beams of pure sunlight that eradicated any daemon it touched. The small army of Acrus, light shapers, Aiden's secret acolytes. They were the only force that made any difference in the horde of daemon, but they alone would not win the battle.

Aiden's power flared, making it impossible for her to see anything but him. Alishia could hardly process the images as she watched the boys. Last she knew them, Aiden could create armor and a hammer and manipulate the flow of light to hide or project their image elsewhere. Now, he made constructs five times his size and channeled Light at a magnitude unthinkable by the boy she met in Throk'tar. Ethan was the elements given life. He changed between them effortlessly. Not just creating a gust of wind or starting a campfire with a flick of his wrist, but becoming rock and a living inferno.

Alishia squeezed her eyes tight and opened them to watch Etharis by the edge of liquid mana.

"You plan to stay down here while they slaughter the armies of Poas?" she asked, cringing at her own hollow words. "I know you're only seeing to your duty. Good that you can under such duress."

"It's about priorities,.Chronicler." Etharis stood and brushed his hands together. "Of course, I want to be out there, rending through the daemon armies with fang, claw, and ensnaring vine. Though it's flattering that you think I might make any difference, my place is here. The birth of a Mraasil will always take precedence, no matter what else is happening." He tipped his gaze to the twisting roots descending from the chamber's ceiling. "Any minute now. You should get up there to watch with your own eyes, Chronicler."

Alishia licked her lips, unsure of what she should say next. "Where is Ruvaal?"

"Ruvaal? He huffed away a while ago, all upset about the troops outside the city. I suppose we should be glad for them now. So many will die, but they give some infinitesimal chance the city and tree will survive."

"So he's not in Poas?"

Etharis shrugged. "I'm not his keeper. You're the one that can see the entire realm at once. If you'll excuse me." He nodded and exploded into a cloud of butterflies.

Alishia watched the last phantasmal insect dissolve and turned to weave through the tunnels leading to the surface, hardly noticing the turns. In a fraction of the time it took Aiden to lead them down, she stood in the dappled sunlight before the Symposium. Her stomach knotted when she glanced south at the Exalted looming high in the distance.

There's nothing I can do. I can watch, but how does that help anyone?

She pushed into the Symposium and froze in her tracks.

Protectorate Alaraic and his guard stood near Etharis and the other three Mraasil. Horned Bireal and Withered Celium kept their focus on the archdruid's work, but the last Mraasil, Traitorous Ruvaal, turned to her with a wide grin.

No, she took a deep breath. *I've seen nothing directly to condemn him. I assumed he was Morna's master in the orb. As much as I believe it, I've no proof.*

"Chronicler," Ruvaal nearly sang. "Lovely for you to join us in person. You were there for the first Mraasil birth, and so you will be the last."

The others turned to her with his words, all but Etharis.

"Ruvaal, you should be out on the field, being the competent mage you are." She crossed the cavern to stop a few paces from them.

"This is a closed session!" Alaraic bristled.

"She's a Sundered. She goes where she pleases," said Etharis without opening his eyes or taking his hand from the tree's bark. "Verndari comes," he whispered and took a single step back. "The first Mraasil born since time immemorial."

The light dimmed as lines of liquid ruby drew up from the marble floor, pooling where the roots cut through it. It ran in swirling lines across the roots toward the central mass of the tree before the Mraasil. It collected there, gaining the perception of depth and fluidity like a bubble of pure, crimson light hovering on the tree's bark. With a last surge, the ruby ceased flowing from the floor, and the bubble of light popped. A nude Mraasil with weak lavender limbs and short, pale green hair hovered there an instant before falling into Etharis's waiting arms.

"That's it?" Ruvaal muttered beside Alishia.

"The heart chamber will form soon. We must get her into it before the daemon reach the city," said Etharis.

"Speaking of the daemon," Ruvaal whispered. "Chronicler, let's talk."

35

I'm sorry, Brother.

Magic was returning, but slowly. Lone's shoulders burned as he felled another daemon hound with a horizontal slash. He wiped an elbow across his face to clear the sweat and drew in all the ley energy he could manage. This was not like it had been in Iecil, when, with Kiol's aid, he pulled enough ley energy to shatter the ley lines to heal Bard. The lines still ran strong below his feet here, stronger than any other ley lines, being this close to the world tree. At the same time, they felt obscured, distant, and unreachable, like candy behind glass.

The ley energy trickling through his system was enough to swing at the next imp that came within range, but that same power fueled the daemon's movements. It dodged, parried, and countered with its long, thin blade, meeting force with force. The daemon grinned at him, exposing rows of thin teeth coated with something that was surely poisonous. With a sound like the wheezing of an old blacksmith bellows, it hissed at him before charging in for a thrust. Lone dropped under the attack, and with a gesture, the air behind the daemon flashed blue. He swung at the daemon's legs. It dodged backward, and as it hit and shattered Lone's aegis hovering in the air, it was distracted for the barest instant. Just enough for Lone to thrust upward and into the monster's chest. He twisted the blade as it fell, diverting the corpse from landing on him, and shifted away from the pool of caustic blood.

Lone dropped back onto his heels with barely the strength to raise his sword arm again. Around him, the Tersguard had made progress against the lesser daemon during this temporary reprieve without their magic. That faded as the daemon regained their protection and strength while the svarters grew exhausted. He watched in silent horror as a pair of flying daemon swooped down at a Tersguard only yards away. They distracted her just enough for a hound to sink its jaw around her leg and drag her back into the mob. The tide of battle turned to favor the daemon while he sat in the bloody grass, unable to pull the strength to rise. He rested his sword across his lap.

His thumb brushed against the thick band on his left forefinger. Surely, the sanctum stone would still work; his father's devices never failed. Lone could return to Castle Dracon, refresh himself in the icy stream of the ley nexus there, and return with a mountain of mana crystal and an arm full of featherr'ock steel swords from the Vault. The thought lingered and tempted him. He considered how long it might take, knowing the locks on the Vault under the castle took an absolute minimum of eight minutes to open. Perhaps he could Break that magic and get in faster.

Exhaustion blurred his mind, and he only looked up when his father yelled his name. A flying daemon streaked directly toward him, claws extended forward. Lone raised his sword arm, but his blade lay across his knees. He cast an aegis in the air before him but knew immediately by how the blue light sputtered that it would offer no protection. The daemon's face resolved with frightening clarity: an eyeless thing with a mouth of fanged mandibles. Lone touched the sanctum stone again, about to activate its magic, when his father's face filled his vision. Daelin smiled and wrapped his arms around Lone just as his body shook with the impact of the daemon. His smile faded as his emerald eyes dimmed.

Lone heard Teiris's rage, and a thin beam of white light pierced through the beast on his father's back, obliterating it to dust. She was beside him an instant later, screaming and blindly hurtling blasts of death into the horde. His father's weight pressed against Lone, and he rolled him to the side. Lone stared down at the blood coating his hands, and it was not until he saw the stains of red on the front of his father's quilted armor that reality crashed down around him.

PART THREE

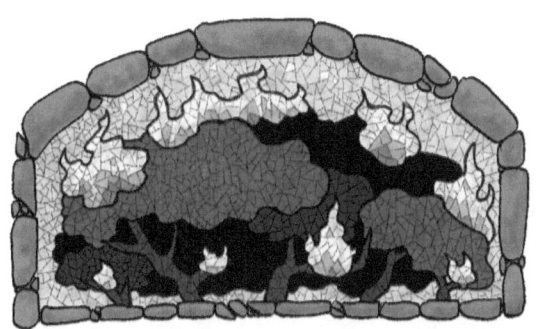

36

Kalvyr society has no obvious hierarchy, yet they get so much done.

Alishia watched the daemon forces clash against the combined human and svarters armies, watched as they steadily gained ground and how they toyed with the soldiers they killed, almost lazy in their slow march forward.

"You know how to stop this," Ruvaal said to her left. "One series of actions led to all the misery daemon and the Gods of Naught have sewn across the tapestry of realms for untold eons."

"I cannot stop the Venatus, Ruvaal," she said around her tears. "No one can stop it."

"Have you tried?"

The swarming cloud of smoke and claws had torn through and around the armies of Poas, leaving only a few pockets of resistance still alive. The daemon neared the bridges to Tidecrest. Sapper engineers ignited their charges, sending the only simple route into the city tumbling into the crevasse below. Undaunted, the daemon climbed down the ravine around the city. The flying beasts continued, dodging the flurry of spells cast by avaryll lining the edges of Tidecrest.

"Untold thousands, millions, numbers beyond your fathoming, have fallen to the daemon," Ruvaal continued. "With their endless reserves, they will flow over this city and corrupt this new tree. Verndari will heed their call and join in ushering this realm into oblivion. What gives you hope that something will stop them here and now?"

Ethan and Aiden still fought against the Exalted, visible as tiny specks against the daemon's unthinkable size. That they still survived gave some rise to Alishia's heart, but how much longer could their strength last? Without them holding the titan back, the Exalted's sheer size would allow it to slither over the city and the rest of Poas, destroying everyone and everything.

I could step away and see the rest of creation before returning to this moment, she thought. *I could step into the future and see how this plays out and decide how to mitigate the worst of it.* She shuttered to consider what road that would lead her down.

Daemon flowed from the ravine around the city, overwhelming the avaryll defenders. The city would not last.

Her eyes flashed with silver light, blinding even her for a breath. When her vision adjusted, she stood where she felt safest, with solid wood under her feet and the silent air lit by an even glow.

"Father..." Lone gasped beside her. His sword dripped with dark ichor, and his face and chest splattered with fresh blood. "Ali? What...?"

"What, indeed, Alishia," came the smooth voice of Etharis. "This is The Stacks, I assume?"

Ruvaal grinned, flashing white teeth. "Brilliant, Chronicler. You were even able to pull in our brothers."

"Ali, I have to go back. I..." Lone said and lowered his sword arm. "Father..."

"Time doesn't matter here. I can send you back the instant I pulled you here," said Alishia. "At least, I think I can. What about Father?"

"Of course you can. You're the Chronicler," said Ruvaal, pulling a small glass vial from his robes. "Nothing is outside of your power."

"Why are we here, Alishia?" Etharis asked, narrowing his glowing eyes.

"She debates doing what you would not, dear brother," Ruvaal answered. "She sees the horrors brought onto the realms by her father's race, horrors that we thought long behind us."

"No..." Etharis's eyes widened, and his brow knit together.

Alishia cut through. "Lone, what about our father?"

"He..." Lone's sword clattered to the floor, and he stared down at the blood coating his hands. He rocked back to sit on his heels, still not taking his eyes from the blood shining in the dim light. "I was too weak. I couldn't stop the daemon, but then Father was there. He threw himself in front of it."

Realization crashed into Alishia, sending her staggering back a step, gasping and clutching at the neckline of her dress. She leaned against the desk on the landing, burying her face in her hands. "I only needed a moment to think."

You should be sad about this, she told herself, but felt only a numbness and distant certainty that sent a chill down to her toes. Etharis pushed past Ruvaal to put a hand on Alishia's shoulder. She raised dry eyes to meet the archdruid's.

"Alishia," he said in a quiet, measured tone and gave a quick glance to Lone. "I am sorry for your loss, but there is nothing to consider here. I admit to my long hours spent considering how I might do the world better knowing what I do now. Even the teeniest, most innocuous change can cause vast, unforeseeable alterations. A pebble tossed into a still lake will cause waves, but considering undoing the Venatus, that would be akin to throwing a boulder into a puddle."

"And after the waves settle, the water is still again," Ruvaal said, pushing Etharis back from Alishia. He held up a dark gem chip between his fingers for her to see. "This is the Ibaerite, the crystallized mana of... here." He turned and waved his arms over the neat, endless rows of books and scrolls beyond the balcony railing. "I had thought it would grant you your powers, but I understand now it only sparked the beginnings of your awakening. That we stand here, rather than amongst the hordes of daemon in Poas is a testament to that."

"You still have the Ibaerite?" Etharis growled. "I ordered you to destroy it."

Ruvaal scoffed. "What power in all the realms could destroy this little gem?"

"And you haven't used it again to enact your plan yourself?"

"No," Ruvaal dropped the gem back into its vial and tucked it into his robes. "It seems I alone lack the power it requires."

"I recognize the energy of that," said Lone in little more than a whisper. "That's the same as what was coming from the Shadow Reaver. What is going on here? Ali, why are we in The Stacks?"

"I'm the Chronicler," she said. "I'm still working on what exactly that means, but The Stacks is a reflection of me. It's weird and complicated."

"That doesn't answer why we're here."

"There was nothing I could do out there. I watched Verndari born, and the daemon overwhelm everything, entering the city."

Lone pushed to his feet, wiping his hands on his baldric. "What does Ruvaal think you're going to do? What is the Venatus?" Alishia noticed the distant spark in her brother's expression of trying to defer grief by focusing on anything else. She saw it often enough after Lium's death.

Ruvaal sighed to the ceiling and strode to the balcony railing, turning dramatically to lean against it. "How many times must I explain it? I forget how frail the memory of humans is. The Venatus, young king, is the daemon's hunt of your people across the realms. It began some impossible-to-calculate number of years ago in the human home realm of Diyar, where the Mraasil Baris guarded his world tree, Safril."

Alishia's breath caught as she recognized the name. "Baris, he was there when the Ascended forged Ethan and Aiden. Thexes banished him to the expanse between the Wheres. I guess that would be, in a way, to here." Her eyes drifted to the endless sea of shelves beyond the balcony as if she might glimpse the violet-skinned Mraasil reading a scroll out there.

"Anyway," Ruvaal continued. "To meet their ever-increasing need for power, the humans sought a new source and found it in the expanse *outside* the Wheres. As I understand it, The Stacks, also called the Lacuna Gap, touches all realms at every point and at all times. Well, imagine a space outside of that. That is where the Gods of Naught dwell. Their very existence is so antithetical to how our mortal minds work that even we Mraasil, the highest of mortal races, cannot adequately understand their nature."

"And Ruvaal wishes to undo that event that first turned the Gods of Naught's eye to us," Etharis said, crossing his arms. "Alishia, he and I toyed with the power of the Ibaerite and traveled back in time within a dead realm. I planted only a handful of spores, and when we returned to the present, an entirely new race of people existed. The world tree of that realm was restored. Do you remember the withered Mraasil Celium you saw at Verndari's birth? They did not exist to us, Ruvaal and I, before planting those mushrooms, yet the other Mraasil have full memory of attending their birth."

Alishia bit her lip, thinking of the frail-looking Mraasil, who shuffled after the others. "But the other Mraasil remembered Celium?"

"Yes," Etharis nodded. "Not only did they remember Celium, but they also remembered Ruvaal and I interacting with them."

"It's like you took the place of your selves that lived the life where Celium existed," said Lone. He pulled his bloody baldric over his head and carefully folded it to place on the desk.

"Brilliant, young king," Ruvaal said with a feral grin.

"The role of the Chronicler is to observe and record," Alishia breathed.

"Who told you that?" Ruvaal chuckled. "Please don't say it was Cazlandt."

Alishia kept biting her lip and looked at her shoes.

"Ali, if you can move through time, you can save our father."

"Or she could save countless millions," said Ruvaal.

Etharis dropped his hands and seemed to grow a little taller, more imposing. "Alishia... Chronicler... I will not stop you by force, but believe me, I have examined a dozen paths the realms may take without the instigating effect of the Venatus. Yes, it was terrible. So many lives have been lost and ruined. But it happened. We will never move forward if we spend our lives regretting and reconsidering every action."

"It was Cazlandt that first told me it is the role of the Chronicler to observe and record," she murmured, only half hearing the archdruid's words. "He was a liar, a murderer, a manipulator."

Ruvaal pushed from the railing. "Would you stop yourself from saving potentially millions on the word of such a man?"

Etharis growled, a low feline sound. "You will erase your entire life, Alishia. Ters will never create the svarters. The avaryll would bore her, and she would be hibernating in Tersil right now, as Uulthra was so long ago. Humans will never spread, and your half-brother here will never be born. As our own experimentation implies, I suspect you two would still exist, orphaned to the changes of time, without an origin. Are you willing to give up all that exists now to save people that were? How could you carry on knowing you effectively killed every human and svarters?"

"No," Alishia shook her head and pushed the loose hair behind a long-tipped ear. "I don't think I could. I don't know if that's right."

"Your father is dead," said Ruvaal with a sigh and gestured callously to the blood-soaked baldric. "Your mother will be once the Exalted kills the boys if the daemon haven't already overwhelmed her. Everything you know and love in this world will be gone within a few hours. We can stay here, frozen in time, hiding, but it only delays the suffering. Unless we can find and defeat Morna Dey, this daemon horde will flow over Poas and into the next world, unstoppable. Human avarice has led to the failure of the realms." He jabbed a finger at Alishia. "Only you can change that."

Her eyes burned on hearing her father's death mentioned in such harsh tones, but her emotion was still muted. She squeezed her eyes tight with a deep breath and released it as she looked up at her brother. His pinched expression and gleaming, emerald eyes were filled with worry but perhaps a mix of anticipation. "I can't save everyone. If I could somehow change things to save our father, you might be dead now, Lone. Then I try again, and Bard dies. On and on, each time, I somehow make it worse. But the Venatus..." She paused and licked her dry lips. "One event that will undo the history of a thousand realms. All that we know is about to be destroyed, so why not try for a better future, even if it never led to us?" She turned to Etharis. "What happened twelve thousand years ago that led to Tersil's destruction? How was the Venatus stopped before?"

The archdruid's expression narrowed even further. "Apparently it wasn't stopped, only paused. We sacrificed a half dozen realms to lure the Gods of Naught here to Poas. Ters destroyed her tree as they made to corrupt her, allowing us to capture the Gods of Naught in a physical form, to shatter and scatter across a thousand realms."

"It took a century to plan," said Ruvaal. "It cost countless lives, and it will not work a second time. Where is Morna Dey that she controls these daemon? Didn't you see her out on the field somewhere?" He paused for a breath before continuing. "No, she hides herself. She knows she is the key to this battle. So long as she lives, this wave of daemon will consume all of Poas and move to the next realm. You're right, brother. We did not stop the Venatus with burning Tersil, only delayed it."

"What happens without her?" Lone asked. "What happens to the daemon if we kill Morna?"

"The daemon go away," said Etharis. "We must still deal with the Exalted, but the shadow beasts have little interest in staying in the mortal realms. They would fade away if not held here."

Ruvaal nodded along with the archdruid's words.

"Wait," said Lone. "If you knew that, why didn't you help me find Morna to fight her directly, Ruvaal? We could have ended this before it started."

"She won't be on the field," said Ruvaal. "The daemon masters never leave themselves so exposed."

"If Morna Dey is the key to this invasion," said Lone, "and if we — you, Ali — have the power to go to any point in time, why not go to when she was summoning the daemon? Or back to Iecil and stop her before she fled? Or go back sooner before she was involved in our aunt's death and Amer's rebirth?"

"Or go back before your father dispersed Amer into the ley lines of Poas?" Ruvaal offered in a mocking tone. "Or stop Cazlandt's military push in Iecil, so he would never have kidnapped the Chronicler to Throk'tar? Or stop him from forging the Shadow Reaver? Or ever found the Ibaerite? Why not just kill Cazlandt's parents before they conceived him?"

"No, you have a point, Lone," said Alishia. "We could decide on the barest single event to alter. Where has Morna Dey been since she was last seen in Iecil?"

"The expanse between the Wheres," Ruvaal answered without hesitation.

Etharis shifted amber eyes to his brother. "You seem very sure of that."

"Of course. Were she in any world with a tree, we would have found her long ago. Where else could she hide for so long except outside the realms?"

"So... here?" Alishia again glanced out past the balcony.

"No," said Etharis. "The Lacuna Gap, the expanse between the Wheres, and, to some extent, the aether, refer to the buffer between the realms, separating them physically and magically. The Stacks exist outside the realms, but that doesn't mean they fall into the same category as the others. Your domain here allowed you to survive the Lacuna Gap and pull us, Uulthra, and the gronyn out after Cazlandt banished us, but that Baris was banished to the Gap does not mean he is here in the library."

Alishia shrugged. "So I cut across time and enter the expanse between the Wheres when Morna Dey is there and we... I don't know... show her the error of her ways."

"No!" Ruvaal spat. "It has to be the Venatus! Have you any idea how long I have spent in considering any other option?"

Etharis turned fully to Ruvaal and cocked his head. "Considering the daemon only entered Poas less than a half hour ago, no."

Ruvaal retreated a single step. "Come now, brother, you know this has been on my mind for months."

"And I told you to drop it."

Alishia's talent for magic was, to her father's chagrin, exceptionally lacking. Nevertheless, she felt waves of power emanating from the archdruid, confirmed by her brother moving to put an arm between her and the Mraasil, waving her to stand behind him.

Ruvaal shied away another step, his eyes wide.

Etharis shot out a hand to grip his brother by the throat. Thin vines grew from his flesh to burrow into Ruvaal's neck and crawl just below the surface of his violet skin, raising him inches from the plank floor. Lone shoved Alishia fully behind him and raised a shining blue aegis.

"No more lies, Ruvaal." Etharis spoke in a voice layered with a feral growl. "You kept that accursed stone with an intention."

"It has to be the Venatus," Ruvaal choked. Etharis's narrowed gaze remained steady on his brother's darkening face. As one of Ruvaal's hands clawed at the archdruid's grip around his throat, the other disappeared into his robes. Alishia watched that hand fumble for something and recognized the intention if not fully understanding what outcome Ruvaal wished to achieve. He pulled out his fist and popped the cork stopper on the vial.

"Ruvaal! No!" Alishia shoved past her brother and through the aegis meant to offer protection from only one direction. She lunged for Ruvaal's fist, prying at his fingers to wrestle away the Ibaerite. Her fingertips grazed the smooth gem.

Etharis gasped and lowered his brother an inch.

"Ali!" Lone's voice distorted behind her.

Etharis dropped Ruvaal and reached for her, but the space between them expanded. She remained in place as the world fell away in every direction. Lone, covered in their father's blood. Etharis breathing heavily over Ruvaal on his knees, gasping and holding his throat. Colors muted and faded to pure white as Lone's cries stretched to a whisper.

Just as quickly, The Stacks collapsed back onto her, the world snapping back into place and flicking to complete darkness.

37

The avaryll subsist mostly on a diet of legumes and ground nuts. Their food would literally kill my mother.

Alishia coughed. Smoke and ash choked the hot air. She heard Lone groaning somewhere nearby and forced her eyes open. She lay on her back, staring at a gray sky with hints of yellow.

"Lone?" she said at little more than a whisper over the dryness in her throat.

He groaned again.

Alishia pushed to her elbows and rolled to see her brother doing the same. Etharis was already standing and offering no assistance to Ruvaal at his feet. "Where are we?" she asked, though she knew the answer.

Etharis inhaled deeply, not taking his eyes from some point in the distance. "Diyar, the realm where humans originated. Though your question should be *when* are we, but you know."

"What's burning?" Lone asked from a seated position a few yards away.

"Everything," said Etharis. "You humans were once far more inventive in your methods of destroying your world." He nodded his chin, and Alishia followed the Mraasil's gaze.

The four overlooked a sprawling city of brick and steel. From the rocky precipice they stood on, Alishia could only see breaks in the city's construction where two rivers flowed through it, joining somewhere near the center and flowing out as one on the other side. Few points of green existed in what must be parks. Smoke churned from a thousand tall chimneys, choking the air and giving the view a hazy, yellow overcast.

"You've done it, Chronicler," Ruvaal said to her left. She had not noticed him rise. "I see people down there, so the event that sparked the Venatus hasn't started yet. Let's speak with Baris. He must know where we should go."

"No," said Etharis immediately. He tore his eyes from the city below and back to Alishia. "I beg of you, return us to The Stacks. You said it yourself: time does not exist there. We could debate the topic for a hundred years until we think of a way to save Poas without altering the past."

Lone sat in a low squat and pointed into the city to a white, cube-shaped building a few stories tall. Smaller than ants at the distance, people milled about in the wide courtyard before it. "That building looks important," he said. "I don't see any other place with that much open space around it."

"Leystrider Industries," Ruvaal said, reading the text in the stylized graphic painted on the building.

"There are some strong ley lines intersecting there," Lone said. He turned and pivoted on a heel to look directly behind them. He whistled and pointed.

Scrubby plains gave way to a sickly forest a few hundred yards away. Rising above that, like a single, thin tower, was Diyar's world tree. Its canopy would barely be enough to shade cafe diners on a cloudy day, but its trunk was visible as it pierced through the thick clouds.

"Safril," Alishia said to no one in particular.

Alishia blinked and let her Sight toss her across Diyar. She saw cities that made the one below look like a rural village. Grander than Tidecrest, populated more densely than Vanaa. Thousands, perhaps millions, of humans lived in this realm and shared in their malaise, in their hunger. Something happened to these people, and recently. She saw more sprawling cities, half empty and abandoned, sensed the peoples' attention and hope focused on the city below her now. The Mraasil Baris worked beside the humans down there. She blinked back to Lone, staring at her with wide eyes.

"Let's go see Baris," said Ruvaal. "We'll stick to the shadows, and he won't notice your wrinkles, brother."

Lone put a hand on her arm. "What is it, Ali?"

"This whole realm is sick. The people are focusing their hope on the success of something in the city below. I almost forgot when I watched the Ascended forge the boys that Baris said he was at Leystrider Industries when it all happened. That's where we have to go."

"To do what?" Etharis crossed his arms. "You expect to walk in there with no plan? Do something that results in a better future? Might I remind you, yet again, that without the Venatus, neither of you will be born? There is no need to undo your father's recent demise because he also will not exist. Welcome to your first trip to a different realm, Lone, but we cannot be here, Chronicler."

"You say you traveled with my future self, yes?"

Etharis and Ruvaal both nodded.

"Then that self already did what I'm about to do, what she did in her past, you—"

"Stop this, Chronicler," Etharis said. "Every moment we remain here, we make the most minor of changes. Perhaps the young king's passive mana cultivation pulls ley energy from someone casting a cantrip elsewhere. Perhaps someone in the city below notices us standing here and is distracted from their duties for a heartbeat."

"No one survived this event to know what happened," said Ruvaal. "Since we're here, shouldn't we try to understand exactly what the humans did?"

"You would suggest anything to get us to stay," said Etharis. "Answer me truthfully, Ruvaal. Did you have a part in drawing the daemon to Poas?"

Alishia looked between the two Mraasil and felt her heart sink with every beat that passed without a response from Ruvaal. Finally, he turned to face Alishia, looking down at her with that terrible, glowing stare. "I have always had an interest in Poas," he sighed. "Naturally, I should, as it comes before my realm in the chain of Trees. I found the Ibaerite and knew from stories you told me long ago, Chronicler, that it was the key to awakening your power. I knew of only one from your realm with the ambition to work with a fragment of such potential."

"You planted the Ibaerite where Cazlandt would find it." Alishia looked down at her empty palm with a wave of panic. Had she dropped the gem after taking it from Ruvaal in The Stacks?

"Exactly. I experimented with the gem for decades but could do nothing to unlock the power of it. I knew you to be Cazlandt's great-granddaughter, so I placed it where the humans might find it and led him there. I set it in the Shadow Reaver myself and arranged the events that ended in Amer imprinting your power onto the Ibaerite."

"But it wasn't enough," said Lone. "You still couldn't use it without Etharis. So you summoned a horde of daemon to siege our world to convince him there was no choice but to return to this moment."

"It was still not enough for the venerated archdruid." Ruvaal's voice cracked as he spoke. "I am a realm guardian. To call for the attack of one realm to save potentially hundreds of millions... While I knew it was necessary, it nearly broke me."

Alishia turned to Etharis, who stood with his eyes closed and arms crossed. "Archdruid?"

She reached for his arm when Etharis did not respond. He jerked away from her touch. "My words mean nothing to you, and I will not take up arms against the Chronicler. Your role is to observe and record, but if you wish to go against that, what can I, merely the first protector of creation, do against you?"

"I'm sorry, Etharis. I didn't mean for us to end up here. Something in the struggle with the gem and, I don't know."

"If you're sorry, return us to The Stacks," Etharis sneered.

Alishia thought of the familiar balcony over the endless expanse of tomes and scrolls, but nothing happened. She had done this dozens of times without effort. She rubbed her fingertips against her thumb, where she had touched the Ibaerite. They felt greasy. She closed her eyes and shook her head.

Ruvaal grinned. "Shall we get down to Leystrider Industries, then?"

Etharis's hand lashed out to grip his brother's shoulder. "Aside from your crimes against your station, I cannot begin to understand the breadth and term of your duplicity. Your punishment will be exhaustive."

Ruvaal put his hand over Etharis's and nodded. "I accept that and know my actions will be justified with our success here. My fate is inconsequential when we return to the realms without daemon or Gods of Naught."

Lone pointed to a place along the road leading into the city. "I can teleport us down there," he offered. "If you'll allow me."

"Again, to what end?" said Etharis.

"We'll do what Ruvaal suggested," said Lone. "We'll watch what was done and see how it might be reversed to cast out the daemon of Poas."

"That's a stupid plan."

"You may teleport me, Lone," Ruvaal said and stepped nearer.

"Ali? Maybe Ruvaal shouldn't come with us," Lone said.

Alishia frowned. "I don't think you should be here, Ruvaal, but I can't return you to The Stacks at the moment. How—" She looked down at Lone's hand on her forearm and up to his glazed eyes as her brother pitched forward. Ruvaal caught him across the chest, and Lone shook his head, pushing his fingers into his temples. "What? What's wrong?"

"It's started," Lone managed.

The clouds began a slow swirl centered over the city, over Leystrider Industries. They darkened and flashed with deep purple lightning.

"What's happening, Lone?"

"Something is drawing all the ley energy to a single point. I can feel the lines narrowing and sputtering. If I'm going to get us down there, it has to be now, before the lines snap."

Etharis sighed and took a single step closer. Lone reached for him, and with a pop in her ears and the sense of a forceful tug forward, Alishia looked up at the regional headquarters of Leystrider Industries, as denoted by the large sign of engraved granite set at the head of the courtyard. The four stood a few yards from a ring of humans wearing matching white, calf-length jackets. In the center, upon a dais, stood a middle-aged woman wearing a form-fitting yellow dress under her open jacket. She worked some unseen interface on the top surface of a metal altar.

The crowd cheered when another mounted the dais from the far side. With dark green hair that flowed in the growing wind and a white jacket that left his deep-violet chest bare, Alishia recognized Baris, guardian of Safril.

***

Lone gritted his teeth and focused on breathing as mana screamed past him. Ley energy focused into the dais fifty yards before him, into that metal device the woman worked with. He assumed the top was covered in runes or dials, something to control and direct the ley energy into a barely visible beam that shot upward. Purple lightning flicked across the surface of black clouds, swirling in a tighter arc with each rotation. The crowd of humans forced him to focus as they cheered the entrance of their Mraasil.

Baris waved at the crowd and bowed dramatically to the woman operating the controls. She returned a nod but did not take her attention from her work. The Mraasil shouted over the ripping of the wind in Lone's ears, but in a language he could not comprehend. It sounded as though a native of a foreign tongue was mimicking Common, poorly. Lone grasped at the mana rushing past him to cast an enchantment of understanding, and the words garbled in his ear as the spell attempted to learn the proper translations.

He felt a change in the workings of the device upon the dais and canceled the failing language spell so he could focus. As he switched his senses to perceive the ley lines, Lone saw the beam of ley energy directed upward, actively creating tiny tears through the ley line nexus under his feet. Each tear wept more purple energy, bleeding into the bright orange he would expect at such a powerful nexus. Lone knew he did not understand what the purple energy meant and wished Jazelyn were beside him to interpret.

Lone tore focus from the ley lines and looked instead to the layers of spellwork upon the dais. He marveled at the interweaving magics' complexity and how one piece supported two or three new fragments. He continued deeper into the spell, navigating through dead ends, and with each false lead, felt it was more complex than may be strictly necessary.

At last, he found the core spell that would tear a hole to the expanse outside the Wheres, invite in the Gods of Naught, and begin the Venatus. The spell upon which a hundred or thousand others were delicately stacked. Months ago, General Miech had given him a cube containing almost this same spell, one for breaking through the barriers erected around his aunt's chambers. Lone had since spent hours studying each of the component spells Miech packed into his little cube. He knew how to cast the magics himself and, to practice his skill at Breaking magic, he learned the counters for them all. Lone traced through that cutting spell, seeing it as a simple web of strings in his mind until he identified the one at the center, the thread that would cause the magic and everything above it to topple like a house of cards.

Lone pulled his mind back to the world of the courtyard and clouds. "I can stop this," he uttered, barely hearing his words over the vortex descending overhead.

"Do it," Ruvaal said to his left.

Lone's mind moved immediately back to that single thread, but he hesitated. *This isn't my power to have, to change history.* Purple flecked from the thread, and Lone severed it. The complex spell matrix collapsed as he pulled his mind again to the courtyard. The thin beam shooting into the clouds sputtered as the magic rebounded, and Lone, along with his sister and everyone else in attendance, was blasted backward by the force.

***

Alishia cracked an eye. Etharis was over her, talking at her, but she heard nothing but a high whine over the archdruid's muffled words. Etharis was gone in a flick of his leather and fur cloak, leaving Alishia alone to push up to her elbows. Where only moments ago, a tall dais stood in the courtyard of Leystrider Industries' regional headquarters, now there was a smoking crater. People rushed around her in panic, seeing to the injured. That she was moving meant she was alive enough to be ignored for the moment.

Lone sat to her left, upright but slumped forward. A wound across his forehead bloodied his left eye, and a dozen smaller cuts covered his face. Green healing magics glowed from both hands cradled in his lap.

"What happened?" she asked.

"I stopped it," Lone breathed around labored breaths. "I found the core magic and Broke it all."

Alishia looked back to the crater and tried to ignore the number of bodies in white jackets lying in awkward poses around the courtyard. "Baris?"

Lone shrugged and shook his head without looking up. "Are you hurt?"

Alishia looked down at her hands, felt her face, and inspected her unmarred dress.

Ruvaal fell into a seated position between them. Alishia saw what looked like amber sap dripping from the Mraasil's fingers. "You did it, Lone. The magic failed, and the device was destroyed. The Gods of Naught won't be entering Diyar today. You stopped the Venatus. Not stopped, because it will never have started. You averted it."

"I'd think you would sound happier about that," said Alishia.

Ruvaal chuckled. "It was too easy. The lengths I went to over so many hundreds of years, and it's over now. It's like a weight has lifted, leaving me hollow."

"You damned my world to death to force my hand here." A shiver ran down Alishia's spine upon hearing her own words. She looked past Ruvaal to her brother's wide-eyed, trembling expression. "Lone?"

"What have I done?"

"You stopped the Venatus! You just saved untold millions of lives! Entire realms!" Ruvaal slapped him on the back.

"What if Etharis was right? What if we will never be born?"

Ruvaal shrugged. "A few lives for so many others."

"Bard..." Lone covered his face and drew his knees to his chest.

Ruvaal breathed in deeply, the air whistling through his nose, and turned to Alishia. "If you allow him, Etharis will spend forever tending to the injured here. You should return us to The Stacks and our own time to see the outcome."

Alishia nodded absently, not taking her eyes off Lone, hugging his knees. She rubbed her fingertips across her thumb, no longer feeling greasy.

Lone or her father never described to her the process of a teleport. What did it feel like to "target" a location? How did they "pull" the ley energy needed, and how did they know how much was required? Her practice of magic, as taught by Cazlandt, was limited to a few basic cantrips creating light or a spark of heat, nothing so grand. She thought of The Stacks and the four that would accompany her, and with no "pull" of mana or sense of motion, she sat in the wing-backed chair before the desk on the balcony. Lone did not move from where he cradled himself on the planks. Etharis rose from a position as if he had been healing someone in a white jacket, and Ruvaal leaned against the desk.

"You certainly succeeded," said the archdruid. "Baris is dead. Safril will wither and die without a Mraasil. The realm of Diyar will follow. If humans stay in their home realm, they will be extinct within a dozen generations."

"Poas has survived without Ters," Alishia said, rising from the chair to move in front of the desk.

"Ters and Tersil are a special case," said Ruvaal. "We made other connections to ensure Poas' continuance after your Mraasil sacrificed herself. Come, Chronicler, let's see what a world we've created."

Etharis crossed to Lone and knelt before him. Her brother's body radiated a calming blue light from where the Mraasil's hands touched his shoulder. "I don't blame you. You saw a puzzle you couldn't help but solve. As powerful as you are, young king, you are still only a human."

Alishia watched her brother and again felt that lingering numbness. Unless humans found another route from Diyar, found some way to restore the history destroyed in that explosion, what might they be returning to in Poas? Through her travels to other random realms, she found the world tree's heart chamber was the easiest place for her to enter. She had yet to run into a Mraasil at work in one, and most of them were hibernating like Uulthra had been in Throk'tar. Alishia imagined the heart chamber of Tersil and found it easy to picture. Her mother's throne was fashioned from the wood of the chamber. Complex swirls of exposed grain made up the walls of a cylindrical space perhaps forty feet across and twice as high. The transition from The Stacks to Tersil was seamless, the walls and books of one blending into the roots and vines of the other.

"Archdruid, what an unexpected surprise," cooed a deep, feminine voice. The iconography of the First High Queen plastered across the House of Enid did her no justice, but Alishia immediately recognized Ters as she rose from a branch that served as a chaise. Her ankle-length, silken dress was slit up both sides to the hip, and the loose straps gave little more than the barest level of modesty. Not that Alishia thought Mraasil cared for modesty or had anything to be modest about.

Ters crossed to them, barefoot, and nodded to Etharis. She looked at Ruvaal with a pinched look of confusion. "Ruvaal, I thought you were sleeping the next few thousand years? Who are your little friends?" She wagged her fingers and grinned, but that faded when she locked onto Alishia's eyes. Ters swept her dress to the side and fell to a knee with her head bowed. "Chronicler, you honor me."

38

Humans are hardly unique in their level of aggression, but with their combination of industry, they're dangerous. The only way to keep them from taking over was to keep them on the run.

Alishia could say nothing for a long moment. Though legend and history had warped the image and role of Ters, Alishia knew her as one to be revered alongside the goddess Enid, whom, she mused, she had met twice, to no great fanfare.

"Please, rise," Alishia said, slurring the words together.

"Ters..." Etharis took the other Mraasil's hand in his and raised it to kiss her fingers. "Pardon the unexpected entrance. We've only come for a moment to see the state of the realm."

Ters let her glowing gaze drift to Lone, huddled among the vines on the ground. "The Chronicler, the archdruid, a sleeping Mraasil, and what have we here?"

"A human archmage," said Ruvaal.

"Human?" Ters pursed her lips and narrowed her eyes. "Why does that word sound familiar?"

"There are no humans in Poas?" Etharis asked.

"No." Ters ran her amber eyes slowly over Lone. "If a human looks like that, I can confidently say there are no others. I'd know about something like this. Where is it from?"

"Humans are native to Baris's realm," said Etharis.

"Baris," she drew out the name in a long breath. "There's a name I haven't heard in a long time. His people destroyed his realm, yes? I remember your cautionary tales, archdruid. Something about the inhabitants inviting terrible powers beyond their ken. *Keep a watch on your mortal races, but do not interfere as Baris did*, you would say."

"That does sound like me," said Etharis. "What happened to them? The humans?"

Ters cocked her head. "Are you feeling well, archdruid?"

"Humor me."

She shrugged. "You could never determine why, but the realm broke itself from the chain of trees and drifted away. You assumed everyone and everything there to be dead now, if the realm still exists."

Etharis glanced at Lone, then at Alishia. "Chronicler?"

Alishia blinked and let her Sight send her across the realm. Rather than the city of Terswood, the world tree Tersil stood sentinel over wild forests that spread miles south to the Alish Ocean. North, beyond the trees, lay the grand cities of avaryll. Sprawling metropolises blended their needle-like towers with meticulously manicured nature. Far to the north, beyond the Eplear Range, in what should have been Dracon, a few avaryll settlements dared to dot the landscape's chill. The southern continent, Iecil, continued the same pattern of towers and trees. Millions upon millions of avaryll lived and worked in peaceful monotony.

No svarters, no humans. Only avaryll.

Also, no daemon.

The cost of meddling stared her in the face. Hundreds of generations of her people, from both her parents' sides, were wiped from existence when Lone Broke the spell. Bard, Uncle Sion, great Aunt Wynlen, Jazelyn and Kiol, Cazlandt, Aiden, and... Ethan. She begged herself to feel an emotion for it all, but perhaps it was too much, her mind too shocked, because she felt nothing. Alishia snapped back to the heart chamber.

"It's all avaryll, this continent and Iecil. Everyone I know... Only Lone is left." The feelings riled within her like a churning school of fish that barely disturbed the water's surface. Lone's face showed what she knew she should feel as he looked up at her with his jaw slack.

Ruvaal cleared his throat. "Tell me, Ters, since I've been asleep a while. Have there been any daemon attacks across the realms? Any horrific invasions by the Gods of Naught that corrupt our trees and spoil our worlds?"

"Gods of Naught?" Ters laughed. "Fey tales. And no daemon since we scattered the Exalted. Well, not *we*. No word that includes *you*, Ruvaal. How long have you been sleeping?"

Ruvaal grinned and faced Alishia. "I say you did it, Chronicler. The realms are safe. We should get back to Tempus Fa to better survey creation, right, brother?"

Etharis said nothing, but his scowl clearly expressed his mood.

"No," Alishia said.

They again stood on the balcony of The Stacks.

"Why are we here?" Ruvaal said while opening and clenching his fists.

"Etharis was right," Alishia whispered and went to kneel at Lone's side. "I won't trade all that was for what we've created." Lone leaned into her, and his quiet sobs shook her frame. Something in that simple transfer of movement crumbled the walls blocking her emotion. Tears flowed from the corners of her eyes.

"You won't trade?" Ruvaal growled. "Ters and the avaryll are alive now, as would so many others without the daemon. All for the cost of a single realm. If you intend to undo Lone's actions in Diyar, you would murder everyone alive now. How can you live with that?"

"How can I?" Alishia jumped to her feet and rushed toward Ruvaal, matching his sneer. Heat flushed across her cheeks and neck. "If changing the past is murder, then I just killed everyone I ever knew and loved. I knew it going in, but..." She relaxed her fists and took a step backward. "This isn't how my power should be used."

"Can it be undone? Or rather, done again?" Etharis asked from where he stood with arms crossed by the balcony's railing.

"Undone? Are you mad, Etharis?" Ruvaal shrieked.

Etharis shook his head. "You have seen your wish fulfilled after so many duplicitous centuries. This goes too far. Mraasil are to protect our realms, not alter others."

"Too far? Ters is alive! So, too, would Felen and Enzrok! Losing Baris that way was unexpected, but he died in our version of events as well. These two are mourning mere memories. Their parents, friends, and lovers are now no more real than dreams."

"There is no justification for erasing one set of lives for another."

"Lives that were moments from being overrun by a horde of daemon and the Exalted." Ruvaal scoffed and turned from Etharis. "Come, Chronicler, send us from here that we may see the fruits of this success."

Like how the Mraasil replaced themselves after altering the Deadloss, Alishia felt confident that, if they returned to that same moment in Diyar, they would replace themselves that undid the summoning of the Gods of Naught, allowing them to repeat the events differently, indefinitely. Even with her shocked emotions muted, she could not go on knowing what was lost. She felt selfish considering it, but there had to be some better solution.

Taking Lone's elbow and pulling him along, Alishia stood. The four were back on the cliff overlooking the city with the regional headquarters of Leystrider Industries.

"No!" Ruvaal raged. "Why do you want millions to die just so you can have your mother? You're—"

Alishia flickered a finger at Ruvaal, and he disappeared.

"I sent him back to The Stacks," she explained before Etharis could ask. "He can read a book or stare at the wall." She stepped before her brother and looked up into his red-rimmed, emerald eyes. "It's undone, Lone. If we do nothing now, the Venatus will happen as it did. Bard and everyone else will be in Poas again."

Etharis cleared his throat. "Not exactly, Chronicler. We've changed the path of time once, and you've now undone it. What if we are meant to have some interaction here? What if we must repeat the next few moments a dozen times before finding what we did in the past that led to the future we know? I am exceptionally long-lived, as is Lone as an archmage. We may be here a *very* long time."

Dark clouds spun in toward the city. The woman in the yellow dress would activate the device at any moment.

Lone shook his head and blinked away his glassy stare. "If we must keep retrying this, maybe we first do nothing and see what happens."

"Sensible," said Etharis. "Try both extremes and work out a middle ground. We can return right now to The Stacks."

"You don't want to see how this happened, Etharis?" Alishia asked. "We could watch but not interfere."

"Not particularly. One of the greatest failures of my kind is the Venatus, and I would rather leave it behind. The longer we are here, the greater the chance our presence will have an effect. The smart plan would be to return immediately."

Alishia looked at the city below and the purple lightning tracing along the dark clouds overhead. "Very well."

"—being selfish and — Why are we back in The Stacks?" Ruvaal waved his arms and huffed.

"We did nothing," said Etharis. "We returned before making any alteration, meaning the young king did not Break the mechanical spell that started every-thing. Chronicler? What present have we wrought?"

Alishia focused on Tersil's heart chamber but could not locate it. That gave her some hope; the place would not exist in her present. Instead, she focused on Castle Dracon, at the point that The Stacks normally exited, but that was also blank. She crossed to the single door from the library, pulled it open, and stared down a long, dark hallway to nothing. Alishia thought of any point in Poas, but it was as though her home did not exist. She tried Throk'tar, Wolvene, the Afterlands, and a half dozen other realms she visited on her own after Cazlandt left, but she felt none of them.

"Chronicler?" Etharis asked again, and she moved to him, taking one of his hands in both of hers. She soaked in the essence of the archdruid's home realm, grounding herself in the absolute destination in her mind.

Nothing.

Tempus Fa was gone, too.

"There's nothing out there." Alishia's knees felt weak as the room spun around her.

"What does that mean?" said Ruvaal.

"I mean, the Gods of Naught must have won. They unmade all realms."

"But that would mean..." Lone touched his cheek, unable to finish the thought.

"We're the only four living beings left," said Etharis. "This is the worst possible outcome, and now we've destroyed the present we know. We've seen the extremes now. Poas is full of boring avaryll, or a trillion lives are snuffed out. Let's find a happy medium."

***

Witnessing the pliability of the past gave Lone hope that they could find just the right series of events that would result in the present he knew. The implication that he would have some role in what would lead to his own birth left him feeling dizzy. Instead, he focused his thoughts on what he remembered of the device on the dais. Baris died when Lone Broke the spell, and the pent-up energy had to go somewhere. Ters said humans went extinct in that version of history. Maybe they tried again to summon the Gods of Naught as a power source. Maybe the realm withered without its Mraasil.

Doing nothing ended all realms as the Gods of Naught and daemon spread unchecked. Perhaps the Gods of Naught burrowed deep into Diyar, infecting the aether that touched all realms. There would be no way to know.

They must have some role in creating their present, but how in the seven hells were they supposed to learn what that is?

He thought of the surge of ley energy as the device was activating and... He jumped to his feet to rush to Alishia, sitting by the balcony's edge.

"Take me back. I have an idea. I think I can fix that device."

Alishia glanced over the railing. "Before or after I sent away Ruvaal last time?"

"Before, I need as much time as possible before they activate it."

She nodded, and despite the stress of the situation, Lone smiled to himself.

In a blink, they were back, overlooking the city.

"Again?" Ruvaal sighed.

Lone rushed to the cliff's edge, followed the ley lines to the courtyard with the dais, and teleported just himself. Without the rush of mana from the device, it was a smooth transition to the pavement surrounded by people in white coats. The woman in the tight yellow dress was mounting the steps toward the control box. Unsure of what else to do, Lone shot a hand toward her and cast one of his stepmother's favorite spells. The woman froze under the Stun, and murmurs rose from the crowd of onlookers. Ignoring them, he ran up the dais to stand beside the controls before releasing the spell and replacing it with one of understanding that he tried and failed here before.

"What is the meaning of this?" The woman was now flanked by three burly men in black jackets aggressively holding short staves in their hands.

"This device will rip apart the fabric of your realm. You—"

"Another extremist terrorist," she spat. "When will your kind learn that the only path to advancement is forward? The world simply does not have enough ley energy to support our needs. Would you rather have another repeat of what happened in the South? Remove him."

The big men advanced, but Lone erected an aegis around himself and the altar, a simple spell with the ambiance of magic at this nexus. The guards pressed against the aegis for a breath before touching their staves to it. Lone could feel how they drained his spell and turned his focus to the altar. He threw his magical senses into it to understand its flaw, but without it first being activated, the device was little more than inert runes.

Lone never saw him enter the scene, but Baris now mounted the dais steps. With hair the color of vibrant moss flowing behind him, his open jacket over a bare chest, and loose trousers were cut low enough to highlight every ripple of the Mraasil's violet abdominals.

"What's going on here?" Baris asked with more whimsy than anger.

"Excellent timing, Lord Baris," the woman said. "Another of Dr. Saint-Enid's followers interrupting our work. He's put up some protective field. It's no matter, now that you're here."

"Is that so?" Baris strode to within a few feet of Lone, just outside the dwindling aegis.

Lone forced his eyes up to the Mraasil's radiant gaze. "No, Lord Baris. I come on behalf of Archdruid Etharis and the Chronicler. I know what this device does and what it will do to the future. I'm looking for the flaw in it."

A dark falcon landed on the dais with Ruvaal a breath behind. Etharis rose, shaking off his feathers, and Alishia suddenly stood beside them an instant later. Lone felt no use of mana in her movement. She simply was there.

Baris dropped to a knee. "Chronicler, you honor me." The woman and her guards mimicked his action, and Lone took the distraction to continue probing through the work.

"Baris, what role did you have in constructing this device?" Etharis asked, drawing the other Mraasil's gaze.

"I was fundamental in its conception, archdruid."

Etharis made a thoughtful noise and continued. "You knowingly and willingly created a device that breached the boundaries of the realms to reach into the expanse beyond?"

"Not at all! The device taps into the limitless energy of the Lacuna Gap. It will siphon the most insignificant fraction to power all of human ingenuity for a thousand years."

"You might want to recheck your calculations," Ruvaal snorted.

Baris rose and took a deep breath, looking between the other two Mraasil. "Not that I mind such a cast coming to witness my grand opus, but might I ask why I deserve the honor?"

"Your device rips a hole to the expanse outside the Wheres," said Alishia. "It invites the Gods of Naught into the realms, destroying creation."

"I... No, that's impossible," Baris stammered but looked unsure of his words. "You've come to stop it, then? To stop me?"

"Not exactly," Alishia said and looked at Etharis.

"The young king here," Etharis waved at Lone, "seems to think his skill exceeds that of you, all your crafters, and greatest minds."

Baris's expression did not change as he slowly blinked at Etharis. "From how far into the future have you traveled to see me, archdruid? I see your signs of aging, however slight."

"That's no matter," Etharis heaved a loud breath.

"And you say my device is flawed? That it will lead to the unmaking of the realms?"

The other Mraasil nodded.

"Then it must be destroyed." Baris frowned. "I had nothing but the best intentions for my people, but not at the cost of others. Stand aside, young king." He reached toward the control panel.

Etharis caught him by the wrist. "We have not come to stop this, but to understand how events will lead to the history we know. Our goal is not to undo these results fully."

"*Your* goals," Ruvaal grumbled.

Lone linked the barest thread of ley energy into the device. Not enough — he hoped — to activate it, but enough to highlight the runes and spells so he may better guess and trace their function. The barrier-breaking spell was at the core, with a hundred others layered atop it. Most of the specifics were beyond his understanding, but he was confident he could fully map the work given enough time to study.

He looked again at the barrier-breaker, set at the core with everything feeding into it in some way. All without a limiter. Lone remembered his father complaining about General Tekin's flawed strength-enhancing bracer prototype that would draw endlessly so long as it was supplied with mana. This device was no different. On a small scale, it may work perfectly. When placed at a major ley nexus, like what flowed beneath his feet, and layered with a hundred spells to enhance it, the results would increase exponentially.

"I've found it," Lone said with a chuckle. The others grew silent to look at him. "It's just missing a limiting rune to specify how powerful it can be."

"That quickly?" Baris asked with a raised eyebrow. "I wish I had you on our staff years ago."

Lone felt the heat on his cheeks. "I'm no brighter than anyone else. I come with a fresh eye and have recent experience with this exact issue." He lowered his aegis and looked at the woman in the tight yellow dress under her white coat. She had a thick notebook in hand, furiously scribbling notes.

Her pen hovered over the page, shaking slightly. "This young..." She looked over Lone, who realized he was still stained with his father's blood. "Young man's theory may have some credit, Lord Baris."

Baris pulled his jacket closed at the neck as his jaw dropped an inch. "Well, that's terrifying. Thank you for bringing his oversight to our attention. Perhaps you could stay on to help with the refit?"

Lone grinned. "I'd love to."

"No," said Alishia and took him by the arm. "We can't stay, Baris."

Alishia tugged on him, and Lone stumbled onto the wood planks of The Stacks balcony.

"Your teleport is somehow more jarring, Ali," he said.

"Did it work?" Etharis asked immediately. "Are the realms restored?"

Alishia's eyes radiated a cool, silver light, and her frown deepened.

"No."

39

The technology of Diyar was a real sight to behold. The humans wanted for nothing, but were left exactly that when it all fell apart.

Humans, everywhere.

Alishia looked over a dozen realms fully populated by her father's race in their cities of brick, steel, and flying ships. They harnessed the power of the Lacuna Gap to power their industry, essentially fueling their works by siphoning power from every other realm at once.

And those works were grand.

Soaring monuments built because they could. Instant travel across realms and between them. The few Mraasil she glimpsed either hid in their trees or worked beside the humans, by their own will or not.

In Poas, the last pockets of avaryll fought a losing shadow war against the invaders. In Throk'tar, the gronyn were traded and sold as a labor class. Kalvyr and Piscinath were hunted to near extinction. No race stood against the humans. Even in Tempus Fa, the infinite home realm of Archdruid Etharis, their presence was significant.

"In fixing their device," she sighed, "humans gained enough power to take over. This is no better."

***

The four returned to that cliff overlooking the polluted city of steel and brick. Lone again uncoupled the device's magic to cause it to fail but without the explosive result. Baris survived. Within a year, Leystrider Industries revealed another prototype containing the same flaw as the first. Humans again went extinct as the daemon overran Diyar.

Again.

Lone broke the first device and the second as well. Human civilization fizzled out as their reliance on ley energy drained their world faster than mana flowed in. Their civilization faltered and fell, and they again went extinct.

Twice more. Another seven attempts. Every time, humans as a species either withered or took over the realms. There was no middle ground similar to the world that produced Alishia and Lone.

"We can't do it." Lone dropped to the plank floor of The Stacks balcony with his back against the desk.

"We already stopped it," Ruvaal growled. "This is a futile waste of time, Chronicler. We saw the best option, the first one we produced with the destruction of their infernal machine. Humans and svarters will be gone, so let the avaryll have Poas."

"No," said Alishia. "Our present happened once. I have to know how."

"Forget that. It's no more than a memory now," said Ruvaal. "Use your power to observe and record this new timeline devoid of the misery caused by the daemon and Gods of Naught. Return us again to Diyar and let the young king explode the device."

"If that's how it was meant to be," said Alishia, "I would have been born in that string of events. There must be a way to restore our world."

An image flashed by Alishia, of standing before the Ascended as they forged the souls of the Taigh brothers into the Hausers. Baris's reaction then gave her a clue about what might have led to her present.

He thought she had tried to warn him.

She blinked.

Alishia yet again overlooked the city beside her brother and the Mraasil. She sighed and closed her eyes. When she opened them a breath later, she stood alone. At the next breath, she stood beside Baris as he waited to ascend the dais and make his grand speech.

"What is the mean—" He gaped at her and dropped to a knee. "Chronicler, you honor me."

"Stand, Baris, we only have a moment."

He rose as ordered, towering two feet over her.

"What do your people know of portal magic?" she asked.

"Portals? Not much. They prefer their grand airships for transportation. I've encouraged that, but many wish for teleportation and portals, but I know the dangers that come with those. The humans are always rushing somewhere, a very industrious people."

Alishia looked up at the growing darkness overhead. "After today, assign some of your top magic people... What do you call them?"

"Ley scientists or rune engineers." Baris grinned, clearly pleased to be teaching the Chronicler a new fact.

"Assign some to the topic of creating cross-realm portals. I have a feeling your people may have the desire to travel to other realms soon."

"Is that allowed? Moving sentient beings between the realms?"

"I don't see why not." The image of an arcing sword in the forest came to her mind, of the humans invaders slaughtering gronyn in Throk'tar.

"Why are you telling me this, Chronicler? Does something go wrong with my work here today?"

"I will only say things will happen as they must. Now, go out there and dazzle the crowd." She flashed a smile.

"Thank you, Chronicler. Will you stay and watch?"

"I'm always watching."

Baris dropped into a sweeping bow and left in a twirl of his jacket. As he ascended the dais, Alishia's shoulders fell with the weight of that simple exchange. Aiden was happy to say how often she meddled in things. Even if she just had no direct action against Baris or his machinations, planting the idea of portal magic would give the humans a means of escaping Diyar when the daemons overran this realm.

While she fretted, the device was activated, and the Gods of Naught quietly released into Diyar. Alishia groaned and returned to The Stacks. Lone and the Mraasil immediately assaulted her with questions, but she ignored them to focus her mind on Poas. She confirmed it existed with humans and svarters, no world tree heart chamber, but looked no further. *Were a few words to Baris all that I needed?* If that was their present, it was still full of a world under siege by daemon brought by Ruvaal's command.

"Do the Mraasil have the power to stand against the daemon in Poas?" she asked over whoever was already talking at her.

"They would," said Etharis. "It would take far more than I was able to rally. Perhaps they would better listen to someone of your stature."

"How many would it take?"

"Perhaps one for fifty daemon. As many as possible."

"And how many of you are there?"

Etharis scratched at his beard. "That's a complex question. There are well over a hundred thousand realms in the great chain of Trees. Only a few have lost their Mraasil and remained connected, and my kind still live in a few disconnected realms."

Alishia balked at the number—over a hundred thousand. A part of her said to toss away the idea brewing in her mind, an idea that would take years, maybe decades, to still possibly fail in the end. If all existence ended in this new wave of daemon, it would make her job easier. Having an earlier end date on the realms would make collecting all their knowledge quicker.

No, though she had not witnessed the end yet, it was a very long way off. This daemon horde would fail. Somehow.

"Chronicler," said Etharis. "If you are thinking what I think you're thinking, this is exactly why we should have never gone to Diyar. I see the plan forming behind your eyes, a plan we would have come to without toying with the past."

"That was an accident, the first time," Alishia said and turned to her brother, clothes still stained with their father's blood. There would have to be a way to fix that, too.

"I'm going to be gone for a while. For you, it should only be a few minutes or hours, but more for me. I'll miss you more than anyone else." She stood on her toes to kiss his cheek. "Before you say it, you can't come with me. I know how sensitive archmages are to changes in ley energy."

"Where are you going, Ali?"

She glanced to the Mraasil and stepped back from Lone with a wry grin. "I'll let them explain."

Without a sense of motion, she stood in a small chamber of twisted vines dripping with a dark, oily substance. A Mraasil in dirty and torn robes stepped from the shadows.

"Chronicler, you honor me. Welcome to Senguosh, home of the Deluge."

Alishia filled her lungs with air saturated with rotten mana and prepared to give a speech that she would have plenty of time to perfect.

***

Lone waved his arms at the empty space his sister had just occupied. "What is she doing?"

Ruvaal walked by him, clapping Lone on the shoulder as he passed. "Whatever she pleases. She's never allowed us in here before. I'm going to poke around down in the books while she's gone." He descended the spiral stairs without a glance back.

Lone looked down as his hands that still ached from Breaking the spells on the device. He must have raised his arms in defense without thinking or remembering. Green energy radiated from his hands as he channeled regenerative energies through them.

Etharis flopped into the chair and propped his muddy boots on the desk. He crossed his arms and closed his eyes.

"You're not interested in going into The Stacks too?" Lone asked.

Etharis sniffed. "I know enough to know I know enough," he said, lowering his chin, looking ready for a nap.

"What is Ali doing?"

Etharis closed his eyes. "When Ruvaal and I traveled with your sister, Aiden, and Ethan, she often raved to them about how smart and powerful you were. Are? Going to be? The tenses get weird. Make use of those smarts now, and I'm sure you'll figure it out before she returns."

"She wanted to know how many Mraasil there are, and if you could beat the daemon in Poas." Lone paused while the pieces fell together in his exhausted mind. "She's gathering the Mraasil. That will take an age!"

"Perhaps two."

"But how—"

"Young king, my kind rarely sleep. When we do, civilizations rise and fall around us. I want to rest my mind and eyes for a moment. I don't want to sound rude, but please go away or stop talking."

Lone bit his lip and frowned. His father's blood was still wet in spots, and the thought of undoing Bard's existence was still fresh in his mind. Then, helping them to fix their work resulted in his race becoming the oppressors of the realms. Things once worked out such that he and Bard were born, met, and fell in love. He would not settle for a present where that was not the case. He thought of his sister's eyes, dark blue, now flecked with mysterious silver. Those eyes haunted with a distant stare.

"I've lost her, haven't I?" The vastness of The Stacks devoured Lone's words.

"What?" Etharis groaned from the chair without cracking an eye.

Lone cleared his throat. "A couple of months ago, she was just my little sister. Half-sister. She finally comes back, and I see the difference in her. She's taller, more..." He gestured and waved his hands down. "She's older, a woman now, and I didn't see it happen. Her eyes are different. That's the worst. What happened to her, Etharis?"

Etharis sighed, opened his eyes, and shifted to sit upright in the chair. "Your sister is the Chronicler, young king. She was born into a mortal shell to allow her to understand the world around her."

Lone's brow furrowed with the odd idea. "What does that mean?"

The archdruid leaned forward with his elbows on the desk. "Were you to watch a game of... What's that one with all the little pieces with their own movement rules?"

"Rooks?"

"Sure, Rooks. Would you know the rules if you watched one game or a thousand?"

Lone shrugged. "I suppose so. I wouldn't be any good at it, just watching, but I could learn the rules."

"Were you to watch a mother sacrifice her life to save her child, would you understand why?"

Lone blinked. "Well, yeah. Any mother would do that."

"Why? Why trade the life of a self-sufficient adult for a helpless child?"

Lone stammered, unsure of how to respond.

Etharis nodded. "Exactly. A mother's love drives that action, not something that mere observation can understand. To someone with no concept of love or grief or anger, it would look like an older being sacrificing itself for another that is weaker, less experienced, unable to survive on its own. These last sixteen years, Alishia has received a primer in the emotions and inner drives of the people she will watch as the Chronicler."

Lone thought of the long hours sitting beside his sister in the old oak tree, watching Myrell rise as he rambled about all the newest events in Dracon. Had her laughs and chiding all been to teach the Chronicler what it felt like to be a person? What had she felt each time she would roll her eyes as he announced his next big project?

"I supposed I haven't lost her." Lone took the simple wooden chair beside the balcony railing and set it beside the desk. "If she was born to become the Chronicler, I never really had her." He sat down and laid his arm out across the desk.

"You can look at this a dozen ways, young king. Maybe cheer yourself up knowing that your time with her shaped the understanding of a being of her magnitude." Etharis patted Lone on the hand.

"You can just call me Lone. I'm not a king."

"As you wish."

Lone put his head down on his arm. "Why is the Chronicler so important? Baris and Ters knew her, but there aren't any legends in human or svarters history about her. If her role leads her to write all the books and scrolls below, what's the point? How does this help anyone's life? Dracon has controlled access to The Stacks for twelve hundred years. No one is benefiting from the knowledge here."

"Twelve hundred years sounds like a lot, but in the context of creation, it's nothing. Time is tricky to estimate between the realms, but consider that when we were just in Diyar, it was fifteen times that from when we consider the present."

Lone crooked his elbow to cover his face. "I hate time travel."

"You and me both. Also, consider this place touches all realms simultaneously. Twelve hundred years of limited access from Poas equates to the sum of unknown millions of years across all the others."

Lone perked up. "Are you saying other realms have some access, like the corridor under the castle?"

"I've witnessed a few routes here, but this is my first time inside."

"And you said there are over a hundred thousand realms. That's mind-boggling." Lone glanced back to where Alishia had last stood before disappearing for her quest. "Can you get us out of here? Can we get back to Poas?"

Etharis raised an eyebrow and gestured to the iron-banded door to his left. "Can you? Whether or not she intended it, she left me in one of the few places where I am completely impotent. As I can't teleport into The Stacks, it seems I cannot teleport from it, either. I'm sorry, Lone. Unless you spontaneously learn your great-grandsire's ability to Realm Stride, we're stuck waiting for your sister to return."

40

*Lone's face just before we returned, that pinch of confusion, almost undid me,
more than anything else.*

Alishia traced a finger along the hard leather bracer on her right forearm and
watched the Mraasil in gaudy red and blue robes speaking into the crystal
ball held between his hands.

"You will find the body in a mountain monastery called Whiteherst Den," said
Ruvaal in a low growl as he attempted to disguise his voice. "Monks are protecting
her and the staff, but they will be no trouble for you. Go now and inform me of
your success." He wiped a hand over the orb and dropped it to the soft grass at
his feet. Ruvaal rubbed at his temple a moment before stooping to pick up the
glass ball and slip it into his robes.

***

"I have not felt this warmth in an age," said the swamp hag in a voice like the
chiming of delicate bells. The tendril that served as her tongue snaked from her
cloak to caress the chip of mana crystal, leaving strands of mucus over Alishia's
hand in its passing. "Is it valuable?"

"Mana crystal is common enough in the few realms it exists," Alishia said,
focused on her shallow breaths, lest the touch of that tongue combined with the
stench of the swamp hut and its occupant overpower her senses. "It is rare by how
few those realms number, and it holds great wealth to those that know the use of
it."

"I accept this payment, Chronicler," said the hag. A skeletal hand wrapped with patches of flaking skin poked from the cloak to take the crystal and draw it back inside.

"Madam Sentra," Alishia started and rolled back her shoulders to stand a little taller, but she still craned her neck to the crowned head of the cloaked hag. "Your kind walk the frail line between worlds. You were born at the edge of the Lacuna Gap and may be the closest to the type of creature I wish to learn about."

"Daemon. You wish to kill them."

Alishia hesitated before shaking her head. "I wish to understand them. I must remove them and the Gods of Naught from the mortal realms before they destroy everything. If I can do it peacefully, I would prefer that."

Madam Sentra's laugh was another clatter of beautiful chimes. "The Chronicler is a pacifist. I honestly did not expect that. Very well, I accepted your payment, though you did not provide a question. Ask it now."

Alishia thought she was prepared for this moment but still did not have the question ready to ask. What could she not find the answer to herself?

"This can't be done peacefully, I know. We will meet the daemon with force, but they are the lesser issue. How do I banish the Gods of Naught from the mortal realms and seal them away?"

Madam Sentra floated silently over the cold firepit for a long moment. She seemed to shrink before finally speaking. "What is it like for you, Chronicler, to live outside the flow of time? That is how it must be for the Gods of Naught, the Teroian as some civilizations call them, to exist outside the physical realms. Even I, who bask in the energy that flows against the Trees here in Urbus, cannot comprehend what such existences would be like."

Alishia frowned at the non-answer, but the hag continued. "It would not be enough to undo what was done to first break down that barrier, to seal the breach to the expanse outside the Wheres. I regret I cannot answer your question with certainty. I wonder if you might hold some power over the Gods of Naught in what makes you unique, Chronicler. They were once nothing that became something and, in doing so, are now beholden to the flow of time. You are not. What if you could overcome them by sealing the Gods of Naught within time itself?"

"I..." Alishia started but touched her chin in thought. "That is an interesting idea, Madam Sentra."

"I regret I have nothing more to suggest."

"Then I thank you for your time. You can keep the mana crystal as a gift to keep you warm."

"Wait, I have one more fragment of wisdom since I could not answer your question," said the hag. "Daemon require a master. If you have an issue with daemon, the true target is the one who called them. With few exceptions, killing their master will disperse their forces."

"What would be an exception?"

"For one, the children of the Exalted are not controlled. We have several of them here in Urbus."

"That may be useful. Thank you again."

Alishia did not wait for the swamp hag's response before she was back, alone, in The Stacks. She thought of Lone and the Mraasil less than a heartbeat away, locked in their own instant of the library, and a smile slid across her lips. Finally, some small inkling of a plan. She marveled at her ability to recall the names and unique features of the thousand Mraasil she spoke with since she stopped counting after a thousand realms visited.

The Chronicler set her eye on Poas. The kalvyr and so-called dirge races quietly thrived to the west while the avaryll dwelt behind their magics. There was no world tree to protect. They just wanted nothing to do with the rest of the realm. Svarters and humans struggled to restore their societies after their war that ravaged the land for a decade. She sighed, wondering how many more tweaks were needed to get to a present where she was born. Once she accomplished that, Amer would blind her and awaken her Sight, Cazlandt would pull her to Throk'tar where her mind and powers would be set free. She felt bad, knowing she would arrange for Cazlandt to abduct her younger self, as if it were happening to a different person. The Chronicler glanced at the bare desk beside her and remembered the note her future self wrote that led to Lone finding their father in the demi-realm.

"Alishia, the workings of the Stacks make it difficult for me to be sure you read this at the correct time but I have done my best. Send aid to the Demi Realm to rescue your father. Be wary of the Mraasil."

She scoffed, thinking of the note. Why did she not write something clearer for her past self?

The Chronicler's role is to observe and record, she heard Cazlandt's words and saw that note as a sort of test. Yes, she could explain everything to her younger self and save hundreds of lives, but that was not the past she remembered. No, she would see that everything happened exactly as they had up until the moment she took her brother and the Mraasil from Poas.

She stared at the desk, where a bloody baldric lay folded in another instant. Everything.

The Chronicler blew out a breath, and the balcony darkened, no longer lit by the ambient light she had grown accustomed to. An open book lay on the desk with her favorite pen sitting in the gutter. Taking it up, she scrawled the note verbatim. Next, she unpinned her ruby brooch and pricked a finger to let a single drop of blood fall onto the page. The scene looked exactly as she recalled. As soon as she left, a young Princess Alishia would come through the door to retrieve her pen, read the note, and... she closed her eyes. That past was still a long way away.

"I'm coming for you, Lone."

***

She held little hope of peacefully ending the daemon conflict in Poas and long ago gave up trying to avoid it completely. A bloody battle in Poas was, regrettably, the best option. If Ruvaal did not see his plans come to fruition, he would find another means to exact them. The Chronicler frowned as she watched the shifty Mraasil stroll through the mana crystal cavern, aiming for a point deep within the twists dug by the human miners. He held the Ibaerite in his fist, and she saw the discomfort the legendary gem caused him. That pain was overshadowed by the smug grin of one knowing their well-laid plans were coming together. He thought of the miserable old archmage he knew well but had not yet met Ruvaal, who would find the gem and eventually lead to the Chronicler's birth. The Ibaerite would grant Ruvaal the power of the Chronicler, able to shift through time and become the master of it.

Ruvaal found the perfect place, surrounded by the tools of workers on break. He picked up a chunk of mana crystal the size of his fist and pushed the Ibaerite into it as easily as one might pierce a needle through leather. Ruvaal rubbed at his palm, where contact with the gem left his blistered flesh with a magenta hue. After so long watching and guiding the Mraasil's hand, the Chronicler could guess his thoughts. He bit back a grin as he saw the future unfold before him. The miners would find the gem. Cazlandt would arrive immediately — Ruvaal left the note for him just moments ago. The archmage would seek help working with the Ibaerite, and Ruvaal would, in some disguise, offer that assistance. There was no way the Mraasil could guess the exact details of a future beyond that, but it was enough to make him feel his machinations progressing.

Since first seeing her in the flesh in Throk'tar, Ruvaal's secret life revolved around some plot that ended in him controlling a portion of the Chronicler's power. He sought the oldest magics from long-faded societies and found power to link him to forces beyond his ken.

As Tersil burned and the Scions of Flayme killed every corrupted Mraasil turned daemon master, a single one escaped to the expanse between the Wheres. Guided by Ruvaal to that timeless place, it fed on the essence of the Mraasil Baris until a cottage appeared, and the daemon master met a powerful aetherwalker named Kethry.

Alishia encouraged and nudged those plots, considering it akin to giving a child matches, only to frown when he burned down the house. Ruvaal had to see his goals met and dashed for him to understand the gravity of his errors. She long ago resolved any guilt felt by her involvement. Ruvaal was set on his plan and would find a means of seeing it through, with or without her silent hand. A quick memory of Lone's quiet sob shaking her body gave her all the motivation to carry on in restoring his present.

***

As she often did, she touched her bracer, running her fingers along the decorative embossing that masterfully disguised the runes across the surface. Since finding it on her bed in Terswood, the Chronicler never went without it, and though she had taken it to a hundred realms, it was as clean and undamaged as when she first unwrapped it from the cloth bundle.

She stared without seeing, her gaze unfocused, looking past the leather bracer to the empty spot on the desk's corner. Upon leaving her brother and the Mraasil, she resolved to return the realms to their state as of when she pulled the three others with her into The Stacks. The barest sliver of the Gods of Naught, no more than a stale breath, entered Diyar that day. Soon, children of the Exalted, uncontrolled and uncontrollable daemon, spilled in after it. Simply suggesting to Baris that his humans explore the idea of portal magic was enough to save the race, as they used their untested spells to fracture the race across the realms. Humans as a species were saved, though cast thin.

***

"I'm busy here," grumbled the Mraasil with violet skin marked with dark splotch-es. "I probably wouldn't even hear the archdruid's call." Wearing filthy robes, she sat up to her hips in the loose, slowly bubbling muck, picking through it to find stones. Some she placed in her lap, but most she tossed away.

"You will hear his call this time," said the Chronicler from a rock just high enough to keep the hems of her dress from the muck.

"Well, like I said, I'm busy." The Mraasil grunted and flicked away another stone. "I might not have the time to spare."

"The Mraasil still remember who would not fight the Exalted at the beginning of time. This will be no different. Ignore this call, and you will forever be an outcast among your people."

The Mraasil touched mucky fingers to her lips and looked down at the pile of rocks in her lap. "I will listen for it. I promise nothing more."

She heard that from most of the realm guardians, a promise to listen. The Chronicler thanked the Mraasil and moved to the next.

***

The Chronicler traveled across the realms until the barriers between each blended and blurred. Time itself meant nothing as she flowed through it at will. With each alteration she made, the result shifted until she came to a single conclusion.

People of any race are nothing but a collection of their memories and the current condition of their bodies and environment. Even the Ascended, beings of energy universally known across the realms, were no better. They were, if anything, worse than the mortals that worshiped them, as each focused fully on the few traits that defined them. Dhumjir responded to everything with conflict and violence. Khizreus strove to be sneaky and necessarily underhanded. Suanh's demeanor was closest to the Chronicler's, also working to gather knowledge. Suanh only valued the accumulation of information with little regard to its organization or application of it. Everything, while wildly complex and seemingly random, would react the same way, given identical stimuli.

Free will was an illusion.

While the realization saddened her, it made her role possible, even manageable. It removed extreme variables. It meant the whole of history across all realms was set. From before Etharis first stepped from Farsil, to the eventual end, everything would happen in a single path of each event leading to the next. Nothing would cause it to deviate except for beings with powers like hers to slide across time.

The Chronicler sighed into the still air of her library and turned her back to the railing. A string of wooden beads lay on the otherwise empty desk. She stepped closer to admire how each bead's grain and color were just a little different, from red and smooth to black and coarse. She bit her thumbnail and traced tentative fingers over a white bead. The image of a man in armor more radiant than the sun seared her mind. She knew what memory this contained and felt the warm tears begging her to leave it be, even as she took up the beads to cradle in her palms.

With a glance to where she last saw Lone and where he still stood at another instant, the Chronicler's mind fell into the Gilded Warrior's.

41

"A Mraasil deserves greater respect."

T otal darkness.

Total silence.

No reason to breathe.

Of all she had experienced across all the realms, this was a first for Alishia.

The first time to experience what it is to be dead.

The whistle of an ax echoed through a memory. That the memory existed at all surprised her.

Next, an emotion. Several. Grief. Loneliness. Despair. All the worst piled onto her, dragging her deeper into the void.

Then, the loneliness abated as she felt another nearby—another who shared a soul with the one she inhabited—two beings who, while individual, required the other.

The two souls orbited one another, creating a dizzying swirl of sparks. The heat built, becoming what should have been unbearable, but Alishia felt no pain of burning, only the intensity of its power.

Her vision snapped to flames licking by her eyes toward a starless sky above. Confusion replaced the initial sense of horror. She felt more than saw who lay beside her in the conflagration, and a weight lifted from her chest. Again, the fire she lay in was nothing compared to what she felt inside. Another breath and it would no longer be contained. As that power erupted outward, the world exploded into chaos. She felt the tug of gravity and a hard impact on the grass.

"Ethan," she heard the choked drawl and saw an arm rise to the other beside her.

Ethan pushed to his elbows and flopped over to his hands and knees. He gasped for breath in the choking smoke. "How?"

Small fires dotted the area for a dozen yards. Through the connection with Aiden's memory, Alishia recognized Chancellor Koughat rushing to their side. "A miracle," he whispered and looked over the brothers for signs of injury. "Elphame rejects your offering."

"By the Divine Gigroot," said another of the council elders. "The Captains Hauser are reborn in flame!"

Aiden locked on to his brother's green eyes, and Alishia felt an unspoken conversation flow between them. *Why are we alive? What is wrong with us? Are we not worthy of sacrificing ourselves?*

Others surrounded the brothers, creating a ring of bellowed prayers and calls to the honored ancestors, pleading for understanding.

A smirk slipped onto Aiden's face, and he fell to his side. He reached to take his brother's hand and fell away into peaceful oblivion.

***

Alishia felt the rough press of floorboards against her cheek long before her mind registered a return to herself. She hugged her knees to her chest and squeezed her eyes tight to let the tears that clouded her vision pool by her cheek. After a long moment, her quiet sobs slowed enough that she pushed to a seated position with her blue dress spread around her. She wiped her palms across her eyes and cheeks before taking a deep, centering breath. Alishia knew her travels deadened some connection to emotion, but what she had just witnessed through Aiden brought it all rushing back, restoring the compassion that she thought faded.

Alishia stood, smoothed her dress, and adjusted the bracer on her right forearm. With another deep breath in, she pushed back her long hair and used deft fingers to work it into a quick plait. As she sighed out, the balcony shifted around her. Etharis reclined in the tall chair behind the desk with his feet propped up and eyes closed. Lone sat in a chair opposite, half lying across the desk and snoring lightly. She took a step toward them, stopped, and retreated. Instead, she turned and silently descended the spiral stairs to the main level of The Stacks.

A few turns delivered her to a clearing dominated by a low table stacked high with maps. She cleared her throat, and the other occupant of the space whirled to her.

"Chronicler, back so soon?"

"Hello, Ruvaal," she said and moved beside him next to the maps.

He squinted and reached to touch a strand of loose, dark hair by her ear. "You've changed again. I see it in your eyes."

"I've been gone a long time."

"Have you done it? Restored the present?"

She gave the barest nod. "So far as I can tell, yes."

Ruvaal's amber eyes flashed wide, and he lunged to grab her by the arms. "Why? Why do you insist on holding onto a version of the world with so much suffering? Why do you choose misery?"

Alishia twitched from his hold and took a step back. "I'm sorry, Ruvaal."

"Sorry? Sorry for what? You have the power to set the realms on a better course. We could all be living in our own utopias if you chose to make that happen."

"You would never be happy."

He scoffed and tossed his arms in the air. "I would be ecstatic. I want nothing more than the happiness of others. My people exist to protect our realms and the people within."

"I'm sorry for what I've done to you."

The Mraasil retreated a step this time while his face pinched with confusion.

Alishia folded her hands before her. "I heard the Chronicler exists outside of time, and I thought that just meant I could travel through it using The Stacks. It's so much more than that. I see how each action chains to the next. As we speak, I know how you'll react, what you'll say and do next. I see the rest of your life laid out as flashes of images in my mind."

"And what have you done to me that you are sorry for?"

"You knew of me, of the Chronicler of legend, before first feeling my power in Throk'tar. Then you saw me across that battlefield, and that legend was suddenly flesh. You have since been driven by a compulsion to possess what I am and use my power to correct past mistakes. You have been so careful, doing all this under the archdruid's nose. I've guided and encouraged that. I am as much to blame as you for those suffering and dying in Poas. More so because I knew how it would all end when I slipped you the Ibaerite."

"Slipped me..." Ruvaal took a deep breath and tapped his fingers on the maps beside him. "I found the Ibaerite on the shores of a dying realm. You had nothing to do with me being there."

"Of course not. You took the stone back to your tree and studied it as an oddity, never guessing its connection to me. It wasn't until I joined your travels with the Scions of Flayme and let slip some details of my past that you suspected the true nature of the dark gem you kept locked up in Nethraanzil's heart."

Ruvaal said nothing, but Alishia saw the tiny twitches in the corners of his eyes. He was rethinking his life and searching for decisions that were undeniably his alone.

"You were a tool used for a lesson," she continued. "As the Ibaerite created physical and aetheric connections from me to The Stacks, I needed you so that I may appreciate the depth of my task. I have the power to alter the flow of time, but I do so knowing how my change will impact the future, a future that should be unknown. After watching how you manipulated events, I resolved only to observe and record, but not interfere."

"I was your little experiment. A puppet to test how far your ethics might bend."

"I'm sorry to have used you like this, Ruvaal. A Mraasil deserves greater respect. By my hand, you have spent so long hoping to undo the past that it has blinded you to ever looking forward."

***

The Chronicler returned to the balcony with Ruvaal sulking a few paces behind her. Lone and Etharis were awake and in conversation when they stepped onto the wood planks. Etharis stopped mid-sentence and nodded his chin in her direction. Lone glanced her way and jumped to his feet.

"Ali?"

It sounded like a question to her, and she smiled back. Lone ran to her and wrapped her in a tight embrace. He acted as though they had spent years apart, though, from his perspective, it had only been a few hours. When he finally stepped back, he frowned down at their father's blood, now smudged across the front of her blue dress.

"I'm sorry, Ali, I—"

"Everything is as it was," Alishia said. "It's time for us to return to Poas and see this out."

"Ali, what have you done? You look... you look older than me now."

"I've been busy." She grinned and touched her brother's cheek. "I did a lot of traveling and thinking."

"And she's chosen to do nothing," Ruvaal huffed from a corner. "You reset the world, only to see it destroyed by the daemon you refuse to stop. My life of careful planning, the millions that will die as the daemon overtake the new tree, all for her misguided spiritual awakening."

"Don't think I didn't try, Ruvaal. I strode to a hundred thousand realms and saw just as many futures play out. It took everything to maintain a connection to why I did it all. Why see a cosmos of realms when I know it will all eventually end? Ethan and Lone kept me going. Between now knowing what I had with Ethan and what will be in our future and knowing yours too, dear brother, I held on and completed my task."

"It'll be hard to pursue your relationship with Ethan knowing the daemon are about to destroy the realm," said Ruvaal.

"The daemon you invited?" Lone said while clenching his fists.

"You have done the unforgivable, Ruvaal," said Etharis. "The Gods of Naught corrupted our people into their agents, but you also did their will. You called for the death of a realm to coerce the Chronicler into action."

"Coercion that she admits to fostering in me."

Etharis looked at Alishia, and she nodded. The archdruid's shoulders fell. "Your actions were still your own. I know you believe the ends justify your means, but you are guilty of the highest crimes."

Ruvaal's lip curled into a sneer before breaking into a sudden laugh. "And what would you do to me, brother? A realm needs its Mraasil. Kill or banish me, and the Afterlands will wither and die. Punishing me would kill my realm, making you no better than I."

"He can stay here," Alishia offered. "After possibly years with Cazlandt in The Stacks, he realized some measure of his guilt. I returned him to more or less the same time he left."

"Would you repent after a thousand years here?" Etharis asked and raised a hand to rub at his beard.

Ruvaal's grin faded again to a sneer. "I'd rather be banished to the Lacuna Gap."

"The Lacuna Gap is a field of inhospitable magics. You'll lose your mind there. No, you'll stay in The Stacks," said Alishia, gesturing to the rows of shelves below the balcony. "Out there, you can learn every outcome I attempted until you one day see why this was the best choice, the only choice. If you take a hundred mortal lifetimes, so be it. I will visit as often as you like."

"Might I, as well?" Etharis asked quietly. "Visit, I mean."

"Of course," she said. "I don't want to be your jailor, Ruvaal, but I know well enough that I cannot trust you in the mortal realms. I will aid you in undoing what I have done all these years."

Ruvaal stood a little taller and gazed down at her with a look dripping with defiance. She blinked, and he disappeared, locked in his own moment without time.

Etharis leaned a palm into the desk and ran a hand through his hair. "I've witnessed the end of many of my kind, but nothing like this."

"He did what I led him to do," said Alishia. "I have as much blame in his actions."

"You can't force a fish to fly. He was born capable of everything. All his actions led us to The Stacks, where you went back and guided those actions. Which actually happened first? You two share a tightly twisted fate, each requiring the other, though not simultaneously."

Alishia put a hand on her brother's shoulder. "I restored everything to how I knew it existed in Poas and Throk'tar. It's time, Lone."

"Bard?" Lone asked with eyes wide.

She nodded. "He's fighting alongside the generals of Dracon."

The corner of his mouth twitched to a grin. "Time to save our father."

Alishia looked down at her hands and how they shook with the chill that spread down her spine. "Please forgive me, Lone." She unpinned her ruby brooch and pressed it into Lone's hands. He looked down at it and back at her with a face pinched with confusion. "You'll know when to use this."

42

I gasped as the knight tossed his magic sword into the pit. What would possess him to cast away such a powerful relic?

L one looked down at the ruby and silver brooch, lauded as the finest piece of jewelry ever created by a true connoisseur of fine things — his mother. The inexpert twists of wire holding the gems in place glared back at him, and he almost ignored the slightly darker tint of the center ruby. He held it up to the diffuse light, thinking it was just a shadow, but no, the gem definitely was a darker hue.

"The ruby's been swapped out," he said.

Alishia put a hand over the brooch and pushed Lone's arm back down. "Don't worry about that."

"Did you embed a spell into it? How will I know when to use it if I don't know what it does?"

"Because I already saw it."

Lone closed his fist around the brooch. "This new you will be hard to get used to, Ali."

"But you will." Her face darkened with a devilish grin. "Take a deep breath."

Lone took a breath to respond, to ask why she had said she was sorry, but The Stacks faded, replaced with blood and ichor-stained grasslands littered with the dead and a horde of daemon. He was exhausted, barely able to lift his hands in some defense as a flying daemon dove at him. He cast an aegis with what little ley energy he could pull, and the monster shattered through it.

His father was suddenly on him, wrapping him in strong, protective arms, and he lurched as the beast struck.

No! Not again!

Lone heard Teiris's scream sounding like it came from a mile away as he focused on his father's fading eyes. He pushed his father to lie beside him and grasped at the ley lines still clouded by the mana bomb, feeding power into healing, but could sense the depth of the wounds and how quickly the poison was spreading. Lone grabbed at his father's quilted armor, gripping handfuls of the stiff fabric, too exhausted to produce tears, and stared into his father's emerald eyes.

Teiris dropped to her knees beside him some moments later, but he barely noticed her.

Lone looked down at his armor, covered in father's blood, both dried and fresh. His right fist held tight to something. He opened it, equally confused and not surprised to see his mother's — Alishia's — brooch. A pale purple light licked from the center gem.

Lone took a deep breath to hold back the tears and pushed back from his father. He held up the ruby brooch in his hand that quivered from the rush of sorrow and anger.

This is why you said you were sorry, Alishia. You weren't going to save our father.

He squeezed the brooch in his fist, ignoring the pain as the wire bit into his palm.

Damn you, Chronicler. You would interfere a hundred times to make things as they are right now, but not to save this one life that really matters.

Lone held up his fist to watch the blood drip from it.

Observe and record, but only when it suits you.

A drop of blood hovered on the edge of his hand, ready to fall into his lap, but instead pulled back into his fist. He opened it to watch as the replaced gem at the center of the brooch drank in his blood.

Pain shattered his mind for an instant, and Lone's arm flared with a green light that drew into the gem before he could think to Break the spell as he had by the mana lake.

"What..."

A light flashed beside him, and he raised an arm from the glare. A grimy Mraasil wearing muck-covered robes stood looming over his father's body. She glanced over Lone and Teiris with shining amber eyes before turning to the daemon horde. A ball of ice blue light formed in her hand, and she threw it at the nearest daemon, where it exploded into shards of crystal that shredded its target.

Lone started and looked up to a swirl of clouds forty feet overhead that cleared to show another Mraasil floating there, wrapped in swirls of loose strips of fabric. They raised both hands and formed a massive fireball that blew apart a clump of daemon on impact.

All around him, Mraasil appeared, each in their unique way. An implosion of fire, flecks of scintillating light, climbing out of the ground, stepping through a red, two-dimensional portal. None spoke as they turned their immediate attention to the daemon invasion. Lone felt the draw of ley energy from the infant tree as the realm guardians called upon Endanlegsil's strength to fuel the daemon's death. Lone lost count at eighty, but they kept appearing.

Butterflies gathered beside Lone, and Etharis appeared a breath later. "I had to see it myself. She did it," he muttered, jaw slack.

"Ali? Did what?"

"Only six came to my call. Hundreds come for her."

"Archdruid!" Lone grabbed at Etharis's long jacket. "My father!"

Etharis dropped to his knees beside Daelin and moved his hands, glowing green, a few inches from the king's body. After a moment, the glow faded.

"I'm sorry. Elphame holds him."

The sounds of battle faded, and Lone heard only those three words echo.

Elphame holds him.

He's gone.

"She should have returned us just a minute sooner," Lone whispered, watching Teiris move through a silent prayer to Enid. "Why didn't she let me save him?"

"As we said in The Stacks, where would it end? Perhaps she has tried a thousand ways to save your father, but something worse always happened. For all we know, she overwrote us a hundred times as she tried other series of events."

The tide of battle quickly pivoted with the might of the Mraasil, with many expressing power greater than even General Kiol, laying out swaths of death against the daemon. They banded together against the greater daemon, taking them down efficiently with blurs of violet flesh and forest-green hair. Within minutes, it was clear the daemon horde would be defeated, which only left the Exalted still looming in the distance.

"The daemon are infinite so long as Morna Dey lives," said Lone. "Where is she? I'll slit her throat myself."

"Remember, she resides in the body of Archmage Jazelyn's daughter. You must find a gentler means of excising the daemon mistress."

"I don't care."

Etharis frowned down at Lone. "Careful, young king. Action from anger and grief leads to regret."

The archdruid's words rang hollow in Lone. Not just anger and grief. *Alishia betrayed me. My sister truly is lost to me.*

"Even if you find and take Morna's head," said Etharis, "the Exalted remains. The Mother of Daemon needs no mistress once called to a realm."

Lone pulled himself from his spiral long enough to ask, "Can your people kill it?"

Etharis frowned again as his shoulders dropped. "I don't think my people will get a chance."

43

My mind is rarely still, always considering where next to travel and explore. I look forward to the quiet moments.

"C hronicler!" Bireal and Celium gasped as they dropped to a knee.

Etharis considered her with the whisper of a grin.

"There's no time for that," Alishia groaned, waving the Mraasil to stand. "Verndari, is she awake yet?"

"Only just," said Celium. "I have fed her dew, and she seems to know where she is."

The three Mraasil parted to reveal the third behind her. Dressed in a loose shift, Verndari lay reclined on a chaise with her hands folded across her stomach. Her wide, amber eyes moved around the small room without focusing on anything for long.

"I'm proud of you, Alishia," said Etharis as she squeezed past. "It seems you really have restored events to how they were."

Bireal took a deep breath. "You smell of him too, of Cazlandt."

"I'm his great-granddaughter. I know what he did for your realm, and no, I won't accept your debt owed to him."

Alishia sat beside the seven-foot infant and took a violet hand in one of hers, causing the new realm guardian of Poas to focus on her. "Verndari, time is against us. Do you understand my words?"

She nodded and pushed a lock of short, verdant hair behind the long tips of her ear.

"Good. Tell me, can you feel the old heart of Tersil through the roots of Endanlegsil?"

The young Mraasil's smooth brow knit with confusion a moment before relaxing, and she slowly nodded.

"What's going on out there, Alishia?" Etharis asked behind her.

"Poas is losing."

As one, the four Mraasil jerked to attention, their long ears twitching. Alishia felt what they heard as a vibration in the realm's fabric.

"I hear your call, archdruid," said Celium. "How is that possible with you standing beside us?"

"How, indeed?" Etharis locked his gaze on Alishia. "Only I, the archdruid, can initiate a summons."

"What do we do, archdruid?" Bireal asked. "When last you summoned us to Tempas Fa, it was but a fraction of the urgency I feel now."

"Bireal, Celium, stay with Verndari," said Alishia.

Etharis crossed his arms over his chest. "You have fully embraced your role, giving orders to the Mraasil."

"You may want to go, Etharis. See what is happening for yourself."

The archdruid's lip curled into a frown, and he exploded into butterflies.

"Are you sure we shouldn't go as well?" Celium asked with hands covering their ears.

Alishia nodded and turned back to the young Mraasil. "Verndari, call to the spirit of Tersil, ask how she contained the Gods of Naught twelve-thousand years ago."

Verndari's eyes clouded, and her gaze drifted to a point over Alishia's shoulder. *Was that too much to ask of a being less than an hour old?*

Just as she readied herself to repeat the request, Verndari spasmed with a single, long gasp. Bireal and Celium rushed to her side, but the young Mraasil's gaze snapped to focus on Alishia. Her high whisper cracked as she spoke. "Morna's in the cottage." Verndari pushed something into Alishia's palm.

The Chronicler held the sliver of bark up to the light. It was ancient and charred at the edges, but she recognized the geometry of it. *It's the same as the Ibaerite.*

She tucked the piece of bark into her sleeve.

Alishia blinked to activate her Sight, but avoided looking at the battle raging to the south. If the Mraasil had been called, her father was dead. She just visited him in his workshop and would not spoil that tender moment with the reality of her decisions.

Her mind went south anyway, to rolling grasslands that lacked depth or dimension. Rather than a horde of daemon and the towering Exalted, a single occupant stood in the space with flaming red hair, lips, and a hunter-green dress that flowed in the light breeze.

"Chronicler," Morna Dey said as Alishia stepped into the demi-realm a dozen paces before her. "Come to observe and record my little bubble?"

"Not exactly, no. I've come on behalf of someone who has always been kind to me."

Morna's right eyebrow raised in anticipation.

"Kethry's mother wants her daughter's body back."

Morna spread her arms, then ran her hands down her sides. "I'm afraid you'll have to tell her it's already in use, and I've grown quite fond of the curves."

"You'll lose the battle, Morna. You called too many daemon and spread your command too thin while you hide in this bubble realm."

The daemon mistress shrugged. "Even if they wander a bit, I'll replenish the daemon as they're cut down. They're endless, unlike the mortal soldiers."

Alishia took a slow breath, steeling herself for the confrontation she knew would happen any instant.

"Oh, sweetie," Morna chuckled and pointed to the fist Alishia had not realized she clenched. "You surely don't mean to fight me. Even with whatever you are, you're still a little girl, and I control one of the most powerful archmages ever to walk the realms."

"No," Alishia's voice cracked. She cleared her throat. "No, not a fight."

"Good," Morna said with a wry smile. "I'd hate to destroy a being such as the Chronicler."

Alishia swallowed the threat. She felt the moment drawing nearer. "Of course, I'm no fighter, but I can offer you a shell with greater potential than Kethry's."

She turned away from Morna Dey and pulled the silver of bark from her sleeve just as Lone fell next to her with a hard thump.

44

The Great Beast Kelngarn stretched almost two hundred feet long. I never imagined something larger until I saw the Exalted.

Aiden groaned up at the Exalted towering into the clouds before him. The largest head in the center was probably the one it ate with, but why would it want to eat him? Why would he want to be eaten by it?

"If not the head, you could try getting inside it through the other end," said Ethan.

"Get me up there again," Aiden grunted.

Wind swirled at his ankles and gripped around his torso. With more precision than the first toss, Ethan raised his brother into the air. They flew toward the Exalted's heads, dodging scythes, until they were close enough for Aiden to see the deep cracks in the monster's largest face. It looked like a porcelain mask, but the cracks shifted and reformed when the beast opened its mouth to scream at them. Ethan's windy form blessedly bent the sound, and only the smallest fraction made it to Aiden's ears. That was enough to turn his stomach and darken the corners of his vision.

"Ready?" said Ethan.

Aiden took a deep breath before realizing that it was his brother he was inhaling. "As ready as I ever am. Love you, Ethan."

"I love you too, Aiden."

A spear of light shot from Aiden's chest to impact the Exalted's mouth. The air around him burst into flames, and Aiden channeled the light and heat into a wedge. Sweat poured down his face, and his hands shook as he pried at the monster's mouth. It stopped resisting and opened wide to scream again at them.

Ethan seized the opportunity and wrapped tight around Aiden, flying them down the Exalted's gullet. He pressed deep into the creature until the contracting muscles made further progress impossible. Lit by the fire still clinging to Aiden's summoned armor, Ethan reverted to his human form. Aiden struggled to hold the beast's interior at bay for another breath. He stared into his brother's eyes and extinguished the light. The Exalted contracted, and the darkness was absolute.

***

They held each other in the nothing, the only two beings of note in this vast void. Eternally bonded, each required the other for survival after the gods lashed their souls together. The nothing resolved into raw elements. The strength and substance of stone, a fluidity from air's breath, the passion and renewing force of fire. With it came the shadow and light to highlight and hide the world forming around them.

***

Lone lacked the will or strength to stand. He could activate his sanctum stone to return to Dracon, but even that was too much right now. Anywhere was better than looking at his father's body, so he watched the Exalted. He watched the minuscule dot that, by how it glowed gold, must have been Aiden rise into the air, zipping around the Exalted's scythes and flying directly toward its faces. The Exalted opened its maw in a silent scream. Light flared, and it screamed again. Lone gasped as Aiden flew into the daemon's mouth.

His heart caught in his throat.

"Wait," said Etharis. "Ruvaal and I traveled with those two, calling ourselves the Scions of Flayme while we trained them. You are about to see the origin of that name."

Lone had enough of mystery, of cryptic, half-spoken truths, and his eyes drifted back to his father. Lone sidled closer and reached for Teiris's hand. She took it and looked up at him with eyes that slowly resolved to focus on him.

"Watch," said Etharis, and Lone and Teiris turned.

Red and yellow light leaked from the Exalted's joints, giving it the impression of being surrounded by a hazy glow. It froze and, one by one, dropped its scythes, which dissolved into shadow before reaching the ground. Light and fire burned through the eyes of the smaller heads, and it opened its mouths to scream. The ground under Lone's feet shook as the Exalted lashed its serpentine tail and raked at its face with all its clawed limbs. Each gash it tore open spilled more fire and light until all its faces were ruined.

"Shields!" Etharis yelled, and his smooth voice carried effortlessly across the field. Mraasil paused the battle to create a wide net of interlocking defensive spells.

The Exalted's arms drooped. One tense heartbeat later, the upper half of the Mother of Daemon exploded in a ball of heat and light. Fragments pelted against the Mraasil's defenses. Lone lowered the arm he raised without thinking and looked in awe at what remained. The Exalted's torso and heads were gone. Instead, floating in the space, blazing with intertwining auras of red and gold, were two figures too small to make out. Though Lone did not understand what happened, he knew who those two were.

Lone brought a hand to his mouth with a gasp. *This is absolutely unreal.*

"I suppose that solves the issue of the Exalted," Teiris said without enthusiasm and looked back to Daelin, brushing a finger across his cheek. "He was doing so well these last few weeks. I thought we'd have more time."

"Me too."

"You should go to Bard," she said without glancing up.

"They're going to fall," Etharis said quietly but with enough alarm to pull Lone's attention. He looked back to where the Exalted had been. The fiery auras surrounding Aiden and Ethan were fading. Etharis ran forward and jumped, taking flight as a falcon.

Lone acted without thinking. He drew in a quick burst of ley energy, and with the familiar pop and tug, he was in freefall with the air ripping past his ears. The remains of the Exalted rushed toward him two hundred feet below, with Aiden and Ethan unconscious or dead in the space between, their arms wrapped about each other. Lone reached for them, twisting his body to fall faster, trying not to notice how very close the enormous body now was. With another stretch, Lone's finger brushed Ethan's ankle. The quick contact was enough for Lone.

Ethan's body crushed on top of him, blasting the air from his lungs. Lone rolled him to the side and sucked in deep breaths to catch his wind. He put an ear to Ethan's chest and blew out a deep sigh at the sound of a heartbeat. Sitting back on his heels, he saw Aiden's fingers twitching into a fist.

"How are they alive?" Lone asked no one.

As one, the brothers jerked to an upright position with a sharp intake of breath. Lone fell back with a cry of surprise.

"Did we get it?" Aiden gasped with his amethyst eyes wide as he and Ethan craned their necks for a sign of the Exalted.

"I think you did," Lone stammered.

"Great," Aiden grinned, looking exhausted, and leaned back onto his palms. Ethan dug through his satchel until he found two small towels. He tossed one to his brother and wiped at his face with the other.

"What are you two?" Lone asked as he pushed to his feet with a groan.

"We are not entirely sure," Ethan said.

A falcon landed, and Etharis reverted to his normal form beside them. "Quite a display, young king. Nice catch."

Lone noticed for the first time where he had brought them after the teleport. The remains of the Exalted lay a hundred yards away, with the armies of Poas twice that beyond.

"When did all the Mraasil get here?" Aiden asked, squinting at the distant battle.

"They came in response to a call just as I would make," said the archdruid. "Though, unlike my call, others actually came to this. It feels... orchestrated."

Lone's finger grazed the brooch that he still somehow held in his hand. He brought it closer to stare into the darker center gem.

Etharis whirled to him and inhaled deeply. The archdruid took Lone by the wrist and snatched the brooch from his palm. "Where did you get this?" He brought the piece of jewelry close to his nose for another deep sniff.

"Ali gave it to me before we returned from The Stacks."

"It reeks of my energy as if I've handled it for a decade. I remember your sister often wearing it on our journeys ages ago, but it wasn't like this. I never enchanted this as it is now."

"Maybe you did," said Lone. "When she returned us from The Stacks, we would have taken the place of ourselves here, yes? Only the Chronicler would know what she had you do differently, which is now lost to your memory. I'm sure you would have prepared such an enchantment for her had she asked."

She did what she knew she must...

"Devious." Etharis frowned and continued his examination of the brooch. "This is what called the Mraasil."

"I need to get to Ali," said Ethan.

"She was with Verndari when I came here," said Etharis.

"Thanks." Ethan nodded and took off toward the city at a sprint.

"I need to get back to Dracon," Lone said, scanning the distant battle for a sign of the battle standard to set his direction. Seeing none, he closed his eyes and focused his mind north searching for Bard's void, finding it immediately. With a tug and a pop, he stood behind two Mraasil as they landed the killing blow on a greater daemon. Bard stood between them, unarmed and covered in dark ichor. At Lone's feet, Jazelyn lay unmoving, and Kiol on his side next to her in a pool of crimson blood staining the grass.

45

Lone saw their flaw right away, not because he's any smarter, but because he lives in a realm where a single spell can snap a ley line.

"**L**one!"

His eyes snapped from the fallen generals for just an instant to see Bard limping the few steps to him and dropped to check the archmages for signs of life. Lone rolled Kiol to his back and felt his heart settle from his throat when the spellslinger groaned. He sucked that breath right back when he saw Kiol's right arm end in a ragged tear of flesh at the elbow.

"General Jazelyn said she would search for the daemon mistress," said Bard. "She laid down right here with General Kiol over her."

"She aetherwalked right here? In the heart of a battle?" Lone felt Jazelyn's neck and noted her shallow breaths coming in short, quick gasps.

"The daemon turned on us, seeming to double and triple in numbers and strength."

Lone looked up and finally saw the mounds of dark daemon bodies mixed with the pale blue of Dracon royal guard armor and the outlandish colors of archmages. He pressed his eyes tight and forced his gaze back to Jazelyn. They would tally the dead later.

"Jazelyn needs an anchor. She'll never find her body with all the magic flying around here. Mraasil!" To his surprise, the two realm guardians turned and looked down at him with cold amber stares, one with bright tattoos over their right eye and the other wearing light chainmail armor. Lone's confidence shrank with their glare. "Please, see to Kiol." Without a word, the armored Mraasil dropped to a knee and suffused Kiol with a gentle, green light. The other turned back to the battle as if standing guard.

Lone looked back to Jazelyn and remembered his research on anchors for scrying and aetherwalking. He placed the palm of his left hand on her forehead and the other on the right side of her ribs, over where he assumed her liver was. Lone never found an explanation for the placement of contact points, but someone must have decided this was optimal. He pulled from the ley lines to press energy in through her head. For a long moment, Lone felt like he was threading a needle blind, searching for that strand of ley energy within her body. Finally finding it, he pulled the energy from her with his right hand, completing the circuit.

It only took a moment, and Jazelyn's eyes flashed open with a deep, ragged breath. "Morna Dey is in a demi-realm with the Chronicler."

"Where?"

"Directly overlapping us here. Go, Lone." Jazelyn's dark eyes equally pleaded and commanded him. She saw the Mraasil hovering over her husband and crawled to his side, lifting his hand in both of hers.

"Go to her," Bard said. "Stopping Morna Dey is the only way to end this." He placed a hand on Lone's chest, over his heart, and slipped the other behind his neck. Bard's kiss started gently, but Lone pressed into it as all that had happened since coming to Isolis crashed into the front of his mind. Alishia returning, looking five, then fifteen years older. Traveling through time and to another realm to undo all of human history. His father died on top of him, twice.

Lone gasped back a sob and pressed his forehead into Bard's.

"I love you, *menf*." The words, spoken in Au, rolled gently from Bard's lips.

Lone let the words seep into his mind while he searched for the demi-realm with his eyes closed. The last time he teleported into one with Bard, it had been an accident while tracing distant and unknown ley lines. Now, he searched for something without idea of what it might look or feel like.

He found nothing and opened his eyes with a sigh of resignation.

"Just go to your sister," said Bard. "She will draw you to her."

Lone smirked. Bard did not understand the laws of teleportation magic but had a masterful understanding of the power of relationships. "I'll try." Lone kissed Bard again briefly and leaned back. "You're the best thing to happen to me in ten years, Bard. I love you."

Darkness in the sky beyond Bard pulled Lone's attention. A dozen black tears rending the air in the distance. Daemon poured forth, reinforcements to redouble their numbers to replenish whatever progress the Mraasil may have made. By how far away those portals appeared, Lone knew it would only be a few moments before the daemon clashed against the remainder of the Poas armies and Mraasil, overwhelming and ending them.

The Mraasil standing guard in front fired a volley of dark magic at a stray daemon, reminding Lone of the urgency. Without drawing the moment out longer, he thought of Alishia as the little girl beside him in the oak tree, rolling her dark blue eyes at his stories.

Pulling at the ley lines and squeezing his eyes tight, he fell, but 'down' shifted with each frantic heartbeat. Lone landed hard on his side and immediately pushed to his hands and knees. He knelt in the dry grass that waved in a steady wind. Tidecrest appeared hazy and flat in the distance, more like a massive painting than reality. Turning, he saw Alishia with her back to Morna Dey a dozen paces away.

"More company?" said the daemon mistress. "It's getting crowded here."

Alishia stepped beside Lone, her long blue dress sweeping the grass, and placed a steadying hand on his shoulder as he rose.

"Is he whom you suggest?" Morna Dey ran both hands through her fiery hair and shook the springy locks.

Lone reached for his sword, which was not there, then pulled at the weak ley line running through the bubble realm. "She's summoned more daemon, Ali. Poas only has moments left."

Alishia locked her eyes on Lone with a palpable sadness. "Morna Dey, will you leave Kethry's body in exchange for another?"

Lone stepped away from his sister and glanced between her and the daemon mistress. "Ali?"

"Are you offering his body for Kethry's?" Morna tilted her head back and laughed. "A hardened war mage for an inexperienced whelp of a boy?"

"No," Alishia said quickly and turned back to Morna. "I offer myself. Morna, I know Kethry still fights you. I offer myself to you freely as you vacate Kethryane en Salo."

Morna Dey grinned and laughed again. "You think she is so worth saving? That there is even anything of her left to save?"

"Ali! You can't—" Lone started.

She silenced him with a raised hand. "Do we have a deal?"

Morna touched a finger to her red lips. "Kethry's mother must mean a great deal to you. I would think you came with some plot to stop me. You must know enough about the nature of daemon to know they require a master; that to stop me is to stop them all. Well, all except the Exalted. Not a single daemon will leave the field in the time I take to control your body."

"I am aware," said Alishia. "My role as Chronicler is to observe and record, but I also want to understand. Growing up as Princess Alishia gave me one perspective. Now, I will see another."

Lone watched his sister in profile, barely recognizing the woman she had become. He watched her for some sign of a double cross but saw none.

Morna crossed her arms and nodded to Lone. "Why's he here?"

"To return Kethry to her mother after. I assumed she would be too weakened to do it herself."

Lone stepped between the women. "Ali, you can't be serious. We want to save Kethry, but not at this cost. I won't let you."

"You won't *let* me?" Alishia stepped forward and grabbed his leather cuirass by the neck, pulling him down to her eye level with surprising strength. "I will do as is required of me. You will not and cannot stand in my way." She tossed Lone aside, and he tripped to the grass.

"Morna Dey, do we have a deal?"

A devilish grin spread across the daemon mistress's ruby lips. "This vessel is powerful, but I would be a fool to pass on the Chronicler's mortal body. We have a deal."

A sour taste filled Lone's mouth as he stared at what his sister had become. "Our father's dead. I could have stopped it if you sent me back a minute sooner. You may as well have killed him yourself."

The Chronicler's eye twitched, but her focus remained on the daemon mistress.

Lone looked on, helpless, as power flowed into the two women, swirling around them like wisps of smoke and lifting them from the ground until the toes of their shoes barely touched the grass. Something dug painfully into Lone's chest, distracting him enough to dig into his well-fitted cuirass, where Alishia had grabbed it a moment ago. He pulled out a shard of charred bark. He looked up at his sister with his emerald eyes wide, holding the bark in trembling fingers.

A black miasma flowed from Morna, coiling and knitting around her in a pattern that became less complex with each passing breath. As it unworked itself from Kethry's body, the polluted energy flowed from her like a heavy fog on the ground, growing thicker and darker as it unfettered itself.

What in the seven hells am I supposed to do with a piece of burnt wood, Ali?

It flowed over and through the grass, which withered and decayed as it passed. It reached Alishia's slippered feet and hungrily grasped onto her as the last tendril came free of Kethry.

Lone threw his will into the piece of bark, testing it for some means of magical activation, but everything about it reacted like a normal, mundane piece of wood. His heart jumped to his throat as the wisps of darkness encircled Alishia's leg and moved upward.

Another agonizing moment passed as Lone ran through a list of spells to throw at the disembodied daemon mistress that looped around his sister. She trusted him with the bark that clearly would play some role, and he failed to understand what.

The charred, ancient bark. Bark from a tree long dead.

Lone pulled at the meager ley line and pushed regenerative magics into the bark. It glowed a soft green, but he knew it would not be enough.

The mist circled Alishia at the waist.

The tattoos down Lone's right arm flared a little brighter. Without a clear plan, he ended his spell and tied the runes on his arm to the single ley line. They flared brilliantly but without pain this time as the ley line dimmed to a fragile wisp, ready to shatter. Lone shunted the power in his arm to the splinter in his hand, but rather than giving it formless healing energy, he did as Etharis had taught him.

"See the body as you wish it to be."

He imagined a world tree soaring over the forests of Terswood, casting its shade for miles.

The charred bark pulsed in his hand. Again. Faster.

The dark tendrils slowed their advance with a strain to resist the call of the old world tree that imprisoned the other daemon masters. The shard jolted in Lone's hand, and the essence that was Morna Dey sucked into it like a quick inhale of smoke. The magic ended itself as the only ley line cracked and shattered.

Alishia dropped the few inches to the ground and calmly brushed her hands on her hips. She pulled a cloth from her belt to take the splinter from Lone's palm.

"That'll work for a short while. It's a piece of Tersil," she explained.

"Yeah, I got that."

"The new world tree touches the roots of Tersil, allowing Verndari to absorb much of the knowledge left there by Ters, such as how to imprison figments of the Gods of Naught. I have to get this back to her."

Her nonchalant words and easy movements grated on his frayed nerves. "Ali, please, I'm so tired. Physically and emotionally drained. What happened here?"

"I promise I'll explain, but for now, we have to get out of here."

Lone looked around the tiny realm. Maybe it was his imagination, but the flat paintings that made up the edges felt closer, the city more hurriedly sketched.

"How? Last time I teleported from a demi-realm, I used Cazlandt's amulet, and it just sort of worked."

Alishia's shoulders dropped with an exasperated breath. "You got here. Just do the opposite. Follow the ley line out or focus on the concept of something or someone outside."

Lone frowned at her patronizing tone and shook his head. "The ley line shattered. The only magic left in this little realm is..." He looked down at the steady glow from the runes down his right arm. "This won't be enough for the three of us."

"Two," Alishia said. "Just Kethry. I can get myself from here."

Lone narrowed his eyes. "You pulled us back and forth from The Stacks over and over without breaking a sweat. Help me get us out of here. Pull Kethry and me back to Poas."

She shied a step away from him with her eyes downcast. "I'm sorry, Lone."

"*Sorry?* For what? Letting our father die, and now you're going to leave me in a tiny, magicless realm?"

"Lone..." She looked up at him while keeping her chin low. "Life is nothing but a series of random events stringing together to create some semblance of sense. Every event that happens around or to us, along with our actions and reactions, weaves a delicate tapestry. Misplace one thread, and it falls apart. Look how many times we meddled with the Venatus before I realized nothing but the slightest nudge was needed. Don't you think I wanted to save our father? But that would lead me down a path of sculpting perfection, which is impossible."

Lone's vision dimmed with the throbbing pulse through his temples. "Fuck your perfection," he hissed through clenched teeth. "I just want my father back."

Alishia inhaled deeply through her nose and blew it out before raising her chin to meet Lone's gaze directly. "You don't think I tried? *Our* father died saving you. I adjusted that, and he died saving my mother instead. Then, my mother died, and our father drank himself to death within a year. The daemon overran the Dracon army, and I watched Jazelyn and Bard slaughtered. I killed Morna Dey where she hid in the Lacuna Gap so that Ruvaal could never call her to Poas. I killed her before she helped Aunt Lilan with her rituals and again before she entwined Kethry's spirit. Or Baris's. I killed Ruvaal before I met him in Throk'tar. When I left to enlist the aid of the Mraasil, I overwrote you more than thirty times trying to save our father. I tried so many iterations of history and ended up doing nothing. Or rather, doing only what I already had."

She stepped toward Lone again and gestured at the faint glow in his tattoos. "It's not far back to Poas. That is enough to get you and Kethry there. I know it is because I've seen this moment happen. Your tattoos hold all the power you need. You channeled a ley nexus through them to heal Bard and a pouch of mana crystal to teleport from the Western Isles. I can't help you now because you must believe you can do this yourself. Think of Bard. Go to him."

Lone chewed on his cheek and felt an ache behind his eyes, the beginnings of a migraine. As much as he wanted to believe everything Alishia — no, the Chronicler — said, she admitted to only thirty attempts at saving his father. Why not forty or a hundred?

He turned from the Chronicler to move to Kethry, placed a hand on her shoulder, and closed his eyes to focus. Images of Bard flooded his mind along with the shock and terror he felt after altering the past, knowing he caused an alternate history where the man he loved never existed. He saw Bard in perfect clarity, knew how that image would feel and smell, the intricacies of how he moved and what made him laugh, the taste of his lips and skin and sounds that escaped him as they made love. By Lone's senses as an archmage, he knew the unique feel of Bard's people and, after his attempts at healing the islander, knew how his body reacted to magic. Lone said the words often enough, but in that moment, he realized how deep his love for Bard ran. Even after such a short time, he knew the man as well as he knew anyone else in his life and, in this moment, wanted nothing more than to return to his arms.

Lone grasped for the ley energy lingering in his right arm, tying it to a teleportation, unsure it would be enough, but the runes continued to feed his spell. Within a moment, the mana flowed from him, more than he would need, and he cast his spell, not to a location, but to the one he held in his mind, to Bard.

The last time, the transition from a demi-realm knocked Lone unconscious in a burning city. This time, he and Kethry appeared inches from the ground beside the Mraasil still working a healing on Kiol, Jazelyn wringing her hands beside them, and Bard with a sword in his fist, keeping a wary eye on what remained of the daemon forces. Lone counted far fewer Mraasil than a moment ago but also saw no standing greater daemon. The remaining realm guardians fought beside the armies of Poas to dispatch the last of the daemon horde, who seemed to have lost their drive to fight.

The Chronicler appeared in front of him.

"Princess Alishia... Chronicler," Jazelyn said in barely more than a whisper. She pushed to her feet and stumbled a step to her side. Lone caught her by the elbow but almost took them both over with him, weary as he was. Jazelyn saw her daughter lying in the grass beside Lone and dropped to her knees. She held one of Kethry's hands in both of hers as tears flowed down her cheeks.

Bard turned and rushed to Lone, dropping the sword along the way. Lone wrapped his arms around Bard's waist and pulled him close for a deep kiss. Everything was exactly as it existed in his image of the islander.

"I have done all I can for this mortal," declared the unnamed Mraasil and stood with a clink of their chainmail.

Lone turned to the Mraasil and stood a little straighter to look up into those glowing amber eyes while keeping his left hand linked with Bard's. "Thank you."

The realm guardian glanced across the battlefield before focusing back on Alishia. "It seems we have won the day. Does this conclude our contract, Chronicler?"

Lone knew being surprised about his sister was a waste of time, but his jaw still fell slack with the question.

"The fight is not over, but your part here is. Thank you, Tesoti."

The Mraasil snapped to attention and bowed. Their skin took on the appearance of soft flower petals before blowing away.

"How is he?" Lone looked down at his friend and to Jazelyn.

"His arm is lost," Bard answered. "But he will live."

"The daemon defeated, the Exalted blown apart, Morna Dey imprisoned, and Kethry rescued," Lone said. "The armies of Poas decimated, my father..."

"What of your father?" Bard asked, and Lone could not form the words. He hoped his expression would be enough.

"Don't celebrate just yet," said Alishia.

The ground shuttered, causing Lone to fall against Bard. "What now?" he moaned.

With the daemon horde beaten down and dispersing, Lone could clearly see the Exalted over the mounds of corpses. Its massive frame shuddered, noticeable even at this distance. It pushed upright on two thin, pale arms, its entire top half having regenerated in the ghastly colors of a bloated corpse. Its five faces merged into one, resembling a jawless human.

"Shields!" Etharis shouted from somewhere, and the few remaining Mraasil turned to throw up their magical protections. Lone moved in front of his group and spread his arms to cast an aegis with all the mana he could channel. He thought of the explosion caused by Aiden and Ethan. If this beast regenerated in a few hours from that, there would be no killing it.

A bright red orb of power formed in front of the Exalted's face, and from it swept a beam of energy across the battlefield. It cut through all protections like a hot knife through lard, obliterating at least two Mraasil that Lone saw, dozens of human troops, and wounding countless others. The attack missed his aegis by a dozen yards, but he still felt the force and heat of the attack. A second or third blast would end all resistance in Poas. He dropped his aegis, knowing it would be a wasted effort.

"Chronicler, if we assume Morna Dey summoned this thing, can we tap into her power in the bark to unsummon it?" Lone felt clever for a moment until the Chronicler shook her head.

"This is out of your hands now, brother."

Lone looked beyond her to notice a trio of Mraasil coming from the city. He recognized the horned Birael and shuffling Celium immediately, implying the third was Verndari. The new guardian of Poas moved with long, confident strides, wearing a loose dress that billowed behind her.

The Exalted blasted another line across the field, but Lone did not see the carnage with his back to it; he only felt the heat and wash of power. He focused on Alishia jogging to join the three as they passed through the remaining forces. Heads turned, and the path cleared for her. Verndari slowed as Alishia neared and handed her something. The shard of bark. Verndari doubled her pace, and the other Mraasil ran to keep up.

"Exalted," Verndari said in a high, delicate tone. The Mother of Daemon paused, and the red orb before it dissipated. "We lack the power to evict you from our realm, but you will be bound here."

It stared down at her for a long moment, and the red orb appeared again, preparing to destroy the Mraasil only hours after her birth.

Verndari gestured, just a smooth twist of her wrist and a curling of her fingers, but something responded deep in the ground, vibrating beneath Lone's feet. The Exalted swept another line of death across the field. Lone watched impotently as it passed doubly close as the last beam and felt the wave of searing intensity that came with it. Only an instant before it reached Verndari, roots burst from the bloody earth. Tree roots as large as a mountain obscured Lone's sight of the Exalted, blocking its attack or ending it by upsetting the behemoth's stance. Dirt and boulders flew high and wide as the roots coiled around the Exalted, holding it firm with constricting tendrils.

"I bind you, Exalted," Verndari said quietly, though her voice carried effortlessly across the field. "With the bones of my sister left behind when she bound your masters, I bind you."

Lone watched with a mix of awe and horror as roots, vines, and mountainous shards of rock pierced the Exalted, thrusting through its enormous bulk. It writhed and opened its mouth in another silent scream as its movements slowed and the vines covered the last inch of decayed flesh. The Exalted spasmed once more as, like a wave of white flowing from the ground upward, flowers bloomed from the vines that dragged the Exalted into the ground. It only took a moment before the fertile soil closed up around the Mother of Daemon; the softly rolling hills giving no hint at what lay beneath.

Sometime during the display, Etharis had joined the Mraasil, and he now stood with a supporting arm around Verndari's shoulder. The archdruid still held the young Mraasil as he directed them toward the city.

Lone looked across the battlefield and at the scores of dead or dying. He wanted to go out and offer what succor he could, but exhaustion strained his thoughts.

"King Lone," said Jazelyn. Lone looked down at her, hovering between Kiol and Kethry. "I see the weakness within you. You are nearer to breaking than you realize. Let us return to Tidecrest or Dracon and allow the medics and healers to practice their art."

"Can you get them back to Dracon?" He gestured at the other two on the ground.

Jazelyn nodded.

"Then go. I have to see what I can here. Terswood, Dehset and Isold within the city." Lone quickly scanned across the remaining Dracon forces. "Lieutenant Dreyma? Have you seen her?"

Bard shook his head. "She was guarding the generals and overtaken by daemon."

Lone blew out a long breath, forcing himself not to let emotion overtake him. It would take time to tally the losses from today. It takes longer to realize the scope of the loss.

He looked to the east toward what remained of the Terswood encampment.

"Lone..." said Alishia, and he focused on the Chronicler standing beside him.

"All part of your plan?" Lone looked down at the gouges in his palm from gripping the brooch too tightly. The archdruid never returned it after taking it to identify its magics.

"I'm sorry, brother. I hope you'll accept my word that this is the best outcome. For me and for you."

"Our father's dead." Lone still stared at his empty palm.

"But you aren't."

His shoulders fell with a sigh. "What about the Gods of Naught? How do we defeat or push them back so this doesn't all happen again?"

"We don't," said Alishia. "They are so far above us, there is nothing we could do to affect them. Imagine your workroom, Lone. Your messy, tragically disorganized workroom. If I moved anything in there, would you notice?"

Lone shrugged. "I don't know."

"Say I rotated an inkwell in the corner one-eighth turn to the left. Would you notice it?"

"No." He resisted the urge to chuckle at the thought, the inanity of it, but did not want to give her the satisfaction.

"That's us. The spark that sundered the Primes, created the Ascended, which manufactured the first world tree that gave solidity to our realms. All we have been — since before Etharis was born to the eventual end of it all — amounts to nothing more than an eighth turn of an inkwell in a crowded workroom. The daemon draw attention to us, wanting us to be turned back and undo our existence. The best we can hope for is to continue without further notice. A sliver of the Gods of Naught exist beside us, within us, but barely notice us."

"That's... bleak."

Alishia hummed thoughtfully. "Fables of the Gods of Naught have been passed through history, painting them as a malevolent force bent on our destruction. When in reality, we're nothing to them. As much as *they* are a thing."

"I thought the Scions defeated the Gods of Naught along with the destruction of Tersil."

"A portion of their presence in the realms was, yes. As much as if I bottled a single of your breaths. That would be enough to destroy everything we have been and ever will be. Such is their place above us."

Lone closed his eyes and slowly shook his head. "What's next for us? For Poas? How do we recover from this?"

"I..." Alishia turned to him. "I don't know."

"Really?" He turned to her. "The Chronicler knows all and knows best. This could have ended a hundred better ways with your knowledge."

"I don't expect you to understand, Lone. There's a war in my soul. I fight that urge to look ahead and play the role of one that would determine the path of all lives across all realms. And to what end? Life always finds a way to inflict misery and wrongdoing. I have spent more time than I could estimate coming to the conclusion that my role must be passive, lest I go insane."

Lone stared into her silver eyes, flecked with dark blue. Despite how she looked now, he easily envisioned his little sister. He remembered holding her only minutes after she was born, how the seething annoyance at his father and Teiris melted away at the sight of her. She had been his reason for visiting Terswood over the last fifteen years. More than for politics, he learned Svarters to talk with her once she began to form sentences. The sleeve of runic tattoos down his right shoulder and arm was done in the svarters style that he silently meant as a connection to her. Lone could only guess what pain still lingered behind those eyes. He fought against holding the Chronicler responsible for the inactions that left the field littered with thousands of dead, including their father. He pushed that resentment onto the Chronicler, away from his sister. Though they may be the same person, he needed Alishia's strength to move forward.

"Lone, do you trust me?" She extended a hand to him.

The question slapped him across the face like a wet fish. He stared at the woman before him, no longer his baby sister, but a cosmic being of knowledge incarnate. Possibly the being worshiped by Bard, the being called Au.

Someone capable of living with the knowledge of inaction.

He looked down at her hand and reached to take it in his own. "I want to, Ali. I really want to."

"There's one more thing to be done before you rest."

46

Despite what he did, his people later erected a memorial in honor of all that he was up until the very end.

As his fingers touched hers, Lone's body ached with exhaustion, and the surroundings shifted to a crimson lake under a thousand roots reaching down from above, the mana lake under Endanlegsil. Protectorate Alaraic stood fifty yards away with arms raised and fingers splayed, his cobalt hair whipping in the pressure of the mana he commanded. Thirty guards in white armor, two-thirds bearing swords and the rest with thick tomes floating in the space beside them, spread around the protectorate. At least another dozen lay dead, mixed with avaryll in darker robes and wood masks etched with gold.

The Einingu.

"Regent King."

Lone jumped at hearing his name and turned. Tanathil limped toward him from behind, cradling his left arm that freely dripped dark blood. Ten others squatted behind him, tending to their wounded, clearly routed.

"The protectorate..." Tanathil squeezed his eyes tight and sucked in a breath through clenched teeth.

"I see him. The quantity of magic he's channeling is obscene. What is he doing?"

"He's going to burn Endanlegsil. He..." Tanathil winced and took a few quick breaths. "He thinks without it, the daemon will leave."

"The daemon are defeated. Their mistress and the Exalted imprisoned using the remaining might of Tersil. Why—" Lone turned back to Alaraic and rushed forward. The avaryll guards tightened the grip on their swords and deepened their stances. "Alaraic! This is madness! The war is over. We've won!"

"It will never be over! I will save my city by removing what the daemon seek. The world tree must burn."

Ley energy ripped past Lone as it had in Diyar with the activation of the device that ended with the Venatus. It roared through Alaraic and channeled upward into the main trunks of the world tree to spread through the twisting branches that spread to shade the farthest edges of Tidecrest. Lone studied the spell for a few long breaths, seeing how the ley energy leaving Alaraic felt fundamentally different. Without taking longer, he could only guess at the protectorate's intention: to fill the world tree with the mana he marked, then ignite it as one. How long would it take to fill a world tree in such a way? A few minutes? Days? How long had he been at it already? Lone knew there was no time to delay.

Tanathil limped to Lone's right side, and the Chronicler stepped to his left. The protectorate's guards bristled but did not advance.

"Tanathil, do you have anything left? A single firebolt or just a slug of raw mana?"

"Barely, but to what end? The mages maintain an aegis. They will tighten it the instant anything comes their way."

"That's what I want."

Lone reached his senses toward the mages' aegis, searching for the strand in its spell matrix that determined its direction. "They're only holding the aegis between us and them, not the far side. Aim for the protectorate's hands."

Blood dripped from Tanathil's palm as he shakily raised it. A sphere of red energy formed and shot forward, lethargically, toward the protectorate. Lone felt the aegis strengthen, felt where the beam of Alaraic's spell penetrated it in the direction allowed by the protection. Lone strained his mind to touch the spell and, as he had against his aunt in Terswood, changed the direction.

Tanathil's weak attack passed through the aegis to hit Alaraic's hands, and the magic pouring from the protectorate rebounded against the shield. Dark energy filled the aegis, obscuring any view of the avaryll guards, and blasted from the unprotected backside. Lone felt the aegis fail as the unfettered energy ripped apart all within it. He grabbed Tanathil's arm and teleported.

47

Lone never told our grandnan about our father, nor do I think he should have.

L one remembered his mother's red and gray wolfhound that died when he was six. Something warm and wet ran across his face again as he struggled to recall the wolfhound's name. He opened his eyes to a white-haired human woman wiping his face with a damp sponge.

"Siraas?" he asked and tried to push up to his elbows. She easily pressed him back down.

"About time you woke up, Regent King," she whispered and tossed the sponge into a bowl by his head. "I'm not a nursemaid; I have a list of very important things I could be doing right now."

"Where...?" Lone started but recognized the plain stone of Castle Dracon. "How did I get here?"

"General Jazelyn forced me from my tower to see to her daughter and husband. We found you and *him* in the Grand Hall on our way back."

Lone rolled his head to the left and recognized Tanathil by his pure-white hair in the cot beside him. Kethry lay to his right; a burst of fiery hair on the pillow with her face turned away.

"Curing your physical wounds was a waste of a skill like mine," Siraas continued, "but Kethry is an interesting patient and, of course, the avaryll. I haven't had the chance to study one before, obviously. The runes on your arm are fascinating." She lifted Lone's right arm and ran her fingers over the faint green runes. "They seem tied to your cultivation now, like the avaryll's golden tattoos."

Lone became aware of his nudity under the thin blanket and pulled away from her touch. "Where is Bard? Jazelyn?"

"All their weeping and clutching at blankets and begging me to work my magic became grating. I tossed them out."

"I'd like to see Bard. Get him for me, please."

Siraas heaved a sigh and rolled her eyes. "Yes, Your Grace." She left in a swirl of her white and red coat.

Lone pushed to his elbows and scanned the room for a pair of pants. Tanathil groaned a few feet away, swung his legs over the edge of his cot, and sat upright, resting his forearms across his knees. Linen wrapped most of his chest and arms, as well as around his head, and covered his left eye.

"Tanathil, I'm surprised you're here."

A weak smile flickered across the avaryll's tired face. He groaned again and pushed to his feet, the blanket falling away to reveal the loose gray trousers he wore. Tanathil crossed to a small table by the door and poured a glass of water from the decanter. "You brought me here. I thought it would be rude to leave before you woke. Besides, I didn't want to leave your healer's cheerful grace." He returned on slow legs and handed Lone the glass.

"Thank you. How long was I out?"

Tanathil glanced out the window at the gently drifting snow beyond the warped glass. "Two weeks."

Lone choked on his water while the avaryll moved to a low dresser and returned with a plain tunic and trousers. Tanathil sat back on the edge of his cot while Lone winced and carefully pulled the long, sleeveless tunic over his head. Everything hurt, and what did not hurt ached. He pushed himself higher in the bed and leaned back against the cold stone while keeping the blanket pulled high. Pants would be a project for later.

"Two weeks... What's happened out there?"

"It seems we've won."

"The protectorate?"

"They could identify none of the remains by the mana lake, but Alaraic appears to be gone."

"The other Einingu behind us? There must have been ten others."

"A few survived."

"I'm so sorry, Tanathil. I couldn't—"

"There is nothing to be sorry about, King Lone. We will honor them for their sacrifice. I would have happily gone with them; nevertheless, thank you for the teleport."

"Ali..."

The door burst open, and Bard skidded to a stop beside the bed. He fell over Lone, pulling him into a painful embrace.

"No, no, off!" Siraas followed Bard and swatted at him until he settled on the cot's edge. Lone grinned at the familiar roughness of the islander's calloused hand in his. Bard glanced at Tanathil with a grin that made Lone wonder how many hours Bard had spent sitting in that same position for the last two weeks. The healer moved to Kethry and turned her head so her vacant eyes stared at the ceiling.

"Is she...?" Lone was unsure of exactly what his question might be.

"She's in there," said Siraas. She placed a palm on Kethry's forehead and closed her own eyes. "Six hundred years is a long time, long enough to forget how to use your body. I can feel her clawing her way back to the surface."

Bard answered Lone's next questions, ticking them off with his fingers. "Kiol is recovering, already making jokes about losing an arm. The Mraasil have all left except Verndari and Etharis. No one has seen Aiden or Ethan. Alishia has been in Terswood with her mother. Memorial services for your father will be planned now that you're awake."

Lone tried to keep his expression even. He raised the glass for another drink but lowered it instead. "What of the other nations? How did they fare after the daemon attack?"

"Not well," Bard answered without pause. "Eplear took the heaviest losses, but they brought the most troops. The Serpent King was wounded, but I haven't heard how badly. The Tersguard were nearly wiped out, as were the Dracon Royal Guard."

"That's enough," said Siraas and waved at Bard. "He's still my patient, and I won't have you getting him depressed."

Bard stood and bent to put a hand on Lone's cheek and a light kiss on his lips. "I'll go get you something from the kitchen." He backed away a few steps before turning to leave as Siraas returned to Kethry.

Ali's in Terswood. Lone reached out for the ley lines and was surprised by how they felt. The mana's flow felt cool and crisp, coming to him more easily than two weeks ago. He started tracing the Gran Marc south toward Terswood.

"Feels nice, doesn't it?" Lone jumped at Tanathil's words.

"The world tree did this much in two weeks? The ley lines feel so... clean."

"That and your..." Tanathil gestured at Lone's right arm and his own tattoos glowing a faint gold. "Some of my people are marked in such a way to create a tighter bond with the ley lines. I have a feeling yours were ornamental at first but now serve a similar purpose."

Lone flexed his right hand and watched the green hue shimmer across his tattoos.

"With you awake, I will return to Tidecrest."

"Who will lead the avaryll?"

Tanathil shrugged. "Protectorate Alaraic had no heir. I expect some minor civil unrest between the factions, but we will find our path. Focus on your recovery, King Lone."

"Regent King," Lone corrected.

"If you insist. We will be in contact soon. I am sorry for your loss." Solid gold light poured from Tanathil's tattoos, and he disappeared in a shaft of blinding light.

"Well, that's flashy," Siraas commented.

The healer left a few minutes later, leaving Lone alone with the unresponsive Kethry. He swung aching legs over the edge of the cot and struggled to pull on the loose trousers. As he stared down at the strings to cinch the pants tighter, Lone's mind wandered to what might await him on the other side of that simple wooden door and found himself wanting to stay in those plain, gray trousers and tunic as long as he could.

EPILOGUE

48

The Stacks is not my work alone. I have enlisted the aid of Lorekeepers in some realms to organize the smallest fractions of knowledge.

Lone eased himself into his father's work chair and pushed back into the firm, unpadded wood. A single project was laid out on the bench, a disassembled sphere of a function Lone could hardly guess at in a glance. The tools of a runecrafter were neatly arrayed on either side of it in precise rows. Above the desk were a half dozen drawers, each with the materials for another project. Everything was so well organized. This would all have to be boxed up and sent to General Tekin or the Academy. Lone accepted that task personally and found himself in no great rush to dispose of and disseminate his father's things.

He leaned forward and, one at a time, pulled out the drawers on the side of his father's workbench. More tools, vials and jars of reagents, sheets of schematics curling from age.

Lone pulled out the bottom and deepest drawer to paw through the neatly organized contents. There, in the back, he found a bundle of papers wrapped in green ribbon. Not caring for what else he disturbed in the drawer, Lone pulled out the bundle and set it on his lap, pulling away the tie.

They were envelopes, at least fifty of them, all with a date in the corner and Lone's name written across the front in his father's small, precise hand. He flicked through the pile. The first one dated back to around when his father moved to Terswood.

Lone broke the wax seal on the envelope with the oldest date and scanned the letter that was never delivered.

Caring words from a father, written as a diary entry, told his son of the marvels of a new city and what joys he might have here, other high-born children of similar age, brilliant instructors of foreign magic and science.

He read the last line out loud to the empty room.

"I know you choose to stay in Dracon, so I leave this letter unsent. I miss you, son. I love you."

With a single sob, Lone tossed the bundle onto the desk before him, scattering tools from the unfinished project. He leaned against the chair's armrest and scratched at his beard.

"Twenty years wasted. I would have come if I'd gotten even one of these." He reached to flick the pile. "I thought you didn't want me, but I never asked." Lone leaned forward, gathered the letters, neatly arranged them in a stack, and secured them with the green ribbon.

"Come on, old man," he said to the letters. "I've only begun to clean up the mess."

***

Lone dropped the stack of his father's letters onto the desk in his workshop. Just as messy as Alishia described it, a score of partially finished projects taunted him. He dropped into the leather chair and pulled off his polished stone crown to scratch at his head. Next to the few loose pages of parchment containing his rambling notes related to the teleportation obelisk portal project sat a glass inkwell. Lone reached to turn it an eighth rotation to the right.

Lone leaned back in the chair, laced his fingers on his head, and stared at the ceiling.

"What now?"

He closed his eyes while the worries of threats — political or magical — flashed through his mind. He exhaled slowly and cleared his mind as the images threatened to overwhelm him.

He thought of his father's workspace and Master Arvil's meticulous office and sat upright. He gathered the loose parchment, stacked it neatly, and opened a drawer to his left.

A red envelope with his name in white, looping letters lay there on another stack of parchment—Master Arvil's letter to him he found in the late scribe's office.

"Not another letter..."

Lone reached with trembling fingers and broke the wax seal.

Regent King Lone,

Do not think me a coward for writing you a letter you cannot respond to. I must say what I could not in life: words your ancestors would cry out as treason. You asked my opinion on whether you would make a good king. As I watched you grow and in the short time I served under you, I say with no hesitation or doubt that you are the finest ruler Dracon could ask for, the finest of Poas. But not a king. With a simple suggestion, you brought together the nations of our world. Your aunt hid it well and her father before her, but Dracon is not thought of highly amongst others. They cry out that we horde the realm's magic, as false as that statement may be. As the counselor and scribe to the monarch of Dracon, let me advise you one more time:

Dissolve Dracon

Let her be a beacon of learning and enlightenment, a symbol of unity in Poas, but no longer a sovereign nation.

I will serve you always,

-Master Arvil Rees

The letter fell from Lone's hand, landing beside his crown on the desk.

49

By the time Archdruid Etharis found the last realm whose Mraasil perished in the daemon war, its world tree was little more than a withered husk.

"**C**hronicler," said the smooth, deep voice.

"Archdruid." She did not glance away from the shimmer of the crimson pool as Etharis sat beside her. "I didn't expect to find you down here."

She opened her mouth to respond but instead only blew out a sigh.

"The service was lovely. Your brother's speech moved me. He really has some skill in choosing the right words when he has the time to think them through."

Silence hung between them, interrupted only by the steady drip of mana into the lake.

"Did I do the right thing, Etharis?"

He considered her for another long moment of quiet.

"That's hardly for me to say," he finally said. "You set things to how they were before you knew the extent of your power. In a way, it's not about you doing the right thing because you didn't really do anything you hadn't already done. Though your mother and brother may never agree, I applaud your conviction. I have made brutally difficult decisions in my life, and had I your power, I doubt I would share your restraint. I raged at Ruvaal in the end, yet my curiosity took me to the Deadloss with him not long before. How would you know you did the right thing?"

She shrugged.

Etharis hummed thoughtfully. "I suppose if you looked ahead to see how long things between you and your family work out, you could make changes until all was well. I'm sorry, Chronicler. The rest of us dwell on reliving our past mistakes, but you see all the future ones as well."

"Did you come down here for any particular reason, Archdruid?"

He watched her again for a few long breaths, watched her silver eyes stare unblinking across the mana lake. "No. No reason." Etharis rocked forward and stood, smoothing his leather and fur jacket as he did. "Yours is a heavy burden, Ali. I know you'll find peace."

The Chronicler raised her face to gaze up at the archdruid with tears ready to spill and gave him the faintest of nods with the ghost of a smile. Archdruid Etharis exploded into a million butterflies to return to Tempus Fa.

TALES

I

The archdruid showed me his compendium of teas. I added entries for a few now-extinct, but his research was exhaustive and very complete.

Etharis took a long sip of his tea derived from a dried herbal blend unique to the realm of Throk'tar. Both naturally bitter and sweet, it possessed an odd savory texture that clung to the tongue and throat, making it ideal for soothing a cold. The archdruid felt in perfect health today, but his choice of tea was fitting for who was to meet him soon in the other three chairs set around him beside a roaring hearth in the cozy room. Even if the others did not know the origin of the tea, he did, and that little secret made him grin.

The door swung in, and Ruvaal stood in the doorway. If he could roll his solid amber eyes, he did. "Of course, it's you, brother." He stepped into the room, an apartment in northern Tidecrest near the mountains, and sat beside Etharis. "I should have guessed by how cryptic the avaryll were that came to direct me here, promising urgent business. Shouldn't you be busy with the tree?"

"Tea?" Etharis reached for the pot on the table between the four chairs and poured Ruvaal a cup. "I've not been myself lately, brother. Anger and impulsiveness are strange emotions to me. Between learning how we altered the past and now the world tree here, I... I admit I got away from myself."

Ruvaal sniffed at the tea before taking a first taste. He winced, but the look of disgust quickly melted to one of appreciation. "Who else is coming?" Ruvaal gestured to the empty seats. "Wait..." He took another slow sip of the brew, smacking his lips. "This is kulgha blend, only found in the valleys south of the tree in Throk'tar. You are too intentional with your tea selections for this not to hold meaning."

Etharis bit his lips to hold back the grin. Perhaps his subtle attempts to widen Ruvaal's tea appreciation over the last few thousand years were starting to bear fruit.

"Who else is coming, then? Someone from Throk'tar? I can't imagine what any gronyn would have a stake here, now, in Poas. Who then..." Ruvaal trailed off with a long breath, closed his eyes, and shook his head. "If it's who I assume, I don't think that appropriate."

"They were already here."

Ruvaal's eyes shot open. "Of course. Who else could see to Endanlegsil's growth but the World Tender."

"And the Gilded Warrior," said Aiden from the open doorway. He stepped into the room, wearing a simple white belted tunic and dark pants. He waved at the two seated Mraasil and scratched at his mop of untidy dark hair as the firelight glinted off his amethyst eyes and devilish grin.

Etharis's prized pupil entered behind him with long, dark hair tied back with a strip of leather and calf-length leather jacket over an intricately embossed vest. His green eyes flitted over the Mraasil and to his brother before settling on a spot on the floor.

"Look at us," said Ruvaal. "The Scions of Flayme reunited in the shade of the last world tree. Have a seat, boys." He gestured to the empty chairs.

"Tea?"

Aiden accepted, while his brother refused with a curt shake of his head.

"Imagine my surprise," Etharis started with another long draw from his cup, "when I learned of a new world tree right here in Poas. Of all the countless realms, this new tree is in one I was just in only months ago, yet I sensed nothing of it. When I became aware of the world tree, I immediately thought it was related to how Ruvaal and I had altered time, inadvertently restoring life to the Deadloss." The archdruid leaned forward and refilled his cup from the pot in the center of the room. "Further imagine my surprise when I arrived in Isolis, witnessed the splendor of Endanlegsil, and heard the avaryll gush about her caregiver, one that had been seeing to her for twenty moons, thousands of years, going by the title of the World Tender."

The World Tended leaned forward. "Etharis, I can explain. Ali—"

"You wound me, Ethan," Etharis cut him off. "You had in your hands the first Seed of my dear Farsil, the Seed I was born holding, and you gave it to these people. You spent endless hours here working the very craft I taught you. I have a difficult time not feeling betrayed."

"Ali told us to do it," said Aiden, dropping his cup back on the table with enough force to slosh brew onto the polished marble. "She laid it all out for us, saying things had to happen exactly right."

"Exactly right for what?" Ruvaal asked, leaning back and steepling his fingers under his chin.

Ethan rubbed at the two-day-old stubble on his cheek. "To ensure her birth. Since she exists outside of time, her life is nothing but causal loops and other paradoxes."

"But she is already born," said Etharis. "She is a sixteen-year-old girl in Throk'tar's distant past right now. How can something that is yet to occur affect the past?"

Ethan only shrugged.

"Then it will be that young Alishia that returns to Poas eventually," Etharis said, downed his fresh cup of tea in a single gulp, and blew out a long breath. "If you acted on the commands of the Chronicler, I can hardly be angry at you two, but I am definitely disappointed. To know that you could keep such secrets from me after all we have been through together."

Aiden chuckled softly. "If the last thing she knows of you is from Throk'tar, I suggest you stay out of sight until someone else can break the news to her, Ethan."

Ruvaal snorted into his cup.

Ethan touched his chest with a frown. "I am well aware of that."

"As my conversations usually run," said Etharis, "we're off track. When I figured out the two of you have been pulling strings in Poas so secretly for so long, I had to know why. Now I know. Alishia told you to do it all. Now, I suppose the better question is, how may I lend support?"

Ruvaal started, twitching away from the archdruid with a snarl. "Etharis, you would implant yourself into the workings of a foreign realm? I understand the care of the world tree and her Mraasil is your top priority, but you could just dismiss the World Tender and take command here. You are the archdruid, the first Mraasil, supreme amongst the mortal races."

"You don't have to tell me all that," said Etharis. "I trained the boy, so I may as well let him do my job."

II

The throne passed to Sion's eldest daughter. She served well and her great-great granddaughter was the one to find Elogoh'an.

"We have to do this now," said Jazelyn as Kiol blasted another daemon with a volley of mana.

"Do what?" he asked as he stopped to catch his breath. Even with the Mraasil's aid, the daemon forces kept coming without end. They would make progress and see the corpse of the impossibly huge daemon in the distance, and another wave of portals would open, spilling a fresh horde onto the battlefield. The daemon mistress only toyed with them.

"We must find Morna Dey or our failure is guaranteed."

"Sure, Lyn. And how do you expect to find her?"

Jazelyn's lips parted as she closed her eyes with a deep breath. "I find her as Kethry did. I aetherwalk."

Kiol looked to the horde of daemon and back to his wife. "We don't have the time to go back to the castle and—"

"Then I will do it here."

"You want to aetherwalk in the middle of a combat? Listen to yourself, Lyn! That's insanity!"

"Then let us get on with it and waste no more time fretting." She sat down and laid back in the tall, soft grass.

"No, Lyn, a daemon could pop up right here, and that's it for us."

"She must be close. It will only take a moment." She grabbed his hands to place one on her forehead and the other over her liver.

Kiol pushed mana through his wife as they had practiced a dozen times and stared up at the boundless horde only a few hundred feet away. As he watched, two brave crystal mages stood against a pair of imps. They took down one with an array of colorful magic, but the other ended them both. Rusl, the archmage famed for his illusionary and shadow magic, bewildered a pack of hounds, tricking them into killing a dozen of their kind before they saw through his deceptions and leaped upon him. A pair of avaryll strode past him in long robes and hair of sapphire, stopping two score feet ahead. A massive tome floated between them, and together, they lobbed spells at the daemon that blasted gaps in their ranks. A half dozen daemon rushed the pair, were blasted away, and four times as many tried in a second wave. The two avaryll placed a hand each on the book between them, and a semi-circle wave of energy erupted from them to cut the daemon down and force them back. The pair took a moment to catch their breath as a greater daemon's black energy attack struck, killing them instantly.

"Lyn, get back now!" he urged his prone wife. "We can go back to the city and do this! This was beyond stupid to do right here!"

He looked up at an imp only a few feet away, loping directly at him. A long, slick blade extended from its left hand and dragged the ground in its wake. Kiol lifted his right arm to blast the thing. He felt the fresh, clean ley energy of Poas' renewed ley lines course through him, but rather than forming into a mana bolt at his right hand, the energy flowed through his left and into Jazelyn. The daemon swung its blade. Kiol felt the sting at his elbow but felt more shocked by the sudden appearance of two Mraasil. They cut down the daemon and turned their back to him. Kiol looked down but could not register why he could not put his right hand back on his wife to be her anchor, to let her find her body again after discovering the daemon mistress's location. Where had all the blood on her stomach come from? She hadn't taken a hit.

A moment later, the wooziness overwhelmed him, and he fell forward.

III

The number of daemon across all realms hasn't increased in almost a decade. Maybe their masters are gone forever.

"**I** bind you to me."

The voice in the orb growled more than spoke, and the daemon mistress knew there was no denying the words. He saved her life and soul, something no mortal should ever want to do. Not for one such as she. She ran clawed fingers over the sphere, wishing for little more than to reach through and grab the long-earred purple face that spoke through it.

"Remain there until I call for you."

She was unsure if that was meant to be a threat or a promise. The daemon mistress stood from the thread-bare sheets of the collapsed bed and entered the main living area of the cottage. The other occupant, a Mraasil like the one in the orb, stared out the window to the void beyond.

"I envy you," she said, sitting across from the Mraasil. "I pity you, as well. Brainless little thing that you are. Yes, I'm going to feast on you for a thousand mortal lifetimes, but you don't even know enough to put up a fight. What a simple life and existence you must have."

The Mraasil turned, and his gazeless amber eyes slowly resolved to focus on her. "Felen?" he mumbled. The word — the name — rang familiar, but not one the daemon mistress remembered. At least, she did not think it was familiar.

"The mortals defeated my masters among the realms," said the daemon mistress. "Don't ask me how, but that was the merest gasp of the Gods of Naught's power. I will bide my time, and another opportunity will present itself. The mortals are, if nothing, creatures of cyclical habit."

She stood and paced the small cottage. "What is this place? This stinking little hole in the void? Why are the ceilings so low and the walls so close? Maybe..."

She crooked a finger at the Mraasil and beckoned once. A thin stream of silvery energy flowed from him, and as she breathed it in, the daemon mistress's form shrank. Her hulking, magenta-skinned form paled to ivory, and her linen robes changed to a soft cotton dress. She ran a hand through her bouncing curls and looked around the cottage that now felt four times as large. "Much better," she grinned.

IV

If the Venatus is actually over, I worry that humans, by their very nature, will rise over other races as I watched them do a dozen other times. I hope my brother can rein them in.

D ehset Tekin dropped onto the stool before his workbench and fell forward with his head in his hands. Regent King Lone had spoken in an even tone, choosing diplomatically sensitive language when informing the royal court of his father's death. Even so, the facts were clear. King Daelin died because a mana bomb of Dehset's design malfunctioned.

The remains of the sphere were laid out in an array before him. Other than some scorching around the capacitance rune, the device appeared to be in perfect condition, ready to be used again with a few minor repairs and mechanical resets.

Dehset picked a spudger — a long, metal tool for measuring mana variations — from the bench and prodded the damaged rune. He flipped the device and frowned at the result shown in the liquid metal gauge.

"Negative?" he said to the empty room. Empty except for the long shelves of crates he was slowly bringing to order. "Negative mana? That's impossible."

He touched the spudger to the pouch of mana crystal on a table behind him to confirm the tool was not broken. After that showed a value around what he expected, he touched it to himself and smirked when the gauge showed zero. It went negative again when he touched it to the bomb on his desk. Dehset took another mana bomb from the crate by his foot, noted the tag on it, marking it as used by General Kiol in the battle, and twisted it open. The capacitance rune's value showed a slightly positive value.

He focused back on the bomb responsible for King Daelin's death. "You were meant to use mana to push mana away, yet you somehow contain, not just none, but a deficit."

Dehset thought through the stack of books in the next room, either from his schooling or borrowed from the small library in the castle's north tower. None of them mentioned negative mana, or anti-magic, as he was starting to call it, as a concept to even theorize upon. The guilt felt for King Daelin's demise dissolved with the wash of new ideas. Other than the eradication of ley energy, he could think of no immediate use beyond the academic, but an application could come later.

I've discovered something new! How do I replicate this? How can I store it? How famous will this make me?

Dehset took an unused mana bomb from the crate and twisted apart the chassis to access the runes within. He lost all sense of time, but his eyes burned from the strain when he finally stretched back with a grin. The spudger showed the same negative value on the new bomb's rune after he used a wire of pure silver to transfer the deficit.

"I've moved anti-magic," he declared to no one. "Now, to think of an application."

V

"I am in you. I am in everyone."

"**Y**ou shouldn't have that."

Cazlandt heard the slurred words, and his mind snapped forward. He recognized his son lying at his feet, then saw how his armor caved in at the chest. He looked up to his grandson thirty feet away, radiating a light that burned like the sun. The shambling army of dead, both recently and centuries past, frozen and blasted to nothing. Daelin's body disintegrated before his eyes, and he could sense his own was as well. The Shadow Reaver was present again and collected them both into the gem it held.

Cazlandt blinked. He stood in a pure white landscape, wearing his familiar yellow robes and tall hat. Beside him, Daelin stared at his hands, wearing some clean version of the armor he had worn a moment ago on the battlefield.

"Grandsire?" Daelin asked when he noticed the other. "Am I dead?"

"You very well may be," Cazlandt replied.

"I... I was being stabbed by Amer's undead. I felt them pierce my heart, cut my throat. Then I used your amulet." Daelin looked down again at his empty hands.

The air quivered, and a misty, cloaked figure wearing a jawless skull mask appeared before them.

"Elphame!" Daelin gasped.

"So we are dead," said Cazlandt.

"Well, you are," chimed another voice to their left. A short woman wearing a long black traveling cloak stood beside them. She tossed back her red hair and flipped her cloak over her shoulder to extend a hand. "Minerva, Sundered Chaos."

The two baffled archmages shook the woman's hand.

"Elphame can't talk without killing you, and I owed Her a favor, so here I am to be Her mouthpiece," said Minerva. "In short, Cazlandt, you did something really naughty trying to subvert Her gift. She says She tried to warn you as you did it. So, yes, you're dead. She'll scatter your life force to the next realm when we leave this space. But you, Daelin... Elphame says She owes a favor to one who wants it repaid by returning you to life. Those are some connections you have, though I'm pretty sure I know who it is."

"I knew my time would end soon," Cazlandt sighed. "This means my resurrection failed?"

Minerva glanced to Elphame and back to the archmages with a roll of her eyes. "Yes, of course it failed. A person is made of elements from the six Greater Ascended. You tried to just make a man out of old blood, stagnant mana, and force of will. What do you expect would happen? You created a gross construct with that same desire to bring everyone back to life, even if they weren't already dead. Like a reverse Veil Walker."

Cazlandt looked at his grandson.

Daelin nodded. "Amer. He killed hundreds before Jazelyn found him a year after you gave me the amulet and disappeared. Thousands more perished fighting his undead armies."

"Any last words? I have a thing I need to get to," Minerva said.

Cazlandt turned fully toward Daelin. "Daelin, I have perhaps failed more than I succeeded. As much as I regret, I know I am nothing but a sum of what I have done, for good or not. Tell me... Do you know love?"

Daelin flinched at the question and nodded. "Of course. I love my wife, my son, my sister, and even you."

Cazlandt exhaled slowly. "That may be my greatest regret. I pushed forward with a mind set on advancing knowledge and the betterment of those around me. Let your love for others be the most important light of your life, never to be dimmed by your own passions."

Elphame, Goddess of Death, wheezed, and Cazlandt blew away like sand on marble.

Minerva coughed.

"Touching, but you will probably remember nothing of that," Minerva said while dabbing at her eyes. "Elphame says you will return to Poas fully healed, in your own bed, at more or less the same moment you were taken. Your grandsire is gone, and we recommend you don't worry too hard about that. Live your life and all those nice things your grandsire said, whether or not you remember them. Now, off you pop."

Daelin opened his eyes. He was comfortable in his own room in the eastern residence. Beside him, the covers were pulled back as if Aaislin had just gotten up from bed. Daelin sat up and saw his old wolfhound, Lina, curled by the fire. She raised her head and thumbed her tail once.

Glass shattered at the doorway, and his wife jumped on top of him, smothering him with kisses.

FROM THE AUTHOR

Well, that's it. The Chronicler's Awakening has been told. There's so much more to be said about what will happen next in Poas, but as the series title implies, this is just the beginning. Will Lone dissolve Dracon? Will Kethry recover? Will Dehset become an evil scientist? What happens now to Alishia?

As I finish this trilogy (and the surprise prequel), I wonder when I'll next to return to these dear friends. My next book plan is a collection of silly short stories (with lots of undead and goblins). The one after that involves a young heir trying to recover his family's fortune (with liches and gay romance). I doubt I'll be able to stay away too long from the realms around Poas. Even if the stories are shorter, like *Necromancer of Urbus*, there are more to be told.

About the Author

Author Jamie M. Samland is a mathematician by training, a web developer by profession, and a martial artist and writer by passion. Math nerd, cat dad, gamer. He always loved to write, but what started in force during the 2020 lockdown has become a driving passion. Jamie lives in Michigan with his husband and their furbabies.

As an indie author, he relies on reviews and word of mouth, so please consider leaving a review on GoodReads and at your point of purchase. Find him on the socials or at jmsamland.com.

Also By

Books by Jamie M. Samland:

Realms of Terswood (2020)
Trials of Throk'tar (2021)
Necromancer of Urbus (2022)
Seeds of Farsil (2022)
Ooo Shiny! Volume 1 (2022)
Arcanym (2023)
The Invisible Castle (2023)
Ooo Shiny! Volume 2, Holiday Edition 1 (2023)
Cracking the World (2023)
Grave Mistakes: A Necromantic Adventure (2023)
Ooo Shiny! Volume 3: Vampires! (2024)

REFERENCE LISTS

People

- Aiden Hauser - Captain in the Imperial Gron Army, Ethan's brother, over dramatic light shaper that hates high places and loves food.

- Alishia - Half svarters daughter of Teiris and Daelin, Princess of Terswood and Dracon, Master of the Eternal Library, The Chronicler

- Amer - Necromancer that swept across what life remained in Iecil, his death caused the appearance of Red Bloom.

- Au - Entity of knowledge revered by the people of the Western Isles, unclear if Au is a Prime, Sundered, or something else.

- Bard - Full name Bartriado Hren

- Bismat - Lady and Lord Bismat are the leaders of Jaiketh.

- Blessed Aubreda - Archmage, likes to drink

- Brarlyh Eldn - Archmage, likes to drink

- Cagla Bayram - Sultana of Evkasa.

- Cazlandt - Archmage, called "the first archmage", founder of Dracon, presumed dead with the rise of Amer, known for his mastery of teleportation magics.

- Daelin - Archmage, king of Terswood, married to Teiris.

- Dalbinth the Redeemer - Archetype of the Holy Seat, ruler of Acrus

- Dehset Tekin - Crystal mage, young student of the Royal Arcane Academy and prodigy artificer.

- Delphin Carter - Halberdier Second Class of the Acrus guard.

- Dhumjir - Ascended representing strength and conflict

- Djarcar - Wererat that fights Bard in the Hungered Arena

- Dreyma - Lieutenant in the Dracon Royal Guard

- Elder Grimorc - Gronyn healer shaman that raised Ethan and Aiden.

- Ethan Hauser - Captain in the Imperial Gron Army, Aiden's brother, diplomat and elementalist that is often annoyed by his brother.

- Etharis - Mraasil, guardian of the world tree Farsil within Tempus Fa.

- Elphame - Ascended representing death and inevitability

- Enid - Ascended representing peace

- Eylas & Gael - Twin sons of the late Queen Lilan, heirs to the crown in Dracon.

- Isold - Jazelyn's scribe and assistant.

- Harnoon Ashta - Owner of the Hungered Arena in the Western Isles.

- Jazelyn - Archmage, founding member of Dracon, Dracon general in charge of all archmages across Poas.

- Kethry en Salo - Archmage, Jazelyn's daughter, her mind was lost to aether walking centuries ago.

- Khizreus - Ascended representing corruption and deceit

- Kiol - Archmage, combat general of Dracon.

- Lavin - Soldier turned warlord that lead Cazlandt's charge in Iecil.

- Lone - Archmage, son of Daelin and his first wife, regent king of Dracon.

- Lilan - Archmage, late queen of Dracon.

- Lium - Late prince of Queen Lilan.

- Madllyn - Sundered Chaos.

- Mage Varon - Archmage, founding member of Dracon, teaches at the Royal Acane Academy

- Master Arvil - Head scribe of Dracon.

- Master Scorhara - Summoner that fights Bard in the Hungered Arena.

- Matron Wynlen - Teiris's great-aunt, leader of the Sisters of the Moons.

- Meave - Sundered Chaos.

- Miech - Crystal mage, late artifice general of Dracon.

- Minerva - Sundered Chaos.

- Morna Dey - Daemon mistress in command of Kethry's body.

- Prelen Kaermys - Prelen of Terswood, leader of the Tersguard.

- Protectorate Gundil - Ruler of Tidecrest when the Forged delivered the Seed of Farsil.

- Protectorate Alaraic - Present day ruler of Tidecrest.

- Ruvaal - Mraasil, guardian of the world tree Nethraanzil in a realm only referred to as The Afterlands.

- Sion - Teiris's brother, often forgotten prince of Terswood

- Searcy - Archmage, Cazlandt only child, first king of Dracon, killed at the final battle against Amer.

- Shenraafi - King of Barbarles, called The Serpent King.

- Shenna Quey - Lord Patriarch of Acrus.

- Siraas vass Soss - Archmage, predominant healer and medical expert in all magic-born diseases.

- Suanh - Ascended representing magic, power, and knowledge

- Tair Garriet - King of Eplear.

- Tanathil Neridove - Leader of the Einingu, a faction of avaryll within Tidecrest.

- Teiris - Svarters, queen of Terswood, married to Daelin.

- Ters - First High Queen of the svarters, the truth of her is warped by legend.

- Thexses - Ascended representing leadership

- Uulthra - Mraasil, guardian of the world tree Throkzil within Throk'tar

Realms
- The Afterlands - Ruvaal's home realm, situated in the chain of realms "after" Poas meaning the life energy of the dead from Poas becomes usable mana in the Afterlands.

- The Deadloss - A dead, failed realm.

- Dioscuri - Little is known, only that the Scions of Flayme adventured here with the Chronicler.

- Gasping Seas - The realm of origin of the humans in Throk'tar

- Poas - Home of svarters, humans, avaryll, kalvyr, fey, and the fabled dirge races. Home to Alishia, Lone, and our other heroes.

- Senguosh - Castlereagh's home realm, situated in the chain of realms "before" Poas, ravaged by the Deluge.

- Tempus Fa - The first realm, infinite in size, Etharis's home.

- Throk'tar - Home to the gronyn race, where Aiden and Ethan grew up.

- Urbus - Realm of Death, home of the Mraasil Bireal.

- Wolvenne - Little is known, only that the Scions of Flayme adventured here with the Chronicler.

Places
- Ascalon

- Elogoh'an

- D'Kreti

- Gurrim'Nosh

- Isolis

- Nyphlym

- Perith

- Gilded Basilica

Nations of Poas
- Terswood

- Dracon

- Barbarles

- Evkasa

- Eplear

- Jaiketh

- The Western Isles

www.ingramcontent.com/pod-product-compliance
Lightning Source LLC
Chambersburg PA
CBHW031429240626
47154CB00001B/267